For those who enjoy watching rugby for the 'sport', I know you're lying to yourself. How can you look past the tight jersey and thick thighs in short-shorts? But also for those who grew up watching the NRL with their parents and still love it to this day.

PLAYLIST

Pictures Of You | The Last Goodnight
Forever Young | Youth Group
I Lived | OneRepublic
Body On Me (Ft. Chris Brown) | Rita Ora
Kiss Me | Ed Sheeran
Iris | The Goo Goo Dolls
We'll Be Okay | With Confidence
Kiss Me | Olly Murs
In These Arms | Bon Jovi
I Believe | Jonas Brothers
Everywhere | Michelle Branch
You Found Me | The Fray
She Will Be Loved | Maroon 5
Never Tear Us Apart | INXS
Growing on Me | The Darkness
With Or Without You | U2
Open Your Eyes | Snow Patrol

Series Note

This book is a part of a series set in the same world. Each book has been written as a stand alone, however, you will see the occasional crossover of characters, and each author has done their best to maintain the integrity of characters from other books.

The Sunburnt Hearts series is set in Australia, in the fictional small town of Barrenridge, New South Wales. As Australian authors writing books set in Australia, we write using British/Australian English. If you notice the occasional "mum" or "realise," don't worry, it's all part of the voice. Thank you for embracing it.

Author Note

As an Australian author, this story follows the rules of Australian English spelling, grammar and punctuation, including the use of 's' words instead of 'z'. Some slang phrases might be confusing, but don't worry, a glossary of said phrases is included.

Unwritten Rules is considered to be a standalone and can be read in any order. The prologue serves as an introduction to the town and characters across all six books. You can choose to skip the prologue and it'll have no effect on the overall plot of this book. Refer to the Series Note for further information. Sydney, located in New South Wales, will be the main location for this story. Barrenridge, located within the same state, is a fictional name, not a real place.

Please note that this book contains explicit sexual scenes and language, so reader discretion is advised. A content warning is listed in the back of the book for those who want to check them before diving into the story.

Glossary

Pokies—slot machine
Schnitty and chips—schnitzel and fries
Parmi—chicken parmigiana
Gobby—blow-job
Arvo—afternoon
Clapping cheeks—having sex
Chew my ass out—to scold or berate one harshly
Scull—chug
Footy—rugby
Flapping my gums—talking a lot
Punch up—fist fight
Bonnett—hood of a car
Fuck-eyed—drunk
Legless—also drunk
Shitfaced—once again, drunk
Footpath—sidewalk
Not here to fuck spiders—not here to waste time
Doona—duvet

Built like a brick shithouse—having a muscular body
Trackies—sweatpants

CULT
DAYCARE
POLICE
O'Z MECHANICS
TOWN MARKET
HOLLOW CREEK FARM
SYDNEY
HOLLOW CREEK
HIGH SCHOOL

DIAMOND FALLS
PUB
GOLD MINE
HUGHES FARM
TOWN HALL
PLAYGROUND
MAZE
COURTS
PRIMARY SCHOOL
WELCOME TO BARRENRIDGE

PROLOGUE

SIX YEARS EARLIER

Three hours west of Sydney lay Barrenridge—a small, one-way in, one-way out town. A typical farming community with an old gold mine, the town harboured more than just dust and secrets. Beneath its quiet surface simmered long-forgotten feuds, forbidden love and the kind of heartbreak that never truly healed.

With a population of 2,351 people, Barrenridge was mostly self-sufficient. It had a small, independently owned grocery store and monthly Sunday markets that showcased local meat and produce, as well as handmade crafts and clothing. Anything they couldn't get in town could be found in Rafters Falls, located an hour away.

The warm air, typical for late November, settled around the hall with the graduating class of 2018. Murmured voices and scraping chairs filled the tight space as students and family members waited for Principal Hargrove to approach the lectern. The middle-aged man with a round stomach and receding hairline made his way across the stage. The microphone crackled as he cleared his throat.

"Good afternoon, parents, students and faculty. We are all gathered today to watch our graduates take their final walk across this stage. The last six years at Barrenridge High School have prepared you for what awaits beyond those doors. I wish you nothing but success in your future."

Some students rolled their eyes at his cheesy line—the same line he had used for a decade. Others had tuned him out, while the rest thought about the endless possibilities awaiting them, not just past the hall doors, but the boundary of the town itself.

Barrenridge was too small for some. Tiny even. It couldn't offer the adventures they so desperately searched for. Others simply wanted to escape the fate of being stuck like their parents, unable to adhere to anything more than living the simple life with nothing to show for it.

Some dreams were too big for a small town.

There was a small group of students who wanted out by any means possible. They weren't all friends; some had barely spoken more than a few words to each other. Despite that, they all shared the same goal: to leave Barrenridge. Whether it be to chase their dreams or escape a nightmare waiting to swallow them.

Flanked by her two best friends, **Tatum Collins** watched her graduating class step onto the stage one by one, accepting their certificates with haste from Principal Hargrove, likely keen to get out of the sweltering hall and down to the pub for celebratory drinks. Filled with adrenaline and anticipation for what would come next, she smiled to herself, but it didn't quite reach her eyes. Her father couldn't make it to the ceremony—being the head coach of the North Sydney Wolves rugby team meant he travelled a lot and couldn't attend many events—but her mother was in the crowd, eagerly taking photos of everyone, all smiles and warm energy.

While Tatum waited for her name to be called, ready to start on the long road she had planned for her future, little did she know that a week later, she would receive news that would turn her world upside down and derail her carefully laid out plans.

The air grew thick inside the town hall—too many bodies, too little breeze. The ceiling fans were doing nothing but spinning the heat in an endless cycle. **Sadie Cooper** wiped her palms on her dress as her name was called, the crackling microphone and scattered applause echoing off the brick walls. She stepped onto the stage, took the rolled-up certificate from Principal Hargrove, and turned just long enough to spot her best friend, Logan, in the back row, legs sprawled out, arms crossed and smirking like none of this mattered.

But it did. It meant something. The end of an era. A new beginning. Freedom.

They were leaving at midnight. It didn't matter where, just as long as it wasn't Barrenridge. He'd shoot photos. She'd write. They had a plan.

But when she found him in the crowd afterwards, his hug held something she couldn't name. She didn't ask, but she should have. Sadie didn't know this would be the last time she'd ever touch him.

Across the hall, **Morgan Elliot** was sitting with her mum and older brother, Shane. She had begged her dad to be sober just for one night, but he couldn't do that for her. This is why she was grateful to be leaving tonight. She crossed the stage and accepted her certificate with a beaming smile, knowing her life was truly about to start. Her boyfriend, Ethan, had the car packed, and they were ready to skip the graduation party for a one-way road trip to Sydney. They had everything planned—university, work, marriage and then babies.

Morgan looked out over the crowd and spotted her mum dabbing away what she was confident were fake tears, alongside a bored-looking Shane, and unfortunately, his best friend, Rhys, who had to come along for whatever reason. Rhys was also leaving Barrenridge. He had no plan besides travelling and waiting for what would happen next. Morgan thought he was being irrational, but didn't voice it. Where Rhys was concerned, she tried her best not to pay attention. They had a strict love-to-hate relationship. Morgan was convinced this was the last time she would ever see him. But as the saying goes, never say never.

Noah Sterling was the golden boy of Barrenridge and a Supercars Australia prodigy. Graduating meant he was one step closer to following in his dad's footsteps. Ready to leave high school, he sat with his best friends, Tatum and Nathan, who were also itching to leave.

As the principal called the names of the graduating class, the jitters of freedom sparked through him as he patiently waited. The thing about Noah was that he was more patient than most people and friendly, which was why most people in town adored him. And once he became a signed driver, he would be known nationwide, or so his parents hoped.

Noah had no idea that after scoring the deal he worked tirelessly for and driving for a top team, his life would swiftly turn when tragedy struck, hearts were torn, and new life began in his hands.

Basketball superstar, **Nash Stone**, couldn't wipe the self-satisfied smirk off his face as he crossed the stage to accept his graduation certificate from Principal Hargrove. In three days, he would be on his way to North Carolina, ready to start the spring semester at Duke University. Getting a basketball scholarship to a D1 school in the United States was always his goal, and now he was one step closer to his dream of playing in the NBA and one whole continent away from his overbearing, arsehole father.

Looking out over the crowd, he spotted his little brother, Ryland, sitting on top of their sister, Zara's, shoulders. His mum stood proudly beside them, wrapped in the embrace of his stepdad, Paul. Upon seeing them, Nash's smile turned more genuine. Having his family there to support him meant the world to him. While he was going to miss them, he was always meant for bigger things than Barrenridge. There were too many hidden demons in this small town.

Little did he know that on the eve of signing his first official NBA contract, his entire world would come crumbling down around him, and the demons he thought he'd buried would come back to haunt him.

The resident goth chick, **Dorothy Willmot**, had been looking forward to this day for as long as she could remember. Not because it was graduation, but because she was leaving this place.

Dorothy hated the town and the people who resided there. Or maybe she simply hated her family. Who was she kidding? It was definitely her family. She was counting down the minutes until the town was in her rearview mirror with no intention of returning. But there was a face in the crowd she didn't expect to see. Her estranged step uncle, Damon.

As Dorothy made her way off stage, Principal Hargrove addressed the students once again. Quoting Shakespeare, he finished with, "Some are born great, some achieve greatness, and some have greatness thrust upon them. Be those some."

The town hall erupted into cheers. Everyone was eager to start their newfound lives away from Barrenridge.

As the saying goes, you can never go home again. Unless you had no choice.

Chapter One

TATUM

"I can't believe you're leaving us, Tate. How am I going to survive without you?"

It hasn't been two hours since we left Noah's house, where we had this exact same conversation. I glance at Noah seated across the table, biting back a smile at our friends' dramatics. "Food and water will keep you alive more than I can, Nathan. Besides, you'll have Noah."

"Yeah, but he's boring because he's a dad." Nathan pouts behind the lip of the beer glass nestled in his hand, chin resting on his palm. Ink swirls over very inch of his right arm, getting lost beneath the sleeve of the graphic T-shirt clinging to his broad frame. "He's no longer fun Daddy Noah from high school."

"Hey!" Noah protests beside Nathan with a frown. Folding his arms over his broad chest, he glares at our friend through sandy blonde strands of hair falling over his forehead. "I told you not to call me that."

Nathan shrugs. "With no will left to live, I may as well go out swinging."

Eyes as green as Granny Smith apples lock with mine from across the table. Noah shakes his head, but I catch the amusement swimming in his irises as he pats Nathan's back. "You'll survive, I promise. Tate is only moving to Sydney, not the moon."

"It may as well be Pluto with how far away that damn city is," Nathan grumbles.

I reach across the table and lay my hand on his forearm, my black nails barely visible in the dim lighting of the only pub in Barrenridge. "I will come back when I can to visit, okay? Or you can come visit me. We don't have to go months without seeing each other."

Nathan lifts his head, messy strands of dark hair falling over his even darker eyes. "Do you mean that?"

I flick my attention to Noah, who is struggling to keep a straight face as he watches our friend spiral. "Of course. And I will text you every day."

"You better," he murmurs before sipping on his beer. *Like he needs to be drunker than he already is.* "I never thought you would actually move."

I retract my hand and place it in my lap. "Pictures Of You" by The Last Goodnight filters around the room, mixing with the chatter of other patrons enjoying a drink at the table around us. The air smells of BO, cheap perfume and the delectable scent of a chicken parmi. "Me either, but shit happens, I guess. I can't do much about the only physiotherapist centre in town going out of business."

"Forget Happy Limbs, you could always be Noah's babysitter," Nathan suggests with a hopeful smile.

"And see him more than I have to?" I joke, biting back a smile. "I think I'll pass." I bring the glass of vodka and lemonade to my lips and sip on the delicious liquid. Since arriving nearly two hours ago, I've lost count of how many of these I've consumed. I told myself I would only have two drinks since I'm leaving in the morning, and the drive to Sydney is a bitch, but once Nathan started buying round after round, all logic went out of the window. Not to mention my ability to drive home. Besides, it's the last night I will get to spend with my two best friends before distance stretches between us.

My eyes drift to the beautiful little girl asleep in the pram beside the table. Long lashes feather over her pinchable cheeks and blonde curls cover her forehead, nestling against her shoulders. A stuffed toy is clutched close to her chest as her even breathing gets lost amongst the noise in the crowded pub.

It's amazing how Jade manages to sleep through the chaos, something not many parents have the pleasure of saying. I guess with Nathan as your uncle, you could sleep through the world ending.

"Woah, tell me how you really feel, Tate," Noah comments, laughter coating the edge of his tone.

"You know I love you," I say pointedly, "but my passion has always been to help others, and I can no longer do that here."

"Babysitting Jade is helping out Noah," Nathan states matter-of-factly with a shrug. "Look, I don't make the rules here."

I chuckle and shake my head. "As much as I would love to stay here with you idiots, my dad has offered me a job I simply cannot pass up."

"Ah yes," Noah says, twirling his cup of water. "You're leaving us for the big leagues."

"And by big leagues you mean the fucking NRL," Nathan chimes in. He shakes his head in disbelief. "Who would've thought our little Tatey would leave us to work for the best team in the league."

"Are they?" I ask, head tilted to the side. "I don't keep up with the footy, so I'm not sure which teams are good or not. I stopped watching a long time ago. Hell, I've forgotten most of the rules."

Nathan shoots me a deadpan look and turns to Noah as if to say *is she for real?* "Tate, the North Sydney Wolves have won more grand finals since the team was formed than I can count on both of my hands. And your dad is the cause of a fair few of them."

"Well, you know I wasn't the closest with my father growing up. He travelled a lot for work and never spoke to me about what he did. Sometimes he would throw on a game and try to explain the rules. I got the gist of what was going on, but I couldn't explain the rules to you. It wasn't until I was in high school that I learned he was the head coach for the Wolves."

My mum would tell me stories of Dad when he played rugby. According to her, he was one of the most impressive fullbacks to play the game during his prime. He was wanted by nearly every club in the league, but ultimately settled on playing for the Wolves. Mum said they met at university and had no idea who he was. He was studying sports science and she had dreams of one day becoming a psychologist. She fell in love with him at first sight, and Dad did as well. From there, they were inseparable.

Dad suffered a back injury when he was twenty-eight and was forced to retire. Because he could no longer pursue rugby, he settled down with Mum in Barrenridge and had me. She had always wanted to live in a small town, never one to enjoy the busy city streets. Without hesitation, Dad made that dream come true. Whether it was to distract himself from the career he left behind or not, Mum never said. After they had me, Mum saw how miserable Dad was living the country lifestyle. She wanted him to be happy, and she knew rugby was that vice for him. So, she pushed him to get a job coaching with the Wolves, despite his best efforts to fight her on it. But his love for the game outweighed the guilt he felt about leaving us.

From there, Mum stayed in Barrenridge to raise me while Dad travelled between home and Sydney.

Then Mum got sick and everything changed.

"Well, he's the shit," Nathan comments. He chugs the rest of his beer before slamming the glass down, rattling the wooden table. "And if you can, I would like to request signatures from every man on the team. It's the least you can do for abandoning us."

I roll my eyes. "God, you're so dramatic when you're drunk."

"Speaking of drunk," Noah mutters, standing from the stool. "I better get this one home if he wants to not be hungover when you leave in the morning."

I chuckle. "That's probably for the best."

"I'm not drunk," Nathan slurs in protest. His dark eyes are blown wide as he meets my gaze. He tries to stay upright on the chair, but gravity seems to be non-existent to him at the moment because his body slumps to the side. Thankfully, Noah is there to catch him. "Okay, maybe I am drunk."

"Go home," I urge. Slurping on the straw, the vodka seeps into my bones, adding to the airiness gliding through my bones. "I'll see you both in the morning. I'm going to need the fattest cup of coffee to keep me awake on the drive."

Noah throws Nathan's arm around his neck and lifts him from the stool. Nathan is unsteady on his feet but manages to wave at a group of girls sitting at the bar. He's never one to miss the opportunity of stealing his chances with the ladies. They giggle at him before going back to whispering among themselves.

"Do you need a lift home?" Noah asks, his emerald eyes

finding mine in the dark room, his free hand gripping the handle of the pram. "If I had've known you were going to sink as many drinks as you did, I would've offered to drive your car instead."

"Yeah, look, I didn't think that far ahead." I shrug. "I'm okay, though. I can come back in the morning to grab my car before I start packing it."

He raises a brow at me. "Are you sure?"

I wave him away with my hand. "I'm sure. I'll stay for one last drink before I call it a night. You get the big idiot home and tuck your daughter into bed. My house is only a short walk away."

Noah contemplates his options. I've known this man since I was three, and in all the years of attending house parties or hitting the clubs, not once has he allowed me to stay behind without taking me home. He is the first person to make sure his friends are safe before worrying about himself, and this instance is no exception. But maybe it's the expression on my face telling him I'm okay, and the large mass hanging from his shoulder, that has him nodding in agreement.

"Let me know the moment you leave and the second you walk through your front door, okay?" He shoots me a pointed look. "The last thing I need is for you to be kidnapped, or worse, the night before you leave."

"Well, if I've been kidnapped, I would suggest looking at Nathan as the prime suspect."

"You can't leave us, Tate," Nathan whines. His eyes are closed as he uses Noah's body for support, his head lolling forward. "We'll be lost without you."

Noah shakes his head. "Speak for yourself." He flicks his eyes to me and smiles, the gesture warm and comforting. "Let me know if you need anything, okay?"

"Of course. Night, guys! Get home safely." I smile at my

niece, sadness swirling in my chest over the thought that after tomorrow, I won't be able to drive over to Noah's house and play with her whenever I want or spend evenings with her when he's out of town racing. I'll just have to settle for photos of her, which doesn't feel the same as witnessing her grow up before my eyes.

"Night, Tate. I'll see you in the morning."

I watch with amusement as Noah drags Nathan out of the pub while pushing the pram with ease, attracting a few curious glances when Nathan starts calling my name. Laughter bursts from my lips, and all I can do is shake my head. I leave the table on shaky legs and find an empty stool at the bar. I swear that man doesn't have an embarrassed bone in his body.

"What would you like?" the woman behind the bar asks while polishing a glass. She couldn't be much older than me. I think I recognise her from high school, but in my tipsy state, I can't remember her name.

"Just a vodka and lemonade, please."

She turns to make the drink, and with nothing else to do while I wait, I pull my phone from the little black handbag strapped over my torso. Vision blurring at the edges, I clumsily click on one of the social media apps I check far too often and scroll, eyes skimming the usernames and photos.

Scrolling on my phone for hours was a bad habit I developed while working at Happy Limbs. After long hours at work, all I craved was quiet time on the lounge. I didn't want to talk or see anyone, so going on my phone was my only vice—a way to calm the turmoil of the day. It was also a way to stay updated on classmates from high school—mostly those who left Barrenridge after graduation. Nash Stone is over in America, killing it with his basketball career, and Morgan Elliot is somewhere in Western Australia, living a quiet life far away from this place. I see many familiar faces from my year group around town, but we weren't close enough to strike up a conversation, even six years after graduation.

I'll settle for staying in the loop from the comfort of my phone.

The bartender places my order in front of me, pulling my attention away from the screen and to the condensation sliding down the glass. With great effort—my hands feel too heavy to be attached to my body—I slip my phone into my handbag and reach for the glass. I hate the feel of the paper straw against my lips, but I welcome the ice-cold liquid cooling my insides.

With a sigh, I glance to my right at the people sitting at the bar, sipping on their drinks in silence. The man on the stool beside me catches my eye. He looks familiar, but I can't place him. *Where have I seen him before?* When you live in a small town, you come to learn everyone's faces and names by heart. Barrenridge is not a town you can hide in, and this man is doing anything but hide with the intense presence he's emitting.

I swallow hard at the sight of him. Stunning is one word I would use to describe his appearance. Followed by downright gorgeous. It's not often you see men of this caliber walking the streets of Barrenridge, which is why I can't help but wonder what he's doing here.

Inky strands of hair cover his forehead, making it difficult to see his eyes as he stares ahead. Long, slender fingers hold the base of the whiskey glass firmly while the other drum mindlessly on the bar. Silver rings adorn some of his fingers, the metal glinting under the overhead lights above us.

My eyes travel up from his hands to his side profile. The precision with which the sides and back of his hair are shorter than the hair on top, neatly trimmed around the edges, tells me he takes pride in his appearance. The black athletic shorts and hoodie indicate he's active, which has me wondering what this man does for work or if this is his preferred style.

He is simply breathtaking.

Talk to him, my subconscious screams at me. *This is your last night in town. You should make the most of it.*

I want to scold her for being so brazen in her approach to the mystery man, but I stop myself when piercing blue eyes meet mine. The air in my lungs evaporates at the sight of them. They're like a calm ocean just before dusk—deep and endless with a hint of mystery. I'm drawn to them like a bee to the hive, desperate to keep them locked on mine even if it's to admire them for a few seconds longer.

"Do you have a staring problem?"

His deep voice snaps me out of my trance. I shift my weight on the stool and clear my throat, hoping he can't see the steam of embarrassment coming off my cheeks.

"I'm so sorry. I didn't mean to stare at you like that."

The man's tongue pokes the inside of his cheek, accentuating the sharp curve of his jaw. He's clean-shaven and tanned like he has spent countless hours in the sun. Every inch of his strong features has my core heating up and my stomach rolling with anticipation. A scar slashes through his right eyebrow, only adding to the mystery he alludes to. I want to reach out and drag my finger along the healed skin, but quickly refrain from making a fool of myself.

A lazy grin turns up his lips, fuelling the fire simmering beneath my skin. "I don't mind." He brings the glass he's drinking from to his lips and swallows the liquid. I'm mesmerised by the curve of his throat and how it moves effortlessly.

Jesus. What is wrong with me?

It must be the alcohol making me think these unhinged thoughts.

He clears his throat and places the glass on the table. To my surprise, he turns his body to give me his full attention. "What's your name?"

The dryness in my throat is unbearable, like thousands of cotton balls have been shoved inside my mouth. But somehow, I clear my throat and utter, "Tatum. You?"

"Sinnett, but my friends call me Sin."

"Sin..." I murmur, testing his name on my tongue. "What an interesting name."

He tilts his head to the side, intense ocean eyes roaming over my face, down the base of my throat and stops at the plunging neckline of the little black dress I threw on before I left the house. It was one of the last things I had yet to pack; I was considering leaving it behind since I didn't know how often I'd get the chance to go out on the town in Sydney. But the longer Sinnett continues to stare at my chest, eliciting a burning ache in my core, the more thankful I am that I haven't packed it yet.

I clear my throat for what feels like the tenth time and gesture behind me. "Are you new to town?"

He shakes his head. "I'm just visiting for the weekend."

I want to ask who the subject of his visit is, but Sinnett doesn't strike me as the type of person who willingly shares information about himself. Maybe it's the overwhelming I-don't-give-a-fuck attitude wafting from him. He might be giving me his full attention, but I can tell by his stiff shoulders and clenched fist on his thigh he is reserved.

"Well, welcome to Barrenridge where there is literally fuck all to do."

Sinnett chuckles, the deep sound like music to my ears. It does nothing to ease the tension building in my core. "Yeah, well, if it has a pub then I'm easily occupied."

"Then you're at the right place," I respond, turning to sip on my drink.

I take the pause in conversation to consider what the hell I'm doing. It could be my drunken state or the fact that he's the most handsome man I have had the privilege to lay eyes on, but all I can think about is what it would feel like to kiss him—among other things I can't bring myself to dwell on. He's a stranger, so I shouldn't be thinking this way, but it's hard to ignore when my body is craving his touch.

What the hell is wrong with me?

"Forever Young" by Youth Group sounds through the pub, drawing my attention. I drum my fingers on the bar, intent on listening to the lyrics and not focusing on the man beside me, intense eyes fixed on the side of my face.

"So, Tatum, what do *you* like to do for fun around here?"

My heart slams into my throat as I drag my eyes to meet Sinnett's. He's looking at me with curiosity, but I catch the slightest hint of mischief. The side of his mouth tilts up in a smirk, and I'm seconds away from melting into a puddle at his feet.

I need to get a grip. I don't know this man.

"I, uh... n-not much," I answer, stumbling over my words. "I-I mean, there isn't much to do here other than work or come to the Barrenridge Pub for a schnitty and chips and a slap on the pokies. Maybe if you're lucky, the local pool won't be inundated with children and you can actually enjoy the water without wondering if you're soaking in piss."

My eyes flutter close as heat races up my throat. I need to stop drinking alcohol because it's making me talk far too much, and in front of a man like Sinnett, it's basically social suicide. Maybe I need to stop talking to him in general to avoid making myself look even more like a fool.

Sinnett drags his tongue over his teeth, nodding slowly. "Uh-huh. So you've never done anything... *crazy*?"

I tilt my head to the side, searching his face. The cheeky smile indicates he's referring to a hidden agenda, but I'm clueless as to what. It isn't until he leans forward, rests his elbow on the bar, and glances down at my body do I realise what he's referring to.

Oh. *Oh*.

My cheeks flame at the realisation and my heart thunders in my chest. "I, um... no, I haven't."

A grin spreads across his stunning features. "Well, I happen to think tonight should be the night you let loose. It could be fun."

Maybe he's right. It's my last night in Barrenridge before I move to Sydney. What's the harm in having a little fun with a stranger? I mean, I could be murdered, but it's a chance I'm willing to take.

I should be asking myself why I'm putting myself in danger. On any other day, I would've declined such a request in a heartbeat because the cons of doing this far outweigh the pros. But at this moment, staring back at Sinnett, I can't find one con—only pros.

Sinnett reaches over to rest his hand on my bare thigh, the touch so electric I fear I might go into cardiac arrest. His slender fingers graze across my skin, leaving goosebumps in their wake.

A shiver races down my spine as warmth explodes in my core.

Fuck it.

I square my shoulders and offer him the biggest smile I can muster. "One night of crazy fun?"

Sinnett smirks and grips my thigh. "It'll be a night you won't forget."

Chapter Two

TATUM

"Where are you taking me?"

I glance at Sinnett in the driver's seat, one hand resting on his thigh while the other steers the sleek, dark grey Audi R8. To say I was shocked to see him driving such an expensive car was an understatement, but I didn't question him about it. There aren't many streetlights in the main drag of town, so most of his face is shrouded in darkness. Even with the lack of lighting, I can make out the curve of his jaw and sharp cheekbones.

"Are you going to murder me?"

"What?" Sinnett snaps his head to me, ocean eyes roaming my face before glancing back at the deserted road. "No, I'm not going to murder you. If you thought I would, you wouldn't have gotten in the car with me."

I swallow and nod. "Yeah, no, you're right."

"Livin' On A Prayer" by Bon Jovi filters through the speakers, his deep voice consuming the small space in the car. I take the distraction as my chance to zip my lips and throw away the key because *why can't I stop talking*? Since we've been in the car—which is all of two minutes—I've asked Sinnett what his favourite colour is, go-to pub food order and if he would prefer to get eaten by a shark or stomped on by an elephant. And let's just say he wasn't too keen on answering the 'would you rather' question.

I need to shut the hell up.

Sinnett exhales and runs his hand through his messy hair. "I know a quiet place we can go."

Now I'm nearly breaking my neck to look at him. "What? Why? We can just go back to my place."

"I don't do sleepovers," he mutters and turns the car onto the road that leads to the park on the edge of town. "And I certainly can't take you to where I'm staying."

The further we drive from the town centre, the harder my heart beats in my chest. I feel every thump at the base of my throat, getting louder and louder as the lights of Barrenridge disappear behind us.

Ridge Park is the local hangout spot for teenagers. It's far enough away from the watchful eye of the townspeople that it allows the kids to let loose and have fun without fear of getting in trouble. Noah, Nathan and I would come out here every day after school to hang out and watch some of the guys from our year group ride their scooters and skateboards on the outdoor skate park. The popular girls would sit in the grass nearby, making flower crowns and giggling while watching the guys.

It was almost like a daily routine by the time we graduated from high school. And now that same routine has been passed on to the new generation of kids going through school.

To take my mind off what I have agreed to do with this stranger, I do the one thing I know will distract me: talk and ask questions. Because obviously I haven't done enough of that since being in the car with Sinnett. At this point, I can't help myself. He makes me nervous, but not in a bad way. More like a *why is this man here with me when he could have any woman he wants* kind of way.

Twirling a lock of strawberry-blonde hair around my forefinger, I ask, "How old are you?"

Sinnett glances over at me, brows pinched into a frown. "Twenty-four."

My eyes widen in surprise. "Me too! Well, almost... Woah, we're twins."

"Well, I already have one of those," Sinnett answers gruffly.

I blink at his side profile. "You're a *twin*? What the hell, that's so cool."

"Twin sister," he corrects, eyes focused on the road ahead. "And I don't know if I would categorise it as *cool*."

"Well, it's cool to me," I retort and shift in my seat. "What's your favourite type of music?"

"Rock."

"Do you read books?"

"Not really."

"Do you have a favourite TV show or movie?"

"My guilty pleasure is The Office and I fall asleep to Fast Five most nights."

"Red liquorice or black?"

"I don't eat lollies."

"Favourite chocolate?"

"Cadbury is the only correct answer."

"And do you watch any sports?"

Sinnett's head snaps in my direction, his eyes swiftly roaming my face before looking ahead. "Yeah, rugby league."

"Of course," I mutter with a soft chuckle. Given Sinnett's athletic appearance, it doesn't surprise me that he watches the footy. It's on the tip of my tongue to ask him which team he supports when he parks the car and turns in his seat.

"Do you ever stop talking?"

I blink, taken aback. "Um, yeah... when I'm sleeping, of course."

"Good," he murmurs and reaches between him and the driver's door. The chair slides all the way back, allowing him to stretch out his long legs. "Get on my lap."

My heart thunders as I look between Sinnett and his empty lap. "I-I don't—"

"Did I stutter, strawberry? Be a good girl and crawl onto my lap."

Oh, my God.

What have I gotten myself into?

Sinnett holds my gaze as I unclip my seat belt and awkwardly climb over the centre console. Strong hands find my waist, guiding me onto a hard lap. An even *harder* presence pokes into my ass, blurring my vision. I stare down at Sinnett, my hands resting on his shoulders for support. He hisses out a breath when I settle my full weight on his thighs. The side of the console and door dig painfully into my knees. With this being a smaller car, we're not left with much room to move.

"Are you okay?" I ask, taking note of the flash of pain that crosses his sharp features. "I'm not hurting you, am I?"

He shakes his head. Messy strands of inky hair fall over his stunning eyes. "I'm fine."

Sinnett slides his hands over the curve of my ass in a circular motion before his fingers dig into my hips, holding me in place. Between his dick poking my ass, the warmth of his hand seeping through the material of the thin dress and his eyes looking at me like I'm good enough to eat, I'm having a hard time finding my breath.

What the hell am I doing?

"Are you sure you want to do this?" he asks, voice surprisingly gentle. *Can this man read my mind?* "You can back out now and I'll drop you home. The choice is yours."

Warmth simmers beneath my skin as I tear my eyes from his and glance through the window. It's pitch black outside with not a soul in sight. We're completely alone. Being in an empty park with a stranger I met not even an hour ago is enough of a warning for my brain to throw a red flag up and demand we get out of here. But the alcohol in my system pushes those concerns away, instead filling me with a confidence I didn't know I possessed.

I have never hooked up with a guy like this before. The last time I slept with a man was my ex-boyfriend, Jayden. We started dating not long into my first year at university, after meeting at a club in Sydney CBD. I was studying to be a physiotherapist and he had dreams of being an architect, wanting to design the best building Sydney had ever seen. Jayden was persistent when it came to taking me out on dates and getting to know me. I liked that he was confident, smart and good-looking—it fuelled the attraction I felt for him.

Being with Jayden was easy. He took me out to dinner once a week, we studied together late into the evening and sometimes on the weekends we would catch a movie. Life with him was simple. Three years flew by, and before I knew it, I was twenty-one and ready to return to Barrenridge. Mum got me a job lined up at Happy Limbs, and I was content with starting my career in my hometown. But that's not what Jayden wanted. Sydney was the only city he had ever lived in, so he had no plans of leaving, not when there was an abundance of work for him there.

Our relationship came to a screeching halt. I wanted to leave, and he didn't. Long distance was an option, but with our ambitions pulling us in different directions, it would only delay the inevitable.

The breakup was a mutual decision, and while I had been a sobbing mess in my mum's arms when I returned home, I soon realised it was for the best. We just weren't meant to be.

Nearly two years on, I've been on my own, working and spending time with my friends when I can. Putting myself out there and dating again is so far down on my list of priorities that it's no longer visible. But being here with Sinnett has restored a hunger I haven't felt in a long time—the desire to be touched and taken to heights the deepest part of me craves.

If I leave now, I may regret that decision and be left wondering what could've happened if I had stayed.

The fire burning in Sinnett's eyes matches the wildfire raging in my core. My hips grind against his without my permission, deciding for me.

Sinnett grins, his hands on my waist tightening. "Good choice, strawberry."

His hands drop from my waist to my thighs, travelling up the length of them to toy with the hem of my tight black dress. A burst of nerves tears through me, and without thinking, I grab Sinnett's face between my hands and press my lips against his.

For a brief second, he doesn't move. I inwardly groan. *God, I've messed this up already and we've barely started. Idiot, idiot, idiot.*

I pull away slightly, but Sinnett's hand finds the back of my head, fingers tangling in the long strawberry-blonde strands. He brings my lips back to his and takes the lead, moving against me effortlessly. Electricity thrums in my veins as I hold his face, kissing him like my life depends on it.

His tongue swipes across my bottom lip, demanding access. I greedily give it to him, my hips grinding against his. A deep growl echoes in his throat, making me dizzy with lust. Sinnett's free hand moves from my waist to rest on the curve of my ass and guides my hips forward to meet his.

At the age of twenty-three, I never thought I would be grinding against a man in his car in an empty park. It's like ticking off a bucket list item most people experience in high school. I've always been more of a late bloomer in the intimacy department.

The hem of my dress rides up my thighs, settling just below my ass. Sinnett uses his hand in my hair to deepen the kiss, and I take this as my chance to roam my hands over his chest. Even through the thick material, the muscles are prominent. *Oh my.*

My fingers find the hem of his hoodie and tug upward. The kiss is momentarily broken while I pull the garment over his head, along with his black T-shirt by accident. Inky strands of hair fall over Sinnett's eyes as he stares at me. I'm too distracted to meet his gaze.

"Holy shit," I breathe, dragging my fingers over the deep ridges in his abdomen. "I'm convinced you're carved from stone."

Sinnett bursts out laughing, and I find myself wishing I could collect the sound in a jar and keep it forever.

Black ink curls over the left side of his torso. I can't make out the design because it's too dark in the car. My eyes drift to the shadows cast over his arm. I can just make out the full tattoo sleeve on his right arm. There are far too many interwoven designs for me to see clearly with this limited vision, but it doesn't stop me from trying to picture what the images could be. Sinnett being this tatted was the last thing I expected to see under his casual fashion choice.

And don't get me started on the lean muscles of his torso or the thick veins bulging from his biceps, threading down his forearms like thick vines before stopping at the top of his hands.

Every inch of this man is unbelievable, which makes me

question why he wants to hook up with plain old me. I'm sure I look like shit in comparison to him.

I open my mouth to speak—likely to say something stupid given the state of my shock at seeing the physique of this man —but Sinnett cuts me off by slamming his lips against mine. My fingers curve over his broad shoulders while he lifts the hem of my dress over my hips. The material hugs my waist, leaving me exposed.

I'm internally thanking myself for choosing to wear a nice pair of lacy black underwear. But my top half on the other hand...

Sinnett tugs the neckline of my dress down, exposing my bare chest. He pulls away from the kiss to drink me in, his eyes nearly popping out of his head.

"So you mean to tell me that you're stunned by my tattoos when you're sporting fucking *nipple piercings?*"

I drag my bottom lip between my teeth. Those piercings are the by-product of a wild night out in Rafters Fall—an hour's drive from Barrenridge—with Noah and Nathan a couple of years ago. Before Noah had his daughter, we would go out clubbing most weekends, mostly for fun. One particular night, I lost a bet of who could get the most phone numbers in thirty minutes and the guys said I had to get my nipples pierced. I agreed with the intention that I would take them out once they healed, but after a few weeks, I grew fond of them.

And now I'm thanking past me for that decision.

Sinnett's large hand comes up to cup my breast, massaging gently as he eyes the silver piercing. "Fuck me."

Yes please, I cry internally. Having him touch me like this with a hungry look in his eyes is making the fire in my core grow out of control and the wetness pooling between my thighs embarrassing.

He dips his head and sucks my nipple into his mouth. My

back arches at the same time my eyes roll into the back of my head. The sensation is all-consuming, making me lose my ever-loving mind. His skilful tongue sucks and teases the barbell before moving on to the next one, giving it the same attention.

"Sin," I moan, dragging my fingers to the back of his neck. My arched back allows Sinnett to run his hands over the curve of my spine while he devours my chest.

"Say my name again," he groans after releasing my nipple. Ocean eyes peer up at me through long lashes. "Now."

"Sin," falls from my lips in a desperate cry as my hands move down his chest to the waistband of his black shorts.

"So fucking eager," Sinnett grunts, watching my hands clumsily toy with the material. "You want my cock, strawberry?"

My eyes snap up to meet his. I blink as his filthy words settle into my inflamed skin. Jayden never used to speak to me this way. He is the only man I've ever slept with, and I guess I would describe our sex life as 'vanilla', but I didn't mind it.

But this...

"I need an answer," Sinnett grunts, his hands stilling on the scrunched material around my waist.

"Y-yes," I manage to squeeze out.

He raises a brow at me. "Yes, *what*?"

Oh, my *God*, he's going to make me say it.

Warmth spreads across my cheeks as I peer at him through my lashes. "Y-yes, I want your cock, Sin."

"Fucking hell," he groans, throwing his head back against the leather seat. "It's all yours, strawberry."

I take that as my cue to continue my earlier actions.

Something black is wrapped over his right thigh, catching my eye, but I don't have a chance to ponder the reason why it's there because my attention slips to the bulge between me and Sinnett. My pulse thumps against the base of my throat as I pull back the waistband of his shorts and underwear, quickly finding the source of the hardness that was pressing against my ass. My mouth dries when my fingers skim over the hot skin. The second my hand wraps around the base, my eyes nearly bulge out of my head.

This man is fucking *huge*. Like could tear me apart and kill me huge.

Sinnett drags his bottom lip between his teeth and tilts his head to the side. "What's wrong, strawberry? Are you scared?"

My head snaps up and I meet his amused eyes. "What? No. I-I'm not scared." I pull his dick from his pants, getting a better visual of what I'm dealing with. And just as I thought, he's still huge. "Okay, maybe I'm a little worried you're going to split me in half."

Sinnett snorts a laugh. "I'm not going to hurt you, Tate. Not unless you want me to."

The double meaning behind his words has me swallowing hard.

"Move," Sinnett commands gently. "Or I have no problem taking control."

I hold my hand up to him. "No, no, I've got this."

Sinnett smirks as he leans back against the seat, stretching his long legs out in the cramped space. "Show me what you've got."

Feeling the pressure of his eyes on me, I give myself a mental pep talk. *You've got this, Tate. This isn't your first time, so just act confident, and he won't notice.* If I embarrass myself in front of Sinnett, I fear I won't recover. It would go down in history as the second worst day of my life.

I scoot my ass back in the limited space behind me and bend at the waist until I'm staring directly at the weapon Sinnett calls his appendage. My eyes flutter closed as I inhale a deep breath before diving into the unknown.

The second my lips wrap around the head, Sinnett groans. His fingers thread through my hair, holding me in place as I slowly take him into my mouth. Given his size and girth, I'm unable to take all of him, but I take as much as I can before dragging my head back.

"*Shit*," Sinnett hisses. He uses his hand in my hair to push me back down, guiding me down his length until my mouth is full of him. "You take me so fucking well."

It doesn't take long for Sinnett to assume control, using his grip on my hair to guide me up and down his length at a pace that suits him. I'm not complaining, though. I would rather he find enjoyment in this than watch me make a fool of myself. And if the deep groans falling from his parted lips are an indication he's enjoying it, then I am too.

My thighs quiver as wetness pools between them. It's taking all of my self-control not to touch myself, to relieve the pressure building there. I want Sinnett to be the one to touch me, considering he's the reason I'm this worked up to begin with.

Just as saliva begins to pool at the corner of my mouth, Sinnett pulls my head back, freeing his cock from my mouth with a soft *pop*. I'm breathless as I meet his fiery gaze. His hand slips from my hair to slide between my thighs, grazing my sensitive centre.

Sinnett hums, tracing his fingers over the damp material of my underwear. "You're soaked, strawberry."

"For you," I manage to murmur breathlessly.

His tongue pokes the side of his mouth as he pushes the material to the side and drags his fingers through the wet folds, eliciting a deep shudder from my body. He grins as he pulls his hand away and pushes his saturated finger between his lips, sucking it dry.

"Tastes sweet like a strawberry."

If this man doesn't stop talking, I fear I'm going to spontaneously combust on his lap because *what the fuck*.

"Do you ever stop talking?" I repeat his earlier words, biting back a grin.

Sinnett returns my grin and drags me forward until my bare chest brushes his. "You have a smart mouth, don't you?"

"I didn't hear you complaining when it was wrapped around your cock."

"Jesus Christ, Tate," he groans, rocking his hips upward, forcing his dick to slide against my core. "Maybe I do need to shut the fuck up or else I'm going to come before we've even started."

"Good choice," I murmur and drag my bottom lip between my teeth.

Sinnett grabs my hips and lifts me, allowing me enough space to grab his dick and place the head at my entrance. My skin is on fire as I lower myself on him, slowly but surely taking him inch by painful inch until I'm seated on his thighs.

It's hard to breathe when I'm this full. My eyes find Sinnett, and he's watching me with parted lips. His hands squeeze my waist, indicating I should move. The thought of moving with this monstrosity inside me is terrifying, but with a little bit of guidance from Sinnett, I lift my hips, dragging him along my walls before I lower onto him again.

"Tate, I'm going to need you to ride my cock, okay?" Sinnett holds my gaze, his ocean eyes intense.

All I can do is manage a nod as I dig my knees further into their holds. My hips lift on their own accord, and I quickly find a rhythm that has Sinnett groaning and throwing his head back against the seat. The curve of his jaw and the veins running down his neck make my mouth water, and I fight the urge to run my tongue over the slick skin.

"That's it," Sinnett grunts. His fingers dig into my skin,

using my waist as a way to guide my hips up and down. "You fit me like a fucking glove."

From this point on, I'm pretty sure I lost consciousness. Between the pressure building in my core, the ache in my thighs, and the steam fogging up the windows, I may as well be floating on a cloud, watching myself from above.

Sinnett takes one of my nipples into his mouth, circling his tongue around the perky skin and barbell. Somehow I manage to keep the rhythm while he devours me, but my movements grow sloppy as I rush toward the edge of the cliff, chasing the high I know will ultimately blow my mind.

It's on the tip of my tongue to tell Sinnett I'm on the pill, but before I can utter a word, he grunts as he spills into me. Seconds later, I'm rendered speechless as my orgasm shakes me to my core. For a split second, I lose my vision, replaced by black spots and random shapes. Every muscle in my body spasms as I come down from the high.

I slump against Sinnett's chest breathlessly as his arms wrap around my waist. He's still inside of me, but it's the last thing on my mind. All I can focus on is thinking *holy shit*. That was quite possibly the best sex I've ever had, and I was with Jayden for three years.

Is this what it feels like to have a mind-numbing orgasm? If so, I've been missing out.

"Are you okay?" Sinnett runs a hand over my messy hair.

I nod against his chest. "Y-yeah, I just..."

Sinnett's body stiffens. His hands come up to grip my shoulders, pushing me back until I meet his gaze. "Shit, I just finished inside of you. I didn't even fucking ask if you were on anything or grab the condom I keep in the glove box."

Too exhausted to match his panicked state, I press my finger against his lips, silencing him. "Shhh. It's okay, Sin. I'm on the pill, so you have nothing to worry about. You're not going to have a screaming baby in your face nine months from now, so chill."

He sighs with what I'm sure is relief before dropping his forehead against mine. "Thank God for that. I thought I was fucked for a second there. I'm normally more prepared, but for some reason I just—" He shakes his head. "It's fine. We're all good here."

Because I'm tipsy and filled with endorphins that cloud my judgment, I press my lips against Sinnett's one last time before sliding off him and crawling onto my seat. His gaze burns into my skin as I readjust my dress and catch my breath. By the time I look at him, he has tucked himself back into his pants and slipped on his discarded T-shirt.

The Audi roars to life, and Sinnett has to flick on the AC to get rid of the fog coating the windscreen. He silently clips his seat belt into place before backing the car out of the parking spot and driving toward town.

I'm at a loss for words over what just happened, so I stare out the window, replaying every second of our encounter. It was unlike anything I've ever experienced. And to my surprise, I don't regret a second of it. But that could change when the sun rises in a few hours.

I manage to squeeze out my address when we drive through the main street, and within a minute, Sinnett is parked out the front of my dark house. My gaze sweeps from the house I grew up in to the man I had my first one-night stand with. He's watching me with curious eyes, waiting for me to speak.

"Have you ever done this before?"

He raises the brow with the scar through it. "Had car sex? Never."

I shake my head. "I mean *this*. Sleeping with strangers for one night of fun."

"Oh," he murmurs and runs a hand through his messy

hair. "A handful of times. But you don't strike me as someone who has."

A blush creeps up the base of my throat. "Yeah, well, I wanted to be adventurous."

"I'm not complaining." Sinnett grins. "Thanks for taking a chance on me."

"Thanks for not murdering me," I counter. "Well, I don't know if I can say the same for my pussy."

Sinnett bursts out laughing, and I can't ignore the warmth that spreads across my body when I hear him laugh, knowing it's because of me. It's addicting.

"You really are something else, strawberry."

I hadn't realised the origin of his nickname when he first said it earlier, mostly because I was preoccupied. But now it's grown on me.

My hair glides through my fingers as I try to get rid of some of the knots Sinnett created. "Yeah, well, I guess you're all right, too."

Sinnett tilts his head slightly, eyes roaming over my face. I'm mesmerised by how bright they are even in the shadows of the night. I could stare into them for eternity.

"You don't know who I am, do you?"

I frown at his strange question. "No... Am I meant to?"

His tongue pokes the inside of his mouth. After a moment of silence, he smiles and shakes his head. "No, I guess not."

"Well, thank you for driving me home." A tiny voice inside me is screaming to invite him inside, but I know I shouldn't. Sinnett only wanted one thing from me and now that he's gotten it, we are destined to walk away and never cross paths again. The thought sours my mood slightly, but I swallow the bitter taste and offer him a smile. "I hope I never see you again, Sin."

Sinnett bites back a smile and nods. "I hope not, Tate."

With that, I swing open the passenger door and step out into the slightly warm air. It's bordering on 1 AM, so the early morning shift of cool air hasn't settled in yet. I wrap my arms around my waist and walk up the pathway to the front door of my parent's house. The same house where I lost my first tooth, where Mum taught me how to plait my hair and where I learned what a gobby is, courtesy of Nathan. It's littered with memories that warm my chest, but break my heart in the same beat. Mum's final moments are trapped in the walls, surrounded by every memory—good and challenging—we shared.

Come tomorrow morning, a 'For Lease' sign will be planted in the front yard, and another family will create their own lasting memories within the structure.

Once inside, I turn to see Sinnett's Audi sitting idle on the street. Warmth blooms in my chest at his kind gesture of waiting for me to go inside before leaving. Barrenridge doesn't have a high crime rate, but it doesn't deter the townspeople from being careful.

I wave at Sinnett from the comfort of my home and watch as he drives down the street, turning the corner and disappearing from my life forever.

While I'm bummed I will never see him again, I'm grateful I got the chance to let my hair down and experience something I never thought I was capable of doing. I'm not above being spontaneous, but having a one-night stand is something far out of my comfort zone. And thankfully, it didn't end with me dead in a ditch somewhere.

And Sinnett was right. Tonight will go down in the history books as one of my favourites.

I just hope it doesn't come back to bite me in the ass.

Chapter Three

TATUM

The soil is colder on my bare knees than I thought it would be. I should've considered wearing long pants or bringing a mat to kneel on, but with the unexpected warmth in the air today, it hadn't crossed my mind.

A light breeze rustles through the trees hanging overhead, flowing through the loose strands of hair falling around my face. Exhaling a soft breath, I place the bundle of native flowers in front of the headstone. The dirt has long since been covered over by grass, reminding me of how quickly two years can pass in what seemingly feels like the blink of an eye. But my heart would have to disagree. It has felt every minute of her absence, and I don't know if that'll ever change.

"You know I'm not one for goodbyes, Mum," I murmur, running my hands down my thighs. "So consider this a 'I'll see you soon' instead."

The headstone is starting to see some discolouration around her name and the message Dad picked out. *A loving mother to Tatum and a faithful wife to Phil. A sister, daughter and granddaughter. Avery will be missed dearly.* I've spent countless minutes, hours and days in this exact spot, to the point where I can recite every word written into the stone without looking. Besides the memories I have of her, this is what's left. A headstone and a patch of grass.

"You always told me to follow my dreams and do whatever it takes to make them come true." I swallow hard and close my eyes, willing my racing heart to slow down. "I just hope I'm not making the wrong decision by leaving Barrenridge."

My eyes flutter open to find a white butterfly sitting atop Mum's headstone, unmoving. A sob threatens to burst from my throat, but I manage to swallow it down. Whenever I would visit the cemetery, I would speak to Mum for what felt like hours, talking about my day and whatever else was on my mind. I started asking for a sign that she was here with me, and each time, a white butterfly would appear. I thought it was a fluke at first, but after the fifth time it appeared, I knew it was a sign. Mum was with me.

And she's here right now.

Blinking back the tears in my eyes, I smile. "So I take it you think moving to Sydney to live with Dad is a good idea? That I'm not going to mess my life up by doing so?"

The butterfly stays put, staring at me.

Dragging my bottom lip between my teeth, I nod. "I miss you, Mum. You've heard me say it a million times now, but I don't think that'll ever change."

It's not going to be easy moving to Sydney, knowing she's going to be here by herself. I know realistically that she'll always be in my heart, but I've gotten used to visiting her grave at least once a week for the past two years, so it's going to be an adjustment not sticking to that routine.

"I'll be sure to tell Dad you said hello." Pressing my lips to my fingers, I press them against the headstone and sigh. "I love you, Mum. Wish me luck."

The butterfly flies overhead as I stand to my feet. Glancing one last time at the headstone, I shove my hands into the pockets of my shorts and turn to walk to where my Jeep is parked nearby.

As I'm about to slide into the front seat, the same white butterfly lands on the bonnet of my car, staring at me through the screen. I can't stop the flood gates from opening, and the sob I had tried to swallow, bursts out.

WHEN I PULL INTO THE DRIVEWAY OF THE HOUSE I grew up in—the red brick faded to a dull brown and the bright yellow front door Mum insisted on having to help brighten up the place—my eyes are stinging and the hem of my black T-shirt is damp.

Noah's red Ford ute is parked on the street, which means he's already here with Nathan and Jade.

Exhaling a sharp breath, I cut the engine and trudge up the cement pathway, the edges chipping and the overhanging grass from the lawn reminding me I should've mowed before I left. When I step inside, I'm greeted by the scent of dust bunnies and Noah's woodsy cologne lingering in the air. Cardboard boxes are piled up in the lounge room to my left, waiting for the movers to come by this afternoon to collect what I don't need and put in storage with the rest of the furniture and items I decided not to take with me to Sydney. Dad said that when he gets the chance to travel up here after the footy season ends, we can take a few days to go through everything. We'll need to donate or toss some things, and, of course, sort through

Mum's belongings that I haven't had the heart to touch in two years.

Up until last week, her bedroom had been untouched. To say I was an absolute mess packing away her things is an understatement.

Sniffling, I follow the sound of my friends' voices to where they stand in the kitchen. Three take away coffee cups sit on the empty granite island, the white cups blending in with the white cabinets. Mum renovated the house five years ago, stating she needed a change from the dull wooden cabinets that came with the house. With my dad not around, I think she enjoyed giving herself these projects as it allowed her to keep her mind and body busy.

Noah and Nathan cut their conversation short, their attention fixed on me as I walk further into the kitchen. Jade is sitting on the floor, surrounded by plastic building blocks. Her soft giggles echo off the walls, slamming into my chest. I'm going to miss her so much.

"How'd you go?" Noah asks. He scoops up one of the cups and extends it toward me. "I got your usual."

I accept the flat white and lean my elbows on the countertop, offering a small smile. "Thank you. And it went as well as what you'd expect. I didn't think it would be so hard to say goodbye to her."

"If your red-rimmed eyes are anything to go by, I'm sure it wasn't easy," Nathan says, his usual joking tone hidden. While he is quick to crack a joke, always finding a way to lighten the mood, I'm glad he's reading the room. "But don't worry, Noah and I will make sure to change the flowers out each week. We know Ave loved roses and natives, so we'll make sure she's never without."

Tears sting my eyes again. "She'll appreciate that, guys. Thank you." Clearing my throat, I nod my head at Noah.

"Thanks again for the coffee. I'm going to need it to get through the drive."

Noah raises a brow at me. "Why's that? Late night?"

Warmth floods my cheeks as I'm reminded of the night before. Images of me on Sinnett's lap, his hand in my hair and lips attached to mine seep into my mind, pouring heat into my veins. I had struggled to get to sleep after he dropped me home, too hyped on adrenaline. Now I'm paying the price for that with only five hours of sleep. And I had to make sure I got my Jeep from the pub to go visit Mum's grave, all before Noah and Nathan arrived. It seems my time management skills need improving.

"No," I murmur, rolling my lips. "I only stayed for one drink."

They don't need to know what that one drink led to.

Noah and Nathan share a knowing look, one that says they don't believe me. To my surprise, Nathan grins, changing the subject.

"Well, I'm more interested in knowing about Noah's new neighbour who has him grinning like a fool." Nathan sips on his coffee, eyes flicking between me and Noah.

A surprised gasp leaves my throat. "A new neighbour? Spill!"

Noah rubs the back of his neck, attention fixed on the coffee cup resting in his hand. "It's not a big deal. My elderly neighbour, June, has her granddaughter staying with her. I saw her Friday when she moved in, and then again this morning in town when I was grabbing our coffees."

"What's her name? Is she cute? How old is she?" The questions roll off my tongue with ease, a smile splitting across my face. A blush splashes Noah's cheeks. I haven't seen him react to a woman like this since the day he met Em. It's something I never thought I would see after her accident.

"See," Nathan says, pointing a knowing finger at our friend. "The cheeks say it all."

"Guys, stop," Noah murmurs. "I've only spoken to her once."

"I do recall you saying her name is Mia," Nathan supplies with a shrug. "And that she is, in fact, *cute*."

"Nate," Noah hisses. I can't help but laugh. I'm going to miss these two so much.

"Nate, leave him alone." I push off the counter and take a sip from the coffee, needing the caffeine to kick in pronto. "You know how tough it's been for Noah since Jade was born, so if he is interested in this Mia girl, then let him move at a pace that's comfortable for him."

Noah shoots me a small smile, as if to say thank you for getting Nathan off his back.

Nathan huffs. "Okay, fine. I'll drop it. *For now*."

Clapping my hands together, I jab a thumb over my shoulder. "Now that it's settled, let's get my boxes packed away in my car."

Before I can step away from the island, strong arms wrap around me. I'm engulfed in Nathan's slightly spicy scent, and I can't help but smile.

I chuckle against his chest. "What are you doing, Nate?"

"Keeping you here in Barrenridge," he murmurs against the crown of my head. "Forever."

I melt against his touch. "Nathan..."

"Get in on this hug, Noah," my friend calls out. "I need reinforcement."

Noah's soft laughter echoes off the walls, and moments later, I feel his arms wrap around my back. I smile and blink back the tears forming in the corner of my eyes. I knew leaving my two best friends was going to be difficult, but now that I'm moments away from walking out the front door and watching them grow smaller in my rearview mirror, I'm wishing I could stay rooted to the floor, trapped in their embrace. Maybe then it would mean I didn't have to face the changes that lie ahead on the road to Sydney and my new career path. Or having to rebuild the relationship with my father. And I wouldn't have to leave the two people I trust most in this world.

But I know if I don't, I'll be stuck in this town with no sense of direction, and that's just not an option for me.

"I love you both," I murmur, voice wavering at the edges.

"And we love you," Noah says, tone light.

"No matter what you do or where you are, we'll be here for you," Nathan utters, tightening his grip around me. "Always."

The truth in his words has the tears in the corner of my eyes sliding down my cheeks, and a smile turning up my mouth. Even if Noah and Nathan are three hours away, nothing about our friendship will change. We've supported each other through every new phase in our lives from the moment we were in preschool, no matter how difficult, and this is no different.

No matter what happens, these guys are my family.

"Always," I whisper.

Chapter Four

TATUM

"Tate, are you ready?"

My eyes shift from my reflection in the bathroom mirror to my father standing in the doorway of the ensuite. He has his arms folded over his chest, with his shoulder leaning against the frame. Deep blue irises stare back at me, framed by a warm smile and weathered features.

"Almost," I say, fluffing the end of my ponytail.

Dad exhales a small breath and runs his hands down the front of his black and red polo shirt. "I know you didn't want me to make a big deal of you being here, but I'm glad you are. It's nice having you around."

My lips flatten into a tight-lipped smile as I turn my body, resting my hip against the vanity. "Dad..."

He holds up his hands, a smile tugging at the corner of his lips. "I know, I know. I wasn't going to say anything, but you've been here for a week already. It's been torture keeping my mouth shut."

A chuckle bubbles up from my throat. "I appreciate you trying. And I'm happy to be here, so don't think otherwise."

"Good, good." He smiles and runs a hand over the top of his greying hair. "Anyway, we should get going. You don't want to be late on your first day."

"Well, that'll make two of us then because you'll be driving."

Dad chuckles and pushes off the doorframe. "Touche." He drums his hands on the wood frame and raises his brows at me. "I'll meet you downstairs."

My hands find the edge of the vanity after he leaves, and I drop my head between my shoulders. Nervous tension rolls through my muscles like a tidal wave, which in turn makes my stomach flip. It's been an endless cycle since the moment I opened my eyes this morning.

Ever since I arrived in Sydney seven days ago and stood at the front door of my father's house with a suitcase at my feet and my life packed in boxes in my car, I haven't been able to relax. Not because I'm not happy to see him, but because it's been years since I've spent more than a few days in a row with my father, especially after my mother passed away two years ago. We were once close, having spent lots of time together while I was growing up in Barrenridge, but once he started travelling to Sydney for work, our relationship grew strained.

I didn't resent him for leaving Mum and I alone for weeks at a time, only visiting home on the weekend when his team had a bye week. At the time, I was grateful he took time out of his busy schedule to visit, but looking back, I wish he had stayed longer. I wish he had visited more because maybe then he would've seen the signs in Mum's deterioration sooner than I did.

And now here I am, back living with my father in North Sydney and working for him. If I told younger me that this is what our life would look like, I would've laughed in her face. I never thought I would ever leave Barrenridge for good because I had Noah and Nathan, and now here I am, doing just that.

I exhale a long breath and pick my head up. Tired light green eyes stare back at me through the mirror. Dad said I don't have to wear a uniform, but I figured it wouldn't be professional to turn up to my first day on the job wearing skinny jeans and a baggy T-shirt. Instead, I opted for a black, short sleeved button-up shirt and long black dress pants.

Pushing off the vanity, I smooth a hand down the front of my shirt and inhale a deep breath.

You've got this, Tate. You know what you're doing.

With my shoulders pushed back and my spine straight, I leave the ensuite and collect my handbag from the foot of my queen bed. Waking up just after six in the morning means I had time to make, and re-make, the bed before I forced myself out of the house for a walk, watching the sunrise. I had hoped it would clear the nervous energy racing through my bones, but it didn't work as I hoped. Instead, it gave me more time alone with my thoughts, and I was left in a spiral of *Can I do this? Am I cut out for this job?*

Dad is waiting for me by the front door with his head in his phone.

"All right, let's go," I say when I reach the bottom of the stairs.

He looks up and slips his phone in the back pocket of his black jeans. "Let's hit the road then. Traffic can be a pain getting down to the Shire at this time of the afternoon."

I follow Dad to his sleek black Mercedes in the driveway and slip into the passenger seat. It's a nice car, one that costs a pretty penny given the detailed leather interior and tinted windows. I'm sure it didn't make much of a dent in the salary my father receives.

"I need to get a new car," I tell my dad, turning my head to glance at him.

"Why?" Dad flicks his eyes from the road to me and back again. "Is there something wrong with it?"

"No, Dad, the 2007 Jeep Wrangler you bought me for my sixteenth birthday still runs like a gem." The sarcasm in my voice doesn't go unnoticed by him because he shoots me a pointed look. "All I'm saying is that it might be time I upgrade to something new, especially if I'm going to be living in the city."

Dad hums. "I suppose maybe you're right. Driving in the city is difficult enough, and I would hate to get a call from you because your car broke down on the side of the road."

"My point exactly," I say with a victorious smile. Getting a new car wasn't on my list of priorities, but after her performance on the highway last week, I was convinced it was time for an upgrade. "Let me shop around first, and then we can discuss options."

The tidy suburban streets of Mosman trail behind us as the daunting road over the Harbour Bridge looms ahead. I don't think I'll ever get used to how fast-paced and large Sydney is, especially after growing up in a town like Barrenridge. It'll take some time adjusting to for sure, but even I can't deny how beautiful the core of the city is. The water in the harbour glistens with the sun slowly setting behind the Opera House, and people walk the length of Circular Quay, dipping into bars for an afternoon drink or simply enjoying the magnificent views.

Even as we get further away from the heart of Sydney, I take in every inch of the streets and the people rushing by. I haven't been to Cronulla before, so tonight being my first shift with the North Sydney Wolves at an away game is a treat. The beaches are stunning and the houses expensive; I thought where my dad lives was boujee, but the Shire is a whole other level.

Dad pulls into the staff parking at the stadium and kills the engine. He turns in his seat, lips thinned in a tight-lipped smile. "Are you sure you're ready for this? I know I talked you into taking this job, but you don't have to do this because I asked you to."

"I'll be fine." I swallow the lump in my throat and force a smile, despite the nervous energy consuming every inch of me.

"Okay," he murmurs, nodding slowly. "If you need anything at all, please don't hesitate to come to me, okay? The guys on the team are great, and so is the rest of the staff. You'll feel right at home, Tate."

Home. I don't know where that is anymore. But now isn't the time to have a crisis.

"I promise, Dad."

He smiles and gets out of the car. My eyes drift toward the large bus parked across the lot with the North Sydney Wolves club logo etched into the side. I wonder if Dad usually takes the team bus with everyone else, or if he decided not to so we could drive together.

I slide out of the car and trail behind Dad as we enter the back of the stadium, heading straight for the locker room. My heart races as we pass by people with clipboards and headsets hanging around their necks. Women with heavy makeup, carrying pom poms and duffle bags, pass by in a burst of laughter and smiles.

Everyone feels important, despite not knowing what they do or why they're here—I don't know much about the NRL world and who the top stars are. My dad may be the head coach for one of the teams, but I didn't grow up watching much because he wasn't home to teach me about the sport. Mum wasn't overly interested in rugby—she only cared about it to support Dad. That has left me with not much experience or knowledge, but I'm looking forward to learning.

"This way, Tate."

Dad gestures for me to follow him into the locker room. In the car, Dad informed me that this room is typically referred to as the 'team sheds'. It was his way of educating me on the lingo, or because he knew I'm walking into the job blind with little to no knowledge. Either way, I appreciate the short lesson because I'm clueless as hell about what I'm getting myself in to.

When I step into the room, my eyes round at the edges. There are a *lot* of shirtless men milling about in front of the open alcoves in the wall I can only assume are built in locker spaces. Black, red and white jerseys hang on small hooks within the rectangle space, and random items spill out of duffle bags. Everywhere I look, a new man appears wearing nothing but black footy shorts and long black socks pushed down to their ankles.

What the hell have I just walked in on?

"All right, listen up!" Dad calls out, his deep voice commanding attention.

Within seconds, all eyes are on him. I shrink behind his tall frame, unable to withstand such pressure of having everyone look at me. In school, I was never the loudest in the room. Having every ounce of attention on me makes my skin crawl, much like it is now as a room full of men stare at me.

"I made mention of this last week, but we have a new physio joining the club today." Dad steps to the side, and I'm blinded by the gazes of what feels like a thousand eyes roaming my face. "This is my daughter, Tatum. From now on, she will be focusing on recovery and any injuries that may come up this season. If you need her advice or want to have a one-on-one session, please don't hesitate to ask." A large hand claps my shoulder, and I nearly jump out of my skin. "Please make her feel welcomed!"

The team clap and cheer, but I hardly hear it over the blood rushing in my ears. *This is mortifying.* It feels like I'm in kindergarten being introduced to my new class. Maybe I should've told Dad not to mention our relationship, but I guess it's too late now.

"And another thing," Dad says. I inwardly groan. *What is it now?* "I'm going to make something very clear to every one of you young lads. My daughter is off-limits, okay? I don't want any of you pursuing something with her. She is here to work, not mess around with you lot. You know my stance on eliminating distractions, especially during training sessions and work hours. I don't care what you lot do at home with your missus or in your free time, but when you're in the training facility and sitting on these benches, your focus should be on the game. Nothing else."

If I could crawl into a ball and allow the ground to swallow me hole, I'd dive head-first without a seconds hesitation.

"Dad," I hiss, throwing my elbow into his side. "Seriously, you need to stop."

He frowns, as if unable to comprehend how incredibly embarrassing it is for my father to warn men away from me. "I'm just trying to protect you and my team. I don't want you getting hurt, and I need these guys to keep their heads in the game. No distractions for either of you."

"I'm not looking to date right now, so you have nothing to worry about. Besides, I understand this is your career, your life, so the last thing I want to do is mess it up."

Dad thins his lips. "Well, good. I would hate for you to go behind my back because then I'd have to fire you. Or worse, discipline one of my players. I want the two most important parts of my life to succeed. That includes you furthering your career, and getting my team to the grand final."

Oh, God. Would he really fire me if I hooked up with one of the players? Not that I want to, but still.

I forgot how intense he can be when it comes to this sport and the people he loves.

"I understand, Dad."

He straightens his spine and turns his attention back to the room of people staring at us. "With that said, I need you guys to form two groups and start warming up."

The team nods in agreement and set about pulling on shirts, slightly different in style to their jerseys. Two older men in caps take each of the two groups into the adjoining room and begin warm-up drills. The rest of the staff watch from the edges of the room, but I stay put.

"What do you want me to do?" I turn to Dad, folding my arms over my chest. Out the corner of my eye, I see the team lunging the length of the room before side skipping back to where they started. "It doesn't look like anyone is injured."

"I have one guy out with a quad injury but he's not here yet," Dad says, his focus on his team as they warm up. "For your first shift, I want you to get to know the team and familiarise yourself with the rest of the staff and how we do things."

"I can do that," I say with a nod. "Should be easy enough."

Dad glances down at his watch. "Okay, we have less than an hour until kick off, so why don't you take a seat and observe."

I pull up the closet white plastic chair and set my handbag at my feet. "You don't have to tell me twice."

For the next forty minutes, I watch the Wolves warm up at the direction of the two assistant coaches. Dad is off somewhere talking to this person and that. Seeing this side of a sports team is interesting. Not only do I get to observe how physically fit these guys are, but it allows me to get to know them from afar, too. How they perform during warm up is a good indicator of where they're at physically, and will let me know what to watch out for when the game starts.

Despite my father's warning for his team to stay away from me, some of them have approached throughout the warm-up to introduce themselves. Each of them was kind and respectful —whether it was due to Dad's warning, I'm not sure. The guy with light brown hair, longer on top and short on the sides and the palest green eyes I have ever seen—if it weren't for the specks of emerald, I would've thought they were grey—made me laugh effortlessly with his bad dad jokes. I think he said his name was Khai.

I have no doubt I'm going to struggle to remember all seventeen of these guys' names. Not to mentioned the other thirteen guys on the extended squad I am yet to meet.

My phone vibrates in my pocket. I tear my gaze from the team forming a huddle in the middle of the room with my dad at the centre. I'm sure he's hyping them up the best he can before the game kicks off.

Glancing down at the lock screen, multiple new messages from my group chat with Noah and Nathan appear. I smile as I flick through the messages. It's been hard not living only a few streets away from my two best friends and being able to see them whenever I want. I know they're only a phone call away but it's not the same.

NATHAN: How goes the big city, Tate? We miss you.

NOAH: We really do. It isn't the same without you. And not to mention I have to deal with this guy on my own now, so thanks a lot.

NATHAN: Hey! Take that back, mister. You were just saying this arvo how much you enjoy spending time with me.

NOAH: Yeah, in small doses.

I chuckle. Even if I'm not around, Nathan will find a way to annoy the shit out of us.

TATE: Don't worry, I miss you both, too. And Noah, would it kill you to send a photo of my niece?

Less than a minute later, a photo pops up in the chat, followed by a text from Noah.

NOAH: Sorry, I've been a bit preoccupied. But here is a photo of Jade I took this morning.

I can't help but grin at the image of Jade with Weetbix smeared across her cheeks, arms, hands and the poor high chair that I'm sure Noah would've despised having to clean before work.

It's moments like these that make me miss Barrenridge. Being close to my friends and watching Jade grow up is what I thought my life would look like.

TATE: Such a pretty girl. Give her a big kiss for me.

NATHAN: And what about me???

TATE: Noah, please give this big doofus a kiss, too.

NOAH: God, why is it always me having to kiss him?

I snort a laugh at the same time a hand clamps down on my shoulder. My gaze snaps from my phone to meet my father's eyes. Looking past him, the team is getting ready to leave the team sheds, which is my cue to get off my phone and back to work.

"Is it kick off time already?" I ask, shoving my phone into my pocket.

Dad nods. "I'm going to head to the sky box to watch from above, but feel free to watch from the sidelines and take notes on whatever it is you need to." He reaches into his pocket, producing a dark green lanyard with *STAFF* printed into the material. A clear tag with my name on it hangs from it. "You'll need to wear this while you're out there. It helps identify you to the other staff members."

The lanyard settles over my torso, cementing me in my new position. I get to watch from the sidelines? That could be fun. If I'm going to be working closely with these guys, I need to see their performance from a better angle.

"Okay, yeah." I stand and clasp my hands behind my back. "I'll wait here until they're out on the field."

"Perfect. Have fun!" Dad cheers and spins on his heels, rushing out of the room.

I blow out a short breath and watch the team walk out of the room one by one. The roar of the crowd can be heard from all the way in the sheds, shocking me. How many fans are out there? There must be a lot if they're *that* loud.

Once I'm the last person standing in the room, I make my way out into the hallway and follow it until I reach a tunnel. At the end, I watch as the Wolves run out onto the field to screaming fans. "Enter Sandman" by Metallica blast through speakers around the stadium.

I can't begin to imagine how overwhelming it must be to run out in front of that many people. Not only would they be under a lot of pressure to perform well for the club and the rest of the team, but they don't want to let their fans down, too.

Taking a moment to calm my breathing, I follow the tunnel until I step out onto the field. No one in the crowd or the people standing on the sidelines take notice of me as I find a free chair in the Wolves team area and sit down. My eyes sweep across the fans littering the grandstand, waving their flags in the air. The hill standing area is packed with not a patch of grass in sight. The stadium is a good mixture of Wolves and Dolphins fans, so I can see this being a tough game.

The two teams get into position with a Wolves kick-off. As soon as the referee blows the whistle and the ball is kicked into the air, the crowd goes nuts.

I can't help but smile as I glance around the stadium. This is crazy, truly. How the players don't lose focus because of the screaming fans is beyond me.

The first tackle on a Dolphins player has me blowing out a sharp breath. God, that must've hurt like a bitch.

It doesn't take long for me to fall into a trance of watching the teams fight for dominance on the field, and thankfully, Wolves get the first try of the game. I jump from my seat and clap with the rest of the staff members and fans. The atmosphere after a try is electric—I feel the thrum of adrenaline pumping in my veins.

I'm too enraptured by the Wolves celebrating their try to notice the man approaching from my left. It isn't until he is a metre away from me do I turn in his direction. The second I take in his inky black hair, sharp facial features and that damn slit in his eyebrow, I realise I'm fucked. So incredibly fucked. It's like looking a ghost from the past dead in the eyes, only this man isn't a ghost and is very much real and breathing.

Why is Sinnett, my one-night stand, staring at me with furrowed brows and a clenched jaw?

Chapter Five

TATUM

Out of all the people I could've run into on my first day at work, it had to be him. The same guy I hooked up with in a car in a quiet park and vowed to forget about.

The universe is playing a cruel joke on me right now. I wish it would cut it out because there is no way this is happening. How unlucky do I have to be to run into my one-night stand out of the millions of people residing in Sydney?

"Tatum?"

Shit.

"Heyyy," I greet with an overly large smile that doesn't fit my face. "Fancy seeing you here."

Sinnett shoves his hands into the front pocket of his hoodie and tilts his head to the side. The curve of his jaw is enhanced with each clench of his teeth as if he's fighting the urge to speak what's on his mind or stay silent. Despite the venomous glint in those dazzling eyes and the stiffness in his shoulders, he looks the same as when I last saw him.

"What are you doing here?" His deep voice vibrates

through every inch of my body like a sound wave. "You're not following me, are you?"

My eyes round at the edges. "What? No, I'm not following you. If I wanted to follow you, it certainly wouldn't be to the sideline of a footy game."

Sinnett blinks at me, unimpressed with my response.

God, what happened to the man I met one week ago? Sure, he only wanted to fuck me in his car and never see me again, but he was at least respectful and somewhat kind. Now he's broody and grumpy as hell. Why the switch up?

I exhale a long breath and run my fingers through the end of my ponytail. A whistle sounds behind me, followed by tense voices. I'm not sure what's happening on the field, and even if I wanted to know, Sinnett has my attention held hostage with his intense ocean eyes and looming presence.

"I'm not following you, I promise," I offer with a shrug. "I work for the Wolves."

Sinnett's neatly shaped eyebrows shoot up to his hairline, getting lost behind the loose waves falling over his forehead. "You *what*?"

"Yeah. I'm the club's new physio."

For a split second, I think I see the colour drain from Sinnett's face. But just as quickly, it returns in full force, making me think the lights in the stadium had simply washed out his skin.

"Oh," he murmurs. A hand slips out from the pocket of his hoodie to run through his messy hair. "I didn't know."

"Do you play for the Wolves?" I ask. Why else would he be here? He's not in uniform, so he must be part of the club in some capacity.

Sinnett nods. "Yeah, I do."

My eyes drift from his face, down the curve of his throat,

over his broad chest and down to his jean-clad thighs. The same thighs I bounced on when I was—

I clear my throat as an excuse to redirect my mind to the present. "Are you injured? Is that why you're not playing?"

All Sinnett manages is a nod before he points a finger behind me. "I need to get going."

"Oh, right," I say, rubbing my right hand over my left arm. "Don't let me keep you from your team."

Sinnett drags his tongue over his bottom lip and nods. "I'll see you around, strawberry."

"I hope not," I utter before I stop to think about what I'm saying. It's a knee jerk reaction to our last conversation, when we said we hoped to never see each other again. But now I just sound like an asshole.

To my surprise, Sinnett chuckles as he walks past me, his shoulder brushing mine.

I spin on my heels and watch his broad back as he walks toward the row of white plastic chairs where some of the players are seated. Each step is met with him putting more pressure on his left leg than his right. Did he hurt his leg? He greets each one of them with what I assume is a bro handshake before he settles between two of the players.

My brows furrow as I sit down on my chair, unable to focus on the game. From the brief interaction with Sinnett, I can't see any physical injuries that might require him to be sidelined. But then again, he is wearing a black hoodie and jeans, covering the majority of his skin. The injury must be serious if he's not playing, or he could have a strain that has forced him to sit out for one game.

Despite my better judgment, I glance over my shoulder and find Sinnett is already watching me. Warmth burns in my cheeks the second our eyes clash. Every muscle in my body is yelling at me to look away, but somehow, I'm trapped by his intense stare. We stay like this, watching each other for what feels like an eternity before Sinnett's attention is drawn away by one of his teammates.

I snap my head forward to stare at the field as the two teams come barrelling past. My pulse thumps at the base of my throat and I'm very aware of the blood rushing through my veins.

What the hell was that?

I mean, I would have to be a rock to not be attracted to a man like Sinnett, but that interaction was... different, and unlike anything I've ever felt. If I were to touch my skin, it would sizzle beneath my fingertips. My heart races to the point it might jump from my throat and crawl over to Sinnett like it's offering itself on a silver platter for him to stomp on.

The crowd erupts into a cheer, forcing my eyes off the ground to watch the Wolves celebrate another try. I blow out a deep exhale and lean back against the plastic chair.

Even with my attention now on the game, Sinnett's intense eyes take up space in my mind. It's like I'm looking at the field with blue-tinted glasses.

I groan and run a hand down my face.

Yeah, I'm totally screwed.

I blink at Dad, my mind lost at sea. "Oh, yeah. It was a good win for the Wolves."

After the final siren blared through the stadium, I stood on the sideline and waited for my dad to join the team on the field. Despite being new to the club and staffing team, I enjoyed watching everyone interact with each other after an exceptional 22-8 win over the Dolphins.

Once the players shook hands with the opposing team, they rushed to the fence surrounding the field to speak with family members who drove down for the away game. I couldn't help but smile as I watched each player laugh and joke around with their family. After a big win, I'm sure it would've been nice for them to know their loved ones were watching on in support.

Despite telling myself I wouldn't, I watched Sinnett linger among his teammates. He was called over to the fence by some young fans asking for his signature on their jerseys. Each one of them smiled as if they had met their hero, giddy with excitement. I tried not to watch when Sinnett smiled for selfies with girls not much younger than me, but like a bad car accident, I couldn't look away. His smile looked forced and didn't quite reach his eyes. Not like they did when I made him laugh a week ago.

"The guys played well," Dad says, breaking me from my thoughts. "Of course, there are areas they can improve on, but for now, I'm letting them enjoy the win."

The Dolphins are on the opposite side of the field interacting with their own fans while the Wolves players left for the sheds a couple of minutes ago, leaving only the staff members lingering on the sidelines.

"Did you see anything out of the ordinary when you were watching the team?"

I blink at Dad. Shit. I forgot I was supposed to be observing the players and not stealing glances of a certain someone. "They all looked in good shape to me. But I'll know for sure when I'm doing recovery with them."

"Good, I'm glad to hear it."

Dad's face lights up at something behind me. Every hair on

the back of my arms stand on edge when I turn around and see Sinnett approaching us. His hands are shoved in the front pocket of his hoodie, and within a few long strides he joins my father and I.

Oh, God...

"Sin," Dad cheers with a warm smile. "How are you feeling?"

Sinnett shrugs. "Okay, I guess."

Dad's face falls with what I'm sure is empathy. "I know it sucks watching from the sidelines, but you know it's for your own good. I can't have you going out there before you're ready."

Sinnett scratches the back of his head, unable to look me in the eye. "I understand. I'm doing everything I can in my recovery to ensure I'm fit enough to get back on the field soon."

"Oh!" Dad snaps his eyes to me, as if realising I'm still standing with them. "Speaking of recovery, this is Tatum. She's the club's new physio."

Sinnett sweeps his ocean eyes to me, offering a sharp nod. "Yeah, we met earlier."

"Good," Dad says with a nod, folding his arms over his chest. "Since you'll be working closely with each other, I expect you to treat my daughter with respect."

It is at this moment Sinnett's jaw hits the floor and his eyes nearly bulge out of his head.

Okay, maybe that was a little dramatic, but he does snap his wide eyes to me, as if unable to believe what just came out of my father's mouth.

"*Daughter*?" Sinnett rasps out. "Tatum is your daughter?"

"She is," Dad says, features sharpening. "And no funny business, okay? She's off-limits, and that goes for the rest of the team, too."

Sinnett hisses a breath and runs his hand through his hair, leaving some of the inky strands standing on end. He draws his eyes back to my father, jaw ticking.

I may as well not be here for this conversation since Sinnett and my father would prefer to talk about me rather than directly to me. But what can I say? *Hey, Dad, funny story actually, I've already hooked up with Sinnett.* I would be a dead woman.

All I can do is keep my mouth shut and pray Sinnett does the same.

Sinnett's throat ripples with a deep swallow as he turns his intense eyes to mine again. I suck in a sharp breath, trying to ignore the heat pulsing through my veins. It's on the tip of my tongue to say something—anything—but I'm at a loss for words.

My father has forbidden me from dating any player on the team, yet he doesn't realise he's looking at the rule I've already broken directly in the eye.

"Of course, Coach," Sinnett finally says, his eyes not straying from mine. "I promise I'll keep my hands to myself."

Chapter Six

SINNETT

A chorus of voices echoes through the room, bouncing off the walls and settling deep in my veins, putting me further on edge. Mint consumes my senses, courtesy of the Deep Heat tubes that were passed around the sheds when the team returned from the field. It's a scent I've grown used to after many games, and is a welcome relief from the BO and Lynx deodorant coating the walls.

My biceps bulge as I tighten my folded arms, eyes sweeping across my teammates jumping in the middle of the room. Liquid sprays in the air from someone's water bottle, coating everyone in the vicinity. Thankfully, I'm standing at the edge of the room, out of the crossfire.

"We are the Wolves, we're standing tall. We're here for the win, we'll answer the call!"

My focus shifts to the woman standing on the opposite side of the room, eyes wide like a newborn deer as she takes in the chaotic scene. She drags her plump bottom lip between her teeth—the same lips that were wrapped around my cock a week ago.

Electricity thrums in my veins as I drink her in. Strawberry blonde hair spills over her shoulders in subtle waves, accentuating the curve of her jawline and high cheekbones. Her slender shoulders are pushed back as if trying to feel bigger in a room full of overly large men. It must be an impossible feat considering the number of men taking up space.

What is she doing here? When I dropped her at her house in Barrenridge last weekend, I had expected to never see her face again. Now here she is, invading the space I keep heavily guarded, and reminding me why I was drawn to her in the first place. Why I couldn't walk away without getting a taste of her that night.

Her constant questions and ability to get under my skin weren't a deterrent for me. Nor was the joy emitting from her soft skin every time she did manage to rile me up. If anything, it pulled me closer, my body wanting to see what else this woman was capable of.

It was a change in pace, being with someone who didn't know me or my family. Who couldn't care less about my career or being attached to the Baxter name. At that moment, Tatum didn't know a single thing about me. It gave me the chance to get lost in her softness and forget about my fucking injury. To forget about my overbearing parents and the pressure I face each day from the media and the club.

It was just me and her.

And now I'm facing her again, wondering what the hell I'm going to do.

Coach Phil walks over to Tatum and says something to her. She smiles and nods. My gaze follows her as she walks past me to leave the room. I wish she would look up, to allow me a split second of seeing those jade eyes that have found their way into my dreams over the past week. But she doesn't.

With Tatum out of the room, I release the breath I had

been holding and slump on one of the plastic chairs forming a circle in the centre of the room. My hands fall to my knees, fingers tightening around them as I watch my team celebrate a win I desperately wanted to be part of. If it weren't for this stupid injury and the conditioning team refusing to give me the go-ahead to get back on the field until the six-week recovery mark, I would've been out there with my friends.

"Hey." A large mass I recognise as my best friend plops down on the chair beside me. Strands of sweat-soaked brown hair fall limp over his forehead, matching the moisture slicked across his bare torso. "Why the long face?"

"I don't have a long face," I huff, leaning back on the chair. The movement puts pressure on my right quad, sending a jab of pain down my leg. I bite on my bottom lip to keep from letting on how much that fucking hurt and rub a hand over the swollen muscle.

Khai nudges my side with his elbow. "Come on, man. I've known you a long time, which means I know when you have a long face." He gestures to the team settling down after the celebration. Beers are being passed around, and someone switched on their portable speaker, Kendrick Lamar's voice bouncing off the walls. "Is it because you're stuck watching from the sidelines?"

My jaw clenches at the reminder. "No."

"You're lying to me."

"I'm not lying."

"Yes, you are."

I exhale a breath and run my hand through my hair. "Has anyone ever told you that you talk too much?"

Khai snorts a laugh. "Yeah, you, asshole." He leans back on the chair and spreads his legs out. "Talk to me, Sin."

What the hell do I say to him?

I'm gutted I can't play for at least four weeks, and even then, the timeline of my recovery is still in the air.

I'm angry at myself for getting injured during a tackle.

I'm frustrated with my father and his constant nagging about me getting back on the field.

And don't even get me started on Coach Phil's daughter.

"I don't know," I murmur, dragging my attention from the people in the room to the pale green eyes watching me, waiting. "I have a lot of shit going on."

"I could imagine." Khai's tone is laced with understanding. His shoulders slump forward as he looks over the guys sitting in the circle of chairs around us. "You have a good support network around you who will ensure you recover well. If you push yourself too much, you might do more harm than good. Just take this time to recover properly and we'll see you back out there in the number seven jersey in no time."

I wish it were that easy. But with my father breathing down my neck and the pressure from the club to perform well this year, I don't have time to take this recovery easy. I need to get back out there as soon as possible.

"Yeah, maybe."

Khai claps a hand on my shoulder, forcing my attention to him. A shit-eating grin splits his face, and I groan, bracing myself for what he's about to say. And if I know Khai, I'm in for a ride.

We've been friends since the moment we could walk. Our parents were neighbours, so we grew up on the same street, playing touch footy in his front yard and sneaking food and alcohol at block parties when our parents weren't looking. Peers in our year group knew we were joined at the hip, and all throughout primary and high school, we stayed by each other's side—no matter what. Khai is a loyal friend—one I trust my life and deepest, darkest secrets with. But in saying that, he also knows how to annoy the shit out of me.

"So, how was Barrenridge?" He wiggles his brows at me, and I can't help but roll my eyes. "I know you went up there to help Mia move in with your gran, but *please* tell me you got some pussy to take your mind off everything."

"I did, but I don't kiss and tell."

Khai gasps in feigned horror. "You motherfucker. I thought we had a deal that we would share details like this, and now you're holding out on me."

I roll my eyes. "I only tell you about my hook ups because you don't shut the fuck up until I do."

"Yeah, well, I like to know these things about my best friend." He spins on the chair so his legs are over the side, brushing the side of my mine. "And because you've said it, I'm going to annoy the shit out of you until you give me every last, juicy, gory detail."

"*Fuck*, all right," I groan, shoving a hand through my hair. "But one of these days I'm going to hold out on you."

Khai grins. "It doesn't sound like you're very good at holding out on someone."

I stifle a laugh and shove at his shoulder. "Dick."

"Yeah, I want to know about what you did with yours, so fucking spill it."

"Okay," I mutter, and exhale a deep breath. "I went out for a drink because I wanted to be by myself, and since there is fuck all to do in a small town like Barrenridge, the pub was my only option. It was there I met this girl, and I don't know, man, I just... had to have her."

Khai's gaze stays locked on the side of my face as I stare ahead, like he's listening to the best bedtime story known to mankind. "And?"

"And we had sex in my car," I state simply. My chest

tightens at the memory of Tatum crawling over the center console and seating herself on me like she owned it—like she owned me. "I dropped her home afterward."

A low whistle sounds from Khai's lips as his fist pushes my shoulder. "You dirty dog, Sin. I knew you were freaky, but car sex is next level. I hope you didn't scare the kids in the town."

"Shut up," I grumble with an eye roll. "There's a park outside of town that is deserted at night. No children were harmed."

"Is that all?" he probes. "No details about who she is or what she looks like? I'm sure she was hot. Unless country people look a little... strange, if you know what I mean."

Tatum saunters into the room, drawing the eyes from every player as she passes by, walking toward her dad nestled in the corner of the room with some of the staff members. I trail her, admiring the way her pony tail swishes and her hips sway to the beat of her steps. I'm reminded of her curves hidden beneath the black clothing, and how warm and smooth she felt against me.

My dick strains against the zipper of my jeans, and I will it to calm the fuck down. I can't be popping a boner with my best friend beside me. We're close, but Christ, not that close.

"You want to know who I hooked up with?" I tilt my head to peek at Khai. Curiosity consumes his features. "Well, she's standing beside Coach."

Khai frowns as he swivels his body to find him. "What? I don't know what—oh."

"Yeah."

"You fucked Coach's daughter?"

The pitch of his voice makes me cringe, and I sink lower into the chair, as if it were possible.

"Do you want to say it louder?" I hiss, eyes darting around

the room. "I don't think Coach heard you say I fucked his *daughter*."

"What the fuck, man?" Khai swings to face me again, eyes wide. "Did you know who she was?"

"What? No, I had no idea who she was at the time." I clench my jaw. "I didn't know until Coach introduced me to her after the game."

"Shit," he breathes, chewing on his bottom lip. "I mean, even if he finds out about it, he can't be too mad since you didn't know who she was at the time."

"I didn't even know he had a daughter." Tatum's eyes find mine across the room, and I suppress a groan at how easily they lock me in, pulling me toward her like a siren song. "And if Coach finds out, he's going to hand me my ass."

"Forget handing your ass to you, he might just kill you, Sin."

I swallow hard, unable to tear my gaze away from Tatum. *I'm so fucked.*

"He can never find out. You know how intense he can be, and if he finds out about this, what I did with Tatum, who knows what he might do. My contract is up at this end of this season, and he might use it as a reason to dissuade the club from offering me a new one." My voice is low, almost a whisper in the loud space.

"Do you really think he would stoop that low for his daughter?" Khai questions.

"I'm not willing to find out." Exhaling a deep breath, I run my hand through my hair. "Promise me you won't tell anyone."

Khai holds his hand over his heart, straightening his spine. "Scout's honour."

I chuckle, unable to stop myself. "You're an idiot."

"An idiot who will make it his life mission that you don't

get murdered by our coach for clapping cheeks with his daughter."

I lift my arm to shove at his shoulder when a familiar voice calls my name. My eyes instinctually flutter close and ice floods my veins.

I'm in no mood to deal with this. Or her.

Khai grins. "I would say I feel bad for you, but I did try to warn you about sticking your dick in her last year. I'm pretty sure she has velcro attached to her hip."

My palms dig into the curves of my eyes, and I wish I could pluck them out so I don't have to look at her. "You're of no help."

Khai shrugs. "Look, I can only help you so much before I'm left beating a dead horse."

"Sin!"

Fuck me.

My hands fall to my lap at the same time Zoe steps in front of me. Manicured fingers dig into her hips as she stares down at me with the heat of a thousand suns. If it were possible to be ten feet under from the look alone, I would be.

"Are you deaf?" she hisses, honey eyes meeting mine.

"Nope, just talking."

Zoe folds her arms over her chest, barely contained in the white tank top. "Why haven't you been answering my calls or texts?"

Because I would rather gauge out my eyes than spend a second talking to you. "I've been busy."

"Well, I've hardly seen you since you got injured and I wanted to make sure you were okay."

Why? So you can continue sleeping with me? "I'm fine, Zoe."

Zoe huffs at my lack of interest in speaking with her and runs her fingers through the ends of the brown hair resting on her slender shoulders. I wish she would take the hint that I'm no longer interested in her, but it seems she lacks the brain cells to pick up what I'm so clearly putting down in front of her. Surely my zero communication would be clue enough.

I made the mistake of hooking up with her during last season. We won the first game in week one of the finals, and I found myself celebrating a little too hard with some of the boys on the team. Zoe and her group of friends—who are part of the Wolves cheerleading squad—joined us in the sheds for some drinks. Zoe had been trying to make a move on me all season, so after consuming a lot of alcohol, my senses were lowered enough to throw her a bone. And from there, I was unable to stop going to her house whenever she texted. It was a routine I couldn't get out of because it was an outlet I often needed after games or tough training sessions. But it wasn't until I couldn't stand being around her, even when we were having sex, that I put an end to it. That was last month.

But it seems Zoe isn't on the same page as me yet.

Zoe lowers her arms to her side and tilts her head, batting her eyelashes—a move that no longer works on me. "You seem stressed, Sin. I know something that might help take the edge off." Her suggestive tone reminds me of every other time she would use that same line on me, and I'd fall into her trap like a blind man.

"I'm good." I jab a thumb at Khai, who smiles and waves. "Khai and I are just gonna head home."

Zoe's red-painted lip turns down in a pout. "Come on, Sin. I can't keep playing this cat and mouse game with you."

"You're the only one playing," I point out, tone sharp. "I told you last month where I stand."

If we weren't in a room full of people, I have no doubt she would stomp her foot on the ground like a child who just got their favourite toy taken away.

"What are you even doing here?" Khai asks, voice light.

"Some of the girls wanted to watch the game," Zoe responds, her eyes locked on mine. "And I wanted to see Sin."

"Well, you've seen him now, so you better run along."

I can't stop the grin forming on my face at Khai's dismissal. I may not have listened to him when he warned me against getting involved with Zoe, but I appreciate his effort to keep her away from me now.

A red hue coats the curve of her olive-toned neck. She huffs out a breath, pinning me with her eyes. "This isn't over, Sin."

"I think it is, though."

She groans and spins on her heels, storming out of the room. Multiple eyes track her movements, even the jade eyes in the corner of the room. I can only imagine what Tatum is thinking right now, but I don't have the energy to explain myself, even if I wanted to.

"We should go," I murmur, turning my body to face Khai. "Before I drown between the regret from my past and my most recent decision."

Khai chuckles and shakes his head. "You've gotten yourself into a pickle, haven't you?"

"Don't I know it," I grumble, folding my arms over my chest.

"All right, give me ten minutes."

Ten minutes pass by at an agonisingly slow pace. Khai fucks around with getting out of his uniform and collecting his gym bag. He stands around talking with some of the staff and players while I pace by the entrance to the sheds, even more on edge than I was earlier.

Khai has always been Mr Popular in the team because of his friendly nature and ability to hold a conversation. But right now, I wish he would shut up so we can get the hell out of here.

A presence at my side stops my pacing, drawing my attention to the kid not much younger than me. If you can call a nineteen-year-old a kid. Jace has his gym bag slung over his shoulder, his dirty-blonde hair slick with water after showering after the game. Dressed in black jeans and a white long-sleeved button up, he looks ready to go to a fancy dinner.

"Going out tonight?" I ask, shoving my hands into the pocket of my jeans.

Jace shakes his head. "I'm heading over to my girlfriends house."

"Dressed like that?"

A smirk curls up his lips. "Well, some of us like to dress up for our girls instead of stripping the moment we walk through the door."

The jab at my complicated relationship with Zoe should annoy me, but I can't deny he's not wrong. Every guy on the team knows about Zoe, which doesn't bother me in the slightest. With how much time we spend together each week training, travelling to games and flying interstate, the team is like an open book. It's hard to keep secrets, so them finding out about Zoe was inevitable.

"You got me." I clap him on the shoulder. "You did good out there, J."

Jace's lips thin, the corner of his mouth curling up. "Yeah, well, stepping up to halfback is no easy feat, especially when I'm filling your shoes."

When I got injured two weeks ago, Jace was pulled from the reserve grade team to take on my position until I returned. While I was fucking pissed that I was going to be contained to the sidelines for six weeks, I was at least pleased knowing Jace was going to get some field time with the main squad. At first, I didn't know how he would gel with the team, but to my surprise, he slipped into the role tonight with grace and took on the advice I gave him last night when he called.

I can see this kid going far as a halfback if he refines his skills.

"The Dolphins are a tough side, but you held your own out there," I tell him. "Great job."

The praise lights up his pale blue eyes. I don't know if he was expecting me to offer the compliment after his first game as the starting halfback, but it is well-deserved after the win tonight.

"Can I expect to hear this every week?" he teases, pumping his eyebrows.

I roll my eyes. "Don't get too ahead of yourself. If we start losing, I'll have to come up with other ways to encourage you."

Jace chuckles and claps me on the shoulder. "Noted." He drops his eyes to my leg, rolling his lips. "You all good?"

No. "Yeah, yeah, I'm all good, man. Nothing I can't handle, right?"

He doesn't look convinced, the crease in his brows say so. And honestly, neither am I.

"Well, rest up, okay? Let me know if you need anything."

"Will do."

Jace moves past me, walking out of the room. I exhale and run my hands through my hair; my earlier pacing resumes. I shouldn't be putting this much pressure on my leg, but I need to do something to keep the adrenaline pouring through my veins from exploding.

When Khai finally joins me, Coach Phil and Tatum are walking in our direction. I silently curse Khai for taking his sweet ass time, because now I have to face the one person I can't seem to forget.

"Great job tonight, Khai," Coach says with a warm smile, clapping his five-eighth on the back. "I'll see you on Monday."

"See you then, Coach." Khai returns the gesture with a smile of his own.

Coach turns his attention to me. "Take it easy, Sin. Okay?"

"Yes, sir," I murmur, shoving my hands into the front pocket of my hoodie.

He nods. "I'll also see you on Monday. The team wants to go over your recovery schedule to make sure you're on track. And, of course, Tate will look over your records before Monday so she has an idea of what is going on."

"Yes, of course." I meet Tatum's eyes. She stands beside her father, peering up at me through thick lashes. Electricity crackles between us, embedding itself into my skin and heating my veins. My body aches to feel her again, to touch her skin and feel her warmth. But I can't. Not now that I know who she is. The best thing for both of us is if I keep my distance from her.

"Good night, then," Coach says, directing it at both of us. "Get home safely."

Tatum tears her eyes from me as she follows her father out of the room, disappearing from sight. My focus stays trained on the door long after she leaves. It isn't until Khai's deep laughter sounds in my ears do I crash back to reality.

Khai claps my shoulder as he slips past to leave. "Oh, dude. You're so fucked."

I exhale a breath and follow him.

Yeah, in more ways than one.

Chapter Seven

TATUM

If I were part of the Wolves and my father spoke the way he is right now, I would've burst into tears. Not because he's yelling or belittling anyone, but he's making it perfectly clear to the team that they still have room for improvement after the game on Saturday night.

My gaze sweeps across the room with five rows of plush chairs, kind of like a movie theatre but instead it's a small room in the training facility. Each of the thirty players in the team, dressed in their black and red training sleeveless jerseys and black shorts, listen intently to each word that falls from Dad's mouth.

No one seems upset by his constructive feedback about the game on Saturday night. If anything, they nod along and ask questions when needed.

Maybe I'm the snowflake who wouldn't be able to handle such intense feedback, and I'm reading this interaction all wrong.

I feel Sinnett's eyes on the side of my face from where he sits in the front row. His messy hair falls effortlessly over his forehead, shielding intense blue eyes that pierce through my soul. Today, he's dressed the same as everyone else—a change from his usual hoodie—leaving his toned muscles on display. Each ridge and rivet is masked by black ink embedded into the tanned skin. The different designs paint a picture of what I'm sure Sin holds no personal connection to, likely having gotten them in the spur of the moment. Either way, they add to his already intimidating frame. Even the gap in material under his arm reveals swirls of ink hidden beneath the shirt, just another mystery attached to Sinnett.

What else is this man hiding from the world?

My gaze lingers on the sports tape wrapped across his right quad—a reminder of the injury he's dealing with, and my 'top priority' as my father put it after the game. On the drive home, he had reiterated that it's important Sinnett stays on track with the recovery schedule and doesn't push himself too hard. Dad provided me with the X-ray of his leg, and there didn't seem to be any broken bones, so my guess is that it's purely a muscle issue. I told Dad I would look Sinnett over after the briefing, and that moment is fast approaching.

Nervous energy races through my veins, my knee bouncing mindlessly as I force my gaze to my dad. He's still going over the analytics from the previous game, and I can't help but admire the passion seeping into every word he says. It's obvious how much he loves the sport, considering the many years he put his body on the line to further his career. I'm sure it's not every day someone like him, with a passion and drive for rugby, comes around to coach a team to greatness.

Once Dad wraps up the session, he instructs the team to hit the gym on the opposite side of the building with a focus on weightlifting. I rush to his side before someone from the staffing team has a chance to swoop in and nab his attention.

"That was truly inspiring," I tell him, clasping my hands behind my back. "It's great seeing you in your natural habitat."

Dad pulls a cap over his head, smiling. "Thank you, Tate. Maybe you should tell the team that so they'll listen." There's no malice in his words; instead he framed them with a slight chuckle.

"I'm sure they're doing their best, Dad."

"I know, I know." A smile warms his face. "I'm heading to lunch with some of the staff, so you'll be all right by yourself?"

I nod. "I have my first session with Sinnett."

"Ah, yes." Dad flicks his eyes to where Sinnett stands in the front row with Khai, their voices hushed. "I need you to take good care of him, Tate. He needs to be in top shape before we can allow him back on the field."

"I've got this. Nothing bad will happen to your star player." I wish the confidence in my voice translated to the tremor tearing through my limbs.

He exhales a long breath and drags his attention back to me. "Sin likes to push himself to the limits, and I fear he's going to do the same with his recovery. He's a strong-headed man and loves the game, so I'm going to need you to keep him in check for me."

I wish I knew how to do that.

"I'll try my best."

Dad smiles and pats my shoulder. "You're the best. And if you need anything, you know where to find me."

He follows the rest of the team out, and with Khai the last one out the door, Sinnett and I remain in the room. His intense eyes find mine from across the small space, searing holes into my already fragile body.

I'm reminded of how he looked at me in his car, how he made me feel like I was the only girl in the world, the one person sharing his orbit. And while I feel a similar tension, it feels more reserved, guarded. He's putting up walls between us, and part of me wishes he wouldn't. But the other part knows that with my father as his coach, and the no dating rule in place, he doesn't have a choice.

I exhale a long breath and rush out the door, Sinnett hot on my heels. Each step echoes in my ears as we make our way across the facility to the examination rooms. A buzz of nerves hum in my veins as I push open the door to the room, stepping to the side so he can enter. Cinnamon and cedarwood consume my senses as he moves past me to the table in the centre of the too bright room. His scent melts into my skin, and I have to fight the urge to take a deep breath.

"Lie down when you're ready." My voice cracks, sounding weird to my ears. I fight the urge to cringe as I walk to the table beside the bed, my back turned to him.

Sinnett doesn't say a word as he climbs onto the bed.

If someone were to walk into the room, they could cut the tension with a blunt knife.

"Ready when you are." Sinnett's deep voice sends a shock wave down my spine, and I shiver.

When I turn to him, I keep my eyes locked on his thigh, which could prove to be a bad decision because my goodness they're bigger than I remember. I clear my throat. "So, tell me how this injury occurred."

Sinnett clears his throat and shifts his hands so they're resting under his head, eyes locked on the ceiling. "I took a hard knee to the thigh during a rough tackle. The pain was immediate. At first, I couldn't tell if I had broken a bone or if it was muscle related."

"I did look over the X-ray taken from the day it happened, and there doesn't seem to be any broken bones. Although, I'm sure your previous physio told you that."

Sinnett nods. "He put me on a recovery plan of light

stretches, but I feel like I could be doing more. I *need* to be doing more."

The desperation melting into his voice doesn't go unnoticed by me. He's eager to get back on the field, and I understand why. With this being his career, being out of action means a lot of pressure is likely building on his shoulders. Pressure to come back as fit and strong as he previously was. Pressure that he might be letting his team down because of the injury. Being injured doesn't mean he can sit around and wait for it to heal, not if he wants to pass the physical examination to play. Not only does he need to focus on the recovery, but staying fit, too.

I swallow hard and eye his quad. "Mind if I take a look?"

"Be my guest."

The tremble in my hands is embarrassing. Why am I so affected by him? I need to get a damn grip.

The area appears swollen in some places with minimal bruising, but other than that, it doesn't look too bad. But the muscles could be a different story.

"My dad told me you suffered a grade two quadriceps muscle contusion, based on what the previous physio observed." I trail my fingers over the swollen area, searching for lumps or any indication that something is amiss. Goosebumps rise in their wake, and I fight the urge to smile in triumph at his reaction to me. "What is your flexibility like with movement?"

I'm reminded of how he limped on the field during the game. Sinnett's face was devoid of emotion when he walked, but with the swelling and how early on he is in the recovery period, he should be harbouring more pain than he's letting on.

"Well, I can sit and stand if that's what you're referring to," Sinnett responds, voice gruff.

"And what's the pain level like?" I grab his ankle and gently guide his leg to bend into a right angle. A sharp intake of breath forces my attention to Sinnett. He bites his bottom lip as he stares at the ceiling. "If your expression is anything to go by, I'm going to guess the pain is moderate and uncomfortable."

"No," he rasps, voice tight as I lay his leg flat on the table. "I can manage it."

"Mhm," I hum as I extend his leg and push it toward the roof. Another sharp intake of breath. "And I call bullshit."

Sinnett scoffs, drawing my gaze from his thigh to his bright eyes. There's an emotion swirling behind them I can't seem to place.

"Are you calling me a liar?" he deadpans.

I lower his leg on the table, meeting his eyes. "I'm saying you're not being honest about the pain you're in."

Sinnett pushes himself up on his elbows, biceps bulging as he holds eye contact. His jaw clenches, eyes thinning. For a split moment, I'm convinced he's going to tell me to go fuck myself and storm out of the room. But he surprises me by dropping onto his back and sighing.

"If I reveal how painful this fucking injury is, I might be out for longer than planned."

My chest tightens at his admission. "Sin, if you lie about the pain, I can't help you the way I'm meant to. Knowing exactly how you're feeling and where it hurts will allow me to adjust your recovery plan and make sure you're healed by the six-week mark."

His throat works a swallow. "And if I don't?"

I exhale a low breath. "Then I won't be able to clear you to play."

Sinnett shoves his palms into his eyes and groans.

I can't imagine what it must be like to be in his shoes, not knowing how the injury is going to heal or when he'll get to play again. But these types of injuries make you play the waiting game. Being thrust into the unknown is what makes people take chances and push boundaries that could result in making the injury worse.

"What should I do?" Sinnett rasps out, runing a hand through his hair.

"Follow the recovery plan I make for you," I offer with a shrug. "And if you go at a steady pace and don't push yourself too hard, you'll make great progress in no time."

He exhales a deep breath. "Can I trust you?"

My throat tightens. "I hope so."

Ocean eyes clash with mine, a fire burning within them. His words hold a weight to them that I don't understand or can't comprehend yet. But I do know his recovery rides on my professional assessment, and given Sinnett's status, it's a pressure I'm not sure I'm ready to carry.

Sinnett sighs and pushes himself into a seated position, swinging his legs over the side. I stay rooted to the spot in front of the table, less than a metre from him.

"If you're honest with me, I'll do everything I can to help you," I say, my voice gentle.

He nods and runs a hand through his hair—a habit I'm starting to pick up on. "Well, in the spirit of being honest, when you were riding me last week, my thigh hurt like a motherfucker."

I blanch at his words, colour draining from my face until I'm a character from a black and white film. He did *not* just say that. "Sinnett!"

A smirk tilts his lips up. "You told me to be honest, strawberry."

"I-I know, I just—" I hold up my hand and take a deep breath, steadying my racing heart. "I'm sorry I hurt you."

"No need to apologise. I liked it, remember? Wanted it, even."

I do indeed remember how well we fit together like two missing puzzle pieces and how he called me a *good girl*. Our night together has been on replay in my mind for the past week, so of course, I remember.

"Yeah, well, you should've told me you were injured," I murmur, rubbing my hand over my arm to distract my racing heart.

"And what?" Sinnett presses, tilting his head to the side. "I couldn't take you back to my grandmother's house, and I don't do sleepovers. Besides, I think you enjoyed the car just as much as I did."

Heat explodes across my cheeks. "Yeah, look, about that—"

"Allow me," he interjects, holding my gaze. "I'll be the first to admit that the night we shared was mind-blowing. But knowing who you are... I can't do it. My career comes first, and I don't want to piss your dad off."

My chest tightens with a pang of disappointment. I knew this conversation needed to happen eventually, but hearing the words come from his mouth is a shock to my system either way. We agreed that it was a one-time thing, but ever since that night, my body has craved more, despite me telling it to move on. And now Sinnett has hammered in the final nail on the coffin to something that was always just out of reach.

I swallow hard. "I understand. My father can be... overprotective of me at times."

Sinnett raises a brow. "That's one way to put it. But I respect him as a person enough to listen to his rules."

He stands from the table, his frame towering over me. I tilt my head back to meet his gaze—Jesus, what is this man, like 6'3?—my heart thundering in my chest. Electricity hums in my veins at the proximity of his body, and my fingers twitch at my sides as I'm consumed by his woodsy scent.

"Give me your phone," I murmur.

He raises a brow. Instead of refusing like I thought he might, he reaches into his pocket and unlocks his phone. With the device in hand, I click on his contact list and type in my number. I'm surprised he's giving me such access to his phone without so much as showing a hint of anxiety about what I could do with it—or see on it.

"This is my number." I save the contact name as TATUM and text myself so I'll have his number, too. "If you need anything, don't hesitate to ask. And rest assured, I'll be checking in regularly with you on your recovery progression."

Sinnett accepts his phone when I hand it back to him, an amused smirk tilting up the corner of his mouth. "I'll be seeing you around, strawberry."

"I hope not," I rasp out, voice tight.

A grin splits across Sinnett's face as he steps back, allowing me a reprieve from the tension swirling between us. He simply shakes his head and turns, leaving the room with the grace and confidence of a man who knows what affect he holds over me and my body.

I exhale a shaky breath and slump against the table, trembling fingers gripping the edge to keep my body upright.

I'm going to need to find a way to forget about this man if I'm to make it through this season with my heart intact.

DAD RETURNS HOME FROM WORK TO FIND ME SITTING on the lounge, focused on my laptop screen. He drops his backpack somewhere by the lounge and plops onto the plush cushion beside me, exhaling a sharp breath.

Tearing my eyes away, I turn to him. Exhaustion seeps into his skin, his side profile shrouded in a soft, orange glow from the standing lamp to my right. A hand runs down the side of his face, scratching at the stubble growing there.

"How was work?" I ask. Although I already know the answer—it's written on his face.

"Long," Dad answers. He swivels his head, blue eyes blinking back at me. "But then again, every day is long."

"You need to rest more, which means not bringing work home with you. Don't think I haven't noticed how distracted you've been since I moved in, especially last week before I started working." He spent a majority of yesterday hidden away in his office. Doing what? I have no idea. But after the presentation he gave today going over the plays from the game on Saturday, he was likely in communication with his coaching team while he prepared his notes.

When Dad was home for dinner, we would sit down together, but I could tell he wasn't mentally present. The faraway look in his eyes told me his mind was elsewhere. Whether he was thinking about work or something else, I'm not sure.

It made me realise that I don't know Dad as well as I should. When I lived on campus during my uni days, I made the effort to visit for dinner once a week between classes, assessments and spending time with Jayden. We would talk about what we were up to—mostly uni and Dad's work. The topic of Mum's condition came up a lot. Dad and I felt tremendous guilt for leaving her alone in Barrenridge, but she was as selfless as they came. She all but forced me to move to Sydney for uni, reminding me that I needed to follow my dreams, and encouraged Dad to continue working with the club, knowing it made him happy.

It pained me to leave her, knowing she could deteriorate at any given moment. The three-hour drive home became a fortnightly ritual, and when I wasn't visiting, we'd spend every second-day on the phone. It was the only way I could feel close to her and ease some of the worry I felt. She had her best friend, Kat, just down the street if she needed anything. Mum was never truly alone, but it didn't stop me from texting her every chance I got.

Living with Dad again full-time is a reminder that I have years of catching up to do. There's still so much to learn about him that I never got the chance to uncover growing up.

Dad exhales a sharp breath. "I know, Tate. I'll try to be more present, okay? For you."

More present for me. I longed to hear those words as a child, wondering why my dad wasn't at my assemblies when I received awards or why he wasn't around to help decorate my hat for the Easter parade.

It seems he is trying to make up for lost time, too.

"Just relax more," I tell him instead. "Okay?"

He nods, but the movement is stiff. It's as if he was forcing himself to do it, not believing he'll be able to stick to the promise.

A beat of silence settles in the room, but then Dad asks, "Whatcha working on?"

My eyes flick to my laptop screen open onto a document I have been working on for what has felt like hours since getting home. The sun is no longer hanging in the sky, replaced by the soft glow of the moon. Without realising it, the day slipped out from beneath me.

"Oh, this?" I gesture to the screen with a flick of my wrist. "I've been adjusting Sinnett's recovery schedule. After my session with him today, learning about the injury and how he's feeling, I have a good idea of what plan he needs to follow moving forward."

I haven't seen too many quadricep muscle contusions in my career, mostly because I worked with elderly people at Happy Limbs. Injuries in athletes require far more research and in-depth plans to help aid their recovery—a simple plan of stretches isn't going to cut it for Sinnett.

"It has stretches he needs to complete each morning and night, and he needs to follow the RICE method before bed—rest, ice, compression and elevate to relieve the pain and swelling. He can still lift weights, but cannot put too much pressure on his leg, at least until I'm confident the muscle can handle it. And in between all of that, I have a list of exercises to help strengthen the muscle again."

Dad whistles, eyes flicking between me and my laptop. "Woah, Tate. You've really thought this all through."

I nod. "You told me that Sinnett is my top priority, so I'm throwing everything I can into this plan. Besides, I got the feeling from my conversation with him today that he's keen to do whatever it takes to get back onto the field as soon as possible."

"He's a tough kid, I'll give him that."

"And stubborn," I retort, rolling my eyes.

Dad chuckles. "That, too. But the plan sounds great. Once you're done with it, forward it to Todd, the head assistant coach, for him to review before we pass it along to Sinnett."

I nod. "Will do." A wave of nerves rolls over me. What if Sinnett doesn't like my plan and refuses to follow it after the effort I put into it? A kick to the teeth would hurt less, no doubt.

Dad slaps his thighs and pushes to his feet, eyes flicking to the clock on the wall. "It's getting late. Should we order in something for dinner?"

My stomach growls at the mention of food, reminding me I haven't eaten since lunch. "Chinese would be great."

"Consider it done." Dad leans down behind the dark grey lounge and shoulders his backpack. "You're doing great, Tate, really. I knew you would be perfect for the job."

His words ease the self-doubt clawing at my throat. "Thanks, Dad."

When he leaves the living room, I blow out a long breath and close my eyes. I hope I can live up to Dad's expectations. Working with top athletes is out of wheelhouse, and the last thing I want is to let him down by not looking after his players properly, including Sinnett.

Our relationship is being rebuilt, brick by brick, and I just pray the gust of wind that is my secret of sleeping with his star halfback doesn't blow it down.

Chapter Eight

SINNETT

I see the horde of reporters before they see me. They're lingering by the entrance to the training facility, cameras trained on my car and microphones in hand, ready to bombard me with what feels like endless questions.

Knowing there is no other way to escape them, I heave a sigh and step out of the car. I feel all their judging gazes on me as I reach into the back seat, retrieving my gym bag. Keeping my head down, I focus on my scuffed black and white shoes as I take long strides in their direction. When I'm in earshot, the game of twenty-one questions begins.

"Sinnett, how is the injury?"

"When do you think you'll be back on the field?"

"We've heard reports that the quad injury is so serious that you might not see another game until round fifteen. Is that true?"

"Sinnett, what's your rehab plan?"

"Can you tell us when you'll be joining the Wolves on the field?"

"How do you think the Wolves have been performing without you?"

It's question after fucking question with these people. If they're not asking about my injury, they're wanting to know about my dating life, which is something I prefer to keep private from the public and media. To them, nothing is off-limits. And try as they might, I never answer their questions, no matter how much of an asshole it makes me look. I don't need them twisting my words into a story that suits them.

Lifting my head, I keep my eyes forward as I side step them, dodging their cameras and letting their questions sink into the back of my mind. Cool air whips at my face as the door to the building is flung open. It closes behind me with a soft click, drowning out the relentless voices of those parasites.

The walk to the change rooms is short, and I make sure to wave at each staff member I pass. The rest of the team arrived an hour ago, ready to hit the field to practice some new plays Coach Phil wants to test out. Lucky me, I got to sleep in and arrived just in time for my session with Tatum.

My heart slams into my throat at the mere thought of her name. Of her face. And that damn vanilla and floral scent that is embedded into my skin.

I told her that I respect her father enough to not break his rule, but fuck me is it difficult. She's been in my head since the night we first met, and I don't know why. Every time I try to force her sweet face from my mind, it stubbornly digs its heels in the ground, refusing to go. And then I'm left to replay our interactions over and over and over again. Seeing her today, being so close to her, is only going to make it worse.

Tossing my gym bag onto the bench in front of my locker alcove, I roll my head from side to side, partially relieving the tension pulling at the muscles. It's just one session. I can make it through without wanting to remind myself of how well

Tatum's hips fit in the curve of my palm, or how her sweet scent is like succumbing to a sugar rush.

I find Tatum in her office, hunched over her desk as her eyes skim over a stack of paperback. Leaning my shoulder against the door frame, I watch her for a moment. Her bottom lip is tucked between her teeth, and her brows are slightly creased. Jade eyes sweep across the page, oblivious to my presence. Tapping the pen in her hand against her chin, she releases her lip and exhales a soft breath. My fingers itch to tuck the stray pieces of hair that have fallen from the bun at her nape behind her ear.

Even in a state of concentration, when no one is supposed to be watching, she is still the most beautiful woman I have ever laid eyes. I can't describe the feeling that overcomes me when I gaze upon her, but I know it's far too big for me to dissect right now.

You're already failing and the session hasn't begun yet.

Clearing my throat, I watch as Tatum snaps her head up to meet mine. Biting back a smile at the soft blush sweeping across her round cheeks, I step further into the room. "I hope I'm not late."

Tatum pushes back from the desk and stands, eyes searching my face. "N-no, you're right on time." Clearing her throat, she gestures to the table in the centre of the room. "Have a seat while I grab your recovery schedule."

Following her instructions, I sit on the table, my attention following her movements as she shuffles around some loose papers on the desk. "No need. I have it memorised."

Tatum blinks at me, soft lashes fanning over her cheekbones. "You... what?"

"Todd sent it to me yesterday morning after he approved it, and since then I've memorised that plan back to front." I shrug, running a hand over my right quad. "I must admit, strawberry, that you do know what you're doing because today is the first day since my injury that I'm not met with blinding pain."

Tatum drags her bottom lip between her teeth, eyes searching my face. I keep mine passive, watching her, waiting. Her lips turn up in a half smile as she steps out from behind her desk. "Well, I guess I should take that as a compliment, right?"

"For now," I muse, biting back a smile. "It'll depend on how this session goes, and how well you work me."

Tatum stops halfway across the room, blanching at my words. "*Work* you? Sin, I—"

"You have to help stretch me out, right?" I arch a brow at her, lips turned up in a smirk. God, it's so easy to make this woman sweat. Tatum nods, swallowing hard. Lifting my shoulders in a shrug, I say, "Then it better be a good stretch. I'd hate to have to retract my earlier statement about the plan being great, and therefore you being the best physio I've come across."

"But you didn't say I was the best physio you have come across," Tatum murmurs.

I grin. "Well, *yet.*"

Tatum holds my gaze, her cheeks a light shade of pink. I find myself wanting to always be the cause for her blushes and the sparkle in those eyes.

Get a grip, Sin. In and out. That's the plan.

Clearing my throat, I gesture to my quad. "Shall we get started?"

Tatum exhales a sharp breath and nods, walking toward me. Her vanilla and floral perfume floats around my head as she passes by, and I fight the urge to drink her in. It's as sweet as her.

"So, you said you started the plan yesterday. How'd it go?"

"Great," I tell her. "The swelling had already started to go down before bed."

Tatum places the plan down on the table behind her, eyes skimming the page. Her shoulders are tense, and her hands are tight around the edge of the table as if she's fighting to keep herself upright.

That makes two of us.

My knuckles are bleached where they're wrapped around the edge of the bed. Swallowing hard, I force my eyes down to my quad, skimming over the affected area.

"That's a good sign, Sin." Tatum spins on her heels and gestures for me to lie on my back. I do as I'm told, trying to keep my eyes off her face, instead focusing on the ceiling. "If you can keep the swelling down and continue to strengthen the muscle, you'll start seeing the results you're after. But it's going to take time, and you have to be patient."

"Time and patience aren't in my vocabulary," I grumble, folding my arms over my chest. "But I hear what you're saying."

"Good."

My breath hitches when Tatum's soft, warm hands caress my right thigh, probing the tight and tender muscles in my quad. I drag my bottom lip between my teeth, fighting the urge to watch what she's doing. To see how she's touching me.

"Now, shall we get started on that stretching you so delicately reminded me of?" The teasing in Tatum's voice has me smiling like a fool.

"With pleasure, strawberry."

I hate that I miss her touch the second she steps away.

Tatum gestures to the yoga mat laid out on the floor beside the bed. "We're going to start with a pre-contraction stretch. It'll help relax the muscles and increase muscle tone."

Nodding, I hop off the table and lie on my back

outstretched in front of me. My heart slams into my chest. I talked a big game when I was teasing her about working me out while stretching. Now that I'm faced with the prospect of having her hands on me and her body so close, knowing I can't touch her in return, is going to be torture.

Tatum kneels beside me, her eyes on my leg rather than my face. "Okay, bend both of your legs so your feet are flat on the floor." When I'm in position, she turns her body so that she's kneeling in front of my right leg, her hands flexing at her sides. "Now, extend your leg and rest your calf on my shoulder."

Fuck me. Now I'm the one blushing.

With my leg resting firmly against her shoulder, her right hand comes up to hold the heel of my shoe, while the other snakes around to splay out over my right thigh. Heat sizzles beneath her hand, seeping into my skin. My jaw clenches, and hands flex at my sides.

How can a simple touch from her send my heart into overdrive?

Clearing my throat, I watch as Tatum leans forward slightly, putting pressure on my leg, and in turn stretching the tight muscle. I hiss out a breath at the ebb of pain that shoots across my thigh. I know this is what needs to happen for me to get through this recovery, but *fuck me* does it hurt like a bitch.

"How's this feel?" Tatum asks, her voice soft and gentle.

Fucking painful. "Yeah, good. I can feel the pull."

"Try to relax, okay?"

Nodding, I exhale sharply and blink at the ceiling.

The air between us is thick. It wraps around my chest, squeezing painfully and weighing heavily on my limbs. Needing to cut it, even if just to hear Tatum's voice to distract me, I utter, "Feels kind of weird that we've switched positions."

Tatum's lips part, her eyes darting over to clash with mine. I bite back a smirk. I shouldn't be putting notions like that out there between us, but I couldn't help myself. Seeing her smile has my body feeling like I'm floating.

"You're a menace," she murmurs, cheeks turning pink. *Again*.

"Sorry, Tate, but you're going to have to buy me dinner first. I don't put out easily."

Her lips quirk. "I think I have all the evidence to prove that you do in fact put out easily."

Laughter bursts from my lips before I can stop it. I like that she can take the banter, and dish it out just as good. "You got me there, strawberry."

Tatum holds me in this position for what feels like an eternity but is only thirty seconds, before she walks backward on her knees and lowers my leg down, extended. I exhale a sharp breath, fingernails digging into my palm.

"Are you ready to go again?" Her sweet jade eyes find mine, searching my face for permission to continue.

I nod, and manage to squeeze out, "Yeah."

Tatum slowly pushes my leg toward the ceiling, resting it on her shoulder again as she resumes her earlier position. This is going to be a long session. Having her so close to me, her thighs brushing the back of mine and her hands touching my skin, is going to make me lose my mind. And I can't do that with her. I told Tatum that we need to follow her dad's rule, but the longer she touches me, the harder it's going to be to keep my self-control intact.

"How'd you get the scar in your eyebrow?"

My eyes snap open—I hadn't realised they were closed—and meet Tatum's face peering down at me through her lashes. She offers a soft smile, one that has my insides simmering with heat.

I clear my throat. "You want to know about my scar?"

She shrugs. "I do. I noticed it the first night we met, and I've been curious about it ever since."

I want to tell her that every person I meet has overlooked it, mostly because it's not overly visible. But the fact that Tatum noticed it straight away after meeting me once has me wondering just how deeply she was viewing me, taking in every inch of me.

"Well, I got it during a rough tackle when I was playing with the U20s." I still remember the day like it happened yesterday. The stench of the mud caked on my boots, calves and hands. It had been pissing down rain for days leading up to the game, making the field almost impossible to play on, but the game still went ahead regardless. "A guy accidentally kneed me in the face, which resulted me splitting my eyebrow. Not only did I have mud, grass and sweat clinging to my face, but I also had a river of blood pouring down the side of it." Shaking my head, I exhale a deep breath as Tatum lowers my leg, giving me a brief reprieve before starting the stretch again. "We won the game regardless, but I was left with a lasting memory."

Tatum's face scrunches with what I can only assume is a grimace. "That sounds awful. Was it painful?"

"At the time, no. But afterwards, when I walked into the sheds, the adrenaline had worn off and the pain was unbearable. After a long stint in the ER waiting room, I went home with six stitches and a memorable scar to tell the tale."

My breath hitches when Tatum lifts my leg onto her shoulder again, her hand bracing my thigh.

"If rugby is so dangerous, why do you play it?" she asks. It's such a simple question, but it's one that feels impossible to answer.

"It's complicated," I murmur, hands fisted at my sides. "My dad wanted me to play it, and eventually, I grew to love it."

Tatum hums.

Does she want to push me further? And if she does, will I be able to answer her questions?

Thankfully, she changes the topic.

"What's your biggest fear?" She shoots me a pointed look. "And don't you dare say spiders."

I snort a laugh. "What type of question is that?"

Tatum's tongue swipes her bottom lip, her shoulders lifting in a shrug. "Well, I know how much you *love* my random questions, so I asked the first one that came to mind."

The emphasis isn't lost on me. I had snapped at her in the car back in Barrenridge for asking me random questions, but the truth is, I enjoyed them. It had me wondering what was going through that head of hers, and how she could be so chatty knowing what we were about to do. It was an unusual experience, but one that had me repeating it in my head days later.

"Okay, fine," I say, relenting. "I'm afraid of not being good enough."

Tatum pauses, her eyes snapping to meet mine. "What?"

Exhaling a sharp breath, I press the palm of my hands into my eyes, needing an excuse to tear my gaze from hers. "I don't need your pity, Tate. I'm aware of how crazy it sounds."

Tatum lowers my leg to the ground, her hands disappearing. "It's a very real problem to have, Sin."

My hands fall from my face, and I'm met with the most dazzling eyes staring back at me. Tatum has her hands resting on her thighs, features soft as she watches me.

"What?" I murmur, throat tight.

"If you didn't fear not being good enough, then you wouldn't be human." She swipes her hand over her forehead. "I mean, I have the same fear. What if I'm not good at my job and I let people down? What if I'm no longer good enough for my friends? Or my future partner drops me for someone better? The possibilities are endless, which makes the fear stronger that one day, it could happen."

I push up onto my elbows, holding her attention. Electricity hums in my veins, making the beating of my heart more erratic. Does this woman have a one-way ticket to my brain because what the hell? It's as if she jumped into my brain and plucked those same fears from the box I keep them hidden in, and reread them to me without missing a beat.

"You... you feel the same?" I swallow hard, watching as Tatum fiddles with the hem of her black polo shirt with the Wolves logo.

"Of course. It's okay to be afraid of the unexpected or how people perceive you. Given your career, I'm sure you face it a lot, and your fears of not being good enough differ from mine, but it doesn't make them any less real." Her mouth curves into a half smile. "I find that the best way to fight through the negative thoughts and overwhelming feelings is to breathe."

My brow arches. "Breathe?"

Tatum nods. "If you find the pressure too much, just focus on your breathing, and I promise you that it'll help push away the thoughts, allowing you to think with a clear head."

I open my mouth to speak, but nothing comes out. She wants me to breathe? That's it? The notion sounds far-fetched, but with how she's looking at me, all soft eyes and warm smile, I don't have the heart to tell her that. Instead, I smile and nod.

Talking about something so deep and personal has my heart thundering in my chest, itching to steer the conversation to something less private. I know if I don't, I'm going to get trapped in a web I might not be able to escape from. Because I'll want to know her fears, and that's not something I should want to know, not when I have to keep myself in check.

Clearing my throat, I murmur, "So, uh... should we keep going?"

Tatum nods, and shuffles to her position from earlier. I don't miss the disappointment that seeps into her features as she extends my leg over her shoulder, or her inability to look me in the eye as we continue the session in silence.

I want to get to know her, in every way that makes Tatum who she is. But I can't. Not when her father made it explicitly clear the guys on the team need to stay away from her. And I just know that if I get to know her on a deeper level, one that only a select few have the privilege of doing, I'll be in too deep with no way out.

Remember who she is, Sin. Tatum is off-limits.

I exhale a sharp breath, running a hand down the side of my face. I was right—being this close to Tatum is fucking torture.

IF I HAD TO NAME ONE OF MY LEAST FAVOURITE things to do with my time, it would be eating dinner with my parents. For two hours, I'm forced to listen to my father tell me ways I can improve in my career and how I can set myself up for the future. And then, factor in my mother complaining about my twin sister's good deed of looking after Gran instead of pursuing a career in law, and I'm ready to throw myself into oncoming traffic.

Most people would be thrilled if their parents were so involved in their life, but not me. I can't stand my father breathing down my neck after every game, media interview, or training session. If I'm not playing to his standard, then he's going to make sure I know about it. The lectures are endless, but I've learned over the years to drown out his voice and nod along.

Ever since I joined the league at eighteen and moved up from the reserve grade at twenty-one, my career has been shared with my father in an attempt to live out his glory days. He was forced to retired at twenty-six after a career-ending injury to his knee. I've seen the footage of the tackle, and let's just say it was fucking gnarly. Dad made it his mission to get me playing rugby from the age I could walk, citing it was in my genes to follow in his footsteps. I believed him, because why wouldn't I? I was just a kid who wanted to make his father proud. And now that I'm exactly where he was at my age, my career has become his fixation—something to take his mind off the fact that all he can do in the sport is be a commentator and punter.

Forks and knives clink against porcelain plates, echoing off the high ceilings. It's too white in here—too plain. Mum doesn't like bright colours or anything that could make the house appear "cluttered" or "dirty". Growing up, Mia and I weren't allowed to hang posters on the pristine white walls in our bedrooms for fear of making them dirty, because God forbid visitors glanced into our bedrooms and saw anything other than perfection. Hell, I couldn't decorate my room with anything that wasn't beige, white or cream. I think it's the reason why I can't stand light colours, choosing to now wear black or grey clothes, and have my room be as dark as possible.

"Sin, honey, how is your recovery going?" Mum's airy voice cuts through the suffocating silence.

I drag my eyes from the pile of mashed potatoes on my plate to meet her mossy green-blue eyes across the dining table. Her chocolate hair is pulled back into a tight bun at the nape of her neck, and the beige pantsuit makes her look every bit the part of a successful prosecuting lawyer.

"It's going," I say, my foot tapping the marble floor incessantly.

"And the new physio? Your father and I heard the club hired someone new to fill the previous roll."

From my right, Dad looks up from his plate, pale blue eyes piercing the side of my face. I hold Mum's gaze. "She sounds too young to be taking care of the team, and especially your injury. The club should've hired someone more experienced," Dad says, voice tight.

I was thinking the same thing after my first session, that maybe Tatum wasn't as qualified as I was led to believe. But those thoughts vanished the moment I was presented with the custom recovery plan she whipped together on Monday night. It was far more detailed than the previous one I was given, even down to each hour of the day. That alone had me intrigued to follow it, which was why I started first thing yesterday morning. And to say the results were mind-blowing is an understatement. After I completed the RICE method before bed, I noticed the swelling in my quad had already started to go down. When I was following the other plan, it felt like I wasn't going anywhere with the recovery, but that isn't the case with Tatum's plan. And today, I feel great. The pain is still there, same with the limp, but it's far more manageable.

My jaw clenches, sending a zap of pain down my throat. "Her name is Tatum, and if she weren't any good, Coach Phil wouldn't have hired her."

Dad shakes his head. "Phil shouldn't have hired his daughter in the first place just because he felt bad for her. He needs to get a *real* professional in to look after you."

My gaze sweeps over the wrinkled black suit hiding my father's frame, showing hours of sitting in an office researching player statistics, countless meetings and media appearances. As a commentator, I know it kills him to be the one calling the games and not playing. If he hadn't gotten injured, I have no doubt he would've played long into his early thirties. Now, he's in his late forties, chasing the glory days he'll never get back.

"Would you be willing to tell that to Phil's face?" I deadpan, meeting his pale blue eyes. "Because I don't think he'd take kindly to hearing you say his daughter isn't capable of treating a grade two quadricep muscle contusion."

Dad's jaw ticks as he holds my gaze, knife and fork hovering over the plate. "That's not the point, Sin. I'm concerned she doesn't possess the skill set to be treating a team of thirty young men and ensuring they're in top shape."

After my session with her today, seeing how passionate she is about her job, Tatum deserves far more credit for her abilities than what my father is reducing her to. Don't get me started on the stretches we went through. I had joked about her "working me out" but she made good on that promise and delivered in every sense of the word. When I walked out of her office, my muscles felt lighter and my limp not as noticeable.

"She's more than capable," I tell him, my voice even. "Our session on Monday was far better than I could've expected. She knew exactly what I needed and promised she would do everything she could to get me cleared at the six-week mark. Hell, the new recovery plan she sent through is working wonders already."

I'm reminded of Tatum's gentle touch skimming my injured quad two days ago, assessing the swollen area with precision for the first time. I hadn't expected her to read me like a book and call me out on lying about the pain. I had every intention of downplaying it so I could be cleared early to play, but it seems nothing gets past her. She saw through the tight-lipped smile and recognized the pain I'm still experiencing two weeks after the injury occurred.

If that doesn't scream competent, then I don't know what does.

"Eli, darling, it shouldn't matter the skill level of the girl," Mum interjects, voice calm like the ocean on a summer's afternoon. She raises a curved brow at my father. "As long as Sin is getting the recovery he needs, then that's all that matters."

Dad huffs a breath and returns his attention to the steak he's cutting in to. "Fine. But I will be having a word with Phil to make sure the treatment is up to standard. The last thing you need is to be sidelined for longer than necessary. The longer you're off the field, the harder you'll have to work to get back to how you were before the injury."

It's on the tip of my tongue to remind Dad that I'm more than taking this recovery seriously, and I don't need him to tell me what I already know. But I swallow the words because it's not worth speaking them aloud. If I do, I'll spend the next however long left of this meal listening to him lecture me about the importance of sportsmanship and how I need to put myself first, as if I haven't already heard the same spiel countless times.

I snap my mouth shut and go back to eating. Silence settles in the room again, licking at my sides, threatening to pull me under. And just when I think I'll get through one dinner without discussing my sister's life, Mum has to go and ruin it.

"Have you heard from your sister since she left?" Mum lowers her knife and fork, and pats her nude-painted lips with a cloth napkin. "She's not returning my texts or calls."

"She's probably busy with Gran," I point out, pushing a chunk of broccoli around the plate, my appetite long gone. "You know how Mia is."

"I know she's good at ignoring your father and I." The

bitterness in her tone doesn't go unnoticed. Mum exhales a sharp breath. "Did she seem okay when you helped her move?"

I shrug. "Yeah, I guess. She was her normal self."

"Did she confide in you about anything? Or if she has plans to come home any time soon?"

If only she knew what is really going on with Mia and why she doesn't want to talk to either of our parents.

But my sister's business is not mine to share.

I raise a brow at her. "Mum, she's not coming back. Not while Gran needs her help."

"She needs to be at home," Dad retorts, peering at me over the rim of his wine glass, dark red liquid swirling at the bottom. "Mia should be here studying law, not prancing around in Barrenridge with no direction but a dream of playing the piano."

I drop my hands to my thighs, clenching them to ward off the need to defend my sister with an iron fist. My parents have never understood Mia's goals of playing the piano and her love for interior design. Not once has she ever expressed interest in studying law like our mother or pursuing a dead-end, boring office job. She has always been creative—far more creative than I ever could be.

Mia has been taking piano lessons for as long as I've been playing rugby. My parents thought she needed a hobby while I was playing sports, and Mia expressed interest in wanting to play the piano. I don't think they realised just how into it she would get. And I think it pisses them off more that she's phenomenal at playing the damn thing.

I may have been bored shitless when attending her school performances in primary and high school, wishing I was hanging out with Khai instead, but that didn't mean I wasn't supportive of my sister. If anything, I'm her number one fan, always pushing her to not give a shit what Mum and Dad think about her choices and to do what makes her happy. All the while I should've been taking my own damn advice.

"If I recall, she has dreams of being an interior designer, which is what she went to uni for. Piano is a hobby of hers," I counter, trying to keep my voice even despite the frustration burning in my chest. "If she wants to help Gran, then that's her prerogative. I don't think either of you should have a say in her decisions."

"Excuse me?" Dad lowers his wine glass, tension pulling his weathered skin taut.

"Eli, he didn't mean it." Mum reaches over to pat his hand in an attempt to thaw the ice consuming his rigid frame.

My spine straightens, ready for a fight. "No, I meant every word of it. Mia doesn't have to answer to you about what she chooses to do with her life. If she doesn't want to study law, then she shouldn't have to. If she wants to play the piano for the rest of her life, then so be it. Hell, if she wanted to be a damn astronaut and go to the moon, then that's her choice to make. Not anyone else's."

Tension coats the air so thick, you could cut it with a knife. My skin prickles with the need to scratch it off, hoping the uneasy feeling will dissipate and allow me to breathe properly.

Mum and Dad share a tense look, one that has me wanting to scream. It shits me that they're so hellbent on controlling us. I don't care if they do it to me because I'm already strapped up like a marionette anyway, so I may as well roll with the punches. But Mia has a chance to break free and make her own choices, free from what our parents want. And I'll be damned if they try to drag her into the fucking perfect world they're trying to create.

"Sin," Mum drawls, her voice even as she holds my gaze. "That's not what we're trying to do. We want the best for your sister."

"No, you don't." My lungs burn as I shove the wooden chair back, the fabric napkin on my lap falling to my feet. Pain spreads through my right quad, but I swallow it done and flick my eyes between my parents. "You don't want the best for her. You want to control her. And I refuse to sit back and watch you do so. You can dictate my life all you like, but Mia is a no-go."

"Sinnett!" Dad slams his hand on the table, rattling the wine glasses and cutlery. His heated eyes find mine, burning with anger and frustration. Tension coils the muscles beneath the suit jacket, mirroring my own hidden beneath the black hoodie I threw on before leaving the apartment. "You do not get to speak to us like that."

I bite my tongue, the sting of pain grounding me. There's no use in fighting them on the matter because they won't change. They don't realise the iron thumb they hold over us, and how it impacts our lives. Mia and I are too afraid to stand up to them for fear of what they might do or how they'll react. Neither of them would lay hands on us, but I have no doubt they would find some way to put us back in line.

As much as it pains me to keep my mouth shut and cop it on the chin, I'm willing to do it if it means I can keep the peace —for now.

"Whatever." I step away from the dining table, my parents' eyes heavy on the back of my head. "I'm leaving."

"Sin, wait!" Mum calls out as I trudge through the dining room, shoving my hands into the pockets of my jeans.

"Where do you think you're going?" Dad's clipped tone grates against my ears, surging my steps forward, eager to get out of this fucking house.

"Out," is all I manage as I step into the hallway. I take a deep breath, filling my lungs with much needed air.

In my car, I drop my head against the headrest and expel a

sharp breath. This has to be one of the worst weekly dinners I've shared with my parents. I didn't think anything could come close to topping the dinner where Dad chewed my ass out after getting injured. Yet, here we are.

I rub a hand down the side of my face and reach for my phone tucked securely in my pocket. My thumb hovers over Khai's contact name—which he changed to *Big Dick* for whatever fucked up reason, and I haven't been bothered to change it since—before tapping the screen.

He answers on the second ring. "Did you forget your apartment keys again? I told you to start clipping them to your belt loop."

"That was one time," I respond gruffly, running a hand through my hair. "I don't leave the apartment without them now."

"Yeah, well, I can never be too sure with you." Shuffling on his end grates on my nerves, setting me further on edge. Khai exhales sharply. "What's up, then? Aren't you supposed to be having dinner with your parents?"

"Plans changed." He doesn't need to know about my family issues, despite what he already knows about my parents. Khai has his own family shit to deal with. "Call up some of guys to see if they want to go grab a drink."

More shuffling, and I grip the steering wheel to keep from screaming at my best friend to quit fucking moving.

"A drink, you say? Well, you know I'm always down for a good time. Just can't get too crazy since we have a training session in the morning."

One that I'm not part of.

"That's fine." I jam the keys into the ignition, my car roaring to life. "I'll see you soon then."

TWENTY MINUTES LATER, I'M SITTING AT A CIRCLE table with Khai to my right, Zane—the Wolves' hooker—opposite me, and Nico—a front rower—to my left. Numerous empty glasses of beer litter the table, and deep voices bouncing off the walls of the small bar. OneRepublic's "I Lived" plays from the speakers in the roof, some of the lyrics getting drowned out by the steady flow of conversation and laughter.

I met the guys at The Rusty Barrel since it is the closest bar to the apartment I share with Khai. It is our go-to when we want to grab a couple of beers and don't feel like crossing the bridge to get to the heart of Sydney. Al, the owner, has every sport imaginable playing on the TV screens in the back room, keeping patrons entertained until the wee hours of the morning. A karaoke machine occupies the front room, allowing drunk people who are too far gone to care about their dignity to get on the small stage and belt out the lyrics to "Mr. Brightside" and "Sweet Caroline". I've seen Khai get on that stage far too many times to count on both hands.

"I still can't believe you went home with her," Zane snorts, pointing a finger at Nico, red-faced. "She was fucking *crazy*."

"Yeah, crazy hot and a freak in the sheets," Nice retorts, shoving at Zane's shoulder, who has to grip the edge of the table to not topple out of the chair.

"Let me guess, she blows up your phone every second of the day, wanting to talk to you or come by the training facility?" Khai wiggles his brows, sipping on a fresh beer. I bite back at grin as the colour drains from Nico's face.

Nico expels a breath. "It's fucking constant, I swear. I'm gonna have to change my number soon."

The three of us burst out laughing at the expense of our friend. Nico should've known better than to pick up a super fan and take them home to sleep with. It's a recipe for disaster. Not only do they become attached and obsess over you, but it has the potential to turn into a dangerous situation, one that leaves you having to deal with a stalker.

I mean, I would know, given my current situation with Zoe.

"You need to sort her out, man." I clap Nico on the shoulder, the muscles stiff under my touch. "Or you could find yourself in some serious hot water."

"Yeah, yeah," he murmurs, sipping on his beer. "I'll sort it out."

Zane turns his attention to me, tipping his chin up. "What about you, Sin? How's the quad feeling?"

"Fine," I bite out, rubbing my hand over my thigh. Talking about my injury is the last thing I want to do. It only serves as a reminder that I'm on the sidelines while my friends tear up the field. "I should be back in a couple of weeks."

"If he gets cleared," Khai adds. When he feels the heat of my glare on his face, he lifts his shoulders in a shrug. "What? It's true. But don't worry, you're in good hands with Tatum."

If I could wipe that knowing smirk off his face with the back of my hand, I would.

"Ah, yes, Tatum." Zane's eyes dart around the table. "What's her deal anyway?"

Khai is quick to jab his thumb in my direction, the little shit. "Why don't you ask our good friend Sin here."

"Shut up, asshole," I hiss under my breath, trying to stomp on his foot, but he's quick to pull it away before the heel of my shoe can make contact with his toes.

Nico frowns. "Why? What do you know that we don't?"

"Well, let's just say he knows an intimidate detail or two about our new physio."

Heat burns the tips of my ears, my fingers curling into fists on my thighs.

Oh, I'm so going to kill him when we get home.

Zane and Nico snap their gazes to me, realisation swirling in their eyes.

"You hooked up with Coach's daughter?" Zane all but shouts in the busy bar.

Nico is quick to slap a hand over Zane's mouth before I can reach across the table and do the same, but in a way that would hurt ten times more. His blinks rapidly, as if that'll help him understand the bomb Khai just dropped.

"I thought Coach Phil said his daughter was off-limits." Nico lowers his hand to wrap around his beer. "How did you bag Tatum so quickly?"

I run a frustrated hand through my hair. "That's not what happened."

Khai grins. "Please do tell what happened."

My jaw ticks as I mouth, *I'm going to kill you.*

My best friend laughs like a banshee.

"Come on, don't leave us hanging." Zane shifts on the seat, resting his elbows on the table. "And don't leave out any details."

I huff and lean back on the chair. "It's nothing, really. We hooked up when I was in Barrenridge two weeks ago. End of story."

"That's it?" Nico deadpans, eyes flicking from me to Zane and Khai. "What are the chances of that happening?"

"Very fucking high, apparently," I grumble. To put out some of the flames burning in my chest, I take a long sip of the Carlton Dry beer. Tastes like shit, but it does the job of easing the tension coiling in my back and pressure weighing on my chest.

"You lucky fucker." Nico jams his fist into my shoulder, shoving lightly. "Well, not entirely lucky because if Coach finds out you touched his daughter, then you're dead meat."

"I know," I murmur, eyes focused on the condensation racing down the side of the glass. "Believe me, I know."

"You not gonna share the details with us?" Zane questions, wiggling his brows. "Come on, I thought we were friends. You've never had any issues talking about any of the women you've slept with in the past."

He's right. I'm that asshole who regularly shares intimate details about the women I've slept with because it didn't bother me whether anyone knew about it or not. But for some reason, I can't bring myself to talk about Tatum. When I think about her soft jade eyes and strawberry blonde hair, I'm reminded of that night in my car. At that moment, with her sitting on my lap, getting lost in the depths of her eyes, I forgot who I was for a moment—to the point I forgot to ask if she was on birth control, like an idiot.

I'm more careful than that because I have a reputation to protect, but back then, it was just the two of us. And nothing outside of the car mattered. Not my parents, sister, grandmother, career or public image. It was just me and Tatum. And fuck, I would be lying if I said she wasn't the most stunning woman I've ever met.

"Yeah, well, you're not getting a speck of detail from me about Tate." I scull the rest of my beer, slamming the glass down on the table. "And don't tell anyone else on the team, okay? It doesn't leave this table."

My friends share a knowing look, their silence weighing heavily on my shoulders.

It's Khai who breaks the silence by clapping a hand on my shoulder. "Don't worry, Sin. Your secret is safe with us."

Secret. That's what Tatum is. And possibly all she ever will be.

While I can't get her out of my mind, and my body aches to touch her again, I know I can't. At this point in my career, I can't afford to lose sight of my goals. Tatum is the one rule I can't break, no matter how badly I fucking want to.

Chapter Nine

TATUM

•

Exhaustion doesn't come close to describing the weight in my limbs or the heaviness of my eyes. Who knew travelling around the country and watching men play rugby would be so tiring? I had expected this job to be a piece of cake —something easy with the ability to switch off when I got home—but it's far from it. Turns out, treating thirty men and keeping on top of their recovery and training schedules is far from a piece of cake. It's possibly the hardest job I've ever had.

Don't get me wrong, I love my job and having the ability to help others, especially footy players who need me in order to be able to play their best. I wouldn't say I'm the glue that holds them together—more like one tiny speck—but a lot does ride on my shoulders, especially going into a game day. Each player checks in with me and we go over their charts to make sure nothing is amiss, and they can talk to me about any pains or aches they might be experiencing. And once I've done a few exercises with them and given them the all clear, I move onto the next person who might have a different history and is experiencing something new.

It's a lot of pressure to shoulder, but at the end of the day, I go home with a smile on my face, grateful to be in the position I am. And it's all thanks to my dad.

Even with pain soaring through my bones from being on my feet for multiple hours of the day, and exhaustion clinging to my soul, I have no regrets leaving Barrenridge. If anything, I made the right choice because here, I can grow. And if I didn't take Dad's offer when he handed it to me on a silver platter, I have no doubt I would be working behind the bar at the local pub because in a town like that, there isn't much else to do.

"How are you feeling, Tate?" Dad asks when I walk into the kitchen, pulling my hair into a high ponytail. "You look tired."

"I am," I agree, dropping my arms to my side. With a sigh, I slide onto one of the bar stools at the kitchen island. Dad stands opposite me, back leaning against the granite bench top with a coffee cup in hand. "Should you be drinking coffee this late into the arvo?"

Dad chuckles and sets the cup down beside him. "Probably not, but with a late game tonight I know I'm going to need the caffeine rush to keep me going."

"That makes two of us." A yawn slips from my parted lips and I crush the palms of my hands into my eyes. "I don't know why I'm so tired."

"Well, we did go to Townsville over the weekend with a bunch of rowdy men in their twenties."

I drop my hands to my lap, blinking away the blurriness coating my vision. "Yeah, maybe it's that. Or maybe it's because I've been staying up late revising every player's medical history and recovery plan. Not to mention ensuring my plans coincide with Todd's training schedule. It's a lot of work."

Dad rolls his lips and nods. I swear I don't see this man wearing anything besides a black and red polo shirt with the

Wolves logo stitched into the fabric and black jeans. If he owns other clothes, I haven't seen him wear them since I moved to Sydney, nearly three weeks ago now.

"You're doing a great job, Tate," Dad says, his lips tipping up in a smile. "I've had a chance to speak to every guy on the team and they have all given me positive feedback about you."

I raise a brow at him. "Are you sure it's not because I'm your daughter, which you made abundantly clear on my first day? Who knows, they could be too afraid to tell you that I suck and need to look for a new job."

Dad snorts a laugh and shakes his head. "Trust me, they like you. Even the rest of the staff have sung your praises."

Warmth spreads through my chest. I hadn't realised since starting the job that the rest of the staff members thought so highly of me. When I'm working, I tend to keep to myself because I'm in the zone and have a lot of work to get done, so I do most of my socialising during lunch. To hear the team is already accepting me fills me with a sense of pride that has me smiling like a damn fool.

On my second day, I met Olive during my lunch break. She's not much older than me and oversees the social media aspect of the club, always involving the guys in interviews or playing small pranks on them. Her carefree attitude and warm smile make her approachable and easy to talk to. After spending twenty minutes with her, I realised we had far more in common than I thought. And from there, we couldn't stop talking until we both had to get back to work.

Now, we spend most of our lunch breaks together, and when I'm not with Olive, I'll speak to whoever is in the break room. I love flapping my gums and making people smile, it brings me joy seeing others happy.

"I'm glad because if I wasn't accepted by the people you

trust and admire to help run things smoothly, I may have considered packing my bags and returning to Barrenridge."

Dad waves me off with his hand. "Nonsense, Tate. You're a great addition to the club. Your mother would be proud of you."

My heart stutters in my chest and I have to swallow the lump forming in my throat for fear it might choke me. My fingers flex on my thigh, and I will my lungs to focus on pulling air in at a steady pace and releasing it without a shake.

Talking about Mum never gets easier. I would be lying if I said she's always on my mind, even after two years of her being gone. I feel her in different ways—her calmness in high-stress situations, her support when I'm riddled with anxiety, or her warmth when sadness consumes me. I don't need to think about her every second of the day to prove I miss her or to remember her face and voice. She comes to me when I need her most, and to me, that's far more valuable than lying awake thinking about her. No matter where I am, or what I'm doing, I feel her—watching and loving me from afar.

When the news of her death made its way around Barrenridge, I was inundated with texts and calls from extended family and friends offering their condolences. The most surprising person to reach out to me was Sadie Cooper. We were in the same year group in high school, but never spoke much, unless it was in passing. Her mum passed away just after graduation, so she understood what I was going through at the time.

"It hurts now, Tate, and it might never get easier with time, but rest assured your mum will always be with you, no matter where you go or what you do."

I needed to hear that more than anything.

It pains me that Mum left this world far too young, long

before she was ready. I wish she were here to see me on this new journey and tell me she's proud. Knowing she won't get to witness the big moments in my life fills me with a sadness not many people can understand. But even though she's not here physically, it doesn't take away from the fact that she's standing in the kitchen with Dad and me, a cup of tea in hand and a smile on her face.

"I know," I manage to choke out. "I wish she was here, you know?"

Dad nods, his face twisted in what I can only assume is grief. "Me too, Tate. But she's cheering on from the sidelines. Her voice always was the loudest."

I smile. "Really?"

He chuckles, shaking his head. "Your mother was my number one supporter. She went to every game, even if we were in a different state. Rain, hail or shine, she wore my jersey with pride, never letting the outcome of the score dampen her shine."

"She used to tell me lots of stories about you guys growing up."

Dad raises a brow at me. "Did she tell you the story about the time she nearly got into a punch-up with a fan in the crowd during the grand final of '06?"

My eyes nearly bulged out of my head. "*No*. What happened?"

Dad rolls his tongue in his cheek, folding his arms over his chest. "Well, she told me the wife of one of the Illawarra Sharks was talking shit about me, and in my honour, threatened to beat her ass if she didn't stop talking."

"Mum did that?" I all but squeeze out, unable to believe the words coming from his mouth. "Are we talking about the same woman?"

Dad chuckles, the sound airy and filled with memories

from decades ago. "She was fierce, your mother. And so incredibly loyal that I almost didn't feel worthy of her." He exhales a soft sigh, meeting my gaze. "She was willing to get arrested if it meant standing up for me. What woman does that? But she wasn't just any normal woman. Your mum was brave, outgoing, supportive and so beautiful it hurt to look at her." Dad blinks rapidly and shakes his head. "I didn't deserve her one bit, but she didn't care. She showed up when I needed her the most, and I wish I had done the same for her."

"Dad…" I breathe, voice shaky.

"I should've been there for her, for you. But I wasn't."

"Mum understood why you didn't stay," I try to reason, my heart aching seeing the pain splintering across his features. "You were doing everything you could to provide for us."

"And in the process, I let you both down because I should've been more present, more available. But instead, I let my passion get in the way of the two women I care the most about." Dad exhales a shaky breath and reaches for his coffee, downing the remnants of the drink. He sets the cup down and meets my eyes, tears brimming in his lower lashes. "I can't take back my actions, Tate, but I promise you that I'm going to do whatever I can to take care of you now. And I know your mother is watching over us, offering her wisdom and support. This time, I'm not going to let her down."

Tears sting the corner of my eyes, threatening to spill over the edges as I watch my dad round the kitchen island and stop beside me. Warmth radiates from him as he rests a hand on my shoulder, gentle and supportive. It's on the tip of my tongue to tell him Mum wouldn't want him to feel this way, that she loved him more than anything, but the words die on my tongue, hidden behind the lump forming in my throat.

Instead, I stay silent as Dad offers me a tight-lipped smile. "I better get going. But I'll see you at the game later, okay?"

"Yeah," I say with a nod, voice tight. "Drive safely."

Dad pats my shoulder before dropping his hand to my side. "You too, Tate. That Jeep of yours is a death trap."

DAD WAS RIGHT ABOUT MY JEEP BEING A DEATH TRAP. In the short twenty-minute drive to the Wolves' home ground, I was convinced the engine was going to die on me three separate times, and each time I had a mini heart attack. I don't know what possessed me to take my car, knowing I'm in the market for a new one that won't potentially give out on me on the side of the road, but here I am, putting my life in the hands of a vehicle that needs to be taken to the wreckers.

Tonight is the first home game with me working for the Wolves. I'm looking forward to seeing how a home crowd fairs against an away crowd, and judging by the sea of black, red and white jerseys filing through the gates, I have no doubt the atmosphere tonight is going to be insane, despite it being a Thursday night.

I step out of my car and lock the door behind me. My gaze sweeps across the group of women sauntering towards the back entrance to the stadium, suitcases rolling behind them. Each of them has their hair curled to perfection, makeup so smooth it looks professionally done and poms poms tucked under their arms. Realisation dawns on me.

Since working for the club, I have yet to meet the cheerleading squad. The previous games I attended were away games, which meant the Wolves' cheerleaders weren't needed. But they're here tonight and ready to cheer on the guys.

I hang back by my car, not wanting to walk in with them.

I'm not one to be intimidated by women, but when there are a group of them who are beyond stunning and immensely talented... Yeah, I'm going to steer clear and fly under the radar. I'm sure they're lovely women, but the last thing I need is to feel inadequate in their presence.

"I haven't seen you around before. Are you new?"

My heart slams into my throat at the airy voice behind me. Spinning on my heels, my gaze clashes with hazel eyes framed by curled balayage hair. The woman's features are hidden behind a layer of makeup, but it's not hard to tell she's younger than me—her tanned skin flawless and her fashion choice working wonders for her curves. Everything about this woman is stunning, making me feel anything but in my staff polo and black dress pants.

"Me?" I rasp out, caught off guard by her presence. "I started with the club three weeks ago as a physio."

Hazel eyes take in every inch of me, sizing me up. I fight the urge to fold under her intense stare, and instead square my shoulders in the hope it'll make me feel less small. The woman tightens her grip on the suitcase trailing behind her, pom poms still tucked beneath her arm. Even in black trackies and a tight-fitting black T-shirt, she demands attention from anyone walking by. And I'm helpless to look away.

She surprises me by extending her hand, red fingernails expectant. "I'm Raya. You are?"

I swallow hard and take her hand, accepting the handshake. "Tatum."

Raya releases my hand and tilts her head. "Tatum... that's a cool name."

A rush of relief rolls through me, easing the tension building in my shoulders. It's hard to read this girl, given her stiff posture and standoffish vibes, but I'm getting the sense that she doesn't despise me right off the bat, so I must be doing something right.

"Thanks," I respond, willing the unease to seep from my voice. "It's nice to meet you. I haven't met any of the cheerleaders yet."

"Well, I think it's safe to say I'm the best one you'll meet."

I chuckle, unable to help myself. She had unknowingly answered my earlier fears. "Is there a reason for that?"

Raya raises a perfectly shaped brow. "You seriously don't know?"

A frown creases my forehead. "Know what...?"

She sighs and steps forward, wrapping her arm around my shoulder. Her walking forces me to keep in step, not wanting to fall behind. It's on the tip of my tongue to ask what she's doing, but I swallow the question. *Keep your mouth shut and follow along. Listen now, ask questions later.*

"Since you're new here, I feel it's my job to fill you in on everything that happens behind the scenes with the girls and guys. And let's just say it's a long fucking story."

"How long of a story are we talking here?"

Raya clicks her tongue. "Far too long to give you all of the details, but I can do my best."

We reach the entrance to the stadium, and Raya stops, her body facing mine. Her arm slips from my shoulders and she nods her head to where the cheerleaders walk into a room on our left.

"I wouldn't normally offer a warning like this to someone if I don't trust them," Raya starts, hazel eyes holding my attention. "But I like you for some reason, Tatum."

"Thanks?" I offer, not knowing what else to say to that. "I think."

"Take it as a compliment," Raya says, waving her hand in the air. "Anyway, just be careful with who knows your business, because once it catches wind, everyone will know and it won't be pretty."

Ice floods my veins. "What does that mean?"

"It means that if you hook up with one of the guys on the team, word will likely get around before the end of the day, and once it gets back to the girls, you will wish you had stayed away."

"W-what?" I stammer, heart rate spiking. "I don't understand."

Raya exhales a sharp breath and rests her free hand on my shoulder. "It means that those girls think they own every guy on the team because at one point or another, they've hooked up with one or more on numerous occasions. So if they think a newbie like you is trying to sniff around the guys, it won't be pretty. I'm telling you this because you seem nice and I don't want you to get caught up in their shit. Every single one of them are possessive when they have no right to be. Zoe is the worst of them all. So, just steer clear of them, okay?"

I blink at the girl I just met not even five minutes ago. Her warning is like a siren in the back of my mind, hues of red flashing before my eyes, mixing with her tanned skin. It's on the tip of my tongue to tell her I've already overstepped that line, but the words die on my tongue.

No one will ever know about my one-night stand with Sinnett, and this is proof of why I never want another soul to learn about it.

I had no idea the cheerleading squad would be so possessive of the players. Sure, it makes sense some of them would get together on occasion because good-looking people tend to gravitate towards each other. But this type of warning tells me it runs deeper than a normal attraction between some of the cheerleaders and players. A connection that could cause tension if lines were crossed, and that's not something I want to slap onto my already full plate.

"Okay," I squeeze out, throat tight. "I'll steer clear."

A tight-lipped smile graces Raya's pouty lips. "It might sound crazy, Tatum, but I promise it'll save you a lot of heartache down the track." She throws her thumb over her shoulder at the women's voices drifting out of the room beside us. "These girls are intense and borderline crazy. And don't even get me started on the whole Zoe and Sin situation."

"Sinnett?" I choke out, eyes wide. The world stops spinning as my heart slams against my ribcage, knocking the air from my lungs. Ice splinters across my body. "Does he have a girlfriend?"

"Yes and no," Raya responds with a shrug. "It's a complicated situation, one that us girls don't know all the details to. But from what I do know, it's messy and not something you want to get caught up in."

Oh, God. How the hell have I found myself in a situation where I slept with a guy who has a *girlfriend*?

My mind is so scrambled right now, I can't think straight. Nothing is making sense. Throw in the warning from Raya, and I'm as clueless as a concussed bird.

"Steering clear," I murmur, dragging my bottom lip between my teeth.

"But hey, consider this an official invite to be my friend," Raya says, voice light. "I don't let people in who I don't know well, but you seem like you could use a friend."

God, is it that obvious I have no friends?

"I would love that," I say instead, trying to smile through the inner turmoil of the clusterfuck I have found myself in. "I mean, after the help you've just given me, how could I turn you down?"

Raya grins, all straight teeth and warmth. "Exactly. I mean,

I did just save you from having your eyes clawed out by some crazy woman, so it's the least you can do."

I know Raya is joking—at least, I hope she is—but I don't consider myself out of the woods just yet.

If this Zoe girl catches wind of the fact that I slept with her boyfriend, I'm going to be in deep shit. And if she's as intense as Raya makes her out to be, then I may as well claw out my own eyes and return to Barrenridge.

Chapter Ten

SINNETT

It's fucking hard watching your closest friends kill it on the field while being stuck on the sideline, wishing you were out there with them. Biting my tongue and smiling through every second until the siren blares after eighty minutes is torture. Hearing the roar of the fans when the Wolves won against the South Sydney Titans, nearly blowing my eardrums, and knowing I wasn't part of the teams win tears at my insides, creating a wound I'm not sure I can fix.

Rugby is my whole life, and without it, I feel lost. I no longer feel excited to start the day if all I'm doing is following a recovery plan in the hopes I can be back on the field in three weeks. Each day feels unknown with a multitude of different outcomes that could see me sidelined for longer, and the thought fucking kills me each time. I'm fighting the urge to go off the deep end and say fuck it. Because what am I good for if I'm not there for my team, helping them win or encouraging them to continue fighting?

Nothing.

If it wasn't for Khai keeping me distracted by forcing me

into the gym—a reprieve from the exhausting thoughts circling my mind every second of the day—or reminding me that I need to stay in shape for when I do get cleared to play, I would be rotting away in bed with no purpose. But because he's stubborn as fuck and loyal to a fault, I'm holding myself back from the edge—barely.

It doesn't help that a certain strawberry-blonde with jade eyes continues to pop into my head when I least expect it, demanding my attention when I know damn well I can't give it to her. I need to stay focused, but she's making it fucking difficult to do so.

"You okay, Sin?"

I lift my head at the sound of Khai's voice. He's standing in front of me with his gym bag slung over his shoulder, his dirty jersey and shorts replaced with dark blue chino shorts and a white long-sleeved button-down shirt, the sleeves rolled to his elbows. Water sticks to brown hair, the strands styled neatly atop his head.

I exhale a deep breath and nod. "Yeah, fine."

"Don't tell me you're feeling sorry for yourself again."

"I'm not," I bite out, running a hand through my hair. "I'm just..."

"Thinking too much," Khai finishes for me, not an ounce of judgement in his voice. "I get it, Sin, I do. If I were in your position, I would be the same. Hell, I'd probably be worse."

"How is that even possible," I muse, biting back a smile.

Khai rolls his eyes and shoves his free hand into his pockets. "My point is, you're allowed to dwell on the fact that you're upset about the injury, but don't feel sorry for yourself. If you start doing that, you'll give up, and I refuse to let you throw away your future because you couldn't get through the recovery period."

I open my mouth to respond, but the retort dies on my

tongue because he's right. For once, Khai is speaking words of wisdom that embed themselves deep in my bones.

The more I feel sorry for myself and debate whether or not I can get through this injury, the more I'm digging myself into a hole that I might not be able to get out of. Doubting myself and my ability to recover from this injury is a mental game that could see me out on the field in three weeks or sidelined for longer than planned. If I stop being a fucking bitch and focus, I know I can get through this.

"You're right... for once." I huff out a breath and stand, my quad groaning in protest. "I need to get out of my head."

"Yeah, and preferably under a hottie that makes you forget your name." Khai wiggles his brows at me, lips turned up in a smirk.

I shake my head, shoving my hands into the front pocket of my Wolves' hoodie. "You're an idiot."

"Your favourite idiot, right?"

"No."

"Come on, I know you're lying. You don't need to play hard to get."

I huff a laugh. "How'd you go from offering some top tier advice to being a dirtbag and saying I need to get laid?"

Khai shrugs, a goofy grin consuming his features. "What can I say? I'm a man of many talents."

"I'll say it again, you're an idiot. And I'm not in the mood to hook up with someone."

"Why? Because you have a certain strawberry-blonde on your mind?"

My fists clench, fingernails embedding into my palm. "No."

A knowing smile splits across my best friend's face. "You can't lie to me, Sin. I can see right through you."

"Well, you're wrong this time," I grunt, unable to meet his eyes.

When Tatum walked into the locker room before the game, her shoulders were tense and jade eyes refused to lift from the floor. I watched her walk across the room to where Olive, our social media person, stood on the other side of the room. I couldn't put my finger on why, but Tatum looked rattled. It was obvious by her refusal to meet the team's eyes—especially mine—and how quiet she was on the sideline, body rigid and spine straight as she watched the game.

I had to stop myself multiple times from asking her if everything was okay, but the death glares I received from Zoe, where she sat with half of the cheerleading squad on the opposite side of Tatum, made me think twice. The last thing I need is for Zoe to cause a scene and make Tatum's life hell— and from experience, Zoe has no problem doing so. She's made my life hell since breaking things off with her, constantly calling or texting me, with no clear end in sight.

Seeing Tatum this on edge has me wondering if Zoe has said something to her. My fists tighten again at the thought. If she has, I will have no problem causing a scene of my own.

Khai holds his hands up in defence. "Okay, if you say so. But if you're wound tight and need an outlet to release some pent-up energy, I'm heading out to grab a drink with Axel. Who knows, maybe you might meet someone who makes you forget about Tatum."

I run my hand through my hair, eyes sweeping across the near-empty locker room. Empty beer cans fill the bin in the centre of the room, courtesy of the celebration ritual post-game. Most of the alcove spaces are cleared out, with only a few players remaining as they gather the last of their belongings. Todd, our head assistant coach, lingers in the corner of the room talking with Axel, our fullback. Coach Phil left ten minutes ago, but I haven't seen Tatum for at least thirty minutes. Not that I'm keeping tabs on her…

Okay, maybe a little.

"I might pass," I say, flicking my eyes back to Khai. "I should probably get some sleep."

Khai raises a questioning brow. "Are you sure?"

I nod. "Go have fun. I'll see you when you get home."

Khai claps me on the shoulder, guiding me out of the sheds and into the hallway. "If you hear strange noises coming from my room, don't be alarmed, okay?"

"Khai, I've heard you have sex enough that I know far too much about the 'strange' noises that come from your bedroom. So, believe me, I will be falling asleep with my headphones in."

A snort sounds from my best friend's throat. "Sorry not sorry, Sin. I can't control them the same way you can't control how weak you are for always going back to Zoe. We're only human."

"I told you I'm done with Zoe." My voice is tight and harsher than I intended as we step through the back entrance of the stadium, the air cool against the exposed skin of my legs. May weather in Sydney makes no sense to me. The mornings and evenings are chilly, but the sun is a blistering bitch throughout the day, making it impossible to gauge what the temperature is going to be or decide what clothes to wear. "If you've heard otherwise, then you're mistaken."

Khai turns his body to me, only an inch shorter than I am. "We both know Zoe talks an unbelievable amount of shit. And while I have heard her saying to her friends that she plans on winning you back, I know you've already checked out."

"I was never checked in."

He chuckles. "That was probably for the best. I would've hated to see you get caught in a web of feelings for that girl."

"You and me both." I exhale a deep breath. "Call me if you need anything, okay?"

Khai hoists his gym bag higher on his shoulder and nods. "As my emergency contact, I expect nothing less from you."

"Yeah, yeah." I bite back a smile as I watch him walk to his car across the lot. "You should really get that changed."

"To who?" he throws over his shoulder.

"I don't know, maybe either one of your parents."

Khai waves me off with his hand. "Not a chance. You're not getting rid of me that easily, Sin. Nice try."

I chuckle and shake my head, watching as he throws the gym bag onto the front seat of his black Range Rover and tears out of the car park, leaving me alone with my thoughts.

My phone vibrates in my pocket. A burst of light blinds me in the darkness when the device flicks to life, revealing a text from my sister.

MIA: I saw the results of the game tonight. I miss seeing you out there.

SIN: Trust me, I miss being out there.

MIA: I hope so… How's the recovery going? Surely you're on the mend.

SIN: It's going as well as I can hope. My new physio's schedule has done more in the past ten days than my previous schedule. If all goes well, the six-week check-in appointment should yield good news.

MIA: I'm so glad to hear that. Gran has been asking me how you're doing. You should call her more.

SIN: I know, I know. I've been super busy with training, and don't even get me started on Mum and Dad.

MIA: That bad, huh?

SIN: Ever since you moved to live with Gran, they've been insufferable. More than their usual amount.

MIA: I'm sorry you have to deal with them alone. You know how hard it is for me to talk to them, especially Mum, with all things considered. I just need some time to figure everything out.

SIN: I can handle them, so you don't have to worry about it, okay? I've got this.

MIA: Thank you, Sin. I appreciate it.

SIN: All you need to do is focus on being there for Gran, doing things for yourself that make you happy, and not crushing on your neighbour.

MIA: Sin! I don't have a crush on Noah.

SIN: Mia, we're twins. Did you think I wouldn't notice the eyes you gave him in the cafe before I left or pick up on the way you speak about him?

MIA: I don't have a crush on him.

SIN: If it helps you sleep better at night, you keep telling yourself that, twinkle fingers.

MIA: UGH! You're so annoying.

SIN: Only to you.

I chuckle to myself as I slip my phone into the pocket of my jeans. When I helped Mia move to Barrenridge, the last thing I expected was for her to be neighbours with Noah Sterling—a Supercars driver for Reign—much less be hired as his babysitter all within three weeks. I warned her not to go there with him, not because I don't trust him, but because I'm not sure if she's ready to let a man close to her heart again after her dickhead ex-boyfriend fucked her over.

It's hard having her so far away, but I know she's safe from the pressure of our parents and the ghost of her past. And as long as she's in Barrenridge, she has the freedom to finally figure out who she is and what she wants to do. I might not physically be there, but I'll be by her side every step of the way.

With a sigh, I walk to my car, my path lit by the streetlamps lining the outside of the car park. Few cars are left, likely belonging to the stragglers inside, but one car does catch my attention. I can't make out the colour from here, but it appears to be a Jeep. Someone has the bonnet flipped up and is digging around, balancing on their toes.

I detour from the direction of my car and approach the Jeep, hands shoved deep in the pocket of my hoodie. "Do you need some help?"

The person gasps and spins on their heels, oil splattered across their face and neck. My stomach does somersaults when my eyes clash with jade, flooding my veins with a fire I only feel with her.

Tatum wipes her hands down the front of her shirt, chest heaving. "What are you doing here?"

I raise my brows at her. "The question should be what are *you* doing here? I thought you left ages ago."

Tatum pops a hip, her hands finding them easily as she holds my gaze. "Keeping tabs on me, are you?"

Yes. "No," I answer too quickly, hating how eager I am to talk to this woman. "Is everything all right with your car?"

"No," she huffs, throwing her hands in the air. "This piece of shit won't start. I've tried everything I know to get it running again, but nothing. The drive here earlier was foreshadowing her impending death."

My body tenses at her choice of words. "What happened on the way over here?"

Tatum flicks her eyes up to meet mine, having to tilt her head back to do so. "Well... let's just say it wasn't the safest vehicle to be in."

"Jesus, Tate." I run my hand through my hair and gesture to the Jeep with the other. "I'm not letting you get back in that thing if it's not road safe."

"Well, I couldn't even if I wanted to." She shrugs and folds her arms over her chest. "I guess I better call my dad so he can come back to pick me up. I'm sure the first words out of his mouth will be, 'I told you not to drive that thing again.'"

I roll my tongue in my cheek, and before my mind has a chance to catch up with my brain, I spew the words, "I can drive you home."

Play it fucking cool, Sin. Jesus.

Tatum holds my gaze, as if waiting for me to take back the offer or reveal an ulterior motive. When the silence between us stretches too far, realising my offer stands, she sighs and drops her eyes to the ground. "You want to drive me home?"

I nod, jaw tense. "I do."

"Why?"

"Because I very well can't leave you here to fend for yourself."

Tatum glances around the lot, worrying her lip between her teeth. "What if someone sees us?"

Let them, I want to say, but swallow the retort. Instead, I clear my throat. "All I'm doing is driving you home, okay? There's nothing for you to worry about."

She opens her mouth as if to say something, but snaps it closed just as quickly, offering me a nod. "I appreciate it, Sinnett. Thank you."

I take it upon myself to lower the rusted bonnet, clicking it back in place while Tatum grabs her handbag from the front seat of the car. My heart hammers in my chest for some ungodly reason when we walk in silence to my car on the other side of the lot. Electricity crackles between us, making it hard for me to focus on keeping one foot in front of the other and not the head of strawberry-blonde hair beside me, her vanilla and floral scent making my knees weak.

God, what the fuck is wrong with me? I need to get a grip.

With a click of a button, the Audi beeps open and I slide into the front seat, the cool leather doing little to ease the heat consuming my skin. Tatum settles into the seat beside me, her scent and presence getting in my head.

The last time she was in my car, I made her crawl over the console and ride my cock in a quiet park. And now she's sitting there covered in oil and looking just as beautiful as she had the night we met. It should bother me that the oil could stain my seats, but the thought barely crosses my mind as I flick on the car, the engine roaring to life.

Tatum runs her hand down her thighs, her eyes sweeping across to meet mine. "I didn't think I would be back in this car."

I lean my arm on the door and turn to her, taking in the

shadows across her face and the softness of her eyes. Sometimes, I find it hard to breathe in her presence, which confuses the fuck out of me. I don't know why I'm so affected by her, but I very well can't allow her to know about it.

Not wanting to breech the topic of the insane sex we had the last time we were in my car, I clear my throat. "What's your address?"

Tatum's eyes round. "Oh! Right." She rattles off her address, and I put it in the Navman, waiting for the route to appear before pulling out of the car park.

I lean back in the seat, one hand on the steering and the other on the gear stick. The car is an auto, but I need to give my hand something to do. My fingers drum mindlessly on the wheel as I fight the urge to look over at my passenger staring ahead, listening to "Want You Bad" by The Offspring. My phone's Bluetooth connected to the system when I got in the car, but I made no move to cue songs or worry about what Tatum might think of my song choices.

"You can change the song if you like." My voice comes out gruffer than intended, and I fight the urge to clear my throat for the tenth time since leaving the stadium.

"I like this song," Tatum says, surprising me. "My dad used to play it in the car when he would pick me up from school in the afternoons."

I raise a brow. "I didn't peg Coach Phil as a punk-rock kind of guy."

Tatum chuckles. "Apparently, you guys don't know much about my dad in his heyday." She leans back, her mouth tilted up in a smile. "He would pull up to the school with the windows down, rock music blasting from the speakers, and a smile on his face. The teachers were appalled by his behaviour, but the kids in my class thought he was the coolest dad ever."

The memory twists painfully in my stomach. I wish I could

say I shared a similar notion with my father growing up, but he was never carefree or allowed anyone to see a side to him that wasn't professional. When Dad would pick Mia and I up from school, he drove a flashy car and wore the best suits. No music came from the speakers, and he certainly gave a fuck what everyone thought about him. If Dad is so much as perceived in a way he doesn't align with, he'll go out of his way to change that persons mind. All of the teachers and students in our year knew Dad as the 'strict one'.

I hated it.

"I've seen him pull into work with the windows down, singing at the top of his lungs to whatever is on the radio," I tell Tatum, which makes her smile in return.

"Classic Dad," she murmurs, smiling. "He always was the brightest in the room."

The song ends, the leading notes making way to "Iris" by The Goo Goo Dolls. Tatum gasps, and reaches for the volume knob. Twisting it to the right, the speakers fight to keep the lyrics steady and not be drowned out by the woman beside me.

I fight back a smile as I listen to Tatum belt out the lyrics, each word cutting deeper than I expected. My hand tightens on the steering wheel.

"I take it you like this song?" I yell over the music, glancing over at her.

Tatum smiles and turns the nob to an acceptable volume. "Like it? It's my favourite song *ever*. I heard it live last year and I swore I melted into a puddle right there on the floor of the arena."

"Why do you like it so much?"

"Everything about it is raw and beautiful. The lyrics, the music, his voice..." Tatum blows out a soft breath and smiles. "I'm sure everyone has connected with it in one way or another."

I contemplate whether I have or not, and when I come up empty handed, I shrug. "Not me."

"Seriously?" Tatum deadpans. "Only a robot would say that."

"I guess I'm a robot then."

"Maybe you're just not thinking hard enough about it," she offers. "And once you do, try and tell me you don't feel every lyric in your bones or the meaning weighing heavily on your heart."

I want to tell her that it's just a song, but the look in her eye, something resembling warmth and acceptance stops me from spewing the words. Instead, I offer a half-hearted shrug. "When that day comes, you'll be the first to know."

Silence stretches between us as the song fades out, replaced with MGK's "I Think I'm OKAY". My fingers drum on the steering wheel, head nodding with the beat of the drums. Headlights from oncoming cars illuminate the space, casting bright shadows over Tatum's features. The further we drive into Mosman, the more my heart sinks. I like having Tatum in my space, which isn't something I can say about most people, especially women. But something about Tatum has me wanting to explore her deeper, to see what she's really like and if she is someone I can trust.

"How'd you enjoy Townsville over the weekend?" The question reveals itself easily, filling the small space.

Tatum glances over at me, searching my side profile. "It was fun. I vaguely recall your buddy Khai being dared to run naked down the hallway of the hotel by Axel, and let's just say Dad was pissed."

I snort a laugh, the image far too clear in my head despite my not being there. "One thing you'll learn about Khai is the man has no shame. Zero. You ask him to do the most embarrassing shit on the planet, and he'll do it without hesitation and a goofy grin."

Tatum laughs, the sound soft and sweet. "Why doesn't that surprise me?"

"Because it shouldn't. He's a nutcase."

"A nutcase whose ass I saw flying past my room at one in the morning."

I grimace, knuckles bleaching around the steering wheel. I should smack him upside the head for putting her in that position. She shouldn't have to be subjected to that kind of thing from the guys, but at the end of the day, I wasn't there to stop it. I was sat in the apartment fighting the urge to go down to the bottle shop to grab myself the biggest bottle of bourbon I could get my hands on, just to give myself *something* to do. Instead, I had jumped on Khai's computer, hoping he wouldn't notice I touched his things.

"I apologise on his behalf," I settle on saying. "He's an idiot, but I guess he's my idiot."

"How well do you know each other?"

I exhale a long breath. "Where do I start? We've been friends since we could walk. Our parents were neighbours before we moved a few streets away. After high school, when we joined the reserve team and were in uni getting our degrees in sports science, we couldn't bear being apart, so we found an apartment and moved in."

Tatum hums. "So, he's your best friend?"

"The one and only."

"That's sweet." After a moment, she says, "You're chattier this time around."

I raise a brow at her. "How so?"

"Well, the night we met, you weren't too keen on answering my questions, but now you seem a little more open to sharing details of yourself with me."

I exhale sharply and run a hand through my hair. It's unnerving how well she can read me, and pick up on subtle cues I don't realise I do. "I was a dick that night, I'll admit. I was tired and needed to blow off some steam."

"I could tell," Tatum comments, voice gentle. "Do you need to do that a lot? Blow off steam?"

I drag my bottom lip between my teeth, and nod. "It was worse because I was injured and couldn't hit the gym like I normally would. So I apologise for how I spoke to you."

"No need to apologise. I think you might recall that I rather enjoyed it."

My pulse jackhammers at the base of my throat, and I fight the urge to reach across the console and touch her.

"I think it's safe to say we both enjoyed that night." My voice is thick and words low, setting off the fire licking in my veins.

Tatum hums, the sound doing nothing to ease the warmth blooming in my chest. This woman is too much. She has somehow embedded herself into my skin, and like a cat trying to get rid of fleas, I can't seem to shake her, no matter how hard I try. She's in my head when she shouldn't be, and my body craves her at the most inappropriate times. I shouldn't want her—nor am I allowed to, courtesy of her father—but my mind and heart haven't quite gotten the memo yet.

The Navman tells me I have arrived at the destination, and the car crawls to a stop out the front of a house similar to that of my parents. Its modern exterior is hidden in the depths of the shadows, and trees line the property, making it difficult to get a visual of the rest of it.

My eyes sweep across to Tatum, who is already looking at me. I exhale a long breath, needing to choose my words wisely, because when I'm with her, I'm nothing but a fucking mess. Before I can get the words out, Tatum beats me to the punch.

"Thank you for the lift home." Her voice is warm, wrapping around me like a gentle hug. "I appreciate it."

"It's no problem at all," I squeeze out, chest tight.

Tatum's hand lingers on the door handle, her back to me. Seconds later, her eyes appear over her shoulder, soft irises melting into mine. "And if you ever need to blow off steam or get out of the house, listening to music and driving the streets does wonders."

I raise a brow, caught off guard by her words. "You've done it before?"

"Barrenridge only allows so many activities before you're bored shitless. My friends and I used to do it a lot in high school, and I found it was a great way to calm whatever turmoil I had going on with exams or personal issues." Tatum shrugs, the movement breezy. "If you ever find yourself in need of quiet company and a killer playlist, you have my number."

And then she's gone. Just like that.

My eyes track her path up the sidewalk, stopping in front of a white door before slipping inside. A soft orange glow from the light on the porch illuminates her enough that I see her wave goodbye before closing the door, disappearing from sight.

I close my eyes and drop my head against the headrest, the palms of my hands digging into my eyes.

I don't know what just happened, but being with Tatum does something to my heart that's foreign and fucking terrifying. Her sweet voice and even sweeter smile are enough to bring me to my knees, as pathetic as that sounds.

What are you doing to me, strawberry?

God, I'm so fucked.

It's getting increasingly more difficult to stay away from her. My heart is at war with Coach Phil's warning, and to my surprise, the instructions to steer clear of his daughter are being drowned out by the way my heart fucking beats for her.

Chapter Eleven

TATUM

Raya's warning about steering clear from the Wolves' players two days ago, especially Sinnett, evaporated the moment Sinnett appeared in the parking lot after the game and offered to drive me home. I should've declined and called my dad instead, knowing I needed to keep my distance since my one-night stand has a girlfriend.

And like the fool I am, not only did I accept the lift home, but then my big fat mouth had to dig my grave deeper by offering myself as quiet company whenever Sinnett needs to blow off steam.

What the hell, Tate?

I've replayed the drive home that night in my mind for the past forty-eight hours, trying to pinpoint the moment I lost my damn mind. Sinnett has been a constant fixture in my mind for three weeks and no matter how many times I tell myself I need to keep my distance because too many factors come into play that could cause issues down the line, I can't get his damn ocean eyes and infectious smile out of my head.

And don't even get me started on what he did the next morning.

I had woken up ready to get an Uber to the stadium and call a tow-truck to get my car, when I saw a text message from Sinnett.

> SIN: Don't worry about your car. I handled
> it for you.

Beyond confused, all I could do was stare at the screen, searching my brain for a possible explanation. When I couldn't come up with anything, I asked him directly.

> TATE: And by handled you mean...?

> SIN: I had my mechanic grab it this
> morning before you could even think about
> returning for the death trap. My guy is
> going to give it a lot of love and hopefully
> by the time you get it back, it won't be on
> the verge of killing you.

All I could do was blink at the screen because *what*. Sinnett went out of his way to contact his mechanic, get my car towed and have it looked at. I didn't ask him to do that nor did I expect it, but it didn't stop my heart from slamming against my ribcage at his kindness.

> TATE: Sin, you didn't have to do that. I'll
> pay you back every cent.

> SIN: Don't even think about it, strawberry.
> It's the least I can do to ensure you're safe
> on the road. At least until you get a
> new car.

> TATE: Don't even think about buying me a new car. This is more than enough.

> SIN: I won't... Not unless you ask me to.

The more I dwell on his kindness, the tighter my chest gets and the faster my heart beats. I need to remind myself that Sinnett Baxter is not someone I want to get involved with. Not only does he have a girlfriend, but he leads a complex and rigid lifestyle that is often in the eye of the media. Having that kind of spotlight on me makes my skin crawl. Strangers are relentless at the best of times, but dealing with the pressure of being attached to his name and not knowing how others perceive you is too much for me to handle.

But it doesn't change how my stomach flips with excitement whenever I see him around the training facility, catching his eye no matter what he's doing. It's made worse when we're working one on one and I'm surrounded by his cinnamon and cedarwood scent, and large presence. I'm only so strong.

Explaining to my dad how my car got to the mechanic so quickly was hard. I managed to pull Raya into the narrative, telling him she drove me home after the game and offered to get it taken care of by her brother who is a mechanic. Every part of the story was a lie, but Dad bought it with ease.

A sigh escapes my parted lips as I flick through Khai's chart, eyes scanning the words on the page. My brain doesn't retain a single word and I inwardly groan.

"You okay there, Tate?"

I lift my gaze to where Khai sits on the table, thick thighs hanging over the edge. His hands rest on his lap, pale green eyes steadily holding my gaze. Strands of mousy hair lift in different directions, soaked with sweat. The Wolves training jersey hugs the muscles on his chest, leaving his bare arms on display. It's impressive how muscular yet lean rugby players can be. They have muscles in all of the right places that allows them to have the strength to tackle hard and take big hits, but not too much mass that it slows their agility and speed.

"Look, if you're still scarred from what you saw in Townsville, just know that I only feel slightly bad about it."

I bite back a smile. "Oh really?"

Khai nods. "Yep."

"And this doesn't have anything to do with Sinnett, right?"

"...No."

I chuckle and shake my head. "Look, don't take whatever Sinnett said to heart. I thought it was funny."

A shit-eating grin splits across the five-eighths face. "Are you hitting on me right now, Tate? I can't wait until Sin hears about this."

"You're impossible." I drop my gaze to the chart and blow out a low breath. "From what I can see in your recent stats, and notes from our last session, the condition of your muscles and joints are looking solid. If you stick to your current training and general muscle recovery plan after training and games, I have no doubt you'll continue down this path."

Khai stands from the table, his six-foot-two frame towering over me. "And are you sure the tweak I felt in my lower back is nothing?"

"If it's not causing you any pain or discomfort, I would say it was likely caused by improper lifting during weight training. Be sure to keep your posture and not push yourself too hard, okay?"

Khai lifts his hand to his forehead in a salute, and I fight the urge to burst out laughing at his antics. "Your wish is my command."

I turn to put his chart on the table behind me as a way to

keep him from seeing the smile slip onto my face. Khai is by far the most outgoing and carefree guy on the team. While the rest of the players are polite and offer friendly conversation whenever they come into my office, I can tell they're reserved, with their heads screwed on straight and their minds focused on training and improving themselves. Khai, on the other hand, will crack a joke at every chance he gets, and he never fails to light up the room when he enters.

Before Khai can leave, I spin to face him. "Can I ask you a question?"

Khai shoves his hands into the pockets of his black athletic shorts, pale eyes peering at me from behind limp strands of hair falling over his forehead. "If you want to ask me out on a date, I'm not sure how Sin would feel about it. I mean, I'm sure he'll be pissed at first, but he might eventually give us his blessing."

I snort a laugh and wave off his comment with my hand. "I'm not asking you out on a date, Khai."

He gasps, feigning upset as he slaps a hand over his heart. "You wound me, Tate. I don't know how I'll possibly recover from this."

My eyes roll involuntarily, a smile lifting the corner of my mouth. "I think you'll survive. Anyway, I wanted to ask you if... well, um..." I fold my arms over my chest and exhale a sharp breath, needing to get the words out that have been plaguing my mind the past two day. "Is Sinnett dating Zoe? From the cheer squad?"

Khai's brows raise in what I can only guess is surprise.

Panic floods my system, and words spew from my mouth before I can stop them. "I know it's not my place to ask, and I wouldn't have said anything but Raya kind of got into my head before the game on Thursday."

Khai rolls his tongue in his cheek and leans back against the table. "Consider yourself lucky that Raya warned you at all.

She isn't one to take kindly to new faces, especially someone she doesn't trust."

"Yeah, she said that," I mumble, cheeks warming.

"But her warning does ring true."

"How so?" I question, voice tight. "I mean, I haven't met Zoe yet..."

"Let's just say that she thinks her shit doesn't stink and because of that, she believes she controls the entire cheer squad, and the guys on the team, too," Khai explains with a shrug. "And Sin is just one of the poor suckers who got caught in her web."

"I don't..." I swallow hard, the words getting caught in my throat.

"If Raya told you to steer clear, I would for the sake of your sanity. Zoe has been known to have a ruthless streak, mostly with those she doesn't like or feels threatened by. She's possessive as fuck, and will go to great lengths to keep everything in her life the way she wants it," Khai says, eyes searching my face.

My pulse jackhammers in my throat. What does he mean by that? Sweat slicks my palms, and I wipe them down the front of my polo, distracting me from the speed at which my heart is racing. "I-I don't understand. This whole thing is confusing."

Khai chuckles, the sound warm and inviting. "Believe me, if you're confused, I'm confused. And if we're confused, then Sin is fucking lost." He offers me a shrug. "Look, I think it's best if you speak to Sin about this. I love talking about my best friend, but if you want the real story, he's the best person to ask."

I exhale a sharp breath and nod. "Yeah, no, you're right. I feel weird asking him about his personal business because he's... well... Sin."

Knowing exactly what I'm referring to, Khai chuckles. "Too fucking right. But trust me, if you ask him what's going on, he'll tell you." He claps his hands together and gestures behind him. "I better get back to the gym before your father or Todd has my nuts."

I want to question why he believes Sinnett would be willing to talk to me about his girlfriend problems when we hardly know each other, at least on that kind of level, but I don't.

"Remember what I said about your posture and pushing yourself too hard," I say pointedly.

Khai smiles. "You can trust me."

When I'm alone in the room, I sink against the table behind me and sigh. The conversation with Khai has left me more confused than I was ten minutes ago. I'm nowhere closer to finding out what is going on between Sinnett and Zoe, and now I'm starting to wonder if it's any of my business at all. Even if I find out the truth, it won't change the fact that Sinnett will always be just out of reach, unattainable.

My phone vibrates in my pocket, pulling me from my thoughts. Needing the distraction, I reach into my pocket and retrieve the device. Noah's name appears on the screen, and my heart leaps with excitement.

"Noah!"

"T, it's so good to hear your voice." A giggle-squeal sounds in the background, and my heart squeezes knowing who it belongs to. "How are you?"

"Better, now that I'm hearing from you." I smile, dragging my bottom lip between my teeth. "How are you doing? And my sweet niece, of course."

"We're both good. Missing you, of course."

"I miss you both, too." I pace across the room to my desk nestled in the corner. It's not much, only the essential office supplies and a desktop computer, but it's more than I need. Dropping into the black leather chair, I lean back, relishing in the pressure dissipating from my feet. "What's new with you? It feels like forever since we last spoke."

"It's been a week, T."

"Yeah, a week too long. Now spill, Noah. How is everything going with the new neighbour you don't shut up about?"

Noah chuckles. "She's fine." A cupboard closes in the background, and I picture Noah moving through the kitchen, cleaning up after Jade, no doubt. "And the neighbour has a name, you know."

"Yes, I know. Now talk to me about her."

"Well, I hired *Mia* to babysit Jade two days a week."

My eyes nearly bulge out of my head. "What!"

"I know, I know. But hear me out. The daycare was dropping its trading days, and I was desperate to find an alternative. Mia offered to look after Jade, and, well... I took her up on the offer."

"I get that," I drawl, blinking slowly. "And is it going well? How does she get on with Jade?"

"Jade took a liking to her almost immediately. It's like my daughter forgets about my existence whenever Mia is around."

I snort a laugh. "She's replaced me already, I see. Well, that will change whenever I visit next."

Noah laughs with me. "I have no doubt. You're still her number one, T."

I smile. "And how are you with having her in the house? I know it's been hard for you since Em, but don't think I didn't see how smitten you were with this Mia girl when you mentioned her the day I left town."

Noah exhales a sharp breath. "Mia is... great, T. Not only is she beautiful, and a mystery I want to unravel, but she brings out a side to me I haven't known since Em."

"And that's a problem because...?"

"It's not," my friend clarifies. "It's both terrifying and exciting."

"So what I'm hearing is you have a crush on her."

"Tate," Noah groans, and I fight the urge to laugh. "Mia is a reserved person. I can't just go in guns blazing when we barely know each other. She's timid, like she's fighting a silent battle."

"It still doesn't change the fact that you like her, Noah," I point out. "Just accept it."

He sighs. "It doesn't matter what I think or feel."

"You just have to break her walls down," I offer with a shrug. "It's an easy solution."

"What if she doesn't want that?" His words are filled with uncertainty. "I don't want to push her."

"Just let destiny take its course, okay? If it's meant to happen, it'll happen. You deserve to be happy, Noah. After all you and Jade have been through, I want this for you."

"Me, too," Noah murmurs, voice low.

"Anyway," I utter, needing to change the topic before Noah starts to spiral in that head of his. "How is Nathan? He texts me every morning and night asking if I can get signatures from everyone on the team."

Noah chuckles, and I'm reminded of the years of memories we share. "That sounds about right."

For ten minutes, I'm transported back to Barrenridge with my two best friends. Noah tells me about Nathan and how he's doing at work, running an organisation that coaches basketball to kids outside of school. He shares stories about Jade and how business at the mechanics is steady, keeping him busy. Even though Noah is sharing menial stories that most wouldn't care about, I'm beaming with appreciation for my friends and how supportive they are of me following my dreams in Sydney. It's hard to come by friends like them, and I couldn't be more grateful.

When Noah asks about my new job, I have to keep from mentioning Sinnett. They don't know about my night with him and I'm not sure I'm ready to share the details with them yet. I trust Noah and Nathan with my life, but with how confusing everything has been since that night, I need more time to figure my shit out.

A knock at the door pulls me from the conversation, forcing my eyes to meet ocean ones. I swallow hard at the sight of Sinnett standing in the doorway, shoulder resting against the frame with his legs crossed at the ankles. This man is all hard muscle, lean frame and an intensity that melts my insides. The tattoos covering his right arm are visible due to the training jersey—a far cry from the hoodies I see him wearing a majority of the time.

My eyes linger on the wolf head inked into his toned forearm. The detail on the design draws me in, tracing each line with precision. The haunting treetops of a forest below the wolf has me wondering if there is a deeper meaning to the design or if he simply likes it and wanted it to be permanently on his body.

"Tate?"

My heart leaps into my throat at the sound of Noah's voice. I exhale a sharp breath, pulse racing. "Y-yeah, sorry. Look, I've got to get back to work, but I appreciate you calling."

"Anytime, T," Noah responds, followed by words of warning to Jade not to put the building block in her mouth. "Talk to you soon, okay?"

"Of course."

Noah and I say our goodbyes, my eyes never leaving

Sinnett's. He strolls into the room as I stand, hands trembling at my sides.

"Who was that on the phone?" Sinnett's voice is deep, but the question holds no accusation.

I clear my throat and roll my shoulders back. "Just a friend from back home."

"A friend?" He flicks his eyes to mine, curiosity seeping into his features.

"We've known each other since we were three. His name is Noah."

A frown creases his brow. "Noah... Please tell me you're not talking about Noah Sterling."

Now I'm frowning. "Yeah, I am. How do you know him?"

Noah has been racing Supercars since he was just out of high school, so it would make sense if that's where Sinnett had seen him before. I know it's a popular sport these days. But it doesn't explain the frown deepening in his forehead.

"Your friend is neighbours with my sister. Your *friend* hired my *twin sister* to be his babysitter."

My eyes widen as the colour drains from my face. "What? Is your sister Mia?"

"Yeah," he murmurs, folding his arms over his broad chest. "Your friend better not fuck around with my sister."

"He would never." I'm quick to come to Noah's defence. "He's a great guy, I promise. Probably the kindest person I've ever known, so Mia is in good hands with him."

"He better be," Sinnett grunts. He walks further into the room and leans his hip against the bed, eyes locked on mine. "Mia has been through a lot, so the last thing I need is for him to make things worse."

It's on the tip of my tongue to ask him about his sister, and why he's so protective over her, it goes beyond just normal sibling care, but I don't. The tension in his shoulders and the hardness of his features tells me it's not my place to ask such personal questions.

Tension crackles between us now, weighing heavily on my chest at an almost suffocating pace. How is it possible that this man can render me speechless with so much as his presence?

"What can I help you with?" I choke out, folding my arms over my chest.

A frown creases his forehead. "We have a session booked, remember?"

My eyes round at the edges and I scramble for the desk calendar on the right of the desk, my schedule for the day as clear as day. I inwardly curse myself for being distracted the past two days and forgetting about this appointment.

"Shit," I murmur, and straighten my spine. "Well, I guess we better get started then."

Sinnett rolls his tongue in his cheek. He hoists himself onto the edge of the table. "Yes, we should."

My movements are rigid as I round the desk and move toward Sinnett. His eyes track my path, and I fight the urge to shudder under his intensity. My hands tremble as I gesture to his quad, wrapped up with sports tape.

"How are you feeling?" I ask, keeping my eyes downcast on his thick thigh that could easily burst open a watermelon if he tried hard enough. "I hope the plan I created for you has been beneficial in your recovery."

"I feel great." Sinnett rubs his hand over the thigh in question. "The swelling seems to have gone down a lot."

I inspect the area that was angry and swollen not even ten days ago, but is now calmer and less inflamed. My heart swells with pride knowing my knowledge and hard work have led Sinnett on a road to recovery that could see him back on the field in three weeks, if he keeps going at this pace.

"Impressive progress," I murmur.

"It's all because of you, strawberry."

I lift my eyes to his, my insides melting at the warmth swirling in the sea of blue. "I can't take all of the credit when you're the one putting in the hard work."

Sinnett runs a hand through the messy strands of hair over his forehead and nods. "Either way, thank you. I might actually be able to get back on the field soon."

"I will say it's looking like a possibility." I take a step back, needing to put some distance between us so I don't inhale more of his addictive cologne. "But don't get ahead of yourself, okay? This is the halfway point, so as long as you keep to the schedule, you'll see positive results."

Sinnett's hands curl around the edge of the table, knuckles bleaching as he nods. "Yeah, no, you're right."

Clearing my throat, I ask, "Ready to get started? Today I'll be focusing more on mobility of your knee to see how the muscles in your quad react to the movement, and then I'll finish up with a massage."

The thought alone of having to touch Sinnett has warmth spreading across my body.

"If you wanted to feel me up, Tate, all you had to do was ask."

My cheeks flame at his words, and I'm unable to meet his eyes. "Are you going to say that every time I need to massage you?"

He smirks. "Maybe."

My body tingles, eyes flicking to his. Sinnett is watching me with an intensity that feels like too much. Too much warmth in my muscles. Too much heat in my core. And too much electricity racing down my spine.

I tear my eyes from him, cheeks burning. Sinnett stifles a laugh, watching as I shuffle to his side, hands reaching for his right leg. Silence settles over us as I grip his calf, using it as leverage to extend his knee. With each movement, I study Sinnett's features for a physical reaction—a good indication of his pain scale. His face stays deadpan, eyes locked on my hands.

I swallow hard. "What's the pain like right now?"

"Not too bad," Sinnett murmurs.

"And your limp?"

"Better." He sucks in a sharp breath when I move his knee toward the bottom of the bed, trying to push it past ninety degrees. "Manageable."

I hum, letting his leg fall naturally. His gaze is hot on the back of my head when I turn and reach for his chart on my desk. I make a note about the mobility of his knee as a reminder to update his plan with exercises that will help get his range closer to one-twenty degrees.

Setting the chart down, I return to Sinnett's side. His hand runs over his thigh, likely to help soothe the pain settling in his quad muscles. Ocean eyes find mine, and I swallow hard, trying to avoid them as much as I can.

"I'm going to update your plan with some new exercises for you to try out that will help with the mobility around your knee. But, overall, the muscles don't appear swollen at the moment, which is a good sign."

Sinnett exhales a long breath and nods. "Thanks, Tate."

"My pleasure." I gesture to the table. "Ready for that massage?"

He nods and lies down, long legs stretched out over the table. I swallow around the lump forming in my throat and reach for his thigh. The second our skin connects, a zap of electricity races down my spine—similar to the spark I felt the night we met. Sinnett must've felt it too, because his eyes flick to mine. A fire blazes in the depths of his irises, and I force my gaze to his thigh where I work the muscles slowly, hoping to relieve some of the tension in them.

Silence settles over us for all of ten seconds before my brain decides to fill it by asking, "Any plans for tonight? It's Saturday, after all."

"I think some of the guys were talking about going out."

"Are you going with them?"

"Maybe," Sinnett drawls. "I haven't made up my mind yet."

"Do you go out often?" I can't stop the question from coming out. Warmth spreads across my cheeks at the lack of self-control I possess.

Sinnett rolls his lips, not fazed by my question. "More often than I should. I try to keep Khai company, he has a habit of going out a lot because of his jinx."

I arch a brow, meeting his eyes. "Jinx?"

He shakes his head. "Trust me, you don't want to know."

"Is that good for you all?" I ask instead. "I mean, surely your nutritionist doesn't want you drinking."

Sinnett shrugs, hands coming up to rest on his stomach. "One or two drinks won't kill them, but Khai likes to take it to the extreme, so there's no telling with him."

"That doesn't surprise me," I chuckle. "He's... a lot."

"You're telling me." Sinnett's mouth tilts up in a half smile. "He's insane, but I wouldn't have him any other way." Dragging his tongue over his bottom lip, his eyes find mine. "Look, about the other night..."

"It's fine," I cut him off, not sure if my heart can take whatever he's going to say. "I get it."

Sinnett's brows crease. "You do?"

I shrug. "Yeah. You helped me out and I appreciate it. But I know now that you have someone, so I need to stay in my lane. I understand. I'm not looking to break up a relationship."

The muscles in his arms ripple as he grips the material of his jersey. "What? That's not—"

A sharp knock at the door saves me from this awkward as hell conversation where I have no doubt Sinnett would've tried to let me down gently and put me firmly in the friendzone. Axel stands in the doorway, eyes flicking between me and where Sinnett lays on the bed.

"Is everything okay? I can come back," Axel asks.

I wave Axel into the room, ignoring Sinnett's sharp eyes on the side of my face. "Nonsense. Come in, please. We were just wrapping up the session." The lie tastes bitter on my tongue, but I need to put some distance between me and Sinnett, for the sake of my heart.

Sinnett's jaw tightens as he gets off the bed and stalks across the room. I track his movement, watching as he runs a hand through his hair, the muscles in his back coiled tight. Within seconds, he's gone, taking with him the breath from my lungs.

I sag against the table as Axel takes Sinnett's spot. Words leave his mouth, but I don't register a single one of them.

What was that reaction from Sinnett?

And why do I feel like I said the wrong thing?

Chapter Twelve

SINNETT

The second the glass slams down onto the wooden table that is as unsteady as my heart, I'm itching to go to the bar to order another. My veins thump in time with the beat of "How Deep Is Your Love" by Calvin Harris, the alcohol swimming through them doing nothing to ease the tension rolling in my shoulders.

"Ease up there, cowboy. Save some alcohol for the rest of us," Khai shouts over the music, the sound grating on my already fragile nerves.

My fingers flex around the glass, and I fight the urge to clench my jaw for fear of snapping a tooth. There are only so many times you can do it before it becomes a concern—one that my dentist might have a problem with.

Strobe lights blur at the corner of my vision, making the already small club feel tiny. Sweaty bodies brush past my back, eager to hit the dance floor with a drink in hand. Drops of what I can only assume is alcohol land on my back, seeping into my tense muscles. I fight the urge to grimace at the scent of cheap perfume, stale beer and smoke. What else would you expect from a club in North Sydney?

The Vixen is one of the most popular clubs in the city, and on a Saturday night, it's almost impossible to get in after 10 PM. Maybe it's the happy hour house spirits that bring in the crowds, or the killer DJ that plays every weekend, but it's packed in here, making it hard for my already struggling lungs to breathe.

I'm going to need more fucking alcohol if I want to get on a level that has me feeling as light as a feather.

"Is everything okay?" Khai asks when I don't respond. "You seem... tense. Hell, you haven't so much as blinked at the women who have stopped by the table in the past hour to get your phone number, or, I don't know, have a friendly conversation with you."

"I'm fine," I grit out, using the same two words each time my friend asks about my wellbeing. I'm sure he's tired of hearing the same shit as much as I am of saying it. "I just needed a drink."

"Or five," Khai snorts, sipping his own drink. "I mean, I'm not complaining. After Zane and Nico bailed on me for a night in to play video games, *fuckers*, I was glad you changed your mind so I wasn't left to my own devices. You know how I get when I'm drunk and alone."

"Yeah, you go home with the first man or woman that locks eyes with you."

Khai leans over to wrap his arm around my shoulders, pressing me against his side. "And since you're here, you'll be the only man I go home with."

I bite back a snort. "Yeah, lucky me."

"But who knows," my friend says as he releases me and returns to his seat, "I might still go home with someone. The night is still young and the stars are yet to fully shine."

I tilt my head to the side, catching sight of Khai's shit-eating grin. "You're a menace, you know that right?"

"And yet you still love me."

"Love might be a strong word."

"You know you love me, Sin. Don't make me shout it out in front of everywhere here."

I reach over and slap my hand over his mouth. "Don't you dare, asshole."

Khai grins beneath my hand, cheeks lifting. "Don't tempt me with a good time."

Pulling my hand from his mouth, I shove myself up from the stool. "I'm going to get another drink. Do you want one?"

"If it's your shout then consider me thirsty."

Leaving Khai to laugh to himself, I push my way through the crowd cast in shadows and multi-coloured strobe lights. Stray hands graze over my chest and down my arms, but I ignore the touches, my sights set on getting another drink in me to calm the storm raging in my mind.

After what felt like an eon standing at the bar, I have two drinks in hand, pushing through the crowd and praying no one pumps into my quad. The last thing I need is for some drunk idiot to ruin the steady progress I've been making.

When I break through the crowd, I stop dead in my tracks when my eyes land on the head of strawberry-blonde hair occupying my seat. Heat thrums through my veins as I watch her from afar, like a fucking creep. Her head tips back, laughing at something Khai said. Beside her, Raya flips her hair over her shoulder, eyes pinned on my best friend.

My fingers tighten around the plastic cups, and I'm grateful it's not glass because I have no doubt they would've shattered under the pressure.

What is she doing here?

Of all the places she could be right now, why does it have to be here at this very moment when I'm balancing on the edge of losing my goddamn mind?

I consider retreating into the crowd and sculling the drinks in my hands, but Khai catches my eye, and gestures for me to approach. *Shit.* This is not good. I came here to get my mind off the strawberry-blonde, not have her invade more of my mind than she already has.

Gritting my teeth, I take, slow, deliberate steps towards the table, ignoring how my pulse races with the overwhelming need to get the fuck out of here.

"There is he!" Khai cheers when I set his drink down in front of him. "I thought you might've gotten snatched up by a lucky lady at the bar and abandoned me."

I grunt in response, taking the seat beside him and across from Tatum. Her eyes trail over my face, leaving tiny fires in their wake.

Don't look into her eyes. Don't look into her eyes. Don't look into her—

Fuck. I have the willpower of a fucking toddler.

Jade eyes lock with mine, holding me hostage. God, she's beautiful. Even in a filthy club with awful lighting, Tatum manages to steal the little air left in my lungs. I flex my hand around the cup, needing to do something with them.

"There was a long ass line," I squeeze out, jaw flexing. "What did I miss?"

Khai gestures to Tatum and Raya with a smile that could light up the moon. "I saw these two lovely ladies enter and thought they could use our wonderful company."

"Did you think that maybe they might want to spend time together?" I deadpan.

"I take offence to that," Khai says with a frown. "Either way, they're here now, so let's get fucked up."

"I second that," Raya says, running her fingers through the

ends of her two-toned hair. "I don't have anywhere to be tomorrow, so I plan to be fuck-eyed come morning."

Khai reaches across the table and the two high five. "That's what I like to hear! What about you, Tate? Keen on getting legless with us?"

Tatum's mouth tilts up in a half smile. "Yeah? I guess."

A shiver races down my spine as my eyes sweep across her body. Besides the night we met in Barrenridge when she wore the most insane little black dress I had ever seen, and a polo and long pants at work, I haven't seen her dressed casually. If you call blue jeans and a white spaghetti strap top casual. And don't even get me started on the outline of her fucking nipple piercings showing through the thin material.

I swallow hard and tear my eyes away. If I continue to focus on her smooth skin and the tiny freckles scattered across her shoulders, I'm going to lose my damn mind.

"Then let's get this fucking party started!" Khai jumps to his feet and leans down to plant a kiss on Raya's cheek. She bursts out laughing. "First round of shots is on me." He scurries through the crowd, hands thrown in the air as he goes. Damn my best friend for thrusting me into this situation.

After my session with Tatum today, I struggled to keep my self-control around her composed and intact. I've grown to enjoy her random questions and how easily I relax in her presence. It's as if all the tension and pressure weighing heavily on my shoulders disappears when I see her face—so sweet and calming. I've started looking forward to going to our sessions, wondering what question she might ask me next or what I can learn about her.

Discovering that Mia is neighbours with Noah Sterling, Tatum's friend, was a shock, to say the least. I was ready to tear Noah to shreds and demand Tatum keep him in line, especially after the bad luck with men Mia has dealt with in the past three years. But she told me I could trust that my sister is in good hands with him, and I believed her words. Call it intuition, but I believed Tatum. I just hope that what she said about Noah is true, and he doesn't fuck over my sister.

"Long time no talk, Sin." Raya shifts on the seat, eyes meeting mine. "How have you been?"

"Same old, same old," I respond with a shrug. I take a sip from my bourbon and Coke to consider my next words. "My new physio has got me on this intense recovery plan, so I spend most of my days living and breathing by her words."

The corner of Tatum's mouth twists up at my words. And God do I wish I could take a picture of it.

Raya grins, her eyes flicking between me and Tatum. "So I've heard. I heard she can be real hard ass."

"Oh, yeah, the biggest."

Tatum takes a swipe at Raya's arm, her friend laughing in response. "Hey! I'm not that much of a hard ass."

"Says the person who has me icing my quad and then stretching it for what feels like hours." I bite back a grin, but it's hard when she looks so cute and annoyed. "But I will say she has her moments."

Raya bumps her shoulder against Tatum, who smiles in return. "Yeah, she's pretty. And totally off-limits, Sin. In more ways than one." The tone of her voice is neutral, but I'm no fool who can't read between the lines. My hands flex around the cup again, the brief good mood slipping from my bones.

I've known Raya since she joined the Wolves' cheerleading squad two years ago. From the moment she walked through the door on the first day of practice, Zoe swept in like a wrecking ball and took the girl under her wing. Zoe did everything she could to drag Raya into her clique of mean girls, and I could see Raya was resisting, but knowing she had no other choice—it was either join them or be on the outs—she gave in. Whenever we got the chance to talk, Raya expressed disinterest in being Zoe's friend, but we both knew how persuasive Zoe could be. I don't know why she confided in me, but I didn't question it.

Raya has been there from the start of my fucked-up relationship with Zoe—if you could even call it that. So her warning just now comes from a place of knowing what Zoe is like. For the best interest of myself, the team and Tatum, I need to keep my distance.

I despise the fact that Zoe thinks she has any say in what I do. I've made it clear to her on multiple occasions that I'm no longer interested, and still she's trying to pull claim over me behind my back. And while I understand Raya is trying to look out for me, I can fight my own battles.

"Raya…" Tatum starts, but I cut her off, not wanting to go down this road when I'm not nearly drunk enough to deal with it.

"It's fine, Ray. I hear you."

Khai returns to the table with a tray of shot glasses filled with a mysterious pink liquid. He sets down two in front of each of us before taking his seat, a shit-eating grin split across his features.

I eye the shot glasses. "What the fuck is this?"

"A wet pussy shot," Khai answers, fingers already reaching for the one in front of him. "And don't even think about bitching out now."

"Well, a free shot is a free shot." Raya lifts one of the glasses to her lips. "Bottoms up!"

Khai and Raya down a shot each. But my focus is on Tatum, who is watching me, big eyes blinking slowly.

I offer her a shrug and reach for a glass, knowing that if I don't drink this, Khai will force it down my throat, and that's not something the public needs to see. "You don't have to drink it if you don't want to."

Tatum lifts one of the glasses, inspecting the bright liquid. "I've never had one of these before. It looks... interesting."

"It's fucking delicious!" Khai cheers before tipping his head back with the second glass pressed between his lips. A gasp of relief slips from his mouth as he slams the glass down on the table. "Damn, that's the best wet pussy I've ever had."

"Oh, I'm sure it is," Raya muses, mouth tilted in a smirk. I snort a laugh and consume one of the shots. The liquid seeps into my veins, and warmth rushes to my head, easing the ache beginning to form at my temples. Loud music and the tension in my shoulders is not a good combination, but the alcohol makes it bearable.

Tatum exhales a sharp breath and drinks one of the two shots. She grimaces as she swallows, desperately trying not to show a reaction to the strong alcohol. I smirk, watching as she reaches for the other one and consumes it.

"Drink up, Sin," Khai says, shoving my last shot into my hand. "The night is young, so buckle yourself in for a good one."

KHAI DROPS INTO THE SEAT BESIDE ME, SWEAT pouring down his temples. Out of breath, he reaches for the beer he left on the table before joining Raya and Tatum on the dance floor thirty minutes ago. "The Anthem" by Good Charlotte thumps in the back of my mind, rattling my bones, and I find myself bopping my head along with the beat of the song.

My gaze tracks Tatum where she hovers at the edge of the dance floor, dancing with Raya. Her hands fly into the air and her features light up with a smile, followed by laughter I can't hear over the music. I wish I could. It's become one of my favourite sounds.

"I don't know how they do it," Khai wheezes, and sucks in a deep breath. "Like shit, I thought playing rugby was hard."

I snort a laugh. "You're acting like dancing is the hardest thing ever."

"I'd like to see you try, Sin. Trust me, my calves are on fucking fire and my hips ache."

"You mustn't be working hard enough on the field then if you're fucked after thirty minutes of dancing."

Khai blows out an irritated breath. "You're just a hater, I get it. I'd like to see you try keeping up with those girls."

"Not a chance," I say with a shrug. "Over my dead body will you ever catch me dancing in a club."

Raya wraps her arms around Tatum's neck, their body swaying to the beat—carefree and effortless. My eyes linger on Tatum, taking in every curve that makes me want to lose my mind. She has no idea what she's doing to me. How much she affects me. But it doesn't change the fact I can't have her.

"God, you're like a lost puppy waiting for its owner to come back from war."

I snap my attention to my best friend, who is hiding his smile behind the rim of the beer glass. "What?"

Khai sets the glass down, his eyes locking with mine. "You're so obvious it's almost painful to witness."

"I'm not following..."

He slaps a hand on my shoulder, his body shifting closer to mine. "I know you like Tatum. Hell, a lot of guys on the team have the hots for her."

Ice floods my veins. "They *what*?"

"Calm your tits, Sin. Jesus. It's like you've done more than just hook up the one time with how you're acting over the girl."

"Am not," I bite out, hand flexing around the half empty cup.

"Are too." Khai shifts his body to face me, but my eyes stay locked on Tatum. "Look, you either need to go for it and accept the hellfire Coach Phil will rain down on you, or you need to let her go and walk away. With you being back on the field in a couple of weeks, you can't afford to be distracted over a girl."

God, he's right. I know he is, but it doesn't change the fact that I can't walk away from Tatum. It's as if I'm drawn to her in a way that has me desperate to be around her, but my mind demands we keep our distance because I can't afford to go to war with her father over her—not when I enjoy playing for the Wolves and want to stay with the club beyond my contract at the end of this season. But if I break Coach's one rule, or even think about touching his daughter, there is no coming back from that. Remembering the seriousness of his warning, I have no doubt he would do anything to protect his daughter.

I shove a hand through my hair and exhale a deep breath. My jaw clenches as I find the right words to express the turmoil raging inside of me. "I know, I just—It's hard, okay? I don't understand why I can't stop thinking about her, and I'm even more confused about what I should do."

Khai slaps a hand on my shoulder, drawing my attention from the dance floor to him. "I get it, I do. And while I want you to be happy, I know that if you stay in this strange limbo of not knowing what the fuck to do, you're going to spin out, and it won't be good for you or the club. We need you in peak condition, both mind and body, when you get cleared. No distractions."

I wish he wasn't so damn perceptive.

"I know," I grunt, my chest aching with the weight of a decision I'm not sure I'm ready to make yet. "I just... It's something about her, man. I seriously can't put my finger on it."

"Maybe it's worth finding out why you feel this drawn to her," Khai says, tone far from joking. "And if it doesn't work out, then at least you know you tried."

I open my mouth to respond when out of the corner of my eye, I see two men approach Tatum and Raya. One is blonde with a crooked nose, and the other has frosted tips, like he just walked out of a 2000s rom-com. Every muscle in my body tenses as I watch the preppy fuckers dance their way into the girls' space, slapping on what they think is a charming smile, but I have no doubt their intentions are anything but pure. Jaw clenching, I watch as the men separate Tatum and Raya. My blood boils.

"You okay?" Khai asks, waving a hand in front of my face.

I point at the dance floor. "Those two fuckers separated Tate and Ray, so I'm keeping my eye on them."

Sensing the concern in my voice, Khai shifts so he's got a clear view of the scene unfolding before us.

It's taking every ounce of self-control I possess not to march over there and tell them to get lost. Could they not see the girls were happy dancing with each other?

Tatum smiles at the frosted tips guy dancing with her friend, but the gesture feels forced, not quite reaching her eyes. His hands are on Raya's hips, but she doesn't appear uncomfortable. My hands drop to my thigh, and I fist the material of my jeans to channel the anger tearing through my veins. If this fucker so much as puts a hand on her—

The edges of my vision scream red.

Tatum spins so her back is to the blonde guy, hand

clutching her drink, and the motherfucker drops something into the liquid so quickly I almost missed it. Tatum turns to face him again, and the guy smiles, clearly pleased with himself.

Time moves at a snails' pace and everything around me ceases to exist. I'm pulled back to the night my sister knocked on my door and told me what her boyfriend had done to her. How he *hurt* her. I've never known fear quite like that moment, wondering the extent of what Ryan had done to her. I wanted to kill him. I really did. But Mia insisted that I let it go because she had no plans to ever see him again. It wasn't good enough for me, knowing he could do the same thing to the next girl. When she fell asleep, I drove to his apartment, ready to beat the shit out of him, but unsurprisingly, he wasn't home.

For the sake of my sister, and not wanting to be thrown in jail for assault, I left it alone like she asked. I walked away when I should've done more. Said more. But I didn't.

This time is different. I refuse to sit back and allow that asshole to hurt Tatum when I can do something about it. I'm not walking away this time.

Shoving the chair out from under me, I ignore Khai yelling over the music for me to stop, to think about what I'm doing, but I don't. My attention is focused on the blonde fucker who has his hand on Tatum's hip as they dance, wearing a shit-eating grin, thinking he's about to get lucky tonight.

Not on my fucking watch.

He doesn't sense my presence before I'm shoving him to the side, pushing the slimy fuck as far away as I can. Tatum gasps, her eyes rounding at the edges as they meet the side of my face. But I don't look at her. No. My eyes are set on the blonde guy who stands a few inches shorter than me, crooked nose flaring like a raging bull.

"What the fuck is your problem?" he roars, squaring his shoulders. His friend leaves Raya to back up his buddy.

Lucky me. Two dickheads for the price of one.

"You better get the fuck out of here before I waltz my ass over to the bouncer and tell them you slipped something into her drink."

His face pales at the same time Tatum gasps, peering down at the drink in her hand. The tremble in her hand doesn't go unnoticed by me, and now I'm reconsidering my decision not to beat this guy's ass.

"I don't know what you're talking about." His posture is straight and confident, but his voice quivers at the edges. "You had no right to touch me like that."

"I could've done a lot more than shove you, so consider yourself lucky." I reach out and wrap my hand around Tatum's wrist, tugging her behind me. "You better get the fuck out of my sight before I change my mind."

The blonde's hero friend steps up to bat, puffing out his chest like it will help make him taller. It's laughable, really.

"Don't talk to him like that," the guy with frosted tips grunts, folding his arms over his chest. "You can't just come over here and demand we leave without proof of what you're accusing him of."

Khai steps beside me, cracking his knuckles. I'm grateful for his presence because I'm going to need some back up if shit hits the fan.

"So if I force her drink down your throat, nothing will happen, right? Go on. Be my guest."

The preppy guys share a knowing look, but neither of them seem willing to back down or admit they're in the wrong. Unfortunately for them, neither am I. If anything, I'm just getting started.

A crowd is starting to form around us, curious eyes

investigating the nature of the showdown. Once a phone appears, I'll need to get the hell out of here. The last thing I need is for some drunk fool to recognise me and Khai and upload a video to social media. Coach Phil will have a fucking field day with this, not to mention his daughter being involved.

"That's what I thought," I continue after the weight of their silence settles over me, adding fuel to the fire growing beneath my skin. "Don't make me repeat myself."

The blonde guy who had been touching Tatum sneers at me before turning his attention to where she's hidden behind me, her hands gripping the back of my leather jacket. "Whatever. You're not hot enough to fuck anyway."

Blood rushes in my ears as ice floods my veins. My first instinct is to put my fist in this assholes mouth to stop him from spewing more shit or consider breaking his nose, but someone beats me to the punch. My eyes round at the edges when dark liquid splashes in his face, drenching his hair and white T-shirt. His hands fly to his face, wiping the liquid off his mouth while his friend glowers over my shoulder.

"You bitch!" the blonde roars, face twisted in anger. "I can't believe you did that."

Tatum peeks out from behind me, her spiked drink running down the features of the asshole in front of me. If I weren't a live wire ready to spark at any second, I would've laughed and given her a high five for that move. Instead, I stick my arm out in front of her chest, keeping her as far away from these guys as possible.

"You're lucky that's all she did, asshole," I seethe, muscles coiled tight. "Now get the fuck out of here before I break every finger on the hand I'm sure you'll use to fuck yourself with tonight."

The blonde huffs and runs a hand through his wet hair. He shoots a heated glare at me and Tatum before stalking off the dance floor with his friend hot on his heels, hopefully to the exit so they can't try to hurt another woman here.

Tatum sags against my side. I spin to face her, wrapping my arms around her back. Her cheek meets my chest, the gesture easing the tension in my shoulders. Vanilla floods my senses, and I sigh at her familiar scent coating the air around us.

She's here. She's safe.

If I hadn't been watching and missed him slipping that pill into her drink, tonight could've ended vastly different. The thought alone floods my body with unfamiliar rage. If he had hurt her... God, I don't know what I would've done.

It scares me what I would do for this girl, even if it means ruining myself in the process.

Chapter Thirteen

TATUM

Raya stumbles onto the street with Khai's arm hanging around her shoulders, wobbly legs barely able to keep him up. Khai certainly wasn't kidding when he said he wanted to get legless tonight. I had thought it was a saying, but apparently, he took the word literally.

"God, you're heavy," Raya huffs as she hoists a giggling Khai higher. One wrong move and he'll tumble from her barely tight grip. "What the hell do you eat?"

"Meat. Lots of it," Khai mumbles, eyelids dropping. He presses a sloppy kiss to her cheek, and Raya scowls at him. "Thank you for looking after me, RayRay. I don't know what I would do without you."

"Yeah, yeah," she mumbles, tightening her grip around his back as she makes a move for the black SUV sitting idle on the curb. "You owe me big time, Khai."

Khai grins as she swings the door open and guides his lethargic body into the back seat. "Anything for you."

With a sigh, Raya closes the door and turns to face me on the sidewalk, with a quiet Sinnett standing to my right. "Are you sure you don't want to get in this Uber with us? I'm sure the driver won't mind making a detour on the way."

I shake my head and wrap my arms around my waist, fighting off the chill from the cool evening air. It's nearly one in the morning, and now I'm regretting my choice not to bring a jacket with me. Dad told me I would need one, but I brushed him off as I raced out the door. Now I'm starting to wish I had listened to him.

"I'll be okay. My house is a twenty-minute walk from here, so it'll be fine."

"You're walking?" Sinnett's deep voice sends a shiver racing down my spine. "Like hell you are."

"Sinnett..."

"No," he bites out, shoving his hands in the pockets of the black leather jacket hugging his frame. "I'll walk you home."

Warmth spreads across my cheeks. "Oh, you don't have to—"

"It wasn't a question, Tate." Sinnett turns to Raya and nods. "Get Khai home safely, Ray. He keeps the keys to the apartment in his right pocket."

Raya drags her bottom lip between her teeth, her brows creasing as if wanting to say something. But she doesn't. Instead, she nods and steps toward the passenger door. "Got it. Make sure you get this one home safely, okay? And behave yourself."

Choosing to ignore her last comment, I wave at her. "Night, Ray. Thanks for inviting me out tonight."

"It was fun." She smiles and points toward a passed out Khai in the backseat. "Some of us had more fun than others, though."

"Is he going to be okay?" I direct the question to Sinnett.

"He'll be fine," he responds with a shrug. "Not the first time he's gotten shit-faced and it certainly won't be the last."

"Well, either way, it was still fun." *If you take out almost getting roofied*, I want to say, but swallow the words instead. I'd prefer to forget about the showdown between Sinnett and those guys, and what could've happened had he not been there. "Get home safely, Ray. Make sure you text me."

Raya swings open the door, the Uber driver patiently waiting in the front seat. "Same goes for you, okay?"

I smile. "Of course."

Sinnett and I stand in silence, shoulders barely brushing as we watch the SUV pull away from the curb, tail lights disappearing in the distance. A chill washes over me, and I'm helpless to fight the shudder. I need to get home quickly before my teeth start chattering.

"Here." Sinnett steps to the side and shrugs off his leather jacket.

My eyes round as I lock my attention on the rippling muscles of his biceps. *Good lord.* "Sinnett, no. I'm okay, really."

He doesn't say a word as he steps into my space and drapes the large jacket over my shoulders, the material swallowing my frame. His woodsy cologne clings to the material, and I fight the urge to inhale deeply.

"Sinnett, I'm okay, I promise."

Sinnett steps back and shoves his hands into the pockets of his jeans. A grey-washed Guns N Roses T-shirt clings to every hard ridge and curve of his torso, not leaving much to the imagination. Not that I have to think too hard when I've seen what's hidden beneath the thin material.

"Tate, I can clearly see you're cold, and with a twenty-minute walk ahead of us, I'd prefer you stay warm."

"What about you?" I squeeze out, throat tight as I relish in the warmth spreading across my arms.

Sinnett shrugs. "I'll be fine. The walk will keep me warm."

I drag my bottom lip between my teeth and nod. Silence

settles over us as we walk side by side in the direction of my house. Groups of drunk partygoers litter the streets, their high-pitched laughter and slurred speech echoing down the street after us. It isn't until we're a block away does the nightlife of North Sydney fade into the background, leaving space for my elevated heart rate to pound at the base of my throat.

Our footsteps set my nerves on edge further, and I rack my brain for something to say. But when I come up empty, I heave a sigh and shove my hands into the pockets of the leather jacket Sinnett all but forced me to take—which I'm grateful for now because it's getting colder by the second—and focus my attention on the footpath.

"Are you okay?"

Sinnett's deep voice catches me off guard, and I jump like an alley cat. Heart beating rapidly against my ribcage, I snap my head to the left, gaze sweeping over his side profile—all sharp jaw and smooth skin. Piercing blue eyes meet mine, and I struggle to force air into my lungs.

"W-what?"

"I asked if you're okay," he repeats, shifting his focus to the footpath shrouded by bursts of light from the streetlamps. "I mean, after everything that happened tonight..."

"Sinnett, please," I rasp out, throat tight as the memories from earlier tonight slam back into me. "We don't have to talk about this."

"We do," he grits, muscles tensing beneath the thin material of the band T-shirt. "We absolutely do, Tate. That fucker tried to hurt you, and if I hadn't seen him slip that pill into your drink—" He shoves a hand through his messy hair, tugging at the roots. "Tonight could've ended badly."

"Yeah," I breathe, swallowing hard. I shift my focus to the empty suburban street. "I appreciate you looking out for me."

Sinnett doesn't owe me a thing just because we had a one-night stand and now work together. If he wanted to, he could've given me the cold shoulder on my first day, and we would've never spoken again unless absolutely necessary. But he didn't, despite my initial thought that he would. And now we've found ourselves in this strange position where we have shared an intimate moment and don't know what to do from here.

At the end of the day, my father's warning to the team about staying away from me still stands, and no one in their right mind would go against their head coach. Sinnett's career hangs in the balance; it rides on him sticking to the rules and keeping his head in the game.

"I'm not going to sit back and allow some low-life to hurt women like that. He's lucky I need to think about my career, otherwise, I don't think I would've held back as much as I did." His eyes pierce the side of my face, and I fight the urge to meet them. "I would never let someone hurt you, strawberry."

My stomach flip flops at the meaning behind his words.

God, what is this man doing to me? I can't get a grip on my damn heart, much less my mind. I'm in a confused state where I know I need to keep him at arm's length, but also want to get closer to him so I can unravel what goes on in that complicated mind of his.

"Well, thank you," I murmur.

Silence settles over us, the seconds ticking by slowly. We've been walking for not even five minutes, and knowing what I do about Sinnett, I'm not sure he would be down for much small-talk. With an urge to fill the silence and distract my mind from thinking about the man beside me, I reach into my handbag and retrieve the corded earphones, tangled in a haphazard ball.

I push one of the buds into my right ear and offer the left one to Sinnett. "Do you want to listen to some music with me? It'll make the long walk go quicker."

Sinnett eyes the bud before looking at me. His jaw clenches, chest heaving as if fighting the urge to say something. But ultimately, he doesn't. He silently accepts the bud and slips it into his ear before shoving his hands into the pockets of his jeans again.

My heart thunders in my chest as I scroll through my music catalogue. When Sinnett drove me home after the game on Thursday, I learned that while he listens to music, he doesn't necessarily connect with it. So, on a mission to make his hard exterior feel *something* from lyrics, I tap on one of my favourite songs. The Calling's "Wherever You Will Go" sounds through the earphones, the opening notes settling the tension in my bones. I nod along to the beat.

Sinnett stays silent as we walk, the song carrying our footsteps in the direction of my house. As each second ticks by, I relax a little more in Sinnett's presence. Hell, he even nods along to the song. It's on the tip of my tongue to ask him if he's heard it before, but not wanting to ruin the moment, I let the song trickle into the opening notes of "3AM" by Matchbox Twenty.

My shoulder brushes against Sinnett's tattooed arm, the contact sending a jolt of electricity down my spine. The designs are hidden in the shadows of the night, but the wolf head sticks out to me even in the darkness, the lines detailed and deliberate. My fingers itch to trace the curves of the body, but knowing that would be a bad idea, I flex them in the pocket of the jacket and keep my eyes trained ahead.

"I like this one," Sinnett comments when we're five minutes from my house.

Trying to not sound surprised by his admission, I keep my voice even as I ask, "You do?"

He nods. "It's catchy."

"And the lyrics?"

"They're okay." He shrugs. "Nothing to write home about."

I fight the urge to groan. "Sinnett, come on. The lyrics are beautiful. And so heartfelt."

Again, Sinnett shrugs. "I guess so. But I still don't feel a connection to it."

"Well, maybe that's because you need to find a personal experience of your own that closely relates to the lyrics."

He hums in response as the closing notes simmer out. "How do I know the right experience to use?"

"You don't," I answer, scrolling through songs to pick another one. "You just... feel it. Embrace it. If that makes sense?"

Before Sinnett can respond, my finger skims over a song I had no intention of choosing. My cheeks flame when I register the title of the song, and my current situation with a man I have an intimate history with.

"Oh, shit, sorry," I rush out as I try to find a different song to replace Ed Sheeran's "Kiss Me". "I wasn't supposed to pick that one—"

"Let it play," Sinnett interjects, eyes lowering to meet mine. "I haven't heard this one before."

"Y-yeah, but—"

"Tate, please." He chuckles, ignoring the panic seeping into my features. "Just relax."

God, I wish that were possible.

With hot cheeks and my sense of pride seeping away, I slip my phone into my pocket and allow myself to listen to the lyrics despite my racing heart thumping in my chest. Sinnett's arm brushes mine again. He wasn't kidding when he said the walk would keep him warm—I can feel the heat of his skin through the leather.

Sinnett pulls out his phone, scrolling and walking in

silence. I try to catch a glimpse of what he's doing, because I'm a snoopy person at heart, but every time I look away from my feet, the thought of stumbling and ripping the ear bud out of his ear is too embarrassing, so I leave him to his scrolling.

Turning onto my street, with my father's house in sight, Sinnett slips his phone back into his pocket. I find myself wishing the walk had been longer. Listening to music with Sinnett brings a wave of calmness I have needed since arriving in Sydney. It reminds me of being home in Barrenridge and hanging out with Noah and Nathan. Music has always been a comfort of mine. Mum used to play P!nk every Saturday morning when she would clean the house, and I would end up dancing with her in the kitchen instead of doing chores. It was something that brought us closer, our shared love for the same genre and songs binding us tight. Now, when I hear the opening notes to "Who Knew", I have to fight the urge not to cry because it was one of Mum's favourite songs.

As we reach the driveway to my house, a sheet of rain drenches us. My eyes widen as I stare up at Sinnett, his head dipped low, watching me with intense eyes. The song continues to play in our ears, blocking out the sudden rain shower. I really should've checked the forecast before leaving the house.

"Shit," I mutter, holding my arms above my head as if they'll stop the rain from seeping into every inch of my body. "I better get inside. Here, take your jacket."

"Wait," Sinnett rasps, holding his hand up.

I drop my arms to my side, no longer caring about the rain. How could I when Sinnett is looking at me like that? Ocean eyes hold mine hostage, and I fight the urge to shudder when his hand comes up to push strands of wet hair off my cheek. The moment his skin brushes against mine, a full body shiver racks through my bones.

One touch. That's all it takes from this man to make me come undone for him. One. Touch.

"Sin..." I breathe, heart rate spiking to the point a doctor might be concerned about the condition of my heart. "What are you doing?"

"I'm embracing the moment," he murmurs, deep voice mixing with the rain falling heavily around us.

I blink through the rain. "You are?"

"I am." He nods. "And it's fucking terrifying."

My heart squeezes in my chest. "Why?"

"Because I shouldn't do this," he squeezes out. "I have so much on the line that could blow up in my face, but at this moment, I can't find the energy to care."

With Ed Sheeran's voice singing in my right ear, Sinnett holds my cheek in his hand. And like a child with no willpower, I lean into his touch, relishing in the warmth radiating from his skin. I'm afraid that if I speak or make a move, the moment will be ruined.

"I shouldn't want you, Tate. But I do. *Fuck*, do I want you." Inky strands of hair fall over his forehead, shielding his ocean eyes from me. "But the question is: do you want me?" From this angle, head tilted back as I look up at the man I should be keeping my distance from, I see the war raging in his features. A battle I can't help him fight.

Do you want me?

No matter how many times I repeat the four words in my head, the answer is always the same. Sinnett is right when said he has a lot on the line—we both do. If we break the rule keeping us from toying the edge of this forbidden cliff, if I give in to my desire for Sinnett, we would be betraying my father. Sinnett has his career to think about, and my job and relationship with Dad would be on the line.

Wait.

I'm an idiot. A stupid, forgetful idiot.

"But you have a girlfriend," I squeeze out. My hands fist in the pockets of the jacket—a jacket I shouldn't be wearing—my nails digging in my palm.

Sinnett's features twist with anger as his brows crease. His hand slips from my cheek, and I hate that I'm the reason for the loss of touch. "A girlfriend? What are you talking about?"

"Zoe," I murmur. "Isn't she your girlfriend?"

"No," he bites out, and runs a hand through his hair. "Who told you that? Did Zoe say something to you?"

With the music in my ear now silent, I have nothing to distract me from the fury festering in Sinnett's features.

Oh, God. I really put my foot into it this time.

"No. Raya told me. She said you and Zoe have a complicated relation—"

"We're not together."

"But she said—"

"Tate, I don't care what Raya told you," Sinnett interjects roughly. He groans and runs a hand through his hair. "We never dated. We used to—"

"Fool around," I finish for him, my voice barely above a whisper. "I get it."

I'm not surprised that Sinnett isn't one to commit to a woman wholeheartedly. Being a professional athlete means you have the pick of the crop whenever you want it. I'm not naive enough to believe Sinnett isn't potentially seeing other women. Hell, he was probably hooking up with Zoe around the time we got together. And while the thought stings, I can't let it get to me.

Sinnett exhales a sharp breath. "Yeah. Whatever bullshit Zoe is spinning about us, it's not true. I haven't been with her in months."

"You don't have to explain yourself, Sinnett. You don't owe me anything."

"I at least owe you the decency of telling you where you stand with me."

My eyes round at the edge as I stare up at Sinnett. "What... what are you talking about?"

Sinnett's chest brushes against mine. The proximity sets my skin alight, and causes my skin to erupt with goosebumps. "I haven't been with another woman since I was with you, Tate."

"You haven't?" I whisper, not trusting my voice.

"No, I haven't," he responds, voice hard yet gentle. "Because I'm not lying when I say my head has been fucked since meeting you."

"It has?" My heart slams into my chest, drops of water gliding over the curve of my lips, which Sinnett keeps lowering his eyes to. "I haven't either."

I'm not the type of person to sleep casually with men, but he doesn't need to know that.

"You haven't?" he breathes, tongue darting out to lick the water from his bottom lip. "Good."

"Good," I repeat breathlessly. "That's good."

"Then believe me when I say that I can't walk away from you, Tate." Sinnett's hand slides through my hair, resting at my nape. His touch prickles my skin in a delicious way, and I have to fight the urge to groan. "No matter how many times I talked myself down from the edge only to return the next day, waiting to see if anything would change. But it didn't. I shouldn't want you, but I do. Every word, every touch, every damn look. I want all of it."

My chest tightens with an emotion I can't place as I stare at the man who has taken up every part of my brain for the past three weeks. I should push him away with a reminder of Dad's warning, but at this moment, I can't bring myself to do it. Fighting the connection forming between us, fuelled by the small moments we've shared, has been far more difficult than I thought. I don't think I have the strength to continue, not when being together feels so *right*.

"I want you, too," I whisper, the words getting lost in the rain falling around us. "All of you, Sin."

"You do?" he rasps, eyes searching my face for any sign I'm lying.

I nod, fighting back a smile. "I do."

"I can't promise you this is going to be easy, or that it won't get messy down the line, but I can promise you that you'll have every part of me. The good and the bad." He lowers his head until our lips are almost touching. "I do know that I breathe a little better when I'm with you, and while I don't understand why that is, I don't want to continue living without my source of oxygen."

Oh, my *God*. This man and his words.

"You don't have to," I breathe, the words melting into his lips.

Sinnett's lips brush against mine, slow and deliberate at first. They're wet from the water falling around us, but it doesn't take away the sweetness of the bourbon and Coke he had been drinking tonight. I want more of it. Of him. I want more than I got the first night we met.

Throwing my arms around his neck, our chests flush, Sinnett deepens the kiss. His tongue swipes over my bottom lip, begging for entrance. I give it to him, and the moment our tongues collide, electricity shoots through my veins, hitting every edge of my body.

I don't know what I'm doing when it comes to Sinnett Baxter. He's complicated and reserved, but has a softer side to him that he doesn't show others. Hell, I'm only just now starting to see it. But it doesn't change the fact that I don't know how to navigate this man. What I do know is that this feels right. Kissing him feels right.

Sinnett groans as he presses himself against me, one hand tangled in my hair while the other firmly holds my waist. I moan into his mouth, relishing in the warmth exploding in my chest. If he wasn't holding me up, I would be in a crumpled heap at his feet, getting lost in the puddles forming around us on the footpath.

Sinnett pulls away long enough to breathlessly whisper, "This moment right here."

"What about it?" I ask, lifting my eyes to meet his.

He grins. "The lyrics of the Ed Sheeran song you played me? Yeah, this moment right here is going to be what I think about any time I want to kiss you or listen to that song."

Oh, *God*.

How am I meant to survive a man like Sinnett Baxter when my heart is already a goner?

Chapter Fourteen

SINNETT

I kissed her. I fucking *kissed* Tatum last night. Hours later, I feel the lingering touch of her lips on mine and smell her vanilla scent on my skin. It's as if she's imprinted into my skin, and every inch of her has embedded itself deep within my soul. I don't know how she's done it, but I'm helpless to fight against it. Not that I want to.

I don't know how long we stood in the rain; my hand tangled in her wet strawberry-blonde hair while her fingers slid through mine. It was as if our lips refused to part for fear of ruining the moment. Every inch of me craved Tatum, and in equal parts it excites and terrifies the fuck out of me. And while I want to do this with her, push the boundaries of the unwritten rules set in place for us, I'm afraid she's not going to like the side of me I keep hidden from everyone around me. The side that holds the weight of my parents' standards and constant pressure from the media, the club and Coach Phil.

What if she doesn't like that side of me? What if she only wants the side that can give her what she wants? What she needs. Am I capable of giving her what she deserves?

What I do know is that I refuse to let this woman walk away without knowing if this is the right move. Not only for my heart, but my career. Because if it all goes to shit, I could lose both in the process. But I'm willing to take a chance on her. Hell, I've come to the realisation that I would do a lot for her.

I hadn't expected Tatum to bring up Zoe. Shocked was the word to describe how I felt at that moment. I don't know why I expected Zoe to take my rejection lying down when she has never been the type of person who lets someone dictate her life or have a say in what she wants. While I had hoped she would back off and get the hint, it seems she is hellbent on getting me back in her bed.

From the very beginning of our messed-up fling, I knew she only wanted me because of the name attached to my number 7 jersey. If it was up to her, she would've thrived off hanging on my arm at award dinners or be attached to my side during any public outing. Zoe has always been the centre of attention in her world, so adding me to the mix would brighten her light, getting her name and face out there by simply riding my tail coat. When I made it clear that I had no interest in showing her off to the public, and was only interested in no strings attached sex, she was pissed. And while I should've run for the hills before I got too deep, I needed the momentary distraction from the stresses of my life—too blinded by the temporary release to see who Zoe really was.

My lapse in judgement has landed me in some serious hot fucking water, and now I have to deal with the fallout of the choice I made. And there is no way I can save Tatum from the crossfire, not when Zoe fires on all cylinders.

Heaving I sigh, I rest my elbows on the railing and take a long sip from the rapidly cooling black coffee I desperately needed when I rolled out of bed. My eyes sweep over the suburbs of North Sydney and the Sydney CBD. From up here in the penthouse, the view is fucking incredible. When Khai and I moved in three years ago, we had just finished university and joined the main squad for the Wolves, having been brought up from the reserve grade team. The moment I stepped foot into the apartment with my best friend beside me, the view through the floor to ceiling glass windows took my breath away. Even three years later, I'm still amazed by the beauty of the city.

The sun is rising on the horizon, and I marvel at the watercolour display it's putting on. Pastel pink and red hues streak across the sky, creating a path for the sun to continue rising. I smile to myself and sip on the coffee again.

I set my mug on the table behind me and pull out my phone, eyeing the text message chain with Mia. After the conversation I had with her yesterday morning about Mum wanting Mia to return her calls, I'm worried about my sister. She has been dealt a difficult hand the past three years, and with her being so far away, it's harder for me to keep an eye on her. To make sure she's safe.

SIN: Did you get yourself an iced latte this morning?

MIA: What are you doing awake?

Her reply comes quickly, which isn't unusual since she's typically up at the ass crack of dawn. I turn to the almost-empty mug of coffee on the glass table behind me.

SIN: Couldn't sleep.

MIA: That's weird considering all you do is sleep.

SIN: Ha-ha, very funny, twinkle fingers.

MIA: Is everything okay?

SIN: I should be asking you the same thing.

MIA: I'm fine, Sin. You don't need to worry about me.

SIN: But I do, Mia. After everything you've been through, and are working through now, I want to make sure you're okay. And don't lie to me.

The three dots linger for a minute before her next reply comes.

MIA: I promise you I'm fine, Sin. Noah is great and he makes me feel safe. If I'm ever in any danger, you'll be the first to know.

I exhale a sharp breath and run a hand through my hair. The hardest thing about being a twin is being away from your other half. Besides Khai, Mia is the closest person I have in my corner. She understands me better than I do myself at times, so it's hard for me not to worry about her, especially when she's alone.

SIN: Okay, I believe you. Just… be careful, please.

MIA: I always am.

SIN: Good. Also, tell Gran I'll call her this week, okay?

MIA: She knows. I swear the woman waits by the phone for you.

SIN: God, I love her. I look forward to listening to her gossip from around town.

MIA: And she loves telling it. Talks my ear off every day about it.

SIN: Oh, I have no doubt.

SIN: Random question, but what's your favourite song right now?

MIA: Why?

SIN: I'm just looking for song recommendations.

MIA: "With or Without You" has been on repeat lately. I love it.

I hum as I consider the lyrics of the song. We both love rock music, and U2 is one of our favourite bands, so I'm not surprised she has them on repeat.

SIN: I should've expected that from you, twinkle fingers. But thank you.

Heavy footsteps from behind have me shooting a quick message to Mia telling her to have a good day, before slipping the device into the pocket of my black trackies. Glancing over my shoulder, I spot a shirtless Khai in only black briefs stumbling through the open-plan living room, rubbing at his head.

"Fuck me," he groans, stepping out onto the balcony. His shoves a hand through the strands of hair sticking up in different directions. "I feel like I've been hit by a goddamn train."

I bite back a smile as I lean against the railing, folding my arms over my chest. "You certainly look like you have."

"Shut up," he grumbles, reaching for my coffee mug. Without asking, he sculls the last two mouthfuls and scowls. "God, this is fucking lukewarm."

"Yeah, because I've been drinking it for twenty minutes."

Khai squints and meets my gaze, fighting to keep from spinning out from the raging hangover I'm sure he's battling, and the piercing sun as it rises slowly. "What're you doing up so early?"

I shrug. "Couldn't sleep."

He raises a brow at me as he drops into the black egg chair to the right, surrounded by random pot plants he bought six months ago when he wanted to be a 'plant dad'. "I may have been drunk when I left the club last night, but I wasn't blind. You didn't come home with me in the Uber."

"No, I didn't."

"Where did you go?"

My jaw clenches. "I walked Tatum home."

"You *what*?" He rubs at his temples, eyes squeezed shut. "Is that the reason you couldn't sleep?"

"Maybe."

Khai gives me a deadpan look as he folds his arm behind his head. "Don't pull my cock, Sin. What happened?"

I swallow hard and look to the right, focusing on the view and not my best friend's interrogation about my whereabouts last night. "Nothing."

"Sin," he groans. "Come on. Tell me what happened. If you do, I'll shut up about it."

"You should shut up anyway."

"Sin!"

"Fuck," I groan, shoving a hand through my hair and meeting his curious eyes. "I may have sort of... kissed her."

Khai jumps to his feet, eyes wide and hangover clearly forgotten already. "What!"

I grimace and drop my head in my hands. "I couldn't sleep because, well... I don't know if I fucked up or not by stepping over the invisible boundary we had put in place."

"You kissed Tate?" Khai repeats, more to himself than me. "Jesus. If Coach Phil finds out—"

"I'm a dead man," I rasp, throat tight. "I've been up all night thinking of different ways he might try to kill me for touching his daughter."

"Shit, man." Khai exhales a sharp breath and pushes out of the egg chair. He steps up to the railing beside me, leaning his elbow on the metal. I keep my eyes on the interior of the apartment. "I mean, I'm proud of you for finally deciding on what you want, but now you're in a pickle."

"The make or break of a burger," I mumble, something I would say to my sister growing up. "Yeah, I know."

"And is she okay with this? Tate?"

I nod. "She's all in."

Khai whistles low and nods. "Okay, well... I guess you're going to have to play this cool. If Coach so much as catches wind of this, or anyone in the club for that matter, you're fucked. The both of you."

"Yeah, man, I know." I exhale a sharp breath and turn to face the view, focusing on the cool air seeping into the exposed skin of my chest. "Is it bad that I don't care? I mean, if we get caught..."

"It means you're happy," Khai says, turning his head to the right, pale eyes searching the side of my face. "It's what you deserve."

"Do I?" I question, rolling my shoulders back. "Do I deserve Tatum?"

"Probably not," my best friend offers with a shrug. "But she clearly makes you feel something you've never felt before."

I drag my bottom lip between my teeth and nod. "Yeah, I guess."

"Don't be so hard on yourself, Sin. Just live in the moment, okay?"

There is that saying again. Tatum had said something similar when talking about embracing moments in life and relating them to song lyrics. And now Khai is saying the same thing.

When the lyrics of that Ed Sheeran song settled over me, and I saw Tatum staring up at me with her big eyes and kind smile, I couldn't hold back anymore. The string pulling us together had tightened to the point I couldn't breathe unless I kissed her. Felt her against me. It was impossible to breathe, let alone get the words out that I needed to.

And when she kissed me back... *Fuck*, it ignited a fire deep in my soul that is still burning as I watch the sun rise.

If I hadn't been in the moment, and allowed my desire to take over, I would be having a different conversation with Khai right now.

"What if I mess it up?" I murmur, chest squeezing inward. "I don't know if I could handle hurting her."

"Then don't," Khai says simply, like it's the most obvious answer to my predicament. "You've got this, Sin. Keep doing what you're doing and everything will work out."

I want to believe him. I do. But nothing is ever easy in my life. Just when I think everything is going well, I'm blindsided by something else that knocks my world off its axis.

"Yeah," I breathe, my voice barely above a whisper. "I hope you're right."

DINNER WITH MY PARENTS IS STILL THE WORST PART of my week. Not because I don't love them—I do—but they have no boundaries when it comes to my personal life or career. They are always finding ways to slip through the cracks in the wall I put up between us, embedding themselves and their opinions under my skin. I know that at some point during these dinners, they will find a way to bring up the inevitable instead of steering the conversation to normal topics like the weather, what they've been up to and how the extended family is. Hell, I would take my mum telling me about a case she's worked on or my dad talking about the latest Supercars race than be put under the spotlight. *Again.*

I know not to hold my breath with my parents because they will always find a way to steer the conversation to either me or Mia. And tonight is no different.

After the disastrous dinner last week, I haven't spoken to either of them besides a few text messages here and there. I hope they got the hint that they fucked up by overstepping the line with Mia. She has been through a lot, and while they don't know the finer details of the situation, it doesn't excuse their behaviour. And don't even get me started on how Dad spoke about Tatum.

For the most part, the conversation over dinner—the same

roast we have every week—has been tame, but it doesn't take long for Dad to ruin the evening.

"Sin, I apologise for my words last week."

"It's not me you need to be apologising to, Dad," I mutter, eyes focused on the half-eaten steak on my plate.

"We can't get ahold of her," Mum interjects from her seat across the table. "She won't answer either of our calls or texts. I'm worried about her."

"Mia is fine," I grit, rubbing my hands up and down my thighs, careful of my injury but needing to do something with them. "I spoke to her this morning. She's been busy helping Gran and getting settled in." The details of her babysitting for Noah are not something I'm willing to share right now. It's not my place to tell them.

Dad heaves a sigh, and I look up to see him running a hand down the side of his face. After commentating for a game earlier this afternoon, he's still dressed in one of his freshly pressed black suits. "She can't continue to shut us out without telling us what's going on."

"Did you tell her to call me?" Mum asks.

"Yes," I bite out, annoyed with my parents' questioning about my sister when I'm sitting right here. She could be asking about *me*.

"I just want to know she's okay," Mum adds, her voice sharp. "After the break up with Ryan, she hasn't been the same."

My hands form fists on my thighs, nails digging into my palm as my knuckles bleach white. "Don't speak his name. He's a piece of shit, and I'm glad Mia got away from him."

"Language, Sin," Mum scolds, and I fight the urge to roll my eyes.

"What are you not telling us?" Dad probes, pale blue eyes

searing into the right side of my face. "You and your sister are very close, so I'm sure she's told you what's going on with her."

Refusing to throw my sister under the bus and air out her business, I shrug. "I don't know what's going on with her, Dad. As far as I'm aware, until she figures out her path in life, she wants to stay in Barrenridge with Gran."

My heart thunders in my chest, the truth of my sister's past weighing heavily on my shoulders. Mia asked me not to tell our parents what went down with her ex-boyfriend, and as much as I want to get revenge on the fucker, her happiness means more to me. Even if carrying the burden of her secret feels impossible at times, especially when our parents know something is up, I would do it for the rest of my life until she's ready to share her story.

Dad hums and pushes food around his plate.

Mum, on the other hand feel, isn't satisfied with my response.

"I told Mia not to hang around those friends of hers in uni, or go anywhere near that boy because I knew he was trouble." She huffs, shaking her head. For once, she's not dressed in a pantsuit—opting for a more casual look of a knitted sweater and dark blue jeans, with her hair in a ponytail at her nape. "But did she listen to me? No."

"Look, I'm not having this conversation with either of you," I say, unfurling my fingers. A jolt of pain shoots up my forearms. "We can either talk about something that doesn't involve Mia or my career, or we can sit in silence. The choice is yours."

Part of me hopes they'll want to talk to me, their son, not their athlete son, like we used to before. We would spend hours sitting around the dining table talking about random things or playing board games, getting lost in the feeling of being together as a family. But now that I'm older and have more responsibilities, not just for myself but the family name and my father's legacy, the family dynamic has shifted. And I'm an idiot for thinking it could go back to how it used to be.

My parents share a heated look before zipping their lips closed and throwing away the key, casting the room in total silence besides the utensils tapping against the porcelain plates.

I groan inwardly and slump in the chair, my appetite gone. Just another family dinner gone wrong. What else is new?

Not caring about my mum's 'no phones at the dinner table' rule, I reach into the pocket of my black athletic shorts and retrieve my phone. Tatum's phone number appears on the screen under the contact name 'Strawberry' and I smile to myself. I changed it the night she put her number in my phone.

> SIN: Are you free right now?

Tatum's response comes quicker than I thought it would.

> STRAWBERRY: That depends on what you're about to ask me.

I stifle a smile as I tap on the screen, my father's eyes boring into the side of my face.

> SIN: Are you up for a drive? I could use the company and killer playlist you promised me.

> STRAWBERRY: Well, you're in luck because I'm as free as a bird.

> SIN: I can pick you up in thirty minutes?

STRAWBERRY: Perfect. Gives me time to curate the best damn playlist I can.

I drag my bottom lip between my teeth and slip my phone into my pocket, ignoring the not-so-subtle glances of my parents.

This fucking dinner can't end quick enough.

Chapter Fifteen

TATUM

Sinnett's car is waiting for me when I close the front door. With my hands shoved into the front pocket of the dark green hoodie I threw on, I make my way down the path, unable to wipe the grin from my face.

When I got the text from Sinnett, I had been lying in bed reading a book. After the events of last night, I needed time to myself to process everything that happened. Dad knows I'm hungover, so he wasn't surprised when I told him I was going to Maccas to get some greasy food. The fast-food joint is a ten-minute walk, and he offered to drive me, but I played it off by saying I would be meeting Raya there and she'll drive me home. He smiled and told me he was happy I was settling in well and making friends.

Guilt burned like acid in my stomach, the lie having slipped easily from my lips without much thought. I don't like lying to my father, especially since we're rebuilding a relationship that weathered away from years of minimal engagement. But he can't know about Sinnett. If he even slightly catches wind that I'm spending time with him, or anyone on the team for that matter, he will lose his shit.

Keeping him in the dark is best. At least, that's what I'm telling myself as I slip into the passenger seat of Sinnett's car.

I'm immediately hit by a puff of cinnamon and cedarwood, and the most stunning man to ever walk this earth. Sinnett's right hand grips the steering wheel while the other rests on his thigh, rubbing the area in slow circles. Even in the dark, with minimal lighting from the streetlamps, his ocean eyes are bright. Just being this close to him, feeling the warmth radiating from his body and happily drowning in his familiar scent, a shiver races down my spine.

"Hi, Sinnett."

"Hi, Tatum." Sinnett pulls the car onto the street, driving with no destination in mind. "Thanks for agreeing to come for a drive with me."

Warmth spreads across my cheeks as I shift in the leather seat. "Are you okay?"

His eyes flick from the road to me. "Why wouldn't I be okay?"

"Well, you're gripping the wheel so tightly your knuckles are as white as a ghost, and your shoulders are tense." I shrug. "A drive like this means something is bothering you."

Sinnett's jaw ticks. "How is it that you can read me like a book?"

"I'm very perceptive."

He exhales a sharp breath. "Maybe a little too much."

"Is it about last night?" I squeeze out, my chest tightening. "Because if it is, we can forget it happened."

Sinnett's eyes widen as he snaps his head in my direction. "What? No. Tate, this has nothing to do with what happened last night. If it was, I wouldn't have asked you to come with me."

Relief floods my system. Thank God.

We haven't spoken since he kissed me out the front of my house, soaked to the bone from the rain. He sent a quick text to let me know he had gotten back to his apartment, but after that, I passed out. And when the morning rolled around, I was far too tired to be on my phone, instead choosing to flip between sleeping, watching a trashy reality TV show and reading my book. I had considered texting him to see how he was doing throughout the day, but ultimately decided not to. Sinnett made the first move with the kiss, so I wanted to allow him to make the next one, giving him that time to decide if what he did was a mistake or not.

If my current position is anything to go by, I would say he's not filled with regret. Yet.

I shift so my back is pressed against the door and my right leg curls into the seat. "Then what's going on? If you want to tell me, of course."

"I might need your killer playlist to get through this," Sinnett rasps.

My eyes widen. "Oh, right! I forgot."

"Too distracted by me, strawberry?" Sinnett wiggles his brows while I fiddle around with the built-in car system.

"No," I mumble, heat pooling at the base of my throat. "Not at all."

Sinnett hums in response, and within a minute, my phone is connected to the car Bluetooth. I tap on the playlist I finalised seconds before Sinnett told me he was outside. My usual playlist I created with Noah and Nathan for our late-night drives isn't exactly Sinnett's vibe. He enjoys rock music and leans more toward an alternative sound, so I made sure to include as many as I could. I did throw in some curve balls though, hoping he'll enjoy them.

"November Rain" by Guns N Roses blasts through the

speakers. Sinnett drums his hands on the steering wheel, a smile tilting the corners of his mouth.

"I love this song," he says, nodding his head along to the opening notes. "A masterpiece, if you will."

"My parents danced to this as their first dance song at their wedding," I say, smiling. "All eight minutes of it."

Sinnett smiles. "Really?"

"Really really. My dad loves this song, and while my mum wasn't overly into it, Dad let her pick the rest of the songs for the ceremony, so she let him pick their first dance song."

"How cool," Sinnett breathes. "Coach Phil just keeps getting cooler and cooler."

"He is." I clear my throat and shoot him a pointed look. "No more distractions," I scold playfully. "Tell me what's on your mind."

Sinnett heaves a sigh and drags his bottom lip between his teeth, as if choosing his words carefully. He isn't the type of person to open up about himself easily, if our past conversations are anything to go by. But I've slowly been breaking down his walls so that I can catch a glimpse of what he keeps close to his chest.

"I had dinner with my parents tonight."

I raise a brow at him. "And that's a bad thing because...?"

"Because they don't care about me," he offers, voice tight. "I mean, they do care about me, but not in the way that matters."

"Keep going," I press gently, my full attention locked on the man struggling to find the right words to say. "Take your time."

"I, um..." He swallows, grip on the steering wheel tightening. "I don't know how to talk to them and vice versa. All they care about is my career and trying to mould my sister into the perfect daughter with a high paying career. No matter how many times I tell them that they can't change Mia's ambitions or ask them to stop breathing down my neck, it falls on deaf ears. It's exhausting."

And there it is. The weight that has been pressing down on Sinnett's shoulders makes sense. I might not fully understand what he's dealing with, but I'm empathetic enough to know that the kind of pressure he's referring to is more than one person can take. Not only does Sinnett have enough on his plate in terms of his career and now his injury being in the spotlight, but throwing parents in the mix who are overbearing and don't understand boundaries would make any normal person want to scream.

"They don't want to know about me, the *real* me, and it hurts," Sinnett continues, voice strained. "All they care about is making sure I thrive in my career, uphold my father's legacy in the league and make good on the Baxter family name."

"That's a lot of pressure to shoulder," I offer, keeping my voice level. "You're doing a good job of keeping your head held high."

"But I'm fucking drowning in the process and they can't see that."

The ending notes of "November Rain" gives way to the start of "Demons" by Imagine Dragons; a coincidence given the nature of the song and the conversation at hand. I reach across the console and place my hand on Sinnett's thigh, needing to comfort him in some way because what do I say to that? I expect him to stiffen under my touch, but he surprises me by releasing a breath he had been holding and sinking into the seat.

"I shouldn't even be telling you this," he murmurs, voice deep. "This is far from a first-world problem."

"Yes, you should," I urge. "You need to tell someone,

because the longer you hold onto these feelings, the worse it's going to get down the line."

"I don't like airing out my dirty laundry."

"All you're doing is getting the pressure off your chest to make room for fresh air and a clear mind." I squeeze his thigh, and his hand covers mine. Warmth explodes in my chest at the feel of his rough skin against mine. "If you let the weight of your parents' expectations push you down, you'll never get back up again. At the end of the day, you're living this life for yourself, not anyone else. You, Sin."

Sinnett swallows hard. "I hear you, Tate."

"Good." I lean over to press a chaste kiss to his cheek, the short stubble he hasn't shaved off yet prickling against my skin. "Now let me hear you say it."

He frowns. "Say what?"

"That you're not going to let your parents push you down."

Sinnett sighs. "Tate..."

"Please?"

"Okay, fine," he huffs. "I won't let my parents push me down."

"Like music to my ears," I drawl as pride spreads through my body. "Now let's listen to some music, okay? It's what I'm here for, right?"

Sinnett sweeps his gaze over me, eyes lingering on my lips. Half of his face is shrouded in darkness, while the other dances with tiny fires that makes my stomach flip flop like I'm on a rollercoaster.

"Sure, strawberry."

For the next hour, Sinnett drives around the suburbs of North Sydney with only the songs from my playlist to guide us. His confession about his parents has me wondering what it was like growing up with them and if they were always this hard on their kids. I don't know much about his sister's situation, but I can't imagine what Sinnett has had to deal with since going pro. He's not living this life for himself anymore, and it shows in the pressure he bears and the self-doubt that lingers at his edges.

Sinnett pulls the car into the car park overlooking Balmoral Beach. With it approaching 9 PM, there is not a soul in sight—just the crashing waves of the ocean and the whistle of the wind whipping against the car. The piano notes in "I Don't Wanna Miss a Thing" by Aerosmith wash over me like a comforting hug. I smile as I lean back in the seat, enjoying the quiet company from the man next to me and the vast stretch of ocean ahead.

"Why did you study to become a physiotherapist?"

Sinnett's question catches me slightly off guard, my mind lost in the waves. I shift my body to face his, only to find he's already watching me. His arm rests on the steering wheel, and slender fingers covered in silver rings tap in time to the beat of the song. The warmth in his eyes smooths over me, wrapping around my body. Genuine curiosity gleams in his eyes, and I can't help but smile.

"I want to be able to help people," I answer simply. "I'm not cut out to be a nurse. The thought of seeing the inside of a person freaks me out to the point I'd probably pass out. So physiotherapy was my next best option." I shrug. "Besides, I get to work with all kinds of people in various stages of recovery. There's never a dull moment."

Sinnett hums, nodding slowly. "Is there a specific reason why you want to help people?"

My lips roll as I consider his question. Pulse thumping at the base of my throat, I exhale a sharp breath and turn my eyes to the rolling waves. "My mum, she... I didn't want to feel helpless, you know? Being in a situation where you feel as though you could do everything in your power and it still wouldn't be enough to fix the problem is a feeling I can't stand." Gaze flicking back to Sinnett, I murmur, "By being in a position where I can help someone, whether it be with mobility, rehab or helping to ease muscle tension, I would no longer feel helpless."

Tears sting my ears, remembering back to the week after graduation when Mum was delivered her diagnosis. Seeing the colour drain from her face, all the while keeping a kind smile in place, was gut-wrenching. I hated that there was nothing I could do to help her. All I could do was sit back and wait for the cancer to take her, no matter how many days, weeks or years that took. And every second of it was the most painful thing I've lived through.

I never want to feel that helpless again.

Sinnett reaches across the console, scooping my hand in his. The gentle squeeze has me blinking back the tears forming in the corner of my eyes. I don't think it'll ever get easy talking about Mum.

"Well, for what it's worth, you're incredible at what you do," he tells me, voice soft. "I mean, all the proof is in my quad after following your plan for nearly a week. I couldn't have done it without you."

Warmth spreads across my cheeks and down my throat, seeping into our intertwined hands on my thigh. "You mean that?"

"I mean every word of it." The confidence in his voice has my heart rate spiking. Sinnett leans forward, capturing my gaze. "You're amazing, Tate. Don't allow yourself to think otherwise."

I drag my bottom lip between my teeth and nod, because that's all I can manage. I'm afraid that if I speak, the words will fall out in a mush of gratitude.

Sinnett leans down to press a chaste kiss to my hand before releasing it. I miss his warmth already.

"I should get you home."

I arch a brow at him. "You keen to get rid of me?"

"What? No." He runs a hand through his hair and sighs. "I don't want you to leave."

"Then I won't," I say with a shrug. "The night doesn't have to end here."

While the comment was meant to be innocent, the hidden meaning isn't lost on me. Warmth spreads down my throat at the same time the air between us grows thick. Out the corner of my eye, I notice Sinnett watching me, jaw clenched.

What is he thinking?

Was I too forward with my suggestion and now he's having regrets about last night?

Panic squeezes my chest and throat.

"I-I didn't mean it like that," I utter, backpedalling. "I was trying to say—"

"You don't want the night to end here?" Sinnett rasps.

I shake my head, unable to find my voice.

He swallows hard. "Neither do I."

My eyes round at the corners. "You don't?"

Electricity crackles between us—the same as the night we spent together three weeks ago. I had thought it was because we were about to have a one-night stand and tensions were high, but it hasn't dissipated since seeing Sinnett again. If anything, it's only gotten stronger the past two weeks.

Sinnett shakes his head. "I don't."

"Then what are we gonna do?" I whisper, throat thick. "Any suggestions?"

He drags his bottom lip between his teeth. Ocean eyes stare back at me from the darkness, holding me hostage. My heart rate spikes at the thought of what could happen next. Was he serious about wanting me last night?

"Whatever you're thinking, stop," Sinnett says, voice hoarse. "We don't have to do anything you're not comfortable with."

I know what he's saying. If I don't want to take the next step with him, and cross boundaries we can't take back, the call is mine to make. But I have no desire to back down now, not when my body is alight with tiny fires and my core has liquified like melted gold.

"I don't want to stop," I whisper, blinking slowly. "Do you?"

Sinnett runs a hand through his messy strands. "Christ, *no*, I don't want to stop, Tate."

I lean across the centre console, fuelled by adrenaline and the need to be close to this man, to feel him against me. My lips brush against his as I murmur, "Then don't stop."

"*Fuck*," he groans, the sound vibrating deep in my bones. "What am I going to do with you?"

I grin. "I think you already know the answer."

"Yeah," Sinnett rasps, his hand coming up to rest on my cheek. "I do."

Chapter Sixteen

SINNETT

I wasn't kidding when I said Tatum is too much. Her scent, her warmth, her fucking ability to bring me to my knees with that damn smile. When I'm with her, I can't think straight. I spilled a truth about my parents I haven't told Khai —he knows the basics but not my true feelings—and yet a woman I've known for three weeks was privy to hearing part of myself I keep hidden.

Why?

Why Tatum?

What is it about her that makes it so easy for me to open up, to reveal parts of myself that I don't want to be made known?

My surroundings are a blur when I pull into the underground parking garage of my apartment. One second, I'm sitting in the car with Tatum, her presence too much. And the next, I have her pinned to the wall in my bedroom with my hands tangled in her hair and my lips attached to hers. Her hands tug at the roots of my hair, forcing us impossibly closer.

I vaguely recall Tatum asking if Khai is home, and me

responding that he's out with some guys from the team. It's hard to think straight when she rolls her body against mine, eliciting a wildfire deep in my bones. Her hands are frantic as they tear at my black hoodie, forcing the material over my head.

My lips leave hers to tease the skin at the base of her throat, while my fingers work the material of the black leggings down her smooth legs. Her breath comes out in small pants as I lift her hoodie over her head, leaving her standing against my wall in nothing but an oversized band T-shirt, her hair a wild mess around her shoulders.

"God, you're beautiful," I murmur, breathing heavy.

A red hue coats her round cheeks. "So are you."

I smirk. "You think I'm beautiful?"

Tatum drags her bottom lip between her teeth and nods slowly. "Yeah, I do."

Being called beautiful by a woman is a first for me. I've gotten every other compliment under the sun, but this is a new one. And it happens to be my favourite coming from her sweet mouth.

My fingertips trace the edge of her T-shirt before dragging it over her torso, the material finding space on the large floor, along with the rest of her clothing. With eyes sweeping over every curve and inch of her body, my lungs fight to force air into them. Because *holy fuck* I don't deserve this woman. Not a single part of her.

I nearly choke on the saliva in my mouth at the sight of the deep red lingerie set moulded perfectly to her body. It's all lace and fucking see-through. Somehow, my cock grows impossibly harder, blurring the edge of my vision.

I can't help but touch her waist, relishing in the goosebumps forming under my hand. Tatum watches me the entire time, waiting for me to do or say something. But how can I when I'm at a loss for words? She leaves me defenceless and while I hate the feeling of not being in control of my actions, I'll gladly hand over the reins to her if it means I have the pleasure of being in her orbit.

"You really are too much," I rasp, throat tight. "But in the best way possible."

Tatum grins as she slides her hand over my pecs, taking her time tracing each ridge, before lowering her fingers over the pane of my six-pack. I fight the urge to shudder under her touch as she traces each line, smiling to herself.

I allow her to touch me, to really see me. And boy does she.

Tatum isn't here to fuck spiders, her fingers reaching for the waistband of my athletic shorts. She holds eye contact as she lowers the material down my legs, forcing me to step out of them. Then, her eyes find the tattoo on my left side, curving from my hip to my back.

"You have so many tattoos," she murmurs, fingers gently tracing the large design. "What is it?"

"A Japanese dragon."

Her eyes round at the edges. Even in the shadows of the room, partly illuminated by the lamps on my bedside tables, I don't miss the intrigue coating her irises. "Why a dragon and cherry blossoms. And why so big?"

I chuckle, my hands finding her hips. "Let's just say I had too much money when I was twenty-one and thought a dragon would look sick."

"I like it," she whispers, dragging her eyes to meet mine.

And I like you.

"And these?" Tatum continues, drawing her attention to the tattoos on my right arm, not a blank piece of canvas in sight.

"I've always liked tattoos," I say, never taking my eyes off her. "I consider it art."

"It is," she agrees, voice barely above a whisper. "It just adds to your beauty."

I inwardly groan, my heart unable to take many more compliments from her.

She's too much.

"Tate..."

She smiles and leans up on her toes to press a chaste kiss to my lips. Before she can pull away, my hands are in her hair and my lips mould against hers. Tatum moans into my mouth, and unable to keep hold of my self-control, I spin us and walk towards my bed.

Tatum giggle-squeals when the back of her legs hit the mattress and we topple onto the dark grey doona. Her hands find my shoulders as I suspend my body over hers, not wanting to put too much weight on her.

Heart pounding wildly in my chest, I take in the woman below me. Strawberry-blonde hair fans out like a halo above her head, chest heaving as she sucks in deep breaths. She wriggles under my gaze, and I can't help but smile.

"Eager, strawberry?"

"Yes," she admits without hesitation. "Last time we, you know, was in your car. This feels... different."

I drag my fingers over the curve of her jaw, before resting at the base of her throat. Her pulse thuds rapidly against my skin, and I'm sure mine mirrors it perfectly.

"Tell me what you want," I rasp. "You set the pace and I'll follow."

"Oh, you don't—"

"The last time we were together, I took from you what I wanted, which was wrong of me. I want you to take whatever it is you need from me and I'll be right behind you."

Tatum blinks at me as my words settle deep into her skin.

There is no denying I was a dick the night we first hooked

up. I was so intent on finding a distraction from my injury and getting off as a means to ease the tension in my shoulders, that I didn't stop to think about what Tatum wanted. And now that I have her here, lying beneath me, I have no intention of fucking this up.

"What's it going to be, strawberry?"

Tatum swallows hard before scooting out from beneath me. I watch with bated breath as she settles against the pillows, a knowing smile on her lips. Her legs fall open, baring her soaked core to me. It doesn't take a rocket scientist to understand what she's asking for, but I'll admit that I'm an asshole for wanting to hear the words come out of her mouth.

I lean back on my shins, mouth tilting in a smirk. "What is it that you want?"

Tatum drags her bottom lip between her teeth. "I want you, Sin."

"Where?"

Her cheeks turn a shade of red that has me smiling like a damn fool.

"Here." She points to her parted legs, and I'm fighting the urge to dive headfirst to give her what she wants. "Please."

"You want me to lick that pretty pussy of yours?"

Tatum nods. "Yes, I want you to lick my pussy."

Fucking hell.

Her eyes follow my movements as I crawl across the king-sized bed until I'm nestled between her thighs. The air in my lungs evaporate when I pull the lace material down her thighs, tossing them over my head. She is fucking soaked. My throat tightens as my mouth loses any moisture it once had.

With my hands gripping her thighs, I lean down and swipe my tongue over her centre. Tatum shudders at the touch, spurring me on. With each flick and swipe of my tongue, moans slip from her parted lips, her hand finding support in my hair.

She's so fucking delicious that I'm finding it hard to think straight. I don't notice the ache in my jaw as I continue to work her over, nor do I take note when I slip two fingers inside. All I can focus on is the sounds falling from her sweet mouth and how I never want this moment to end.

"Sin," Tatum cries out, her legs shaking as I up the speed of my tongue and fingers. "I-I'm going to—"

I lift my head, meeting her lust-hazed eyes. "Come on my tongue, strawberry. I want to taste every last drop of you."

My tongue swipes over her core, and that's all it takes for her to fly over the edge. I don't slow my movements as an orgasm consumes every inch of her body. Seeing her this way, writhing under my touch and crying out my name, has me feeling like I'm on cloud nine. Knowing I did that to her, made her feel that way, brings me a pleasure I never knew possible.

I have never found giving head to be enjoyable—until this moment. With Tatum, it just feels... right. Like every other aspect of being with this woman. I don't know how else to explain it, nor do I understand it. But I'm willing to see where this goes.

"Holy shit," Tatum breathes, eyes finding mine as she sinks into the bed. "That was... insane."

"The best you've ever had?" I raise a brow, a smirk tilting up my mouth.

"By a long shot." Tatum pushes her hair out of her face and lifts up onto her elbows. "I can, you know, help you—"

"Don't even think about it," I warn, crawling up her body until we're eye to eye. She releases a tight breath, tucking her lip between her teeth. "I did this for you. I don't need anything in return."

"But I—"

"But nothing." Balancing on one hand, I use the other to trace a line down the valley of her full tits, stopping at her waist. "I owed you one for the way you blew my socks off with the head you gave in my car."

Tatum smiles shyly. "Okay."

"Now," I say, lowering my head until our lips are brushing. Her wetness coats my lips and tongue. "What are we doing next?"

I wasn't kidding when I told her to take the lead. Whatever she wants to do, or wherever she wants to take this, I'll follow. If she decides she wants to end the night here, I'll drive her home without complaint. But if she wants to take the next step, I'll take the leap with her.

"I want you to fuck me."

I blink down at her, my heart stilling in my chest.

Did I hear her correctly? Did those words come out of her mouth?

"Only if you want to," Tatum quickly adds, as if worried she took it a step too far.

I slam my lips against her, pushing my tongue between her lips, forcing her to taste herself. She moans against my mouth as her arms come up to wrap around my neck, deepening the kiss. This woman drives me to near insanity with little effort, and I'm helpless to fight it.

I pull away from the kiss long enough to squeeze out, "Your wish is my command," before my lips find hers again.

We're a frenzy of tangled limbs and discarded underwear, our lips fighting to stay together. As soon as I have Tatum sprawled out beneath me in all of her naked glory—and those fucking nipple piercings—I waste no time entering her, shoving in all the way until I bottom out. Tatum clutches my shoulders and cries out, her nails digging into my skin. Her muffled cries against my skin remind me I need to take this slow, to allow her to adjust to me before I turn into a maniac.

"You okay?" I rasp, afraid to move for fear of hurting her.

"Yeah," she strangles out, body tense and thighs hugging my waist. "I forgot how big you are."

"Can I move?" I ask, voice tight. "Because if I don't I fear I might come without so much as starting."

Tatum laughs, the sounds sweet and airy as she nods. My hips pull back and roll forward at a slow pace, allowing Tatum to get used to me. My forearms strain from holding my body over her; the angle giving me a deeper position to fill every inch of her.

Our moans echo off the white walls, and I have to fight the urge to slam into her with the desperate need to feel closer to her than we already are. Each stroke and thrust has my vision blurring at the edges, and a low growl falls from my parted lips.

"You fit me fucking perfectly," I grunt, chest tight. "Every inch of you was made for me, Tate."

"I told you to fuck me, Sin," Tatum squeezes out, jade eyes searing into mine. She arches her back, somehow allowing me to slip deeper inside of her. "So do it."

Don't come yet. Don't come yet. Don't come yet.

Fucking *hell*.

"Jesus, Tate," I grunt, my right hand coming up to toy with the metal bar through her nipple. "Too much."

Tatum grins as she digs her nails deeper into my shoulders, meeting me thrust for thrust as I pick up speed. I must black out because one second, Tatum is lying beneath me, and then the next, I have her bent over the edge of the mattress, driving into her from behind.

This woman makes me feral in every sense of the word. Reckless is another word I would use when I'm with her. It's as if I become a different person—someone I don't recognise.

Not in a bad way, by any means. I don't feel like myself, but maybe that's the point. Being someone else entirely when I'm with her means she doesn't have to deal with the bullshit that comes with my life and she can just have *me*. The real me.

"Fuck, Tate," I growl, fingers digging into her hips. "What the hell are you doing to me?"

Tatum fists the doona and moans in response. Her legs shake as her pussy clenches around me, nearing the edge. And fuck if I'm not right behind her. Literally.

With a deep thrust, we come at the same time. It's both intense and fucking magical. My vision blurs at the edges as every muscle in my body coils tight. The air is knocked from my lungs at the sensation of her walls squeezing me, taking every last ounce of energy I possess.

We fall into a tangled heap on the bed, with Tatum tucked under my arm. She hums as she hooks a leg over my left thigh, careful not to touch the right, I notice. My skin is slicked with sweat, but Tatum doesn't care, nuzzling her face in the crook of my neck.

Hooking my right arm under my head and wrapping the other around Tatum's back, I heave a sharp breath, staring at the ceiling. "Holy shit."

"Holy shit indeed," Tatum murmurs, followed by a soft chuckle.

A wave of emotions I can't recognise press down on my chest. I swallow hard, voice raspy as I murmur, "I'm both terrified and intrigued by you, Tate."

Tatum lifts herself up onto her elbow, jade eyes meeting mine from above—like a fucking angel. "Why?" Her hand caresses my cheek, and I lean into her touch.

"Because I'm confused."

"About me?"

I nod. "There are so many factors stacked against us and

rules that could have lasting effects if broken. And while I want to break them—fuck do I want to break them… I'm also torn. The need to protect my career and you—"

"I understand," Tatum murmurs, voice light. Not a hint of anger lingers in her words at my admission. "You have a lot on the line, Sin. We both do. And if you want to end things here… I get it."

"God, no." I push up onto my elbow, body turning to face her. Her nipple piercings brush my chest, sending a shiver down my spine. "I don't want that."

"But you're confused," she points out. "And it's okay to be. I'm confused, too."

My hand slides up to cup her cheek, needing to feel her to know she's real, because right now, it feels like I'm having an out of body experience.

"It doesn't change the fact that I still want you," I strangle out, voice tight. "I just…"

"Me, too," Tatum interjects. She smiles, and it's brighter than any star in the sky. "Should we be confused together and see where it takes us?"

I can't help but smile, despite the pressure baring down on my chest. "Confused together. I can make that work."

A sultry look gleams in Tatum's eyes as she gently pushes at my shoulder, forcing me onto my back. My eyes track her movements as she slides down the bed, her face centimetres from my cock, which is hard again. I swear it has a mind of its fucking own.

"What are you doing?" I murmur, fisting the doona at my sides. "Tate—"

"Shhh," she whispers, tongue darting out to lick her plump bottom lip. "I believe I have a favour to return for that skilful tongue of yours."

Before I can utter another word, her mouth wraps around

the head of my cock, taking me all the way to the back of her throat. A moan slips past my parted lips, and I'm helpless to stop it. My head drops onto the mattress, relishing in the feel of her tongue sliding over my skin, sucking and teasing with precision.

I don't know what I did to deserve this woman walking into my life, but I'm determined to keep her by my side, even if she is my downfall.

Chapter Seventeen

TATUM

"How are you adjusting to the new job and being in Sydney?" Dad asks as we pull into the car park behind the Wolves' home stadium, located in Brookvale. He kills the engine and flicks his eyes to me. "I only ask because you've been acting a little... off the past week."

Despite my best efforts, heat floods my cheeks and I shift in the seat, unable to meet my father's eyes.

How can I tell him the truth? If he found out I'm sleeping with his star halfback, there would be no coming back from it. While I don't agree with his need to enforce a 'no dating' rule on his twenty-three-year-old daughter, there isn't anything I can do to change his mind. Not that I've tried. And even if I did, he seems adamant with his stance.

With how busy Dad has been this past week, he didn't bat an eye when I would leave to go for a late-night drive around the suburbs with Sinnett. Each time I left, he would either be in his office working on game plans for the round ten match against the Redfern Raiders, or he'd be passed out in bed.

Dad isn't the kind of father who watches everything I do

218

with a keen eye, but I have no doubt there is a slight concern in the back of his mind that I'll go against his rule of steering clear from the players. Whether it's because he doesn't trust I can keep a promise—turns out I can't—or because he doesn't want to see me get hurt. Either way, he gives me the breathing room I need to live my life, but keeps close enough to take note if anything is out of the ordinary.

And apparently, I'm not as slick as I thought I was.

"Y-yeah, I'm adjusting well, Dad." I clear my throat and slip a smile onto my face.

He raises a brow at me. "And you're okay?"

I nod, not trusting my voice.

God, am I really that obvious?

Dad's knowing eyes search my face for any sign I'm lying. If this were Mum, she would notice straight away I'm not being truthful. She pointed out my 'tell' when I was ten and being questioned about a broken pot plant in the backyard. I broke it by accident when I was kicking around one of Dad's old rugby balls, not realising the ball would go in the complete opposite direction when not kicked correctly. As soon as Mum noticed I was picking at the skin around my left thumb, she knew I was lying. Apparently it was something she had picked up on over the years, but didn't say anything until that moment.

I still my hands, snapping my head down to see my pointer and thumb fingers hovering over my left thumb, the skin around the nail raw.

Shit.

Flattening my hands on my thighs, I force a bright smile that doesn't quite touch my eyes. "I promise I'm okay. You know how this job can be. I'm just tired."

"You have been spending more time with Raya lately, so that could also be adding to the tiredness," Dad points out.

Relief washes over me and I sink back into the seat. "Yeah, that's probably it."

"And I've noticed you've been spending extra time with Sinnett outside of his scheduled session slots this week. Is he needing extra support with his quad?"

Oh, crap.

I definitely haven't been as slick as I thought. I didn't consider what others might think seeing Sinnett and me together at work. From the outside looking in, the interactions could be passed off as nothing more than friendly, or Sinnett asking his physio for advice. But if Dad is taking note of it, based off what he has seen with his own eyes or what the other staff have told him, then I need to be more careful around Sinnett moving forward.

I clear my throat and plaster on a smile. "Oh, he's fine. You know how he is with following a schedule. It's non-stop questions with him, which I don't mind answering." The lie tastes bitter on my tongue. "He's doing great, recovery-wise."

Dad nods. "That's great to hear, Tate. Just remember what I told you about not dating the players. I'm not doing it to be annoying or unfair. I made a promise to your mother to protect you, so that is what I'm trying to do."

I swallow hard and nod. I'm in desperate need of fresh air. "Yeah, sure. I understand, Dad."

"Also, when are you getting your car back? The mechanic has had it for ages."

Shit. I had forgotten about my damn car. Sinnett hasn't given me an update on the status of it, other than his guy is working hard to get everything fixed, but because it's an old model, he has to order parts in, which could take time.

"Soon," I answer, voice wavering at the edges.

"Well, we should look at getting you a new one like we talked about," he says, not fazed by my vague response. Dad glances down at his watch and reaches for the car door. "We better get inside before Todd starts to wonder where I am."

Phew. Dodged a bullet there.

As we approach the back entrance to the stadium, the echo of voices from the crowd filing into the space thumps in the back of my mind. It'll never cease to amaze me how passionate and dedicated rugby fans are, especially the Wolves' fanbase. Each week they show up, no matter if it's an away or home game; they're always there to support the team with their cheers and chants. It's a dedication I've never witnessed before.

"What is your favourite game night of the week?" I ask, following Dad down the long hallway to the Wolves' locker room.

"I would say tonight, Fridays."

"Why?"

"It's always a good crowd," he tells me, glancing over his shoulder. "A lot of fans travel from work straight here, and families bring their children hoping to have a fun night after school."

"That's commitment," I comment. "What's the crowd meant to be like tonight? Is it a sellout?"

"I've heard from Todd that it's close to being sold out."

I exhale a sharp breath and step into the sheds behind my dad, my view blocked by his large frame. He spins on his heels to face me, crisp polo shirt in place and black dress pants recently dry-cleaned. I tilt my head back to meet his eye, ignoring the feel of a certain pair of ocean eyes watching from across the room.

Even without seeing him, I feel him. Like my body is drawn to his, seeking out his touch. It's a strange feeling, and not something I've gotten used to—even after spending the past five days with him in some capacity. Late-night drives have become a new routine for us.

"I'm going to need you to keep an extra eye on our centre tonight, Tate," Dad says, clutching at the clipboard under his arm. "Todd said Ryder was having some aches and pains during training this week, and while he's been given the all-clear to play, just observe him throughout the game. If you see anything of concern, just let Todd know."

Right. I have a job to do when I walk through the doors to the stadium. This is what I signed up for when I agreed to leave Barrenridge. I've been so distracted by Sinnett that I almost forgot that the well-being of everyone in this room relies heavily on me.

I swallow hard and nod. "Absolutely."

Dad smiles and pats my shoulder. "Thank you, Tate. Have I mentioned you're doing a great job?"

I chuckle. "Just every morning over breakfast."

"Well, you better start believing it." Dad takes two steps back and claps his hands. "I'll see you later, okay?"

I nod and wave him off, watching as he walks across the room to where Todd and some of the other staff members are standing. Olive has her phone held up in front of Axel, no doubt asking him pre-game questions to put on social media.

My chest aches with the breath I'm holding on to. I'm annoyed at myself for being distracted by a man to the point where I had forgotten about my purpose here and why I moved to Sydney. Much like the team is now—warming up, listening to music and stretching—I need to get my head in the game and *focus*.

No more distractions.

Refusing to look at where Sinnett sits beside Khai, who is stretching on the ground in his pre-game jersey, I walk over to where Ryder sits in front of his locker space. He lifts his head at the sound of my approach.

"Hey," I greet with a warm smile. "Phil said you're worried

about some aches and pains. If you're up for it, I'd like to have a chat before the game to make sure you're okay."

Ryder stands, his frame towering over me. Brown eyes narrow from behind wispy strands of blonde hair as he touches his right shoulder. "I'm worried I've done something to my rotator cuff."

"Not a problem. I can help with that." I gesture to the chair behind him. "Take a seat and I'll take a look."

For twenty minutes, I go through some stretches and exercises to determine if there is something wrong with Ryder's rotator cuff, ending the impromptu session with a massage and taping up his shoulder to give it extra support throughout the game. I make a mental note to switch up his recovery plan to help with the issue moving forward.

With a sigh, I drop down in my usual seat in the corner of the training room. As it gets closer to kick off, the players start moving around the open space, going through their warm-ups and getting changed into their jerseys. At first, I was self-conscious about seeing the team half-naked because I didn't want them to think I was checking them out or being weird. I was respectful and kept my eyes down when I could. But I quickly realised that they don't care who sees them in this state, especially if you're part of the staff. Which makes things easier for me because now I don't have to endure neck pain from constantly looking down at my phone.

A vibration in my pocket alerts me to a new notification. When I retrieve the device and see the name on the screen, liquid pools in my core and my pulse jackhammers at the base of my throat.

SIN: Are you avoiding me?

I slowly lift my head to see Sinnett standing on the

opposite side of the room, ocean eyes locked on mine while his fingers hover over his phone. How is it possible for him to look as good as he does in an all black outfit of athletic shorts, a hoodie and a backwards cap?

TATE: Do you think I am?

Sinnett rolls his tongue in his cheek, flicking his eyes up to meet mine. The fire burning in my core intensifies as I'm reminded of what his tongue can do.

You're at work, Tate. Relax.

SIN: Don't answer my question with a question, strawberry.

TATE: I don't know what you're talking about.

SIN: Well, I think you're avoiding me because you secretly love me and can't bear to keep your hands off me.

TATE: Ha-ha, you're so funny. Has anyone ever told you that?

SIN: No, just you. Now tell me, Tate. Are you avoiding me?

I exhale a sharp breath and run my fingers through the ends of my slightly curled hair.

TATE: I've been so distracted by you the past four days that I forgot why I'm really here.

SIN: Ah, right. And here I am once again distracting you while you should be working. If you need an excuse to talk to me, I can tell Coach my quad has been playing up this past week. Because I don't know if he'll appreciate the other reason being I simply can't keep my hands off his daughter.

Heat bursts across my cheeks and down my neck as I re-read the text. This man says *I'm* too much?

TATE: Yeah, look, I don't think he'll appreciate it one bit.

SIN: Yeah, maybe not. Was a nice try though, right?

TATE: The best. And if you really want to see me, I can find you after the game before Dad is ready to leave. With all the media stuff he has to do afterwards, we'll have plenty of time alone.

Sinnett smirks, dragging his bottom lip between his teeth.

SIN: Tate, are you suggesting we have time to make out in my car?

TATE: Those are your words, not mine.

SIN: Well, consider it a date then.

Dad's voice filtering across the room tears my attention away from the flirty text messages and the racing of my heart. I slip my phone into my pocket and watch as the team shares a last-minute pep talk with Dad before getting ready to head out to the field for kickoff.

I stay as close to the corner of the room as possible, knowing the sheds are being broadcast on TV, showing the team making their way out to the field. Their team song blasts through the speakers around the field, followed by the deafening cheers of the fans. I don't think I'll ever get used to the sound, and even now, with this being my fourth game, I still get a flutter in my chest watching the team run out through the tunnel.

By the time I make my way to the Wolves' staffing team and benched players on the sideline, Sinnett is already seated with them, watching intently as the game gets underway.

Settling down on a free chair, I do my best to watch the game, keeping my focus on Ryder as he finds himself in some intense tackles. He doesn't seem to be favouring his shoulder, so it must be holding up all right for now. I jot down some details on the notepad I keep in my pocket, wanting to see him for a more intensive session next week just to be sure nothing is wrong.

By the time the clock nears forty minutes, half-time on the horizon, my leg bounces with anticipation of seeing Sinnett after the game. He might be sitting ten metres away from me, but it's not the same as when we're alone.

The more time we spend together, the closer I am to seeing the real him. Even now, I've learned from our late-night drives around North Sydney that he can't stand tomatoes or mushrooms, he and Khai would sneak out of class in high school to kick a football around the oval because they wanted to practice their skills as much as possible, and his favourite part of the day is watching the sun rise.

I've shared details about myself, but I can't bring myself to mention my mum in much detail. It's been on the tip of my tongue numerous times, but I could never get it over the line. I want to talk about her, to keep her memory alive, but maybe I'm not ready yet to share that part of me with Sinnett.

We don't speak every time we go for a drive; sometimes we'll sit in silence and listen to the playlist I curated. If I'm too tired to hold a conversation, and Sinnett has other things on his mind, we'll get lost in the music with his hand on my thigh and drive for what feels like hours. It's calming in a way, having a quiet support system that is comforting and familiar. And now I crave it whenever I'm stressed or need company that isn't my father.

The whistle blows for half-time, and I exhale the breath I was holding. As the Raiders and Wolves leave the field, the score sitting at 8-2 with the Wolves in the lead, I hang back and wait. Sinnett leaves with the rest of the team, a knowing twinkle in his ocean eyes as he passes by with his hands shoved into the pockets of his shorts.

Oh, yeah. We're so on for a make-out session after the game.

A presence behind me has my spine straightening. Whoever it is doesn't speak, so I spin on my heels to face them. A woman I don't recognise stands at eye level, her honey irises filled with a fire I can only describe as annoyance. She gives me a once-over before tilting her head to the side, pom poms hanging limp by her hips.

"You're the new physio, right?"

I swallow hard, eyes sweeping over the curled brown hair sitting just above her shoulders, and the perfectly applied makeup to her sharp and stunning features. She's dressed in the Wolves cheerleading uniform of black leather mini-shorts, a long-sleeved black and red crop top, with toned calves hidden beneath fishnet stockings and skin-tight knee-high boots.

Behind her, I spot Raya in the same uniform, watching us

with a worried expression. She's standing with the rest of the cheerleaders, likely getting ready for their half-time performance. But even as some of the other girls try to talk to her, Raya keeps her attention on us.

"I am," I squeeze out, and clear my throat. "And you are...?"

"Zoe," she bites, mildly offended I don't know who she is. "So, you work with the team?"

Oh, shit. This is the same Zoe who has the complicated history with Sinnett, and who Raya warned me to stay away from. How I managed to avoid her until a month into the job is beyond me, but maybe that goes to show how little she cares about the staff members.

But now the question becomes: why is she talking to me?

I nod. "Yes, I do."

"So that means you work with Sin?"

Oh, God. Where is this going?

"Yeah, I'm helping him through the recovery process of his injury," I tell her, not wanting to give her too much information as it's private doctor-patient confidentiality.

Zoe folds her arms over her chest, giving me another once-over. It's clear by her posture and the way her lip curls upward that she would rather be anywhere else than talking to me, but she has a hidden agenda that keeps her rooted to the spot in front of me.

"Has he mentioned me?" Zoe finally asks, jaw ticking.

Not wanting to get on her bad side, I shake my head. "Not that I know of."

Zoe clicks her tongue, her features twisting in annoyance. "Funny he didn't when we're seeing each other."

"You are?"

Sinnett explained the situation with Zoe, and he has never

given me a reason not to believe his word, so I'm going to humour her to see what she's playing at here.

"We are," she confirms, voice sharp. "So if I were you, I would remember that when you work with him next. Sin is hot and lots of women want him, and I understand it's hard to resist his charm, but he's taken, hun. He's all mine."

It's on the tip of my tongue to tell her that if Sinnett really is her boyfriend, it would be a red flag that she can't trust him enough to the point where she feels the need to warn other women away from him. I know they're not actually dating, but it seems like she has an underlying fear of him seeing other women even while they've been hooking up.

Is that the type of guy Sinnett is?

"I hear you loud and clear," I murmur, throat tight. "I'm just his physio, nothing more." The lie settles heavily on my tongue, but I swallow it down.

A smile slips onto Zoe's face, as if she's just won the lottery. "Good. Because if I find out you or anyone else has gone near my man, there will be hell to pay."

I blink at her, my heart thundering in my chest. Before I can respond, Zoe is called away by her friends to get ready for the performance. I lock eyes with Raya who offers a sympathetic smile before walking to the centre of the field.

My shoulders slump as worry works its way into my bones. Sinnett didn't tell me Zoe is still hung up on him to the point she thinks they're together even after he's reiterated that they're not hooking up, nor were they ever officially together. It's clear she refuses to let go of what they have, but if she does find out I'm sleeping with him and I lied to her face, I'm going to be in some deep shit. Because although I don't know Zoe from a bar of soap, her air of confidence and intensity is an indicator that she stands by her words and promises.

Not only do I need to keep whatever is happening between Sinnett and I from my father, but now Zoe has been added to the list. I'm not sure this is going to end well for either of us.

Chapter Eighteen

SINNETT

The second half is tense, to say the least. The Raiders are a strong side, and have been pushing hard against our defensive line with each play of the ball. It's almost as if their coach lit a fire under their asses during half-time, and now they're ready to play a strong forty minutes.

Shoving a hand through my hair, I lean forward on the plastic seat, eyes locked on Maximus—a front rower—as he charges into a tackle. The score has changed from 8-2 our way to 12-10. The Raiders are coming for our throats, and with how much pressure the team is putting on us, it wouldn't surprise me if they find a crack in the formation.

"Fucking hell," Roman breathes from beside me, right leg bouncing. "I knew this game was going to be tough, but they're bringing the heat this half."

Roman is on interchange, waiting for his turn to hit the field when one of the other guys needs a break. He's lethal out on the field because he can play any position required of him, and he can do it well. I have no doubt Todd will walk over soon and have him start warming up, because with how gassed our guys are looking, some of them are going to need a break soon.

"When you get out there, tell Axel to tighten up our plays on the wing," I tell him, eyes flicking to meet his. "Their right winger is lacking energy. His movements are slow, and pace off, so if they put enough pressure on him, they should be able to slip right past before he can understand what's happening."

Roman nods, running his hands over his thighs. "Got it."

As if on cue, Todd staunches towards us, pointing his finger at Roman. "Start warming up, Ro. I need you out there in second row so I can bring Dante off."

Without saying a word, Roman jumps up and jogs the half-length of the field to the right, stretching his muscles as he goes.

Releasing a sigh, I rub my hand over my right thigh. Without realising, my gaze flicks over my left shoulder to where Tatum sits a few chairs down, watching the game with her hands tucked under her thighs. The cool nip in the air has me wondering if she's hiding her hands from the cold or if it's to keep her nerves in check.

I want to sit close to her, even if it's to breathe in her familiar scent and feel her warmth that my body craves. But with the eyes of the fans and the rest of the staffing team on us, I force myself to stay put with the notion in mind that I'll be seeing her after the game in my car, where I have every intention of keeping her close for as long as possible.

I clear my throat and focus on the game, watching as Roman runs onto the field, switching with Dante. The play restarts, and Jace passes the ball to Khai. Before he can pass it off, he is tackled by an opposing Raiders player, sending him flying to the ground at an odd angle. My eyes nearly bulge out of my head when I see my best friend reach for his right ankle, face screwed up in what I can only assume is pain.

Oh, *fuck.*

I'm on my feet at the same time as Tatum. My eyes follow her as she rushes out onto the field with Greg, one of the club trainers. The ref gestures for the play to stop just as Tatum and Greg reach Khai, and both teams move to the side, waiting to see what happens.

My heart thunders in my chest, and a sickening feeling seeps into my stomach. I hope the pain Khai is feeling in his ankle isn't anything major. Possibly a sprain? The team needs him because he is one of the best five-eights in the league right now. Being out on injury is torture, and I would hate for him to have to suffer the same fate as me.

My attention shifts to Tatum. She is speaking to Khai with her hand resting on his ankle, while Greg focuses on passing around a bottle of water to the rest of the team, making sure they're okay, too. I wish I knew what was being said. It's killing me that I have no clue what is happening.

Seeing Tatum jump into action like that, so willing to help Khai, has my heart racing in a way I haven't felt before. It feels different than when she smiles at me or whenever she slides into my car, ready to tell me about what song she wants to play me first for our drives. It's deeper than that, and something I can't describe.

Tatum has told me about her love for helping others, and while she hasn't gone into much detail about why, it reflects in her actions and the passion and drive she puts into her position. Without hesitating, she rushed to Khai's side to check on him when Greg could've helped him off the field so he could be examined on the sideline. But Tatum went full steam ahead and rushed onto the field like a bat out of hell. If that isn't a testament to her desire to help others and perform her job to the best of her ability, then I don't know what is.

My heart is in my throat, pounding rapidly as Tatum and Greg help a hobbling Khai off the field. On instinct, my legs carry me to the tunnel, meeting them halfway. Khai lifts his head to meet my eyes. Pain seeps into them—a mixture of physical and emotional.

"Are you okay?" My voice is gruffer than intended, but the worry is all the same.

Khai nods. "Yeah. I'm hoping it's just a sprain, but Tate is going to check me out thoroughly just to be sure."

When I lock eyes with the all-too familiar jade ones I have started to see in my dreams, my heart is ready to jump through my chest. The same feeling in my stomach rushes forth like a tidal wave, threatening to drown me. Warmth seeps into my skin, embedding itself deep in my bones as I hold eye contact with the woman who has my head a fucking mess and my heart forgetting how to beat.

"You've got him?" I murmur, shoving my hands into the front pocket of my hoodie.

Tatum smiles, that sweet fucking smile that nearly sends me to my knees every time I see it. "I've got him, Sin."

God. What is this woman doing to my heart?

I nod, trying to ignore the electricity swimming through my veins. Clapping Khai on the shoulder, I say, "I'll see you in the sheds at after the game."

"*We'll* be waiting for you." He wiggles his brows, and I can't help but roll my eyes. Even facing the prospect of a serious injury, he finds a way to joke around with me. That's a good sign, I suppose.

Flashing a half-smile at Tatum, I murmur, "I'll see you after the game."

A light hue of pink splashes her cheeks as she looks up at me through her lashes. "I hope so."

THE COOL MAY AIR WHIPS AT MY BARE LEGS, MY BACK pressed against the side of my car. I've read and re-read my text messages with Tatum from earlier tonight at least ten times, and each time I smile like a damn fool.

What is this woman doing to me?

Seriously, it's concerning.

I went from hopping between multiple women's bed, desperate for a distraction and a quick fix, to laughing out loud at Tatum's bad jokes and flirty text messages, with zero interest in other women. Hell, I won't look in another woman's direction unless it's a certain strawberry-blonde.

Khai keeps telling me I'm whipped, which results in him getting a smack upside the head because I'm *not*. Thankfully, he doesn't mind when she comes over at night for a couple of hours, unable to keep our hands off each other. Khai says he puts his earphones in and plays the PlayStation, which I'm thankful for. If I couldn't have Tatum over at the apartment, we wouldn't have much alone time besides going for late-night drives.

Those drives have become an escape for me from the stresses of my life. Whenever I feel overwhelmed by my father's constant need to be involved in my life and career, or doubt creeps in that this injury is worse than it is and I might not be on the field in two weeks, I crave Tatum's quiet company and killer playlists. Getting lost in the lyrics of a song was something I couldn't do, but with the help of Tatum and her calming presence, I find myself needing the escape through words and music.

"In These Arms" by Bon Jovi blast through the ear buds jammed into my ears as I scroll through the list of my liked songs. My phone vibrates with an incoming call from Gran, pulling me from the lyrcis. With some time on my hands while I wait for Tatum to finish checking over Khai, I accept the call.

"Hey, Gran."

"Sin!" Gran coos, voice as airy as the cookies she used to make every time Mia and I would visit Barrenridge in the school holidays. "How is my favourite grandson doing?"

"Gran, I'm your only grandson," I chuckle, shoving my left hand into the pocket of my shorts. The car park is empty save for a few cars belonging to the staff and lingering players in the sheds. The moon is high in the sky, surrounded by stars that dull in comparison to the smile of the woman I have looked up to my entire life. "But I'm doing good. Nothing new happening on my end."

"I watched the game tonight. I miss seeing you out there."

Gran watches the Wolves play every week without fail. Besides Mia, she is my number one supporter. Even though she lives a couple of hours away, she did her best to be present for every part of my life, especially in my rugby career. If she wasn't calling every other day to catch up, she was talking to her friends about me and buying jerseys for whichever club I was playing for throughout high school and university. She also owns every Wolves item from the merch shop possible. Even if she isn't physically around, she is silently supporting from the sidelines and never fails to remind me of how proud she is.

"Me too," I murmur, kicking at a rock with the toe of my white Air Force. "I have my six-week check-up approaching, so if all goes well, I could be back on the field for round twelve."

"Oh, darling, that's wonderful news!" she says, excitement laced in her tone. "I'm so proud of you."

"Thanks, Gran." I glance at the exit to the stadium, and

with no sign of Tatum yet, I cast my gaze to my feet. "What's new with you and Mia? Is your arthritis playing up again?"

"No, dear, my arthritis isn't giving me too much grief these days. Having your sister here has been life-changing, and I couldn't be more grateful."

My brows crease into a frown as I read between the line of her words. "Why do I get the feeling there is a *but* you're not saying?"

"But..." Gran drawls, setting my nerves on edge. "Mia did have a panic attack this morning."

Ice floods my veins as my spine straightens. "She what? Is she okay? What happened?"

"It's all right, Sin, she's fine," Gran says, her gentle voice trying to calm the turmoil in my chest. "I spoke with her earlier, and she's doing much better."

"What caused it?" I squeeze out, throat tight. "She's been going to therapy, so I thought she was past this."

"Well, you know my neighbour, Noah Sterling?"

"The guy who Mia is now babysitting for? Yeah, I know the one."

"He left a coffee for her at the house this morning. You know how much she loves those iced lattes to get through the day."

I frown, struggling to understand how Noah bringing Mia a coffee ended with her having a panic attack. "Gran, I'm not following."

Gran exhales a long breath before saying, "She was freaking out because she wasn't expecting Noah to do something like that for her. To know a simple detail about her and respond in kindness. In her eyes, the small gift was crossing into a territory she hasn't navigated since Ryan, hence why she panicked. It was a lot for her to handle."

I blink, processing everything Gran said. It kills me that I can't be there to support my sister through this. I'm the best at getting her to calm down, pulling her from the depths of her mind and that dark place I don't want to ever see her in again.

"I told her to keep her distance from him," I rasp. "But she didn't listen to me."

"Mia deserves to be happy, Sin," Gran says, voice wavering. "And I've known Noah for years. He's a good man who will do right by her. If anyone can give that girl what she deserves, it's him."

Tatum said the same thing last week.

"I don't know..." I run a hand through my hair, tugging at the roots. "I'm worried about her."

"Me too, dear." Gran exhales a slow breath, and I take this as a chance to focus on my breathing, trying to combat the storm brewing in my chest and weighing heavily on my heart. "Mia is a strong woman. I have no doubt that with time, she will get through this. And if I know anything about Noah, he's the anchor she needs to keep afloat."

"I hope you're right," I murmur. "I'll talk to her, okay? Please keep me updated if anything else happens."

"Of course, dear. And you look after yourself, too, okay? I know you shoulder a lot of pressure from your parents, but just remember that you don't have to carry it by yourself."

Throat thick, I nod. "Thanks, Gran."

"Take care of yourself, darling. Talk soon."

Bidding farewell to Gran with the promise of calling her next week, I shove my phone into my pocket, along with my ear buds, and push my hand through my hair. Tension pulses through the muscles in my back as I tip my head to look up at the stars. I need something to ground me before I lose my fucking mind.

Tomorrow, I'm getting Mia on the phone to find out what's going on with her and Mr Thirty-Four Supercars driver.

Because if he thinks he can weasel his way into her life before she's ready, he has another thing coming. Mia is my best friend, so I will do whatever I can to protect her and her heart—no matter what.

Footsteps sound through the empty car park, falling in time with the erratic rhythm of my heart. Lowering my head, I catch sight of the one person I don't want to see right now, much less talk to. She stalks toward me, gym bag slung over her shoulder.

"Sin," Zoe drawls. She stops two metres from me, honey eyes roaming my face. "Fancy seeing you here."

"What do you want?" I bite out, folding my arms over my chest. "I'm not in the mood, Zoe."

Zoe whistles lowly. "It seems someone is in a foul mood despite the big win tonight. I thought you'd be happy."

"And I thought you'd gotten the hint that I don't want to talk to you anymore."

Her jaw clenches at the jab, but I can't find it in me to care if it upset her or not.

"Jesus, Sin, what has gotten into you?" Zoe demands, tilting her head to the side. "Something must be wrong if you're trying to pretend you don't want me, and then go on to ignore my texts and calls."

"I'm not pretending," I say through gritted teeth. "And I'm not having this conversation with you again. We keep going around in fucking circles, and quite frankly, I'm over it. So, if you can't understand the simple phrase *I don't want you*, then that's not my problem. You need to find some other fucker to take my place because I'm done. Are we clear?"

Zoe steps forward, her hand closing the space between us to rest on my chest. Her sweet perfume invades my space, and I find myself remembering the vanilla and floral scent I have grown accustomed to.

"You don't mean it," she drawls seductively, dragging her bottom lip between her teeth. She bats her false eyelashes at me, and I fight the urge to shudder. "I know you still want me, Sin."

"Get your hand off me," I demand, my self-restraint rapidly decreasing the longer she touches me. "Now."

"Come on." She steps closer, her minty breath fanning across my lips. "I'm sure you remember all the fun we had together. I know I do. Which is why I know you still want this. You want me."

"Get. Your. Hand. Off me. *Now*," I growl. "If I have to ask again, it's going to be far from nice."

Zoe lifts on her toes, her lips brushing mine the tiniest bit before my hands find her shoulders. Guiding her away from my body, I stare down at her with a look I can only assume represents the sizzling anger in my bones.

"That's enough," I strangle out, throat tight. "I need you to get the fuck out of my sight before I do something I might regret."

Zoe stumbles back, her gym bag falling to her side. Heat burns in her honey eyes as she stares me down and straightens her spine. She refuses to be made to look weak, and I know handling her that way made her feel exactly that.

"You're an asshole," she spits, venom dripping from her words.

"And you're still standing here when I told you to leave."

Zoe huffs and flips me the bird. She spins on her heels and stalks across the parking lot, leaving me to fester in a pool of worry and fucking anger. Worry that my sister is hours away and struggling, and anger that Zoe refuses to leave me alone.

"Fuck," I grunt, fisting my hands at my side.

I feel her before I see her, and my heart rate spikes in my chest.

"That was... intense."

Tatum steps out of the shadows with her handbag slung over her shoulder. Even in a polo shirt and black zip-up hoodie, she's the most beautiful person I have ever laid eyes on. Or ever will. Her hair is in loose waves over her shoulders, spiralling down her spine.

"You saw all of that?" I rasp, slumping against my car.

Tatum replaces the space Zoe greedily took from me, her scent inviting and so fucking calming. I had forgotten how to breathe when Gran told me about Mia's panic attack, but with Tatum so close, and her voice and scent wrapping me in a tight hug, I inhale a deep breath and close my eyes.

"Most of it," she responds with not a hint of anger or jealousy in her tone. "Are you okay?"

My eyes snap open, greeted by jade eyes peering at me through long—real—lashes. "You're asking if I'm okay?"

Tatum nods. "You seem upset, and stressed."

"Not upset, just annoyed," I clarify, running a hand through my hair. "But I'm okay."

"Are you sure?" she presses, her hand finding my chest, my heart. "If you need to talk about it, I'm listening."

I place my hand over hers, the warmth from her skin soothing away the storm rolling through me. "I'm good. Promise."

Tatum grins. "I'm sure it's nothing a steamy ten-minute make-out sesh in your car won't fix."

I choke on the saliva in my mouth, causing Tatum to laugh. Yeah, she really is too much. But in the best way possible.

"I think you might be right about that."

Tatum smiles and steps between my legs, stealing the air from my lungs. Her hand slides to the back of my neck, tracing gentle circles into the skin. "I can trust you, right?"

My hands find a hold on her hips, chest tightening. "Why are you asking?"

"Just... because," she murmurs, blinking up at me. "Can I?"

"Of course you can," I murmur, tightening my grip on her. "Can I trust you?"

She nods without hesitation. "Absolutely."

The scary thing is, I believe her. Every emotion she makes me feel and how my body reacts to her... It's overwhelming at the best of times, but when it's just us with nothing but the open road ahead and the music seeping into our veins, I have never felt safer with a woman—someone I can be myself with. And it's fucking terrifying.

"Then let's stop wasting time, strawberry. The backseat of my car is calling our names."

Tatum giggles when I attach my lips to the base of her throat, teasing the skin as I blindly reach for the handle of the door.

I'm going to savour every moment I get with her because deep in my soul, I know this isn't going to last. The forces determined to keep us apart will overpower us soon enough, and I'll have no choice but to let her go. And until then, I'm going to commit every inch of Tatum to memory so I never forget her.

Chapter Nineteen

TATUM

"Tate! How is my favourite girl doing?"

I lean back on the desk chair and smile, pressing the phone to my ear. My gaze flicks over the stack of files spread out on the desk in front of me, the light wood blending with the cream manilla files. "Nate, the last time I checked, I'm the only girl in your life."

Nathan scoffs, feigning hurt by my words. "I'll have you know I'm quite the ladies man."

"Does that mean you have a girlfriend?"

I bite my bottom lip as silence trickles down the line. Checkmate.

"That doesn't matter," Nathan finally says, and I burst out laughing, unable to hold it in any longer. God, I miss this man. "I didn't call you to talk about my love life or lack thereof."

"Then why did you call me?" I twirl a piece of hair around my finger, the thick ponytail I threw my hair in this morning lying over my left shoulder.

"Well, mostly to check in on you since you have forgotten how to use your fingers and don't respond to my texts," he murmurs. "And secondly, a little birdie told me something about you that I wanted to ask about."

I playfully roll my eyes. "I always text you back, Nate. It might not be as promptly as you like, but this job keeps me busy, remember?"

"I know," he mumbles, followed by a huff. "But still, I just want to know you're okay and get all the hot gossip about Sydney."

I snort a laugh. "Don't worry, if there is hot gossip to share, you'll be the first to know."

"Which brings me to what the little birdie told me," Nathan drawls, and the hair on the back of my neck stands on edge. "And please don't lie to me, okay?"

"I would never lie to you." I mean that. Nathan is one of my best friends, and not once have I ever kept a secret from him, which is why the anticipation of his question has my heart rate spiking.

"That's good to know," he says, voice confident. "And before you ask, no, I can't tell you who my source is."

I groan and rub at my temple, a low thump forming behind my eyes. "You're a menace."

"And yet you still love me," my best friend sing-songs.

"Please get to the point," I squeeze out, my chest aching with anxiety.

"Okay, so I was down at the pub last night, having a drink by myself as one does since our other best friend is a father and pre-occupied with his new babysitter, and I got to talking with the bartender."

"You just told me who your source is," I point out, voice tight.

"Shit," he mutters. "I wasn't supposed to tell you that."

I stay silent, hoping it'll make Nathan get to his point sooner. If he doesn't, I might start screaming.

"Anyway, when I mentioned you, she told me she saw you talking with a guy at the bar the night before you left town. She remembered you because she watched Noah and I leave with Jade, and once you sat at the bar, you started talking with a guy who was sitting by himself."

My eyes widen as dread floods my veins.

Oh, *shit*.

"To add icing to the cake, the bartender, Penelope—you remember Penelope? She was a few years below us in high school, and her older brother, Rhys, left to go to Western Australia to work on a cattle station or something, I don't know. She was always a wild child around town. Anyway, she recognised said person as Sinnett Baxter, the halfback for the Wolves. And you *left* the pub with him!"

My eyes flutter closed as my secret explodes from the box I have kept it hidden in since leaving Barrenridge. I didn't know if I was ever going to tell Noah and Nathan about Sinnett and what happened the night before I left, only because I knew how they would react. Not only would they want to know every detail—as much as I'm willing to share—but they would make a big deal of it, much like Nathan is now as he continues his spiel.

"Like, seriously, Tate. How dare you hook up with the halfback of a rugby team and have the audacity not to tell us. I thought we were friends."

I lean forward to drop my head on the desk, blinking rapidly as darkness consumes my vision. "It's not a big deal, Nate."

"It is to me," he retorts. "Our little Tate is finally moving on from Jayden, and it just so happened to be with a famous athlete who is fucking built like a brick shithouse. You're one lucky lady. *And* you get to work with him."

"You sound like you want to sleep with him, too," I quip,

needing to find some humour in the situation I've found myself in.

"Don't change the subject." My friend's voice is stern but holds nothing but happiness. "I want to know everything."

"Nathan…"

"Everything," he repeats, leaving no room for argument. "Now, or I will tell Noah. And, as the dad of the group, you'll get more of an ear-full from him than me."

I groan and lift my head, resting my chin on my bent hand. "Fine. But only because I know if I don't, you won't shut up."

"It pays off to be annoying. Now, spill. And don't leave any details out."

Of course, I left some details out. I kept it as PG-friendly as I could while also keeping some more intimate details to myself. There was no way in hell I was going to reveal I'm still sleeping with him because it'll only add fuel to the fire Nathan started.

For now, all he needs to know is I hooked up with Sinnett the night before I left Barrenridge, and now I'm treating his injury as the physio for the Wolves.

"You saucy minx," Nathan says when I finish speaking. "I didn't think you had it in you."

"What?" I quiz, tilting my head to the side.

"A one-night stand."

My shoulders lift in a shrug even though he can't see me. "Yeah, well, I thought I had nothing to lose at that moment. I had no idea who he was when I saw him. It wasn't until a week later that I realised he played for the Wolves."

"The no dating the players rule your dad gave you must suck," he comments. "Knowing you can't do anything about it."

If only he knew the truth.

"Yeah," I murmur. Glancing down at my watch, my eyes

widen. I have a session with Sinnett in two minutes. The man has never been late before, so knowing my luck, he'll appear in the doorway to my office on the dot. "I have to go, Nate. I have a session booked in a couple of minutes I need to prepare for."

"Since you kept your end of the deal, I'll keep mine about not telling Noah. Yet."

I exhale a sharp breath and stand, hand firmly pressed against my hip. "You promise? He has a lot on his plate right now."

"Scout's honour," Nathan responds, and I just know he's smiling like a fool. "I miss you, Tate."

I smile. "I miss you, too. Talk soon, okay?"

"I'll hold you to it."

The moment the call ends, a familiar head of inky hair appears in the doorway, right on time. Sinnett saunters into the room and closes the door behind him, heated eyes locked with mine.

My stomach flip flops like it does every time I lay eyes on this man, and my skin tingles. How he effortlessly makes me want to melt into a puddle at his feet still baffles me.

"If this wasn't our last session before my six-week check-up, I would be all over you, strawberry."

A shiver races down my spine as I step out from behind my desk. I gesture to the table in the middle of the room, my eyes tracking Sinnett's movements as he sits on the edge; his eyes trained on me.

"We need to behave ourselves at work," I remind him, but my heart is racing with the possibilities of what he could do to me in this room.

"I know," he murmurs, lying on his back. The training jersey clings to his defined chest, and the athletic shorts struggle to contain the sheer size of his thighs. Talk about mouthwatering. "But when it comes to you, I can't seem to help myself."

I drag my bottom lip between my teeth as I examine the once swollen area of his quad. When I first checked him over, the muscle was irritated and tender. Sinnett was worried he wouldn't heal in the time it would normally take for a muscle contusion injury, and I understood why, given the state of his quad. But I was determined to help get him back on the field sooner rather than later. And it seems my recovery plan has been working wonders.

"How's it looking?" Sinnett asks, his voice wavering as he folds his arms behind his head, eyes focused on the ceiling. "I've been following your plan to a tee."

I probe the skin, feeling the muscles beneath. "It's looking good," I murmur, and get to work bending and twisting his leg. Sinnett's face doesn't twist with pain when I work the area. "Better than good."

Sinnett's eyes snap forward, searching my side profile. "You're not fucking with me, are you? Because I have a session booked with Ian, the club doctor, on Sunday to see if I will be medically cleared to play again."

I turn my attention to a stressed Sinnett. Without breaking eye contact, I lower his leg down and offer him a small smile. "Sin, trust me, your quad is looking great. From the outside, the skin is no longer discoloured, the muscles are moving as they should, and as long as you're not lying to me about the pain level, then it's a no-brainer that you've done everything you can to heal this injury."

Relief washes over Sinnett's features, and he exhales a sharp breath. "You're serious?"

I nod, watching as he pushes himself into a seat position. He turns his body so his legs hang over the side of the table, conveniently on either side of my hips. His hands find my waist, fingers digging gently into the skin as he holds me. Neither of us speak.

Working with Sinnett for the past month has given me a front row seat to how hard he has worked to get to where he is now in the recovery process. He did everything he was meant to, and now the hard work is paying off.

"Are you okay?" I ask, tilting my head back to meet his eyes. Even sitting on the table, his six-foot-three frame towers over me. "Something on your mind?"

"I'm worried," he murmurs, voice tight as he holds my gaze. "I just... don't know if I'm ready to be cleared. What if Ian finds something you missed and I'm sidelined for longer? What if I haven't been training hard enough in the gym and now I'm not up to the fitness standard? So many things could go wrong, and I just—" He shoves a hand through his hair and groans. "I'm just worried, Tate."

My hand cups his cheek, the light stubble ghosting his skin prickling the inside of my palm. Sinnett's breath catches as he watches me, blinking slowly. Standing this close, I catch the hues of green scattered across his irises, like lily pads drifting on a calm river.

"Sin, listen to me," I urge, voice gentle. "You've got this, okay? You did everything right. Not only did you follow my plan, but you put in the effort to go the extra mile of keeping up with the training schedule and sticking to the nutrition plan. Once Ian gets my letter of approval to have you medically cleared, I would be shocked if you weren't."

Sinnett swallows hard and nods. "Yeah, you're right."

I smile. "Just try to relax, okay? *Breathe.* You've got this."

Ocean eyes blink at me, and I have to resist getting lost in them. Sinnett's hands squeeze my waist, pulling my body closer until my chest is flush against his. My breath catches in my throat, eyes rounding.

Sinnett's lips brush over mine, gentle and tender. Within seconds, my hands wrap around his neck as I melt into the kiss. His lips are soft and taste of Powerade. Heat explodes across my chest as our tongues meet. No matter how many times I kiss this man, he manages to steal the breath from my lungs and cause butterflies to erupt in my stomach.

Sinnett pulls back long enough to murmur, "Thank you," against my lips.

"For what?" I breathe, chest heaving.

"For helping me. For making me believe I've got this."

"You do have this," I reaffirm, my nose brushing his. "You've always had this, even without my help. I just guided you along the way while you did all of the hard work."

Sinnett's fingers flex around my waist. "You've done more for me than you realise."

My brows crease, not understanding what he means. But before I can ask, a knock sounds at the door. With my heart in my throat, I step away, hating the distance between us. Sinnett holds my gaze as we stand in silence, neither of us moving or acknowledging the person behind the door.

Dad pops his head through, eyes narrowing as he flicks them between me and Sinnett. "Am I interrupting?"

I clear my throat and turn to Dad, slipping a smile on my face that hides the pounding of my heart. "Nope. We were just finishing up."

Dad turns his attention to Sinnett. "All good?"

Sinnett nods, rubbing a hand over his right thigh. "Yes, sir. Your daughter has been taking *good* care of me."

The emphasis on good as my cheeks burning. God, I hope Dad doesn't notice. With how bright my office is, a change in hue to my cheeks would be hard to miss.

Dad knocks his knuckles against the door frame, nodding slowly. "Wonderful. The guys are out on the field running drills, so why don't you join them? Todd has a few light exercises for you to go through. We need to start getting you ready to get back on the field, but we'll start small, okay? And once you're ready, and Tate here approves it, you can join the rest of the squad."

A light I only see when talking about rugby explodes in Sinnett's eyes, and he nods. "Yes, of course. I'll see you out there."

I offer Dad a smile. "I'll see you later."

He arches a brow at me. "Thai for dinner?"

Dad hates cooking as much as I do. Mum was always the one cooking up meals worthy of being on a cooking show.

"Sounds perfect."

When Dad closes the door behind him, I expel a sharp breath and rub my forehead. "God, that was close."

"Too close," Sinnett agrees, gripping the edge of the bed. "I know we need to be careful, but it's impossible to keep my hands off you, strawberry."

Unable to wipe the smile from my face, I gesture to the door. "You better get back to training."

Sinnett stands from the bed, his chest brushing against mine as he leans down to press a chaste kiss to my forehead. My eyes flutter close as he steps back, running a hand through his hair.

"I'll see you around, Tate."

I wrap my arms around my waist and smile. "I hope so."

Chapter Twenty

SINNETT

I don't know why Khai insists on having the speakers in the apartment complex gym so fucking loud to the point my eardrums might explode. He says it helps him work out better —needing to feel the base of the music to get him in beast mode or whatever the fuck—but I think it's to drown out the kids squealing and running around in the backyard area outside. The gym shares a wall on the bottom floor of the building with a private playground, and without fail, every time we're in here, we're greeted with children crying and screaming for what feels like hours.

"You're going to send me deaf," I shout over the music, spotting Khai as he attempts to bench press seventy kilos. "If it's such a problem, chuck on some headphones."

Khai grunts as he extends his arms and re-racks the barbell. Sitting upright on the bench, he reaches for the water bottle at his feet. "One of these days we'll get a quiet session in, without those little demons running around."

I snort out a laugh and switch places with him. Settling

onto my back and positioning myself for the lift, I peer up at Khai. "You can't deny that they're cute kids."

"You only think they're cute because you want some of your own. Freak."

I bite back a smile and position my hands on the barbell. The weight is fucking heavy, but I focus on completing three reps before re-racking. With a huff, I stand and turn to my friend, who is glaring at the wall shared with the playground.

I roll my eyes and reach for the stereo controller beside my water bottle. With the volume at a reasonable setting, I ignore Khai's protests to turn it up and fold my arms over my chest.

"I don't want kids yet," I remind him. "I know a lot of the guys on the team are having kids, but they're not on the cards for me. At least for a couple more years."

Khai raises a knowing brow at me. "You looking to make Tatum your baby mama?"

I scowl at him. "No."

"With the noises I've been hearing from your bedroom at night, I would say she's not far off."

The muscles in my back tighten. "You promised you weren't listening."

"I also never claimed to tell the truth one hundred percent of the time," he responds with a shrug and smug fucking grin. "But don't worry, your secret is still safe with me. How Coach Phil hasn't caught on yet is beyond me. It's so obvious you're into each other."

"We are not." I take a long sip from my water bottle to give me time to decide how I'm going to navigate this conversation with my best friend.

"Oh, please." Khai drops onto the bench and lies down, spacing his hands correctly on the barbell to complete the lift. "An astronaut in space could fucking see the heart eyes you give the girl when she's not looking. But hey, I'm not judging here. I just want to make sure you're being careful."

"I am," I mutter as I spot him, keeping my attention focused on the barbell moving through the air. "You don't need to worry about me."

Khai re-racks and sits up, heaving out a breath and glancing over his shoulder. "For both of your sake, I hope that's true."

"Don't you start with me about it," I deadpan, raising a brow at him. "Don't think I don't know about your escapades over the weekend in Auckland."

Khai gasps and jumps to his feet, pointing an accusatory finger at me. "Who told you?"

A shit eating grin splits across my face. "I'm not telling."

"It was Finn, wasn't it? That bastard!"

I chuckle and clap a hand on his shoulder. "I don't need to tell you what could've happened if someone caught you having a threesome two hours before the game in the backseat of a girl's car." My brows crease into a frown. "Actually, now I'm more curious as to how you made that work."

"Oh, shut up, Sin." Khai slaps my hand away and drops onto the bench, head slumping between his shoulders. "If Finn hadn't caught me, my secret would've stayed in the back of that car."

I exhale a sharp breath. "You've got to let this jinx thing go before it starts impacting your career."

Khai rolls his eyes. "God forbid a man be superstitious." He reaches for his phone, plucking it off the floor and slipping it into the pocket of his shorts. "And what can I say? I'm a man who enjoys the company of others the night before a game, which happens to turn into sex and results in me performing well in said game. Sue me, Sin."

"Khai..."

"No, I don't want to hear it," he bites out, standing. "I've told you before I have no plans to abandon the jinx, not unless I'm proven wrong."

"Have you ever considered the fact that you might just be a good player?" I ask, folding my arms over my chest. "Because I've seen you out there. As my right-hand man, you help me in ways no one else on the team can. Which I think is accredited to your skill and abilities, not who you fuck the night before."

Khai runs a hand through his sweat-soaked hair and grunts, casting his eyes to the floor.

When Khai first told me about this jinx of his when we transitioned to the main roster of the Wolves, I thought he was pulling my cock at first. He was always a jokester growing up, so I thought this was one of those times he would try to make me believe something only to turn around ten minutes later and die laughing at what he thought was the prank of the century.

But the laughter never came, and his need to fulfill the jinx grew with each passing game and season.

I've warned him multiple times not to let the jinx get in the way of keeping his head clear, especially the day before a game. The last thing he needed was to get caught in a compromising position—much like he did in Auckland over the weekend— that could see him facing disciplinary action.

"If this has to do with your parents, you don't have to—"

"It's not about them," Khai squeezes out, running a hand down the side of his face. "I don't care what they think about me or my career. Their opinion means nothing to me."

Exhaling a breath, I nod. Growing up, I thought Khai had the coolest parents ever. They were young, fun and always down for a good time. Whenever Khai organised a sleepover with some of the guys from primary school, neither of his parents cared if we were too noisy at three in the morning. His mum made the best chocolate chip pancakes and his dad would sit down with us in the media room to watch re-runs of the footy games from the night before. From the outside looking in, Khai had the perfect life with even more perfect parents.

But then something shifted. Something Khai refuses to tell me about, not wanting to let go of whatever secret he's holding on to. And I don't want to pry—not if he doesn't want to talk about it.

"Just be careful, okay?" I caution with a nod. "Whether you think you have a jinx or not, you're a fucking phenomenal player."

Khai grins and opens his arms, gesturing for me to embrace him. "If you wanted to hug me and kiss my cheek, Sin, all you had to do was ask."

I playfully roll my eyes, refusing his hug before swiping my phone off the ground beside my gym towel. The soft material soaks up the sweat clinging to my face, which is much needed after the intense session I was put through by my best friend. He insisted on getting me into the gym with the excuse that I need to be ready for the round twelve game this Saturday afternoon, on the off-chance I am medically cleared to play.

Two days ago, I had a six-week check-up with Ian while the rest of my teammates were in Auckland. Not having them around, breathing down my neck all desperate to know how the session went, made it a little easier. I'm glad my team cares about me and wants to see me back on the field enough that they're interested in my recovery, but this was something I needed a clear head for.

You've got this.

Tatum's words got me through the session with Ian, and by the time I walked out, my steps were lighter and my head clearer than when I walked in. She was right about me doing all I could leading up to the check-in. Ian didn't say much as he looked me over and went through a physical fitness test with me, but I saw the impressed look he tried to hide throughout. If that's not an indicator that I'm going to be cleared, then I must be fucking blind or seeing shit.

"Let's go get something to eat," Khai says as he gathers up his gym bag, stuffing his bottle and towel into it. "I'm so fucking hungry I could eat a horse. Or better yet, one of those insufferable kids outside."

I burst out laughing as I follow him out of the gym and toward the elevator. "Shit, man, you can't say stuff like that."

Khai shrugs as he steps into the elevator. "This is a free country, Sin."

I shake my head and keep my mouth shut as we ride the elevator to the top floor of the building. When we step through the front door to the apartment, my phone vibrates in my pocket. Like a freak with no self-control, I clumsily reach for the device and drop my bag just inside the door.

I feel Khai's eyes on me as I read the caller ID on the screen.

"It's Ian," I breathe, muscles tight as I stare at the screen.

"Well fucking answer it," Khai hurries to say, gesturing to the phone. "Now, you big idiot."

Snapping out of the trance, I bring the device to my ear. I hope I can hear him through the blood rushing in my ears.

What if he doesn't clear me and I have to continue with Tatum's recovery plan?

I felt confident going into the check-up, but now I'm wondering if I was gaslighting myself into thinking my quad was okay and I was just too blind to see it.

Oh, *God*.

"Sin!" Ian's cheery voice sets my nerves further on edge. "Do you have a minute to talk?"

My eyes lift to meet Khai's, who is watching intently. Clearing my throat, I adjust the backwards cap on my head. "Y-yeah, I can talk now. Is everything okay?"

"Couldn't be better," Ian says, spiking my heart rate. "I wanted to call to say that our session on Sunday went amazingly. I've had a couple of days to go over your file with the results from our session, and consult with Tatum about your progress, and I've come to the conclusion that you're medically fit to return to the field as soon as this Saturday."

Somehow, my heart doesn't burst from my chest and the air in my lungs doesn't evaporate. Instead, my eyes widen and I strangle out, "Really? I can play this weekend?"

"Absolutely. Coach Phil is on board and is excited to have you back out there."

Holy *fuck*.

I did it. I'm cleared to play again.

It's hard to explain the emotions racing through every inch of my body, seeping into my veins and bubbling away under my skin. But my first thought goes to the strawberry-blonde who got me here. If it wasn't for her knowledge and perfectly laid out recovery plan, I wouldn't have pushed myself the way I did, and I certainly wouldn't be having this pleasant conversation with Ian.

I owe this win to Tatum.

"It would be my honour," I rasp, throat tight. "Thank you."

"Just be careful of the quad, okay? It's more susceptible to aches and further injury moving forward, so when entering tackles, be mindful of your positioning. And have Tatum strap you up good before the game."

"Will do, Ian. Thank you."

"Have a good night, okay? I can't wait to see you back out there."

The call ends a moment later, and all I can do is stare at my best friend, silence enveloping us in the hallway.

"You got cleared to play?" Khai asks, his words hopeful.

A grin splits across my face. "Fuck yeah I did."

"Hallelujah!" Khai races forward and lifts me in the air, his laughter bouncing off the walls. "This calls for celebratory drinks."

"Put me down you idiot," I grunt, but the words hold no malice to them. "I would like to step onto the field first before you fuck my quad again."

"Oh." Khai sets me down, smiling. "Not to fear, I will protect you with my life out there. You can count on me."

I clap him on the shoulder, returning his smile. "I have no doubt you will."

"Welcome back, Sin." Khai gestures over his shoulder. "I'll drop my gym bag in my room and get started on those drinks. I think it's time we crack open the good whiskey."

He hurries down the hallway, leaving me standing by the front door with my heart pounding in my chest and one specific person on my mind.

My fingers fly over the screen as I type out a text message.

SIN: You up for a drive tonight?

Her response comes not even thirty seconds later.

STRAWBERRY: What's the occasion?

SIN: I have something I want to tell you.

STRAWBERRY: Consider me intrigued.

SIN: I'll pick you up at ten.

STRAWBERRY: See you then, stud.

Unable to wipe the smile off my face, I pick my gym bag off

the floor and enter my bedroom. Tatum deserves to be the first to hear the good news—apart from Khai—because without her support, I wouldn't be here.

I wasn't kidding when I said she's done more for me than she realises. Not just physically with my injury, but emotionally, too. She has shown me that it's okay to be vulnerable. I had thought it was weak to put your heart on your sleeve, that no one would take me seriously or consider me to be less of a man. But the more time I spend with her, I'm learning to be more open and allow myself time to think about what I want moving forward.

Because at the end of the day, I'm living this life for myself —no one else. And whether my father likes it or not, this is my career, not his.

I just have to start believing in myself, even when it feels impossible.

Chapter Twenty-One

TATUM

Sinnett hasn't spoken a word since I got in his car ten minutes ago. I had half expected him to spill the beans about the news he wanted to share with me as soon as I got into the seat, but was surprised when he had the playlist I shared with him last week on full bore and a cheeky grin on his face instead. I was itching to pressure him into telling me what was on his mind, but quickly figured out that he wanted to keep me on the edge of my seat by purposefully staying quiet.

And because I didn't want to push him, I stayed silent and got lost in the music, but deep inside, I was dying to know the secret he kept hidden on his tongue.

The car rolls to a stop in the car park of Edwards Beach. It's pitch-black outside besides the headlights illuminating a small portion of the tide rolling in over the sand. My fingers flex on my thighs as I spin in the seat to face Sinnett. The grin he wore when I got in the car hasn't slipped once. I'm impressed with his ability to hold it for as long as he has, but it also means the news he wants to share must be epic enough for him to be this giddy about it.

"Sin," I start, reaching for the volume button on the touch screen, lowering the music to an acceptable level, "if you don't tell me what's going on, I might just die from a heart attack caused by anticipation."

Sinnett snorts a laugh and shakes his head. His body turns to face mine. If his torso wasn't hidden behind the same black hoodie he wears religiously, I have no doubt the muscles beneath his inked and tanned skin would've rippled with the simple movement.

"Ian cleared me to play on Saturday."

My eyes widen as his words settle deep into my bones, followed by the rhythmic beat of my heart. Before I can stop myself, my hands dart out to grab Sinnett's cheeks, needing to feel his warmth as I processed the situation.

"You're playing this weekend?" I squeeze out, unable to hide the emotion seeping into my voice. "For real?"

Sinnett smiles—the same smile that has me melting each time he flashes it at me. "I'm being so for real right now. I got the call earlier and knew you were the first person I wanted to tell. Well, besides Khai, of course. But he doesn't count because he was already with me."

A squeal slips past my lips, and I'm helpless to stop it. Within seconds, my lips find Sinnett, and he's quick to pull me onto my lap, planting his hands firmly on my waist, holding me against him while my legs straddle his thighs. We melt into the kiss like we have done so many times before, but this time feels different. Charged with excitement and something I can almost describe as pride, I melt against him, needing to feel every inch of him.

Sinnett kisses me with such force it knocks the air from my lungs, but I hold on, fingers digging into his shoulders.

This man has worked so hard to get to the end of his recovery. Even when he doubted he had the strength or determination to go on, he proved himself wrong by pushing through and reaching the end of the tunnel. Not only is Sinnett a man who knows exactly what he wants, he will do everything in his power to get it, even on the days when everything feels overwhelming and self-doubt eats him alive.

But this moment right here will serve as a reminder to him that anything is possible if he puts his mind to it.

"I'm so proud of you," I murmur against his lips breathlessly.

Sinnett exhales a sharp breath, hands tightening on my hips as his eyes lift to meet mine. "You are?"

I nod, grinning. "Very much so. You fucking did it, Sin. Just like I knew you would."

His throat works a swallow, ocean eyes darting across my face as if searching for a sign that I'm lying. When he doesn't find one, he drops his forehead against mine and inhales deeply. "No one has ever told me that before. Well, besides Mia and Gran."

I frown, lifting a hand to run it through his silky hair. "Are you serious?"

Sinnett nods.

Well, shit. I wasn't expecting his words to form cracks in my heart, but here we are.

"Not even your parents?" I question, voice wavering.

He shakes his head. "Not once."

"Sin..." I breathe. I swallow hard, fighting the lump forming in my throat.

"I accepted it a long time ago," he says, forehead pressed firmly against mine as we hold each other. "Nothing I have done has ever felt good enough for my parents, especially my father. When I was growing up, I did everything I could to make him proud. I got the best grades in school, was the best on my footy team, and I even won countless awards in school, but none of it mattered to him."

I open my mouth to say something, but the words die on my tongue because what is there to say? No word in the English dictionary will change how Sinnett feels at this moment. Nothing I say can change his perception of his father and the lack of support he got as a child.

I can't imagine what it would've been like to grow up with parents who didn't tell their child they were proud of them. If I so much as drew a picture for my mum in primary school or came home with an excellence in participation award for a class I was mediocre at best in throughout high school, Mum would say the same thing.

"This is amazing, sweetie. I'm so proud of you."

Even Dad would say the same thing when I would call him after school some days. It didn't matter whether I was getting terrible grades in my legal studies class or my weekend soccer team was coming last in the comp, he never failed to remind me that he was proud of me.

My heart breaks for the man in front of me, baring the deepest parts of him. Every insecurity and self-doubt he has is laying on his sleeve, and he's trusting me with this information —a part of him others aren't privy to seeing.

The fact that he trusts me enough with this side of him has my heart racing and my fingers trembling.

"Even now, when I'm at the height of my career and in the best shape of my life, before the injury, it still wasn't enough for him. Every try I scored or conversion I kicked didn't faze him. It's as if he's waiting for something I don't know about or simply thinks I'm not capable of achieving, and it fucking hurts, Tate. Not being the man my dad wants kills a little part of me every day."

I blink back the tears forming in the corner of my eyes and release a shaky breath.

"Don't listen to him," I whisper, my lips brushing against his. "You're every bit the man you're supposed to be. I see it in the way you carry yourself, how driven you are and how you treat me. Being a man isn't defined by how physically fit you are or if you're the best athlete in the world. To be a man means to be the best version of yourself in every way. And I would be lying if I said I was looking at anything but a real man right now."

Sinnett slowly lifts his head to meet my gaze. My breath catches in my throat at the intensity of his eyes. They're somehow brighter in the depths of darkness consuming the small space, and a spark of hope flashes across them, melting my insides into liquid.

"Do you mean that?" he rasps out, holding my gaze. "Tate..."

"I meant every word." My hand comes up to cup his cheek, and he leans into it. "You don't need your father's approval to be the man you want to be. At the end of the day, this is your life, so live it without hesitation or the fear of never being good enough. You can't please everyone, Sin. But you can be the best version of yourself for *you*."

"How is it that you see the real me better than anyone else?" he murmurs.

The corner of my mouth tilts up in a half smile. "Because you allow me to."

Sinnett hums, as if mulling over the words. His hands slide over my hips to rest on the curve of my ass. Heat pools in my core and I instinctively rock against him, needing to be closer. I feel him straining against the light material of the black athletic shorts, and my mouth dries.

He grins and leans forward, breath fanning against my lips. "Do you have something else on your mind, strawberry?"

Only Sinnett would go from baring his soul to me to flirting in the blink of an eye.

I swallow hard. "I don't know what you're talking about."

Sinnett slides one hand to the back of my neck while the other toys with the hem of my black leggings. "So you're telling me that if I dip my hand beneath the fabric of these flimsy tights, you'll be as dry as a bread loaf?"

No. "Yes."

His fingers tease the waistband, leaving bursts of heat on my skin as he works his fingers closer to where I need him. And when he reaches the destination, he's going to learn very quickly that I was lying through my teeth.

I want him. There has never been any doubt about that.

Sinnett holds my gaze as he pushes my underwear to the side. My breath hitches in my throat when he slides his finger between my folds, learning exactly what I want. He grins in response and slides his finger into me. I throw my head back, arching my body against his as I take all of him.

"Such a liar," he squeezes out, pumping his finger in and out to the rhythm of my pounding heart. "You're fucking soaked, Tate."

All I can manage is a whimper as he joins a second finger in on the fun. One of my hands slides to the nape of his neck, holding on for dear life as he drives into me. His cock strains against the fabric of his shorts, begging to be touched, but with the pressure building in my core and the lack of vision I have right now, all I can do is let Sinnett take the lead.

Sinnett stills his fingers and angles them upward. "Ride my fucking hand, Tate. Be a good girl and take all of me."

Needing no further instructions, I do as I'm told and ride his fingers. Lifting my hips until his fingers are barely inside of me, I then slam them down. Sinnett groans and reaches for the back of my neck, attaching his lips to mine.

Between the pressure building in my core, the intrusion of Sinnett's fingers, and the feel of his lips moving against mine, it's too much. I can't breathe; the sides of the car closing in on me as I rush closer to the edge, chasing the euphoric feeling only Sinnett can provide.

"That's it," Sinnett utters against my lips. "Come on my fingers, Tate."

I screw my eyes shut and focus on keeping my rhythm from turning sloppy. Pressing my lips against Sinnett, I groan against his mouth. The fire building in the depth of my core is one spark away from exploding. And Sinnett feeds into the fire by sliding his hand around my throat, squeezing gently as his lips attack mine.

Yeah, that'll do it.

My body seizes as an orgasm tears through it. Tilting my head back—with Sinnett's hand still wrapped around my throat—my lips part as a breathless moan escapes them.

Sinnett presses his lips to the side of my mouth, his hand on my throat sliding down my chest to rest on my hip. "You're so fucking beautiful, Tate. God, I'll never get used to it."

My head is too full and my body weightless to do much more than collapse against Sinnett's chest. He pulls his hand out of me and re-adjusts my clothes before wrapping his arms around me, hugging me closer to him.

"Savin' Me" by Nickleback sounds from the speakers, replacing the silence that settles over us. I focus on the lyrics and the warmth radiating from Sinnett's chest. Whenever I'm with him, it feels like the rest of the world falls away. We don't have to worry about responsibilities or the fact that we can never truly be together. But for the couple of hours we spend together in this car, we get to be ourselves.

It's moments like these I've started to cherish the most.

"In case you've forgotten, I'm proud of you," I murmur, turning my cheek to rest on Sinnett's shoulder.

Sinnett runs his hand over my back, the movement comforting. "Believe me, I haven't forgotten, Tate."

"Good, because I'm going to tell you every time you're about to walk out onto that field, and you'll hear it again the second you come off."

His hand stills on my back and he exhales a sharp breath. "I can't wait to hear it."

Chapter Twenty-Two

SINNETT

Getting back into the regular training schedule after taking it easy the past six weeks and following a limited recovery plan is fucking brutal. I had forgotten how gruelling it can be on your body, taking the big hits and running drills for hours, that I'm fucked by the time I drag my ass to the locker room.

I slump down on the bench and reach for my water bottle, chugging the contents of it as if it'll help my lungs from giving out on me. I reach around my back and pull my training jersey out from the waistband of my shorts. The material is cool against my skin as I wipe away the sweat and dirt clinging to each pore.

Footsteps sound in the otherwise empty room, drawing my attention from the real fear I might be dying to the man who mirrors my features. He's dressed in one of his black tailored suits, hands shoved into the pockets of his pants while his dark hair is styled neatly with far too much gel.

Dad eyes me from across the room, and my back stiffens.

Fuck. Here we go.

"Want to tell me why I had to hear from Phil you were cleared to play and not my own son?"

After pulling my jersey over my head, I shove a hand through my sweat-soaked hair and exhale a sharp breath. I'm regretting my decision to step away from training—at the suggestion of Todd so as not to aggravate my quad before the game tomorrow night—for a ten-minute water break.

"I've been busy this week," I grunt, trying to keep my voice even.

The truth is as simple as I didn't want to tell him because I knew he would act like *this*. Ready to control me like the puppet I've always been to him.

"I can see that," Dad retorts, stepping towards me. Each slap of his shoe against the floor sets my nerves further on edge. "But it shits me that I had to wait until the day before your return to hear the good news."

My conversation with Tatum from three nights ago echoes in the back of my mind. I revealed to her my father's inability to express his support for me and my career. At that moment, I hadn't planned on telling her, but as usual, her easygoing attitude and calming presence brought it out of me, and I was helpless to fight it.

Her words made me realise that I've spent far too long living in my father's shadows, hoping I can one day live up to the standard he has been seeking ever since I started playing rugby. I'm starting to wonder if he'll ever be proud of my achievements or if he'll continue to wish for more from me.

"Well, surprise, I'm cleared to play," I deadpan, jaw ticking. "Happy?"

"Sinnett," Dad scolds, brows creasing into a frown. "What the hell has gotten into you these past few weeks? All you do is back-chat your mother and I when we try to talk to you, and don't even get me started on how you react when we bring up your sister."

I focus on my breathing and not the anger pooling in my veins. If I give in to his baiting and fight back, it'll do nothing but prove him right, and I refuse to give him the satisfaction.

"I'm fine, Dad," I say through gritted teeth. "I just don't need you and Mum breathing down my neck every second of every day."

"We're only trying to be supportive of you, especially with your injury." Dad sighs and shakes his head. "I thought I raised you and Mia better than to turn your back on family when all we're trying to do is look out for you."

Breathe, Sin.

If you fight back, it'll only make things worse.

"I'm not doing this with you," I bite out, flexing my hands on my thighs. "I'm busy."

Dad's jaw clenches, his features tight as if he's weighing if he wants to continue pushing me or let it go. Deep down, I hope he chooses wrong so I can let go of everything I've been holding onto for years, but I know it would leave behind a wound that can't be fixed. I'm not sure now is the right time to play that hand.

He rolls his tongue in his cheek and nods, taking a step back. "Fine. But this conversation isn't over, Sin."

"Wonderful," I murmur, holding his gaze.

"Your mother and I will see you at the game tomorrow," he continues, ignoring my sarcastic remark. "With it being your first match back, you better be on your A-game, Sin. Everyone will be watching you. Your teammates are going to rely on you to get them a win, so you better be sure you live up to the standard."

Fucking hell. If I wasn't already feeling the pressure before, now I'm being crushed by an expectation I'm not sure I can maintain, especially returning after an injury.

"I'll do my best," I squeeze out past the lump in my throat. Dad doesn't say goodbye; he simply nods before turning to leave the room, passing Khai as he enters.

Am I going to be the same player I was before I got injured?

What if I hurt my quad again?

What if I let the team and the club down?

My chest aches from the earlier training and the conversation with my dad, but I can't let on to Khai just how fucking worried I am about returning to the field.

My best friend drops onto the bench beside me, gripping his water bottle. His training jersey is smeared with grass stains and dirt, mirroring mine.

"God, that was fucking rough," he groans, slumping forward with his elbows resting on his dirt covered knees. "I swear Todd was tougher on us because you're back and needs to whip you into shape."

"Either way, I think he destroyed a part of my soul," I grunt, and heave in a lung full of air.

"Is everything okay with your dad?" Khai asks, lifting his head, pale green eyes filled with curiosity. "He looked kinda pissed just now."

My jaw clenches. "Everything is fine. He came by to see how I was adjusting to being back at training." I don't want to bum my friend out with the truth.

Khai regards me for a moment, as if searching for a sign that shows I'm lying. If he looks hard enough, he might find it.

He smiles, warming the ice that has found its way into my veins. "It's good to have you back, man. I don't think the rest of the guys will admit it, but we've been a little lost these past six weeks without you. Jace has been playing well, and we've only lost two games, but still. We felt the lack of your presence out there."

Can this fucker read my mind? With how well we know each other, it wouldn't surprise me if he developed a sixth-sense that allows him to read my thoughts through my expressions.

I exhale a sharp breath and clap him on the shoulder. "You better not be fucking with me right now."

My best friend snorts a laugh. "Me? I would never, Sin. But I'm serious. We're all looking forward to having you out on that field tomorrow night."

Despite the turmoil of doubt sweeping through my veins, I manage a smile. "I'm looking forward to getting back out there."

The rest of the team files into the room—conversations bounce off the walls and music from someone's speaker wraps around me. Ever since Tatum told me the proper way of listening to music—to feel each lyric and relate them to a personal experience—it's all I do in my spare time. When I'm not with Khai in the gym or sticking to the training schedule, I'm in my room listening to the playlist she created for me. I often find myself wondering the kinds of playlist she would listen to, and if they're anything like what she makes for me. I don't know how she did it, but each song feels curated to my life somehow. I've spent hours with the playlist on repeat, allowing each song to delve deeper into my bones and reach my soul. It's at the point where I know each song by heart and have an experience I can relate to the lyrics.

Even now as "She's Got Issues" by The Offspring seeps into the walls of the room, all I can think about is my time with Zoe. Khai repeatedly warned me not to go there with her because she is possessive and manipulative, but my stupid ass didn't listen. Instead of thinking with my head, I thought with my dick, and look at where it's gotten me.

Speaking of the devil, my phone lights up on the bench beside me with multiple un-read text messages from Zoe.

> ZOE: I wish you would stop ignoring me, Sin. I'm not letting this go.

> ZOE: Come on, Sin. Don't you remember all of the good times we had? I know I do. In fact, I think about them every night before bed.

> ZOE: Do you think about me?

> ZOE: Please, Sin. Don't make me beg for your attention.

I run a hand through my hair and toss the phone into my gym bag at my feet.

"You've gotta block her number, man," Khai says, eyes flicking between me and her number I, for some strange reason, haven't blocked yet. "Is there a reason you haven't?"

"I know it'll piss her off more if I block her," I grunt. "It's not a battle I'm willing to fight yet."

"Why not?" he questions with a frown.

I run a hand through my hair. "It's complicated. Zoe isn't one to back down from something she sets her mind to, and given I don't know how far she's willing to take this, I don't want to poke the bear."

"Well, I'll save you the hassle and do it for you."

Before I can stop my friend, he's on his feet with my phone in hand.

"Khai!"

Khai darts out of the room and into the adjoining training space we use before games. With his fingers tapping away at the screen, I'm helpless to stop the damage he's undoubtedly causing for me.

Standing in the open space, I watch as a grin slips onto Khai's face. He tosses the phone at me, and I barely manage to catch it before it drops at my feet.

"All done." He claps me on the shoulder as he passes by, acting as if he hasn't rattled the viper that's been waiting to strike from the edge of darkness. "You're welcome."

"Khai," I hiss, slipping the device into my pocket. "Do you have any idea what you just did?"

"Yeah, I saved your ass." Ignoring the rest of the guys hanging out by their locker space, Khai drops onto the bench in front of our spaces with a smug grin.

I drag my hand through my hair and release a pained sigh. "Zoe is going to be fucking pissed about this."

"Good," Khai quips with a shrug. "Maybe she'll get the hint then."

"No, not good, idiot." I groan and drop my head into my hands. "Keeping the line of communication open was my only way of not getting on her bad side. As much as I don't want to be with her in any way, I don't need the woman to rain hellfire on me, man. And now that you've blocked her number, severing the only source of communication she has over me, she's going to do everything in her power to make me suffer."

If there is one thing I know about Zoe, it's that she's as ruthless as they come. She once made one of her teammates cry because the girl was out of sync in the dance routine. Zoe accepts nothing short of perfection, and the poor girl had to suffer the consequences of her iron tongue and cruel words. It was hard to watch while I was training nearby, but I wasn't about to get my head bitten off for sticking up for a girl I didn't know that well.

Zoe is the kind of person to stick to her word, whether it's a threat or a promise. And if she promises to make my life hell for blocking her, I have no doubt she will find a way to do so.

Khai's eyes round at the edges, and he blinks slowly. "Oh, shit. I had no idea." He flicks his hand in the air between us. "Can't you just unblock her and pretend it never happened?"

I shake my head. "The damage is done. She's always on her phone and constantly sending texts. It would be a miracle if she didn't notice the second it happened, but I'm not lucky enough to be blessed with miracles."

"Fuck," Khai hisses. "I'm sorry, Sin."

I slump onto the bench beside him and drop my head in my hands. It might seem shady that I hadn't blocked Zoe's number after I called things off with her, but in my mind, I was doing it to keep her from ruining me and my career. And now that I've blocked her, taking the next step to cut her from my life, she's going to retaliate in ways I'm sure I've never thought possible.

I can only hope Tatum doesn't get caught in the crossfire of Zoe's wrath, because if she does, I'll never forgive myself if she gets hurt.

Chapter Twenty-Three

TATUM

The bed sheets are a tangled mess around my legs, with one foot sticking out and the other trying to find the cool spot on the mattress I have yet to reach. My skin in inflamed, despite the ceiling fan running at full power, and a light sheen of sweat has broken out across my brow and upper lip. The bed shorts and tank top I threw on after the shower feel uncomfortable against my skin, and I'm itching to tear them off in the hope it'll make everything feel less overwhelming.

I don't know what's going on with me. To start, I couldn't concentrate on the words coming out of Dad's mouth over dinner. I didn't need to study his features to know he could tell something was up with me—it was evident in the way I kept glancing at my phone, hoping to see a text message from Sinnett. I knew it was rude to do something like that while eating dinner, but it was a knee-jerk reaction. I couldn't stop myself from searching for any sign of him—however small— when he was the only thing on my mind.

Thankfully, Dad didn't say anything and continued telling me about his day.

"The Wolves are looking good for the game tomorrow night," he told me, a smile touching his lips. "I'm so pleased Sinnett was cleared to play. The guys have been performing well without him, but I know they could be better, especially if he's on the field."

I understand the stress he's under right now, especially with Sinnett returning. The Wolves are sitting on the leaderboard in second place, which is a great spot to be in at this point in the season. However, Dad is a perfectionist, so he will do everything in his power to get his team to the number one position by the end of the season. They'll have to, if they want to win the minor premiership and then go on to win the grand final.

He's always been a driven man—prepared to put his heart and soul into the sport he has loved his entire life. And while I admire his strength and determination, I would hate to see him burnout and lose his spark down the line if he doesn't take it easy. Rugby is his life, and now with Mum gone, he's dived head first into it.

We all need a distraction from the grief and heartache of losing a loved one, but he hasn't slowed down in years, and I worry it'll catch up to him sooner rather than later.

To top off my inability to fall asleep, I have a certain messy-haired, blue-eyed halfback on my mind. Ever since he got cleared to return to the field on Tuesday, I have been a ball of nerves and excitement. Nervous because I'm worried he might aggravate his quad if positioned in a bad tackle and is forced to take more time off to recover, and excited because I finally get to see him out on the field doing what he has worked his entire life to achieve.

Working with him throughout his recovery made it clear to

me just how passionate he is about the sport. Not only does he love being out there, fuelled by the cheers from the fans, but he has a drive about him that pushes him to better himself each game.

We went for a drive around North Sydney last night, and somehow, the topic of conversation shifted to his younger days playing rugby.

"I wouldn't say I was anything special, but I did try my best each game," he had said, his fingers drawing lazy circles on my thigh draped over the centre console, resting over his. Warmth lit up his eyes, and he smiled softly. "After school, Khai and I would toss the ball around in the backyard, looking to improve our skills. At that moment, I hadn't fallen in love with rugby yet."

"When did you?" I questioned, tilting my head to the side.

"It wasn't until I was seventeen and joined the U18s team." Sinnett turned his attention to the crashing waves behind the car. "Coach Stevens took me under his wings after my first training session with him. He saw something special in me. Something I didn't know existed. It was he who taught me to love the sport, accepting each ache and pain after a game and channelling it into a sense of self-worth and pride. And eventually, my mindset shifted from the sport being a hobby to something I wanted to pursue and make a career from."

"Whatever happened to Coach Stevens?"

"We still keep in contact to this day," he told me. "He comes by to watch home games when he gets the chance."

"I'm sure he's proud of you," I told him, caressing his hand resting on my knee.

Sinnett smiled. "I hope so."

It's clear Sinnett was born to do this—to be the star he's perceived to be—but he puts far too much pressure on himself to be the best. I hear it in the way his voice shakes at the edges when he talks about the sport in any capacity. I see it in the way his features harden at the mere mention of transitioning back into his regular training schedule.

He doesn't need to outwardly tell me he's worried about returning to the field and letting his teammates, coaches and club down if he doesn't perform as well as he did before he got injured. I wish I could tell him that he doesn't need to put so much pressure on himself to be the best when all he needs to do is perform at *his* best. From there, everything else will fall into place.

With a huff, I throw my arms down on the mattress at my sides and blink up at the ceiling. Giving up on trying to get a wink of sleep, I stare ahead and attempt to clear the corners of my mind. Maybe I should try counting sheep. People swear by it.

One sheep.

Two sheep.

Three sheep.

Four she—

The vibration of my phone on the bedside table pulls me away from my counting.

Goddamnit.

Abandoning all hope that the fluffy sheep can pull me into a deep slumber, I roll onto my side and reach for my phone. The device bursts to life, momentarily blinding me until I swipe across the screen and lower the brightness. Blinking rapidly, I take note of the time. 3:15 AM.

My heart slams into my chest when I see the sender of the text message.

Sinnett.

SIN: Please tell me I'm not the only one who can't sleep.

The rhythm of my erratic pulse thumps in time with my heart. My eyes linger on his message, fingers hovering over the screen. I haven't spoken to him all day because he was busy with training, and I was getting lost in a mountain of paperwork. I had grown used to seeing him on a regular basis, but now that he's been cleared, our time together has been cut short with only the occasional session to check in on him once a week.

I knew it would come to an end eventually, but I didn't think it would bum me out as much as it has this past week.

Now the question becomes: what do I respond with?

Should I respond at all? If I want to get even a couple of hours of sleep, it would be in my best interest not to say a word, because I know if I do, I'll get swept up in his words like every other time.

Unfortunately, I have the willpower of a six-year-old in a lolly store.

> TATE: Do you have a camera in here watching me? Because yeah, sleep is eluding me.

Sinnett's response comes quickly, sending my heart into overdrive.

> SIN: Do you have something on your mind, Tate?

> TATE: A lot of things.

> SIN: Do share.

I exhale a long breathe and tap on the screen, my fingers a blurry of movement.

> TATE: I can't give away all of my secrets, but I will say you're pretty up there on the list.

> SIN: Me? Well, I wish I could say it didn't go both ways.

My heart thunders in my chest as I re-read the message at least twenty times.

He's thinking about me.

Sinnett is thinking about *me* at three in the morning.

> TATE: All good things, I hope. I would hate for you to be awake this late, thinking of all the ways you could tell me you don't want to see me anymore.

> SIN: On the contrary, strawberry. My thoughts are far from it.

If my skin wasn't on fire before, it is now. I'm afraid to touch it for fear of burning myself. I don't know how this man does it. All it takes is for him to say something as simple as he's thinking about me, and my body reacts like a dog in heat. It's a foreign feeling to me, and not something I experienced when I was with my ex-boyfriend.

An ache pounds in my core, followed by liquid heat pooling at the edges, fuelling the feverish fire across my body. I drag my bottom lip between my teeth, fighting the urge to relieve the pressure building.

Feeling risky, I reach over and switch the lamp on beside the bed and sit up against the mound of pillows behind me. With light filtering across the room, I notice the windows overlooking the backyard are slick with rain drops from the downpour that did its best to lull me to sleep at midnight, but since then, it has stopped, bringing with it a howling wind that rattles the frame with each gust.

With my heart in my throat, I hold the phone above my head with the camera pointed at me. I smooth down the flyaway baby hairs around my face and adjust my tank top slightly. My nipple piercings press against the thin, white material, and the white and pink checkered shorts ride up my thighs, showing off more of my legs than necessary.

I swallow hard and turn my mouth up in a tight-lipped smile, snapping a photo that is far from my comfort zone. My hands shake as my thumb hovers over the send button. Somehow, Sinnett manages to bring out a side to me I never knew existed. Sending a revealing photo like this is not something I would've ever considered doing with Jayden. Even if he begged for it, I would decline because it's not something I'm comfortable doing. But there is something about Sinnett that has me wanting to live life on the edge a little bit, and do something that will have him feeling the same way I do—hot and bothered.

Before I can overthink my decision, I send the photo and type a quick message to follow.

TATE: Well, I'm ready and waiting to hear said thoughts.

I drag my bottom lip between my teeth and stare at the screen. The messages are received as delivered and then seen. I can't help but smile when the three dots appear, eager to see what his response is going to be, but they disappear a moment later. And then reappear. Then disappear. Again and again.

I frown. What the hell is he doing?

Panic surges through me as a realisation washes over me. What if I took it a step too far by sending him a picture of myself? Maybe I misread the tone of the conversation and

Sinnett was searching for someone to confide in about what is on his mind. After all, he does have a lot on the line with the game tomorrow—I guess tonight, actually. And here I am sending raunchy photos of myself to tease him a little.

God, I'm such an idiot.

After five minutes of watching the dots appear and disappear, I lock my phone and drop it onto my chest with a sigh. I'm going to take this as a sign to never step out of my comfort zone again because look where it's gotten me. Embarrassment creeps up my throat and I swallow the lump forming.

Mortified, I kiss any form of sleep goodbye because I'm going to lie awake until the sun rises, constructing a plan of how I can face Sinnett at the game without turning as bright as tomato.

Vibration on my chest has my eyes widening and my hands scrambling for the insistent device. When I see Sinnett's contact name on the screen requesting to *Facetime* me, heat explodes in my core.

Oh, *God*.

What is happening?

Why is he Facetiming me?

I exhale a sharp breath and reposition myself on the mound of pillows before answering the call, hands trembling. Sinnett appears on the small screen—all messy hair, sharp features, bright eyed and no fucking shirt. A soft glow illuminates the room, shadowing half of his face in a warm light.

"Sin..." I breathe, blinking slowly. "What are you do—"

He grunts, jaw ticking as he holds my gaze through the screen. "This is what you do to me, Tate." The camera pans down over the hard ridges of his torso and the lean muscles in his abdomen to where his hand is wrapped around the base of his cock, stroking it gently.

Holy. Shit.

Sinnett reappears on the screen as a I struggle to find an ounce of air in my lungs, but it seems the man has taken my breath away. All I can do is stare at him, mouth parted, as he pleasures himself. To a photo of me. *Me.*

The fact that I can see the muscles in his right arm flexing beneath the inked designs with each stroke has my head spinning and my mouth so dry I may as well have gotten cotton balls stuffed in there.

"Were you trying to tease me with that photo?" Sinnett continues, voice tight. "Showing off those perky tits with those damn nipple piercings you know drive me crazy." He rolls his tongue in his cheek—something he knows drives *me* crazy— and tilts his head to the side. "Because this is what you do to me, Tate. Your smile, your mind and your ability to break down my walls. I crave every fucking inch of you to the point of insanity."

Without realising it, my right hand has slipped between my shorts, pointer finger circling my soaked clit. I drag my bottom lip between my teeth, biting down on the skin to the point I might draw blood. But I know if I don't, a moan will slip through and reiterate to Sinnett what he does to *me.*

"Talk to me, Tate," Sinnett grunts, muscles flexing. "I want to hear that sweet voice of yours."

"Sin..." I squeeze out, dragging my finger through my slick folds. I drop further into the pillows, focusing on his eyes through the screen.

"That's it," he encourages, voice thick with an emotion I can't place. "Touch yourself. I want to hear what you can do to yourself while I watch."

Oh, my God.

The edge of my vision blurs as my focus zeros in on the man who has me so far out of my comfort zone I can no longer see it. But I've never felt safer. Not only does he bring out a side to me that is raw and unrecognisable, but he makes me feel like I'm the only woman he has eyes on. Protected, beautiful, *powerful*. Sinnett gave me something I didn't know I possessed, and that's the ability to be the person I want to be. Before him, I was the Tatum I thought I had to be. It was easy to follow the rules of what was expected of me by my parents—go to university, get a career job and then settle down with a family. But among those rules, I lost sight of what I wanted to be. And that's someone who isn't afraid to take what they want without fear of judgement and live life on the edge without fear of falling.

When I'm with Sinnett, I never worry about being judged or falling, because I know he's going to be there right alongside me, ready to take the leap with my hand in his. We've somehow brought out the best in each other—the real version of ourselves. And it's something I'm not taking for granted.

"Y-you make me feel... beautiful," I murmur breathlessly, eyelids heavy. The grip on my phone tightens as I slide my finger inside of me.

"Because you are," Sinnett is quick to say. He shifts on the bed and releases a deep groan that has my eyes nearly rolling in the back of my head. "You're so fucking beautiful it hurts me, Tate. Every time I look at you, I'm reminded of why I couldn't walk away. Of why I wanted to break the rules for *you*." He moans, head tipping back, throat arching. "And you bring out a side to me I didn't know existed. You opened my eyes to a world I thought was only black and white. And with you... all I see is colour. Big, bright fucking colours."

My back arches as the rhythm of my hand quickens, pushing me closer to the edge. I'm having a hard time processing Sinnett's words when my brain is a fuzzy messy and I can't see straight. But I do feel him—every inch. He might not physically be in the room with me, but his overwhelming presence is palpable as if he were watching from the corner of the room, his words spurring me on.

"I miss you," I squeeze out, throat tight as I continue to work myself closer to the edge. I'm barely hanging on by a thread. "I'd break every rule if it meant being yours."

"*Fuck*, Tate," Sinnett hisses, muscles ready to jump out of his skin as he strokes himself. "I need you to come for me. Close your eyes and pretend that it's my fingers fucking you."

"Only if you close your eyes and picture my mouth wrapped around your cock."

Sinnett groans in response, and I can't help but smile in victory.

Our moans mix together as we close our eyes, racing toward the edge. I feel his hands on me—touching and teasing my skin, and trailing his lips along my inner thighs. His fingers are intrusive as they enter me, filling me completely. I arch into his touch, desperate for more of him. Every flick, every thrust, every goddamn moan sweeps over me in a rush, and with a stifled cry, I'm freefalling, limbs shaking and head spinning.

Sinnett joins me, shouting my name as he rushes with me.

My eyes flutter open, my chest heaving for a breath it can't catch. I meet Sinnett's hooded ocean eyes, his chest slick with sweat and messy strands of hair covering his forehead. He grins at me and chuckles, deep and soulful, melting into my skin.

"Holy fuck, Tate," he drawls, a smirk touching his lips. "I never thought I'd see the day where a woman has the power to make me come on my stomach like a teenage boy."

I snort a laugh as feeling comes back to my body and I'm returned to Earth. "There is no way that's true."

"I'm being serious."

I raise a brow at him and push away the hair sticking to the side of my face, having fallen from the messy bun at my nape. "You are?"

Sinnett nods, tongue darting out to lick his bottom lip. "I've gotten myself off plenty of times before, but never over Facetime and certainly never with a specific person in mind. Until you."

Heat floods my cheeks and I'm helpless to fight the smile that splits across my face. "Well, I guess we're in the same boat then."

"That's what I like to hear." Sinnett shifts on the bed, reaching for something on the floor before settling back in position. "I'm also serious about having a lot on my mind."

The mood shifts from flirty to serious. Wanting to be the person Sinnett needs right now, I shift my focus to what could be stressing him out to the point he's awake at three in the morning. "Is everything okay?"

He shrugs as he reaches for something off-screen. A blush rises up my throat when a box of tissues appears. "Yes and no."

"Talk to me," I encourage, leaning back further into the mound of pillows. "I'm listening."

Sinnett exhales a sharp breath and shakes his head, as if trying to find the right words to speak what's on his mind. "I spoke with my dad about me getting cleared to play tomorrow —tonight."

"And how'd that go?"

"As well as you could imagine," Sinnett murmurs, running a hand through his hair. "No matter what I do out there, it's not going to be enough for him. Being out for six weeks has opened my eyes to the amount of pressure he was putting on me because he wasn't doing it anymore. And now I don't know if it's something I can handle again."

"Sin," I start, keeping my voice even. "You've got this, remember? Forget about your father and what he wants from you. Hell, forget about what my father is expecting of you and just go out there and be the best version of yourself for the team."

Sinnett's eyes meet mine, and my heart stutters in my chest. The stress behind them is evident, and I wish so badly I could take some of that pressure so it's less for him to hold on to. But I know it's not possible, so all I can do is remind him of what's important—himself.

"You're right," he murmurs, nodding slowly. "Sometimes I get so lost in my head that I forget I need to look after myself."

"Well, I'm always going to be right here whenever you need a reminder."

Sinnett smiles, bright and genuine. "How do you do it?"

The question catches me off guard. All I can do is blink. "Do what?"

"Stay so positive all of the time."

A smile touches my lips. "My mum. She was the most positive person I knew. I don't know how, but she could turn any negative into a positive by asking me to look on the bright side of things. If I didn't get a good grade in school, she would remind me that at least I got up, went to school and took the test. Even if it wasn't the mark I was expecting, I still put in the effort, and that's all that mattered."

I glance to the left at the framed photo of me and Mum at my year twelve graduation. She spent weeks searching for the perfect dress, and when she found it, she was so excited she couldn't stop talking about it for weeks. Black always looked stunning on her, making her orange hair pop and emerald eyes sparkle. No matter what room she walked into, Mum could demand attention from any person near without so much as lifting a finger or flashing her award-winning smile.

She had no idea of the devastating news she would receive a week late about her cancer diagnosis.

"No matter what I did, if a negative came from it, Mum was there to remind me of the positives. And, I don't know… I guess it has stuck with me through the years. It's easier to stay positive than get dragged down by the negatives, especially when you can't control it."

"You said *was*," Sinnett murmurs, breaking me from the memories resurfacing of my mum. "Is she…?"

I swallow around the lump forming in my throat and drop my gaze to the hem of my tank top. I wasn't planning on talking about my mum because it's not something that comes easy to me. But when I'm with Sinnett, the carefully constructed walls I had built two years ago come crashing down in an instant. It's as if my body and mind are eager to pull him closer, to reveal to him the deepest parts of me without my say so.

"She passed away two years ago from ovarian cancer." My voice is barely above a whisper, thick with grief. Tears spring to my eyes when images of her lying in the hospital bed the night she left us appear, replaying in my mind like a home movie, reminding me of everything I have lost. The one person who knew me better than anyone else. And suddenly, she was gone.

Sinnett hisses out a sharp breath and shoves his hand through his messy hair. "Shit, Tate. I'm sorry. I shouldn't have asked."

I shake my head, lifting my eyes to his. "You don't need to apologise. I don't mind talking about her, it's just—" I exhale a shaky breath and lift my shoulders in a half-hearted shrug. "I miss her a lot. And being here in Sydney without her reminds me of everything she missed out on when she had me. She never got to travel the world like she had always dreamed of, nor did she ever become a psychologist because she was too busy raising me. If she just had more time—"

Tears burst from my eyes, but I'm quick to wipe them

away, not wanting Sinnett to see me in this state. He has enough on his plate to deal with, he doesn't need me crying to top it off.

"Tate, you can talk about her," he says, voice a soothing chill to the fire licking at my side. Dark eyebrows raise, and I find myself tracing the shape of them with my eyes, noticing how they kink perfectly at the edges without a professional having to shape them. "If you find yourself wanting to tell me about her because she springs to mind, then do it. You have listened to enough of my shit over the past couple of weeks, so the least I can do is return the favour."

And now tears are forming for a different reason.

Sinnett doesn't need to be as kind and caring as he is. We're... whatever we are, which doesn't come with the burden of my fears and grief, but he's willing to let me bare it all to him and he'll *listen*. Granted, I do the same for him, which has me wondering if what we are is more than just a casual hook up. Now is not the right time to bring out that can of worms.

"I'm here, Tate," Sinnett says, voice firm with not a hint of hesitation. "Whatever you need from me, I'll gladly give it to you. I'm all yours."

I smile through the tears and nod. "And I'm all yours."

Sinnett grins. "That you are."

A wave of exhaustion rolls through me, our earlier activity finally catching up to me. Yawning, I stretch my arm above my head and settle back under the covers, the heat fuelling my body dissipating.

"Tired?" Sinnett questions.

I pull the doona up to my chin and nod, eyelids heavy. "Yeah, finally."

"Okay, I'll let you go—"

"Can you stay on the phone until I fall asleep?" I mumble,

sleep trickling up through my toes, threatening to consume me. "Please?"

A heartbeat of silence is followed by Sinnett's deep voice saying, "I'm not going anywhere, Tate. You're safe with me."

To his credit, I believe his words as I drift into a weightless slumber, fuelled with images of him and the memories we share.

Even as I'm falling into the darkness, my gut spikes with fear—a warning that something bad is coming my way. And I'm helpless to stop it.

Chapter Twenty-Four

SINNETT

I never thought I'd say this, but I've missed the media activities before a game. Game days are already hectic enough, so adding media interviews and pre-game segments when I still have to fit in a warm-up is overwhelming, to say the least. But having been out of the game for multiple weeks, I found myself hyped to talk with the different broadcast stations and answer questions about my injury and return. The outpouring of support I received from the reporters and fans online from the moment I woke up this morning was... a lot. In the best way possible.

Nervous energy pounds in my veins as I follow some of my teammates down the tunnel and onto the field, blinded by the stadium lights overhead and the murmur of voices from the crowd. I focus on warming up and practicing my goal kicks, considering it has been several weeks since it's been a top priority for me. But I find myself getting lost in the moment— taking in the faces of the fans watching from the fence around the field, calling my name and cheering for me. The collective boos from the Campbelltown Giants brings a smile to my face.

Fucking hell, I truly have missed this feeling.

Through the fog of adrenaline and the need to get back into my jersey, I feel her eyes on me. They're strong, like an electric current pouring through my veins, demanding my attention. And fuck, do I give it to her.

After kicking the ball through the goal posts, I spin to find Tatum standing on the sidelines with her arms folded over her chest, watching me. From the outside looking in, she's every bit the concerned physio checking on a client who is returning from an injury and needs to be monitored. But in my world—the one where it's just us—I know she's watching with pride, eager to see me in action.

Having her be here by my side, peppering me with encouragement and secret kisses in the hallway when no one is around, is all I need tonight. Not my family, my friends, or anyone in the club. Just Tatum.

She's all I need.

"God, you really are down bad for her, huh?"

I turn back to the goal post to find Khai watching me with a shit-eating grin. He tosses a ball into the air and catches it with ease when it drops into his hands. His hair is styled neatly with gel, but in thirty minutes, it's going to be slick with sweat and matted with blades of grass.

"Is it really that obvious?" I gesture for him to toss me the ball, which he does without hesitation. His eyes linger on me as I position the ball on the plastic holder. Once in place, I stand and take several steps back, focusing on where I want the ball to travel. Ideally, through the centre of the posts.

"Sin, if I can see it, everyone is this damn stadium can, too."

With a sharp exhale, I rush forward and punt the ball as hard as I can. I hold my breath as I watch it fly through the air, moving exactly where I wanted it to. Elliot, one of our centres, catches it with ease, tossing the ball to Finn to run drills with him.

I shove a hand through my hair and meet my best friends knowing gaze. "I don't know what I'm doing, man. Tate has me all fucked up in the head."

"In a good way?" Khai questions, raising a brow at me.

I nod. "Of course, in a good way. *Shit*. I don't know what the fuck I'm doing. When I'm not with her, I'm thinking about her. And when we are together, I'm thinking of ways I can keep her with me forever."

Khai bites back an amused grin. "Yeah, you're down so bad I can't pull you out. I have no choice but to let you drown in your craziness."

"I feel crazy," I admit, swallowing hard. "Crazy about her."

"And what do you plan to do about it?"

God, I wish I knew the answer to that question.

Being with Tatum is so easy and familiar that it terrifies me because I don't want to fuck this up. As much as I want to be all in with her, the stars haven't aligned for us. No matter what way you look at it, this, what we're doing now, is all we can ever be. As long as her father is standing in the way, and with our positions in the company reminding us of our places, being together in secret is our only reality. And I hate it.

I've broken every rule possible for this woman, and I would do it again in a heartbeat if the moments we share—however small—will continue to last for as long as time is willing to give us.

"I have no idea," I admit, voice tight. The lump forming in my throat makes it hard to breathe, but I manage to squeeze out, "There is nothing I can do, Khai. My hands are tied."

Khai flicks his eyes from me to where Tatum stands on the

sidelines, watching quietly. "Surely there is something you can do, Sin. It's clear you really like the girl, so why not just go for it?"

"Uh, because I don't want Coach Phil to bury me six feet under for breaking his rule of staying away from his daughter," I deadpan, as if I haven't laid awake for hours at a time over the past few weeks with the same thought on my mind. "No matter what way you look at it, if I choose Tatum, I could lose everything I worked so hard to achieve at this club. And if I choose the club, I lose the one person who has made me feel like... me again."

I worry my bottom lip between my teeth and roll my neck from side to side, hoping to ease the tension building in my shoulders. I've been in a constant state of stress, not knowing what I'm going to do moving forward. As of right now, everything has fallen into place, and I don't want that to change. But I'm not naive enough to know that the other shoe has to drop eventually, and I'm not sure I've prepared myself for when that time comes.

"You're in a fucking pickle, that's for sure." Khai rolls his tongue in his cheek, nodding slowly. "Okay, I guess all you can do is hope that Coach Phil doesn't find out about you and Tate, and until then, just enjoy the moment."

I nod, shoulders slumping forward. "Until everything comes crashing down."

With a sad smile, Khai claps my shoulder and guides me towards the tunnel. Kickoff starts in less than thirty minutes, and we have more training drills to go through in the sheds. For the first time in six weeks, I get to put the number seven jersey on. I've been looking forward to this moment since I hobbled off the field in round five, my quad in so much pain my vision was blurring at the edges. And now, six weeks later, I've reclaimed my position as halfback, and I'm ready to tear up the field.

My eyes find Tatum as we walk past, and she smiles so sweetly that I have to flex my hands at my side to keep from reaching for her. She's dressed in her usual work uniform of a polo shirt and black pants, but with the cool May air whipping around us, she has my leather jacket thrown over her shoulders—the same one I gave her the night I walked her home. I have no intention of asking for it back, not when it looks that good on her.

Needing to stay focused, I tear my eyes from Tatum and follow Khai down the tunnel. Young Wolves fans call our names as we go, and we stop to give them a quick wave before disappearing out of sight.

Before I can enter the sheds where the rest of the team are, I'm stopped by a hand on my chest and heated honey eyes. Her floral perfume is overwhelming to the point my eyes begin to water in the corners, but I blink it away.

Khai looks between me and Zoe, and I beg with my eyes for him not to leave me. He holds his hands up in defeat and retreats into the sheds, taking with him my only source of defence against this woman.

The audacity of him to fucking leave me when *he* is the cause for the wrath seeping out of Zoe's pores.

Here we fucking go.

"Why the hell did you block my number?" Zoe demands. Her hand slips from my chest, and she folds her arms, holding my gaze with such intensity that I resist the urge to shudder. She's dressed in the Wolves cheerleading outfit, ready to go for the pre-game performance. But, of course, she had to carve out some time in her schedule to chew my ass out.

Great.

"If you didn't text me every hour of the day when I've repeated multiple times that I'm no longer interested, then maybe it wouldn't have come to this, Zoe."

I'm not going to tell her this was Khai's doing. While I was pissed last night when he took it upon himself to block her number so I didn't have to deal with her persistent efforts to win me back, I've now realised that it was the right thing to do. I shouldn't enable her behaviour when I've made it clear where I stand with her. And if she's unwilling to take the hint, then it's no longer my problem.

Despite the makeup covering her face and neck, red splotches appear at the base of her throat and her jaw mashes together. The fire in her eyes is enough to make anyone drop dead, but not me. Zoe can intimidate her teammates and some of the other guys on the team, but I'm not one of them. I refuse to bow down to her every need just because she demands it.

"You've got a lot of nerve to try and push me away," she hisses, voice low. Staff members pass by, their attention focused on whatever task they're doing and not us. "I'm not letting this end, Sin. I don't care what you say. You're *mine*, and I'm going to make sure it stays that way."

Anger bubbles beneath my skin, and I clench my hands at my side to keep from lashing out at her. "You don't own me, Zoe. You never did. All we did was fuck when it was convenient for the both of us. There were no feelings involved and I certainly didn't want to be with you for longer than necessary."

Zoe gasps, her red painted lips forming an O.

My words might have been brutal, but they were necessary. If this is what she needs to hear to leave me alone, then so be it. I'll be the bad guy if I have to. If it means I can finally be rid of her.

"You didn't mean anything to me," I continue, voice dropping low enough that it can only be heard by us. "All you were was a momentary distraction. A quick fuck. And that's all you ever will be."

Zoe's features twist from shocked to downright fucking pissed in the blink of an eye. I don't see her hand before it connects with my cheek, but *fuck* does it follow through with a pain that explodes across my skin and seeps behind my eyes. The force isn't enough to turn my head, but the connection was loud enough that anyone in the vicinity would have heard it.

Yeah, I should've expected a reaction like that.

But I don't regret what I said. If the truth is enough to rid myself of a Zoe sized leech, then I'll take a hundred more slaps across the face until she's gone.

"You're a fucking asshole," Zoe hisses, voice dripping with lethal venom that could kill an adult. "And you're going to regret ever treating me this way."

I chuckle humorlessly. "I'd like to see you try, Zoe."

With a huff, she barges past me, her shoulder digging into my bicep as she storms down the tunnel.

The chatter of people passing by and the gradual volume of my teammates metres away sound in my mind like static. I fight the urge to rub at my cheek which I'm sure is no doubt red, a reminder of what just happened. Every muscle in my body is wound tight, and with the added stress of wanting to perform well tonight, I feel like I'm slowly sinking into the ground—the weight too much for me to bear.

I run my hand through my hair and release a sharp breath. Needing to get my head in the game, I make a move for the sheds, but I'm stopped when a vanilla and floral scent sweeps me up, holding me hostage.

Glancing over my shoulder, I find Tatum standing two

metres away, her round jade eyes moving to the red mark on my cheek.

Shit.

How much of the conversation with Zoe did she hear? More importantly, what did she see?

As if she can read my mind, she says, "What was that all about?"

I open my mouth, but the words get caught behind the lump in my throat. All I can do is watch as she steps forward, closing the space between us. Her small hand finds my left cheek, caressing the inflamed skin. Tatum's touch is gentle and comforting. I fight the urge to lean into it, knowing anyone— especially her father—could walk upon us.

"She got you good," she murmurs, eyes searching my face. "Are you okay?"

I nod. "I'm fine, Tate. It's nothing I can't handle."

"Was that your first time getting slapped across the face?"

A smile tilts the corner of my lips. "By a woman, yeah."

Tatum laughs, the sound defusing the shitstorm raging in my chest. "I'm not going to ask."

"What you saw..." I drag my hand through my hair and exhale a sharp breath. "What I said needed to be heard by her."

"It was harsh," Tatum admits quietly. "But I understand."

"I don't need another person trying to keep us apart," I tell her, voice barely above a whisper.

Tatum drags her bottom lip between her teeth and drops her hand to her side. I crave more of her touch, but now isn't the right time.

"Good luck out there, Sin," Tatum says, changing the topic, which I'm grateful for. "I'm proud of you."

Those four words do something to my heart that I don't understand. It's not something that can be measured with words or a specific emotion. They seep into my soul, wrapping around me like a tight hug. My body screams at me to kiss her, to thank her for everything she has done for me, but I can't—no matter how fucking badly I want to.

This woman is too much. And I love it.

"I'll see you after the game, strawberry."

Tatum grins. "I hope so."

Chapter Twenty-Five

TATUM

Watching Sinnett out on the field—taking hard tackles, guiding his teammates through the six tackle set and pushing for plays that saw them get try after try, and how powerful his legs are when he kicks for a try conversion—is like finding the brightest star in the sky on a clear summer's night. Sinnett was born to play rugby. It's obvious in the way he commands the field and does everything he can to support his teammates.

I understand now why he carries a lot of pressure on his shoulders. His teammates look to him for guidance out there, and Sinnett only has a split second to decide what the play is going to be and how best to get the ball over the try line. And without fail, he puts his body on the line to help the team succeed.

Throughout the first half, I was on the edge of my seat. His earlier confrontation with Zoe and getting slapped across the face melts into the background as I track his every movement. My lungs ached from me holding my breath each time he got the ball for a tackle or kicked a try conversion. While I was ecstatic to see him back in his safe space, I couldn't help but worry about his quad with each bump he took or whenever he kicked the ball. I've never felt stress and excitement wrapped in a tight ball quite like this.

Now, with five minutes left on the clock, the Wolves are ten metres out from their try line. The Giants are desperately fighting to keep them away, and with two tackles left before the ball is turned over, the Wolves might not get over the line. I shift forward on the plastic chair, fingers splayed over my mouth as I watch on with anticipation thrumming beneath my veins.

The score is 36-6 with the Wolves way in the lead. It's been a thrashing of a game, and despite the deflated Giants fans, the Wolves fans are still loud and crazy, cheering for their team every step of the way. I feel bad for the Giants, but it's still early in the season, and I guess tonight just isn't their night.

The fans behind me cheer for the Wolves, and when Sinnett receives the ball on the last tackle, they erupt into a flurry of excitement. They scream his name as he races toward the try line. I watch with my heart in my throat as he slips past two defenders and slides over the try line. My eardrums ring as the entire stadium cheers and the Wolves rush to celebrate with Sinnett.

I jump out of my chair and clap, my hands aching and lungs on fire as I join the fans in their cheering. Adrenaline pumps through my veins as I keep my focus on Sinnett. His smile is wide, teeth on display as he accepts hugs and pats on the shoulders from Khai and the rest of the team. Scoring a try like that is exactly what he needed after returning from an injury. He has put in the hard work for the past seventy-five minutes, so if anyone deserves this win, it's him.

Sinnett sets up for a try conversion on the sideline, just metres away from where I'm standing. One knee is bent while the other rests on the grass, his hands making quick work of adjusting the ball on the plastic stand. Turning his head to the right, his ocean eyes find mine. My breath hitches in my throat when he shoots me a wink and goes back to what he's doing.

My lips part in a silent O as I watch Sinnett stand and prepare to kick the ball, unfazed by how a simple gesture has my heart racing to the point I might have a heart attack. I wrap my arms around my waist, relishing in the woodsy cologne that lingers in the material of Sinnett's jacket. I wasn't going to wear it tonight because it doesn't quite match my work uniform, but I wanted to have a piece of him with me for his first game back.

Sinnett kicks the try conversion with ease and runs to the centre of the field to join the rest of the team.

Before I know it, the final whistle of the game sounds across the Brookvale stadium, and the fans cheer for the Wolves' massive 42-6 win over the Campbelltown Giants. It's a flurry of bodies moving past me—reporters, teammates, staff and the cheerleaders. But my eyes stay locked on Sinnett as he celebrates the win. I've never seen him this happy—all smiles and radiating a warmth that has me wanting to shrug off his jacket and get lost in his embrace instead.

Sinnett is right where he belongs, and I'm glad I was able to help him get back there.

I CLOSE MY EYES AND LEAN MY HEAD AGAINST THE cement wall beside the back exit to the stadium. The fans have long since cleared out, and the team has been busy with post-game interviews, celebrations in the sheds and cool down routines to keep their muscles from growing stiff after a gruelling game.

When Dad joined the team after the game, he couldn't stop smiling. Partly because he was beyond pleased with the results of the game and how the team played, but I think it also had to do with Sinnett's performance. I'm sure it brought him great pleasure to see his top star out there tearing up the field and on fire to the point where he was unstoppable. Dad has his side at full strength, which means he's gunning for the top spot on the leaderboard.

The cool air whips against my cheeks, chilling me to the bone despite being rugged up. Strands of hair from my high pony tail whip around my face, but I don't bother to contain them behind my ears, too lost in thought to care.

My eyes drift to the moon shining in the sky, casting a soft glow across the half-empty car park. Most of the staff and cheerleaders left not too long after the game. I didn't see Zoe afterwards, choosing to keep my distance after what I witnessed before the game. Sinnett hasn't told me much about their relationship, but judging by what I saw, it's clear that Zoe viewed it differently to him. He was only looking for a distraction, and she wanted something more. They're on opposite ends of the seesaw with no way of meeting in the middle.

While Sinnett's words were harsh, he didn't deserve to be slapped across the face. It's something Zoe needed to hear, no matter how badly she refused to listen to him.

"What are you doing out here?"

I tilt my head to the right, spotting Raya approaching with her gym bag slung over her shoulder. Her hair falls around her shoulders in bouncy curls, the only remnants left from her cheerleading persona. Gone is the heavy makeup and revealing outfit, replaced with grey trackies and an oversized black hoodie. The woman even has Ugg boots on, ready to get home and into bed.

"I needed a breather after the intensity of the night," I answer, tapping my thigh. My right foot is pressed against the wall, offering some support as I stare mindlessly at the gravel around my feet. "You know how it is."

"Yeah," she breathes, her shoulder brushing mine as she mirrors my position on the wall. "It was a good game, though."

"A great game," I agree, smiling. "Sinnett was amazing."

"It's why he's considered one of the best in the league," Raya supplies with a shrug. "No other halfback is doing it like him."

"Yeah," I murmur, remembering the smile he wore when he scored the last try of the game.

"I, uh... heard about the fight he got into with Zoe before the game."

I exhale a sharp breath, my good mood crashing down around me. "I saw it play out in real time."

"Zoe is always one to exaggerate stories."

"I don't know what she told you, but it was... rough." I clear my throat and shake my head. "Sinnett told her the truth and she couldn't bear to hear it, so she slapped him across the face."

Raya snickers. "She told the girls she slapped him because he called her a slut, but I know Sinnett and that's not something he would say to a woman. Unlike some men in this profession, he respects us."

I close my eyes and drop my head against the wall. "Either way, I'm hoping this is the end of it. I don't need the added pressure of Zoe lurking in the shadows when I'm already struggling to keep my father from finding out about us."

"How is that going, by the way?" Raya questions, her voice

holding no judgement. "The last you told me, everything was going great."

"It is going great," I murmur. "Better than great, actually."

Raya turns her body to me, leaning her shoulder against the wall. "Why do I get the feeling there's something you're not telling me."

I exhale a long breath and turn my eyes to meet hers. "I'm just scared."

"Of what?"

"Of losing him."

Raya clicks her tongue and nods. "That's a valid feeling to have, Tate. But you can't let the fear of things ending one day stop you from living in the moment. I know I initially told you not to go there with him, but I've seen how you two are with each other."

A lump forms in my throat. I try to swallow it down, but it's a persistent thing and won't budge. "I know, I just... This feels too good to be true, you know? We've been seeing each other in secret for three weeks and in that time, it feels like three months have passed. Being with Sinnett feels right, like it's where I'm meant to be."

"But...?" Raya presses.

"But I know it won't last," I whisper, voice tight. "Time has been against us from the very beginning, and we both knew that. And now I can't shake the feeling that the short time we were given is running out quicker than we realised. If Dad finds out about us... I'm not sure what'll happen."

Raya pushes off the wall and moves to stand in front of me. With her hands planted firmly on my shoulders, the moon casting off her stunning features in a soft, ambient glow, she holds my gaze.

"You listen to me," she says, voice steady. "Don't let the fear of the clock running down stop you from embracing this moment. If being with Sinnett is what makes you happy, don't worry about anyone else and just focus on him. I see the way he looks at you when he thinks no one is watching. That man thinks you are the light that brightens his world and leads him from the darkness. In my eyes, that's a man worth fighting for. And I know he would go to war for you if it came down to it." Raya pats my shoulder and drops her hands to her side, retrieving her gym bag from the ground. "It doesn't matter that you haven't known each other long. When the right person enters your life, you'll know it. And if that person is Sinnett, then take the hand you've been given and don't look back."

My lips part as I try to retain the inspirational words that fell from my friend's mouth. I didn't know she was capable of such profound words, given her tough exterior and reserved nature. Deep down, she must hold on to a lot of emotion she refuses to share with others. And for a brief moment, I got to see a glimpse of the real Raya.

"You're right," I murmur, my lips thinning into a tight-lipped smile. "Thank you. I needed to hear that."

Raya smiles. "As my friend, you get my good advice for free."

I snort a laugh and pull her in for a brief hug. "I don't know what I would do without you, Ray."

She pulls back and winks. "You'll never have to find out."

"Do you have any plans for the night?" I ask, needing a change in conversation. One that doesn't have my head spiralling.

"I'm video calling with my family," she murmurs, eyes darting away.

"You don't talk about them much." Her family is included as one of those emotions she doesn't talk about. "Where do they live?"

Her hands glide through the ends of her hair, tongue dragging over her full bottom lip. "Just this little town three hours north of Sydney. Barrenridge?"

My eyes nearly bulge from my head. "Barrenridge? No way! I was born there."

Raya's eyes widen, the skin between her brows creasing. "Seriously? What are the odds of that."

I'm reminded of Sinnett's connection to Barrenridge—the tiny town I thought no one outside of it's perimeter knew about—and I can't help but laugh. "More likely than I thought."

"Well, they moved to Barrenridge a couple of years ago, but I wanted to stay in Sydney to pursue dance and cheerleading." Raya shrugs. "They tend to keep to themselves, so I'm not sure if you would've seen them around."

I want to question Raya further about her family while the topic hangs in the air, but she drops her attention to her phone, checking the time.

"I better go," she murmurs, lifting her head to meet my gaze. "You all good?"

Disappointment tears through me, but I swallow it and smile. "Yeah, I'm all good. I'm waiting for Dad."

Raya's brows wiggle. "Or are you waiting for a certain halfback?"

I playfully roll my eyes. "I don't know what you're talking about. Now get out of here. I'll see you next week."

We bid farewell for the night with the promise of going out for brunch tomorrow since it's Sunday and neither of us have any plans. I'm in desperate need of some girl time with my friend, and to ask her about her family in Barrenridge. Having two guy friends all throughout high school was good because I always felt safe with Noah and Nathan, but as a girl, I craved the kind of friendship that comes from befriending women and talking about usual girly topics. Noah and Nathan did their best to provide me with that, but it wasn't the same. Now that I have Raya, I'm learning what it means to have a girl best friend, and it's been a fun experience thus far.

Footsteps approach from the side and I look up to find Sinnett smiling at me, his gym bag hanging by his side. Having ditched the grass-stained Wolves jersey and black shorts, he's looking freshly showered in loose black athletic shorts and the same black hoodie he wears every day. I'm convinced he has several of them in his wardrobe that he rotates through each day. I'll have to test the theory the next time I stay over. The hood is thrown up, covering his half-dried hair, the strands messy and slightly curling at the edges.

Sinnett looks every bit the stunning man I have grown to know over the past few weeks. And if he continues to look at me with hunger simmering in those ocean eyes, I won't be able to keep my hands to myself.

"Hi, Tate."

"Hi, Sin," I return his greeting with a smile.

Sinnett joins me on the wall, and we turn to face each other. His cinnamon and cedarwood cologne wraps around me and I fight the urge to step toward him, closing the already small space separating us. I drag my bottom lip between my teeth, meeting his intense eyes.

"Did you enjoy the game?" His voice is deep, vibrating my bones.

"You were amazing out there," I gush, unable to stop the words from tumbling out. "Seeing you score the try and kick all of those conversions—" I chuckle and shake my head. "That was embarrassing. I told myself I'd play it cool."

Sinnett laughs, the sound rich and airy. His hand comes up to rest on my cheek, his touch warm and inviting. "You're cute, strawberry."

"I'm being serious," I tell him, blinking slowly. "You were amazing, and I'm proud of you."

He smiles, the gesture warm and genuine. "If it wasn't for you, I wouldn't have been out there, so thank you."

"You did all of the hard work, not me," I remind him, mouth tilted in a half-smile. "But if you're dishing out credit..."

Sinnett chuckles. "Don't get ahead of yourself, Tate."

I drag my bottom lip between my teeth as warmth pools in my core. Having him this close has my body reacting in a way that is only catered to him. I crave his touch, his smile, his words that make me melt into a puddle at his feet. I want all of this man.

"I must say, the jersey was a look."

A smirk splits across Sinnett's face and he drops his hand from my face to shove into the front pocket of his hoodie. "It was?"

I nod. "You know, I've never owned a jersey for a sports team before."

Sinnett raises a brow at me. "You haven't?"

"Never," I say, shaking my head. "Maybe I need to get myself a Wolves jersey."

"If it doesn't have the number seven on it, then the fabric isn't touching your body, Tate," Sinnett all but growls, voice low.

I smirk and tilt my head to the side. "Is that so?"

Sinnett's hand darts out to grip my hip, pulling me flush against his chest. A giggle escapes my lips as my hands come up to press against his toned chest for support. His nose brushes against mine, his ocean eyes sparkling under the moonlight.

"I won't allow you to wear another man's jersey, Tate." His lips skim over mine, sending a jolt of electricity done my spine. "As my girl, you'll wear my number, no one else's."

My girl.

Liquid heat pools in my core as my heart slams against my chest. Seeing Sinnett show his possessive side has my body thrumming with adrenaline, the desire to get this man alone overwhelming. I hate that we have to keep whatever we are a secret, but it does allow us the space to nurture this growing affection for each other and see where it leads.

"And what are you going to do about it?"

Instead of answering, Sinnett slams his lips against mine, stealing the air from my lungs and the ability to think clearly. My hands loop around his neck, melting into the kiss as his claims me. I let him.

He drops the gym bag at his feet and his free hand comes up to cup the back of my neck, holding me firmly against his body as he deepens the kiss. Electricity sparks between us like a live wire, and for a moment, all I can think about is how perfect this feels. Having him against me, his warmth seeping into my skin, followed be the comforting scent I have grown to seek out in the crowd, and how easily my body responds to each swipe and nibble.

We were cursed from the beginning—orbiting each other's space, and never quite cementing ourselves in it.

Time can be a real bitch sometimes.

Sinnett pulls away breathlessly and drops his forehead against mine. "Get in my car, Tate. I'm going to show you exactly how, and you know I'm a man of my word."

Warmth explodes across my chest as a smile splits across my face.

He doesn't need to tell me twice.

Chapter Twenty-Six

TATUM

Khai isn't home when we stumble through the apartment door. Sinnett said his roommate went out for celebratory drinks with some of the guys from the team, leaving us with the spacious apartment for a couple of hours.

I texted my dad on the way over here and told him I was staying the night with Raya. His response came quick, telling me not to get into any trouble if we go out. The guilt lingers in the back of my mind. For not telling my father what I'm really doing, and for using Raya as a cover without asking. *Again.* With how little friends I have in Sydney, and zero reason to be going out at night, she is my only scapegoat when I need it. I should double check with her that it's okay I use her as a cover, but I don't think Dad would go out of his way to ask since he doesn't interact with the cheer squad. In fact, I don't think they would have a reason to talk *at all*, not when the cheer squad is managed by Liz, who works for the club itself and not necessarily the team. But still, I need to speak to Raya about it.

I wish I could tell Dad the truth about what I'm doing, and *who* I'm doing it with, so I no longer have to hide it from him, but I know the revelation wouldn't go down well with him. He has his mind set on the stupid no dating rule.

When the front door closes behind Sinnett, locking in place, I don't see much of the apartment before I'm flat on my back. The black doona cover is soft against my skin and smells of lavender. The colour scheme of Sinnett's room is dark and cosy, making it difficult to leave every night I've been here, when all I want to do is stay wrapped in his embrace and hide away.

I drag my bottom lip between my teeth and push myself up onto my elbows. Sinnett stalks across the room to the built in wardrobe with sliding glass mirrors. I've caught myself in those mirrors far too many times with wild hair and swollen lips. I would shy away at first, not wanting to see what I looked like after being thoroughly ravished by Sinnett, but I quickly realised that I felt power in that position. Beautiful, even. And now I don't look away when I catch my eye in the reflection, wanting to hold onto the moment for as long as I can.

Sinnett rifles through the dark clothes hanging in his wardrobe—not a single hoodie that isn't black catches my eye —the plastic coat hangers smacking against each other. A moment later, he tugs free a black, red and white jersey. He steps toward the bed, holding it up for me to see.

"Is that an old jersey?" I question, taking note of the worn material and slight change in club sponsor logos.

"It's last seasons jersey," Sinnett tells me, a shit-eating grin turning up his mouth. "Try it on."

My eyes round at his words, and I sit all the way up, tilting my head back to meet his gaze. "You want me to *what*?"

"Put it on, strawberry." Sinnett extends the jersey to me, eyes never leaving mine. "I wasn't kidding when I said you'll wear no other jersey but mine."

I thought he meant just his number in general, not a jersey he wore from last season.

"I-I—seriously?" I swallow hard and accept the shirt, the material smooth in the palm of my hand.

"I'm dead serious. Now stand up."

Doing as I'm told, I stand, my nose barely reaching his chest. Sinnett's hands make quick work of discarding his leather jacket from my shoulders, followed by my polo shirt and pants. All I can do is stare at him, and he's grinning like he's just won the lottery.

Ocean eyes skim over the emerald-green lacy lingerie set I threw on when I was getting ready for work earlier. I had no intention of showing it to Sinnett because we hadn't planned to sneak away after the game. In fact, all of my comfortable underwear was in the basket in the corner of the room, laughing at me when I realised I had forgotten to do my laundry. *Again.* But judging by how Sinnett's pupils dilate and his breath hitches, I know I made the right choice wearing it.

"It's a damn shame I'm going to cover you up," he grunts breathlessly. "But it'll be worth it."

He gestures for me to lift my arms, and when I do, he shimmies the smooth material down my arms. The jersey isn't overly large given how tight-fitted it is to his body, but it's roomy and falls mid-thigh.

Sinnett steps back, his eyes skimming down the length of my body. The heated look in his irises sets my heart into overdrive and my palms grow clammy. The material smells like him and I'm picturing all the times he wore it, running the length of the field, getting lost under bodies during tackles, and sliding over the try line.

Oh, my God.

Did it suddenly get hot in here?

Tongue darting out to lick his bottom lip, Sinnett steps

forward, large hands finding my hips like they've done so many times before. It's like muscle memory.

"I have pictured you in my jersey many times when trying to fall asleep at night, but never did I think you would look this good wearing my number."

My hands find his shoulders, needing to feel his warmth and the confidence he gives me every time we're together. I smile, feeling sexy and desired under his intense gaze. Electricity thrums in my veins, and anticipation pounds in my core, eyes dropping to his full lips.

"I only have space in my heart for number seven." Leaning on my toes, my lips brush against his, sending a shiver across his lean and toned body. "And it's yours for the taking."

That is all the encouragement needed for Sinnett to claim my mouth, taking everything I have to offer him. It's not enough for me to lay my heart on a silver platter for him to take. I want him to feel when it beats for him. I want him to hear when it calls for him. I want him to know that as long as he's willing to protect it with his life and not trample all over it, my heart is his for the keeping.

Our lips move feverishly together, sending my mind into a delirious state as I fight to keep from melting under his touch. My legs hit the edge of the mattress, and Sinnett's body sinks with mine as we sprawl across the king-sized bed. Sinnett slides his hands over my stomach as his body hovers over mine. Every touch, every lick, every nibble fuels the fire raging in my core, making me more desperate to feel him.

"Sin," I whimper against his lips, lungs begging for air.

"Tell me what you want, Tate," Sinnett squeezes out, his minty breath fanning over my lips.

"All of you," I whisper, getting lost in his eyes as they hold me captive. My fingers trace the curve of his jaw, needing to feel more of him. To somehow be closer than I already am.

The glow from the bedside tables cast a soft hue across his sharp features, brightening the slight stubble on his jawline and the scar in his eyebrow. Even in dim lighting, he is the most handsome man I have ever seen. I could get lost in his eyes for hours and never be bored. I'll never tire of tracing every line and curve of his tattoos, like I have done many times already when we've been lying in bed, embracing the moment where it's just the two of us.

"You already have all of me, Tate," Sinnett murmurs, his grip on my waist tightening. "Every last breath in my lungs is yours. So take it."

Our lips meet and it's like an explosion of fireworks has been set off in my chest. My hands thread through his hair as his hands roam over my body. Lips moving in sync, we explore each other's body, taking what we need and searching for what we don't have. A moan sounds in the back of my throat as Sinnett dips his hand beneath my panties and finds my soaked core.

My back arches when he presses into me, and all I can say is I'm grateful Khai isn't home right now, because he would hear every moan that Sinnett effortlessly pulls from me. His skilful fingers pump in and out of me, and I'm helpless to do anything but kiss him back with just as much fervour, and try not to come too soon.

Needing more, I slide my hands to his shoulders and shove at him until he's on his back. Dark ocean eyes track my movement as I crawl up the length of his body and straddle his waist with my bare thighs. His hands clamp down my thighs at the same time my hands find his chest, leaning forward with a smirk.

"What are you doing, Tate?"

"Taking all of you," I answer, voice even. Keeping my eyes locked on him, I reach down to where his cock strains against the material of his shorts, begging to be freed. I palm the bulge, relishing in the wide-eyed reaction from the man below me.

Sinnett groans and sits up, chest brushing against mine. He reaches for the hem of his hoodie and rips it over his head, leaving him bare and at my disposal. My eyes trail over the ridges of his muscles and the smooth skin only I get the pleasure of exploring.

"Can I colour in your tattoos?"

Sinnett bites back a smile. "Is that what you want?"

I nod, smiling.

"Then of course you can," he says, running a hand through his hair. "I'm sure Khai has some coloured markers lying around in his pigsty of a room."

I grin and trail my fingers down the side of his torso, watching as goosebumps follow in their wake. Sinnett's eyes burn into mine as I tease the waistband of his shorts. I bite my lip to keep from smiling as I reach beneath the material and grip his cock. Within seconds, it's standing hot and thick between us with my hand wrapped around the base.

"Take the lead," Sinnett squeezes out. "I'm at your mercy, strawberry."

"I like the sound of that," I muse with a smile.

"But at no point does the jersey come off," he warns, voice low.

I grin. "Yes, Sin."

Sinnett groans in response, hands finding my thighs as I pump my hand up and down his length, eyes never straying from his. My core is on fire and my panties are soaked through, but it doesn't deter me from pleasuring Sinnett, hanging on every moan and grunt of my name.

When I can't take it any longer, I push onto my knees and guide the head of his cock to my entrance. My heart slams into my throat as I take all of him—slow and with a patience I'm barely holding on to. We share a hiss at the connection, and I breathe through the intrusion of his size. I don't think I'll ever get use to how big he is, but I'm not complaining. Not when he's looking at me the way he is—like he could devour me.

"Move, Tate," Sinnett grunts, hands reaching for my hips.

Managing a nod, I find leverage on his chest and rock my hips forward. My head tips back as heat simmers beneath my skin and pleasure floods my veins. Sinnett uses his hold on my hips to guide me up and down, setting a pace that has my eyes rolling into the back of my head and my heart thundering in my chest.

"That's it," Sinnett squeezes out, voice tight like the muscles in his biceps as he guides me down his shaft. "*Fuck* you look so good in my jersey. Wearing *my* number. Crying out *my* name."

As if to prove his point, his name tumbles from my lips in a breathy moan, and he grins, the sight melting my already liquid insides.

Sinnett's jaw clenches as he slams his hips up to meet mine. "I want to hear you. It's just me and you, baby. Cry for me."

My vision blurs at the edges, and the breath is knocked from my lungs. Taking him at this angle has him filling every inch of me. It feels like too much but not enough at the same time.

"Sin," I moan breathlessly, struggling to find a word in the English language to say, and coming up short.

"Ride my cock, Tate," Sinnett demands. His right hand comes up to fist the bottom of the jersey, balling the material in his hand. He uses it as leverage to keep my pace from faltering. "You wanted all of me, so *take it*."

Doing as I'm told, I use his chest as support and rock my hips forward. A light sheen of sweat has broken out across my skin, but I don't let it deter me. Sinnett slams his hips upward to meet my thrusts, and we fall into a flurry of breathless moans and fondling hands.

My core clenches as I rush toward the edge, eager to find a release. If I don't, I might just lose my damn mind. Heat spreads through my chest, seeping into my veins and dipping to the edge of my core, and I'm fighting the urge to stop, to give myself a break in fear of my muscles cramping. But I'm so close. So damn close.

Sinnett surprises me by swiping his thumb over my clit, sending a bolt of electricity across my body. A moan rips through my chest, my pulse thumping at the base of my throat.

"Come on *your* cock, Tate," Sinnett demands, voice raspy. His rhythm doesn't falter as he continues to meet my thrust, the hair falling in his eyes not a bother to him. "Take all of me because it's always been yours. *I'm* yours."

That's all it takes for me to freefall over the edge, muscles tensing and my back arching. Sinnett's thumb traces my clit as my hips still, but it doesn't stop him from falling with me. My limbs feel numb and my head light as the after-effects of the orgasm wash over me.

With a sigh, I slump against Sinnett's chest, his cock still inside of me.

He smooths down the flyaway hairs around my face and presses a kiss to the top of my head. His smooth skin is slick with sweat, but I couldn't care less. My focus is on the rhythm of his heartbeat returning to normal, falling in sync with mine, and the comfort his touch brings me.

"I meant what I said, Tate," Sinnett murmurs above me, stroking my hair. "I'm all yours."

I manage a smile, blinking through the haze obstructing my vision. My heart slams against my ribcage, realising the depths of his words. This is becoming more than just a casual hook-up to him. He wants more. And I'll be the first to admit that I'm on the same page.

But our situation is far from normal. One wrong move and this could all blow up in our faces.

Is that something we're willing to risk?

Despite these fears, it doesn't deter me from lifting my head and locking eyes with icy blue ones that make me feel like I'm lost at sea. I smile, unable to hide the giddiness overcoming me. Sensing my excitement, Sinnett returns my smile and cups my cheeks, his palms warm and comforting.

"And I'm all yours, Sin."

Chapter Twenty-Seven

SINNETT

It's been a long ass fucking day. Getting back into my regular training schedule for the week has been difficult, to say the least. I knew it wouldn't be easy, and both Coach Phil and Todd warned me as much, but my ego was determined to not let it faze me.

Oh, how I was wrong. So fucking wrong.

Muscles I didn't know existed in my body ache with each step, and my legs don't feel attached to my torso. The heaviness dragging down my limbs is the equivalent of having cement poured into my veins, making it difficult to move. If it weren't for the rigorous stretching and cool-down exercises I have to do after each session, I would be as stiff as cardboard.

Despite how exhausted and drained my body feels, I wouldn't want to be doing anything else with my time. I have lived and breathed rugby for as long as I can remember. There hasn't been a time when a ball wasn't in my hands or I haven't been lacing up my boots. The sport is all I have ever wanted to do, and now that I've made it a reality, I never want it to end.

"Are you sure you don't want to go out tonight?" Khai asks

from behind me, rubbing a towel over his freshly washed hair. The Lynx deodorant he has been using since we were twelve years old wafts around my head.

"Do you really think it's a good idea to go out before the game tomorrow?" I turn away from my open locker space in the change room to face my best friend, his usual goofy smile locked in place.

He shrugs and wraps the towel around his neck. "It's never stopped me before."

"I swear to God, if you're hungover on the bus down to Wollongong tomorrow, I'll be pissed."

Khai waves me off with his hand. "I'm not going to be a drunken fool tonight, don't worry. Two drinks max."

"You've said that every other time you've gone out the night before a game. Two drinks turn into five," I deadpan. "How you're not dead on the field, I'll never know."

Khai grins and flexes his biceps. "I'm just that fucking good, Sin. I can handle my alcohol, unlike some of us."

Nico walks past with his gym bag slung over his shoulder, and when he catches Khai watching him, he stops mid-stride, a confused expression slipping over his features.

"What's going on?" he asks, eyes flicking between me and Khai.

"Khai said you can't handle your drink," I offer, biting back a smile. "And for once, I have to agree with him. Although, I don't think he's any better."

"Hey!" Khai and Nico protest at the same time, snapping their eyes to me. I roll my eyes and turn back to my locker. Clothes litter the small space, along with my water bottle and shaker cup with creatine in it. Needing to busy myself, I begin shoving everything in my gym bag while Nico and Khai bicker behind me about where they should go for drinks.

With everything packed away, I pull my phone from the

pocket of the athletic shorts I threw on after freshening-up in the shower, my fingers hovering over the text conversation with Tatum.

It's been hard seeing her around this past week during training but not having the opportunity to get her alone. When we had multiple sessions together throughout the week, it made it easy to steal precious moments with her. In those times, we didn't fear anyone catching us because everyone on the staff team, the coaches and the players knew I was booked in with her. But now that I'm back to my regular training schedule, I only see her when necessary.

God, is it fucking hard.

Whenever I'm not with her, I'm thinking about her. And when we are together, I'm still thinking about her. No matter what I'm doing, Tatum is on my mind, having carved out a space reserved only for her.

We've both been busy this week, so we haven't had a chance to go for our late-night drive. But that changes today.

SIN: Are you free right now?

STRAWBERRY: I'm getting ready to leave for the day. Is everything okay?

SIN: It will be once I see you. Care to go for a drive?

STRAWBERRY: Right now?

SIN: Right now.

STRAWBERRY: Let me get changed first. You've seen me in my work uniform far too many times.

> SIN: I happen to like the sexy polo look on you.

> STRAWBERRY: If that's the case, then maybe it's the next shirt we try out.

I drag my bottom lip between my teeth, biting back a grin. I hadn't intended on fucking her while she wore my jersey last weekend, but when she said she's never worn a jersey for a sports team before, I couldn't help myself. Besides, she looked fucking beautiful wearing my number. And I *will* make sure it's the only number she ever wears from now on.

> SIN: Is it bad that I'm already thinking about you bent over the edge of my bed in nothing but said polo shirt?

> STRAWBERRY: Not at all, stud. I'm thinking the same thing.

> SIN: Too much, Tate. You're too much.

> STRAWBERRY: See you at your car in ten, stud ;)

My tongue rolls in my cheek as I slip my phone into my pocket. Glancing over my shoulder, I zone in on Nico and Khai still discussing where they should go for drinks, as if they're not flushed with options—North Sydney has an array of bars they can go to. I have no doubt Khai will be on the prowl for someone to fulfil his jinx before the game tomorrow.

"What about The Scary Canary?" Khai asks, folding his arms over his chest. "The music is always banging and the drinks flow like a fountain."

"Can't we go someplace closer to home?" Nico whines,

hands gripping the edges of the towel slung around his neck. "We have to be back here early to jump on the team bus, so the last thing I want to do tonight is go all the way into the city."

"But the bars and clubs in the CBD are way better than what we have here," Khai tries to reason. "Please, Nico? I'll owe you one."

Nico's gaze sweeps to me as if looking for advice on what he should do, especially with Khai giving him puppy eyes like a fucking three-year-old. I simply shrug, not wanting to get involved in whatever it is their plans are.

Seeing no way out of this, Nico relents with a groan. "*Fine, we can go to The Scary Canary. But we need to leave no later than midnight, okay?*"

Khai throws his arms around Nico's neck and forces him to bounce on the spot with him. "You're the best!"

I chuckle and pat Khai on the shoulder as I pass by. "Well, you two have fun tonight. And don't wake me up when you come stumbling through the front door, okay?"

Khai wraps his arm around Nico's neck, pressing his side against him. "My lovely friend here will make sure I get into bed safely. Isn't that right?"

Nico playfully rolls his eyes. "Yeah, I will."

"Well don't get too fucked up," I remind them both with a pointed look. "Axel would normally be the one to tell you this, as our captain, but since he's already gone home for the day, I guess the duty falls to me. We need to keep our heads, and Illawarra Sharks are sitting just below us on the table, so it's going to be a tough game."

"We've got this, Sin," Khai says with confidence. *A confidence I don't have myself.* "With you back on the field, we're going straight to the finals."

My lips part, ready to tell him that I can't be the only one to carry the team, but then decide not to. I've carried the weight of expectation since joining the main roster, and while it can be hard at times to shoulder it, I don't mind doing it if it means my teammates are filled with a confidence I don't possess. The confidence they have in me is overwhelming, and I'm fucking terrified of letting them down, but if it helps them to know I have their backs heading into game day, then I don't mind carrying that burden.

"Let's hope so," I murmur, dropping my hand to my side. "Be safe tonight."

"You, too," Khai says, wiggling his brows. "Don't think for a second that I'm not aware of who you're going to meet up with."

"How did you—"

Khai taps his temple, a grin splitting across his face. "I just know."

"How is that going, by the way?" Nico flicks his eyes to me. "You and Tatum."

I hadn't intended for Nico and Zane to find out about Tatum—well, more than what Khai had already told them over drinks that one time—but if there is anyone I can trust on this team to keep our secret, it's those guys.

"Good," I tell him with a nod. "Better than good, actually."

Nico pumps his brows at me. "Do you like her?"

Khai grins and slings his arm around Nico's shoulders. "I think our Sinny boy has the fattest crush known to mankind."

I playfully roll my eyes and head toward the exit, refusing to play into their antics, and because I don't know how to answer Nico's question. "I'll see you guys later."

Khai and Nico call out their goodbyes to me as I walk through the change room and out into the hallway of the training facility. My legs drag with each step to my car, but somehow, I feel light and buzz with electricity. The grip on my gym bag tightens as I step out into the car park, my eyes landing on a head of strawberry-blonde hair leaning against my car.

My breath hitches as my legs falter, taking in her ethereal beauty.

Fucking hell. It's like finding rays of sunshine on the darkest of days.

Before I met Tatum, I saw the world through a black and white lens, believing I needed structure and drive to achieve my goals. And now, she has lit my world up with colours I didn't know existed, and taught me that if I want something bad enough, all I have to do is believe in myself. Tatum has shifted my way of viewing life and my career in such a short amount of time that it scares me at times, but deep down, I know it's something I needed, especially after my injury.

I clear my throat and continue towards her, never taking my eyes off her face. As promised, she changed out of her work uniform into a pair of black jeans, a white graphic T-shirt tucked into the waistband and my leather jacket. Heat spreads across my chest, knowing she's walking around wearing *my* clothes and everyone is none the wiser.

"How was training?" Tatum asks, shoving the tote bag on her shoulder higher.

I fight the urge to pull her into my arms and kiss her. No one is in the car park, so I might get away with it, but I need to keep my head and be careful. To anyone else, this interaction can be viewed as me dropping Tatum home because her car is still getting fixed. Turns out, there is a lot fucking wrong with it, but my mechanic is adamant that she can pick it up tomorrow morning before the game.

I flash her a smile as I walk around to the driver's side. My eyes stay locked on her as I pull open the back door and toss the gym bag onto the seat. "Hard. I don't think my body has been in this much pain before."

Tatum tosses out a laugh as she slides into the passenger seat. I follow suit.

"You've been out for six weeks, so it'll take some time to get used to the rigorous training again." She clicks her seat belt into place and watches me as I do the same. "But you're okay?"

The engine roars to life and I put the car into reverse, needing to get Tatum as far away from this place as possible so we can be alone. My grip tightens around the steering wheel as I lean into the leather seat. Tatum's floral perfume consumes the small space between us, and I fucking love it. If I could die with her scent being the last thing I ever smelled, I would be a happy man.

My hand instinctively glides over my right thigh as I respond, "I'm okay. My thigh felt a bit tight today, but I'll have Todd wrap it well before the game." I toss my gaze to her and grin. "Why? Are you worried about me, strawberry?"

"I'm always worried about you," she says without hesitation. Her hand glides over the centre console to rest on my left thigh. My heart explodes in my fucking chest at the simple touch. "Be careful out there tomorrow, okay?"

My hand drops from the steering wheel to cover hers, the touch warm and electric. "I'm always careful, Tate."

Sliding my fingers through hers, Tatum tells me about her day. Our winger, Jaxon, has been struggling with his hamstring the past week, so Tatum had an extensive session with him to see what the issue was. After talking with Ian, they've decided to keep him from playing tomorrow, which means our wing isn't going to be as strong as it normally is with one of the reserves stepping up to the plate. Jaxon is amazing at what he does, so it'll be some big shoes to fill.

By the time we reach Edwards Beach, the sun is starting to

set on the horizon. Hues of pink, orange and yellow swirl among the thin clouds, creating a marbled look that has me dazed for a moment.

"What a stunning view," Tatum murmurs beside me, equally mesmerised.

I turn my head to the left, eyes locking on the curve of her jaw and the way her hair falls around her shoulders in soft waves. Her mouth is tilted in a half smile, jade eyes sparking as they admire the view.

My heart hammers in my chest. "Yeah, it is."

After a long moment, Tatum slips her hand from mine and reaches for her phone. "So, what playlist should I put on today? Are you feeling a more grungy vibe or something gentle?"

"I was thinking we could sit on the beach and watch the sunset," I say, reaching into my pocket. Tatum eyes the headphones in the palm of my hands, the cord no longer white but grey with age. "And, of course, listen to music."

Tatum grins and leans across the console, nose brushing against mine. "Sinnett Baxter, are you suggesting we do something other than sit in your car?"

I playfully roll my eyes and reach for the handle on the door. "Only if you're up for it, strawberry."

"As long as I'm with you, I don't care what we do."

My heart lodges itself in my throat. I step out of the car and try to clear it with a cough, hoping Tatum won't notice. Thankfully, the late afternoon air whipping around us muffles the sound. A few cars are parked in the lot overlooking the beach with only a handful of surfers bobbing in the waves, hoping to catch a decent one. With it being early June, the weather is far too cold to walk dogs or meet up with friends. Which makes it the perfect scenario for us.

Tatum's shoulder brushes against my arm as we walk to the

water, shoes in hand and toes sinking into the sand. The wind whips at my face and exposed legs, making me grateful for the hoodie I threw on after getting out of the shower. My hand itches at my side, wanting to take Tatum's hand in mine, needing her warmth. Instead, my thumb twists the silver ring on my forefinger.

I survey the length of the beach, and upon spotting an elderly woman walking her small dog along the water and surfers heading into the waves, I think *fuck it*. My fingers slide through Tatum's, and her eyes snap to the side of my face. Not wanting her to stress about my very public action, I look ahead and relish in the warmth her skin spreads up my arm and across my body.

We settle onto the sand and I shove my feet through the tiny grains, hoping to find some warmth for my toes. Without saying a word, Tatum slides her hand from my grasp and reaches for the headphones in my palm. I watch as she slips one of the earphones into her ear and offers the other to me, all while flicking through her playlists.

Tatum clicks play on a song, leans against my side with her cheek resting on her shoulder, and slides her fingers through mine again. The opening notes of "Stop And Stare" by OneRepublic blasts into my ear, and I exhale a sigh of relief.

This is what I needed after a long week of being exhausted. I was in desperate need of some sort of release; not the sexual kind like I would chase in the past with Zoe and random women I would meet out at bars. Being here with Tatum, feeling her calming presence and getting lost in music... Yeah, it's exactly what I needed.

I like that we can go from talking about the most random things about ourselves or topics we find interesting, to sitting in silence. It's the kind of silence that never feels uncomfortable, but can last an eternity and yet, even then,

I'll still crave more because it's with the right person. Tatum has this unique ability to reach into my soul and see me for who I truly am. Not the halfback rugby player, but a guy who is still figuring out life and what he wants. Instead of forcing me down the path my parents desperately want me to take, she has opened my eyes to the endless paths that have always been there but were shrouded in darkness. The paths that I was too blinded by what my father wanted for me to see.

This newfound sense of freedom within myself has been eye-opening. If it wasn't for the woman sitting beside me, hand wrapped in mine while the other taps against my bicep to the rhythm of the song playing in our ears, I would still be the lost guy she met at the Barrenridge Pub.

The song ends, making way for another upbeat one I haven't heard before. I listen intently to the lyrics, nodding my head to the simple beat.

"You like this one?" Tatum asks, tilting her head up to look at me.

I nod. "What's it called?"

"'Kiss Me' by Olly Murs."

Another one to add to the list.

I grin. "Another song called 'Kiss Me'. If I didn't know any better, I would say you're trying to send me a message, strawberry."

Heat floods her cheeks, mixing with the light pink hue caused by the cool air lashing at us. "I don't know what you're talking about."

Unable to wipe the shit-eating grin off my face, I jump to my feet, not carrying that the earphone rips from my ear with the movement. Tatum squeals when I bend at the waist and hoist her onto my shoulder, spinning her with ease. Her giggles catch the air flowing past us, drifting away while her hands find my back, trying to hold on for dear life as I race down to the water.

"Sin!" she squeals, followed by a giggle. "Put me down!"

"I happen to like you at this angle," I respond, chuckling. My arm tightens around the back of her legs while my other hand comes down on her ass. "Yeah, I'm never putting you down."

"Sinnett!"

Laughing like a hyena, I stop short of the water and lower Tatum to her feet. Our eyes lock, sparks catching. My chest heaves as I get lost in her beauty, wishing we could stay in this moment forever. Her hands slide around my neck, bringing our bodies closer. The grip I have on her waist is the only thing keeping me afloat right now, my self-control slipping away rapidly.

"I made you something." My voice is barely above a whisper, the words getting caught on the wind.

Her eyes round at the edges. "You did?"

I nod. "A playlist of all the songs that remind me of you. Of us."

Tatum blinks at me, her lips parted. "When did you do this?"

"I've been building it since the night I dropped you home when your car wouldn't start." I swallow around the lump forming in my throat and drop my head so our noses brush lightly. "You made me a playlist, so it's only fair I return the favour."

"Sin," she breathes. "That's so kind of you."

"Listen to it tonight, okay? When you get home."

Tatum nods, strands of hair whipping around her face. "I will."

Despite the adrenaline and nerves mixing throughout my body, I grin and press my lips against hers. With the sun setting low in the sky and the beach deserted, all of my self-control flies out of the window.

Tatum responds in kind, pushing onto her toes and deepening the kiss.

If we weren't in public, I would stay like this until the sun is replaced by the moon and the air grows too cold for us to stay out here. Instead, I break the kiss and lift her in the air, spinning until I grow dizzy. Her hair flies through the air, followed by her sweet laughter.

It's at this moment I realise that what we're doing is far deeper than casually hooking up. The thought of having to give her up when the time comes physically pains me, my chest squeezing uncomfortably.

At the end of the day, can I have both my career and the one girl forced to stay out of reach?

Chapter Twenty-Eight

TATUM

The Illawarra Sharks' home ground in Wollongong is stunning. Not only are the facilities nicer than some of the stadiums I've visited, but it's located one hundred metres from the beach, bringing with it salty sea air and a cool breeze. I can only imagine what the sunsets are like when watching an afternoon game.

Standing on the sidelines, watching as some of the Wolves players run onto the field, including Sinnett, I gaze at the blue sky, mirroring the ones watching me from the goal post. I wrap my arms around my waist, fighting off the cool breeze whipping around me. Sinnett's leather jacket is now my go-to source for warmth. It still smells like his woodsy cologne, and I refuse to wash it, not wanting to be rid of the last remnants of him.

My gaze shifts to Sinnett as he practices goal kicks, followed by some warm-up drills. Around me, the grandstand is starting to fill as we close in on the kickoff time, and the large hill is packed with not a spare patch of grass in sight. The colours are a good mix of red and black, and blue and white. With this being an away game for the Wolves, I'm pleased so many fans chose to make the trip down the coast to support them.

I was beyond relieved when Sinnett's mechanic called me yesterday to say my car was ready to be picked up. It has been in the shop for weeks now, and I was convinced it was a lost cause with too many things wrong with it. So imagine my surprise when I drove it down here without a single hiccup and an engine that purred. Well, I could only just hear it over Noah and Nathan's voice through the dodgy Bluetooth connector I had installed in the car before I left Barrenridge. I was gobsmacked, and still don't know how I should thank Sinnett for taking care of it for me. I was ready to get a new car, but now I won't need to, thanks to him.

A smile turns up my mouth as I lock eyes with Sinnett, who flashes me an award-winning smile before returning to his training. I don't know how I got so lucky with this man. Not only is he kind, sweet, and a freak between the sheets, but he brings me that sense of comfort I've been craving. He made a goddamn *playlist* for me of songs that remind him of me, for God sake. I'm convinced he's not real but someone I conjured up from a dream.

When he dropped me home last night, he sent me the playlist and told me to listen to it when I got inside. I was ready to do so, but I got caught up with talking to Dad in the kitchen about our day, and by the time I had a shower and crawled into bed, I passed out without responding to Sinnett's 'goodnight' text. Then, following a catch up call with my best friends once I left the mechanics, I haven't been left with much time to listen to it. When I get home after the game, the first thing I'm going to do is put the playlist on and get lost in whatever songs he put in there for hours.

I still can't believe he made *me* a playlist.

Sinnett follows his teammates off the field after wrapping

the warm-up. He changes course and runs up to me, a smile lingering on his lips. My eyes widen as my heart slams into my ribcage.

What is he doing?

"Hi, Tate."

"Hi, Sin," I greet quietly, looking around at the endless bodies lingering on the sideline. They're mostly staff members or punters for sports news stations. "Is everything okay?"

I force my eyes to stay on his face and not roam over the tight training jersey clinging to his biceps and toned abdomen, or the black shorts shaping his thick, muscular thighs.

"I just wanted to see you before the game," Sinnett says, tossing the football between his hands with ease. "You're my good luck charm, strawberry."

Heat shoots across my cheeks. "I am?"

He nods. "I'd like to think so. You did get me back on the field, after all."

"That was all you," I remind him with a smile.

"Either way, I like having you on the sideline. You keep me going, Tate."

My heart squeezes, making it difficult for air to travel from my lungs to my nose. How can those simple words be my undoing? Hearing him say I'm the reason he pushes through each day has my head spinning and my heart threatening to burst from my chest.

"I do?" I squeeze out.

Sinnett nods, tilting his head to the side with a smile. "You have since you walked into my life."

I open my mouth to respond, but the sharp voice of my father has me slamming my mouth close. His shoulders are tense and his face thunderous as he storms down the tunnel in our direction. I didn't get a chance to see him this morning because he left early to catch the team bus with the players and I had to pick up my car. Why he's this angry has me confused.

"Is everything okay?" I ask when he reaches us, voice wavering.

Dad looks between me and Sinnett, eyes hard, and gestures over his shoulder with his thumb. "You two, follow me. Now."

Now my heart is beating for a different reason.

Sinnett and I share a confused look when Dad turns his back on us and walks back down the tunnel, stomping as he goes.

"What the hell is going on?" I whisper, worrying my lip between my teeth.

"I don't know," Sinnett responds, voice deep. "But judging by the look on his face, it can't be good."

Tense silence settles over us as we follow my father into an empty room filled with training equipment, offering a level of privacy for whatever conversation is going to take place. What feels like a hundred different scenarios swarm my mind, but I'm unable to focus on a single one.

Dad closes the door behind him, folding his arms over his chest. He looks between Sinnett and me, standing a few metres away from each other, confused as hell.

"What's going on, Dad?" I ask, voice trembling. "Is everything okay?"

"You want to know what's going on, Tatum?" Dad hisses, his words lashing at me like a physical assault. Oh, my God. He only ever uses my full name when I'm in trouble. "Would either of you care to explain this photo I received an hour ago?"

Sinnett and I share a confused look while Dad pulls up something on his phone, holding it up for us to see. We step closer to get a better look, and once realisation dawns on me, ice floods my veins and my heart drops to my toes.

Sinnett and I kissing on the beach yesterday. As clear as the sky outside and as obvious as the shock seeping into my features.

Shit.

Who took the photo? We were basically alone on the beach, but with how good the quality is, someone must've been lurking in the background that we overlooked. Was it the media? A fan?

I swallow hard as my heartbeat grows erratic, pulsing at the base of my throat. My right hand reaches for my fingernails, picking at the skin around the nail bed. "Dad, I can explain..."

"Explain what, Tatum?" Dad roars, shoving his phone into the pocket of his long pants. The tips of his ears are red, something that only happens when he's ready to blow his top. "I told you not to go there with any of the players, and you went against me. You betrayed me and the trust we shared." He turns to Sinnett, directing his anger at him now, finger pointing at his chest. "And *you*. I made it very clear you were to stay away from my daughter."

"Phil, let me explain," Sinnett says, voice even despite the tension rolling through his shoulders.

"No!" Dad booms. "The photo speaks for itself. I made myself clear about you lot staying away from Tatum, so imagine the betrayal I felt seeing my halfback going against my word."

"Dad, please," I plead, desperate for him to not do this. "Just listen to us."

"How long has this been going on?" he demands, directing the question at me.

"Dad..."

"How long, Tatum? I won't ask again."

I exhale a sharp breath at the same time Sinnett runs a hand through his hair. "A month."

"*Fuck,*" Dad hisses, throwing his hands in the air. "I can't believe this, Tatum. I trusted you, and this whole time you've been seeing him behind my back?"

Tears sting the corner of my eyes, but I don't have the energy to blink them away. Instead, I focus on my father freaking out about me and Sinnett. I knew this would happen eventually; I wasn't naive to the fact that my relationship with Sinnett would have to end eventually. But I didn't think it would happen so soon. I thought we had more time.

I don't want it to end.

"And what about your career?" Dad turns to Sinnett, throwing his hands in the air. "You need to be focused, not frolicking around with my daughter."

"I am focused," Sinnett defends, squaring his shoulders. "If it wasn't for your daughter, I wouldn't be wearing this jersey. She helped me through my lowest time and reminded me why I'm here chasing this dream."

"It doesn't change the fact that you betrayed me," Dad hisses, shaking his head. "I can't fucking believe this. I truly can't."

I step toward my father, the skin around my thumb stinging as my nails dig into the skin. "Dad, don't think for a second that Sinnett isn't committed to this job. He has worked his ass off to get back on the field, despite whatever was going on between us. The Wolves are his life, and you know it."

Dad's jaw clenches as he holds my gaze, deep blue eyes burning with a fire I've never seen before.

"I can't have this under my roof," he finally says, squaring his shoulders. I know what he's referring to. He doesn't want Sinnett and me to be together while at work. "It's not going to work."

"Dad," I warn, voice low. "Please don't do this. *Please*. This isn't what you think it is."

"I know exactly what *this* is." He waves his hands between me and Sinnett, nostrils flaring. "And I don't like it."

"Why?" I plead, not caring how pathetic I sound, tears brimming at the corner of my eyes.

"Why?" Dad repeats, heated eyes finding mine. "Because he's not good for you, Tate! I've heard the rumours about him and how he treats women." He scoffs, shaking his head. "I don't want him to hurt you. The one person I care most about. Not like how I—" Dad runs a hand down the side of his face, scratching at the stubble on his jaw. "A guy like *him* doesn't deserve a woman like you."

A guy like him.

What does that mean?

If he's referring to the women Sinnett has been with in the past, or his complicated relationship with Zoe, then that's not a fair assessment of the man standing in this room. Dad only knows a fraction of the man Sinnett is. He sees the side of him that is an unstoppable force on the field, doing everything he can to help his team out there, and he's heard about the side of him who was lost and finding ways to cope with the overwhelming pressure thrust upon his shoulders, ensuring he's the best version of himself for the club and his parents.

But Dad hasn't met the Sinnett I know. The man who saved me from being drugged in a club. The man who walked me home because he couldn't stomach the idea of me being on the streets alone. The man who listens to music with me and sits through every single one of my random questions as they pop into my head. The same man who lights up my vision with his smile, and forces the butterflies in my stomach to go haywire.

Sinnett is far from the man Dad thinks he knows. I just wish he would allow me to show him.

"He's not like that, Dad," I tell him, voice barely above a

whisper. I'm afraid if I raise my voice even the slightest octave, the tears I'm holding back will burst forward. "You don't know him."

"I know him well enough to know he's not good enough for you, Tate," Dad says, chest puffing out. "This ends. Right here, right now."

I try and swallow around the lump forming in my throat, lungs burning for air. Eyes flicking to Sinnett, I see he's already watching me. Pain seeps into his face, ocean eyes calling to me. His biceps are tense, arms folded over his chest.

It pains me that I can't reach for him or turn back time to yesterday when we watched the sun sink below the horizon, getting lost in the crashing waves and solace of being together.

"Dad, please don't do this." I step forward, hoping he can see the pain in my face. How much this is fucking hurting me. *Us*. "Please."

"My hands are tied, Tatum." Dad holds his hands in the air as if to prove his point. "Make your choice, Sinnett. If you care about this club as much as you claim, then you'll know what to do."

And there it is. The choice I knew would eventually be thrust upon us, namely Sinnett.

It's me or the club.

My heart sinks when my eyes clash with Sinnett. They're filled with hurt and indecision, mirroring my own. It hurts me that my father would put me in a situation like this, knowing he was in a similar position when he was my age and met Mum. If she were here, I have no doubt she would talk him off the edge and knock some sense into him.

But she's not. And the reminder is painful.

"Phil, I—"

I cut Sinnett off by taking another step forward, pulse so erratic I can hardly breathe. "I quit, Dad."

Dad's eyes widen as he stares down at me.

"Tate, no," Sinnett pleads, reaching for me. "You can't do this."

"It's already done," I squeeze out, bottom lip trembling as I lock eyes with him. The man who crashed into my life like a bulldozer and has been slowly picking up the pieces ever since. "I'm sorry, Sin. But I can't let you throw your career away for me."

Dad exhales a sharp breath. "Tatum... I don't want you to throw your career away."

I fold my arms over my chest, anger seeping into my veins. "You didn't give me much of a choice."

He swallows hard, features like stone. Dad turns to Sinnett and gestures toward the door behind him. "You better get your ass into the sheds. Kickoff is in ten minutes."

Sinnett doesn't move, eyes drilling holes into the side of my face. I can't bear to look at him, because if I do, the tears I'm holding back will break free. This isn't just me quitting my job. It's us having to say goodbye to the secret moments we shared in his car, the music we bonded over and the silent support we gave each other to keep pushing through. Now that Dad knows about us, he'll do everything in his power to keep us apart if we try to see each other in secret. It won't be the same as before today when we could be ourselves in private. But everything has changed now.

This is what was always supposed to happen, but it doesn't hurt any less now.

I drag my bottom lip between my teeth, focusing on my breathing instead of looking over at Sinnett. He opens his mouth to protest, but snaps it shut before words slip out. When he realises what I'm doing, he grunts and shoves his hand through his hair. I catch a glimpse of the back of his head as he staunches toward the closed door, flinging it open with such force my hair flies over my shoulder.

When he's out of sight, tears burn my cheeks as they slide down.

Just like that, he's gone—taking with him a piece of my heart.

I'm doing this for him.

"Tatum," Dad murmurs, reaching for me. "Please don't—"

"Why would you do that?" I cry, bottom lip trembling. "Why, Dad?"

Dad's lips thin into a straight line. "You know why, Tate. I didn't put the rule in place to be an asshole. It was for your own good, trust me. Guys like him—" He runs a hand down the side of his face, eyes darting away from me. "They can't be trusted. And I didn't want to see you hurt the way you are now."

"That was your doing," I snap. "Everything was fine. *We* were fine."

Dad huffs, eyes meeting mine again. "And you'll thank me down the line when you realise you were better off without him." He exhales a sharp breath. "You're not to see him again, Tate. I know you quit your job, which we'll talk about at home, but it doesn't change the fact that I don't want you anywhere near him."

I open my mouth to argue, but the words die on my tongue, along with the energy I had moments ago. I'm at a loss for what I should do. At this moment, I don't have the strength to think it through. I just want to be alone.

"I'm going home," I rasp out, wrapping my arms around my waist. I can still smell him embedded into the leather fabric, the last semblance of him I have now. "I can't do this."

"Tatum—"

I rush past my dad, not stopping until the stadium is

behind me and I'm sitting in the driver's seat of my car, staring ahead. The roar of the crowd is ear-splitting as the game gets ready to kick off. I can't begin to imagine the pressure Sinnett is under right now after what just transpired. It pains me that I can't help him through this, like I have so many times before when he's struggling with his emotions.

My bottom lip trembles as I reach for my phone. The air from my lungs dissipates upon seeing the text from him on the screen, time stamped two minutes ago, moments before the team stepped into the tunnel.

> SIN: If you want to know how I truly feel about you, listen to the playlist I made. It speaks volumes that I can't right now.

The playlist.

My hands tremble as I scroll to the playlist saved in my phone, titled 'Songs for Tate'. Thumb hovering over the screen, I weigh my options. If I listen to the songs, I'll be breaking my heart further, knowing I can no longer have Sinnett. But if I don't, I'll never know how he truly feels about me. Is that something I'm willing to walk away from?

Exhaling a sharp breath, I click on the playlist and close my eyes.

Listening to these songs will only bring with them more heartache, but I know I'll regret it if I don't. Call it closure, but I need to hear the words Sinnett hasn't been able to tell me himself.

The opening guitar riff of "Iris" by The Goo Goo Dolls is the straw that broke the camel's back. Tears burst from my eyes in waves, and I'm unable to stifle the sob that tears through me.

Sinnett found meaning in the first song I ever played for him. It's *me*.

And now, when I listen to this song, all I'm going to think

about is that from the very beginning, it was inevitable we would end this way, despite how *right* it feels when we're together.

This must be some sick joke fate is playing on us. And now I'm forced to return to a life before Sinnett with no say in the matter. No matter what way I look at it, he'll have to give up something that makes him happy. I would rather be in the firing line than the career he's worked tirelessly to achieve—no matter how much it hurts to step back.

Chapter Twenty-Nine

SINNETT

I can't fucking focus. Not on the player in front of me, the ball in my hands, the crowd of fans in the grandstand or the damn ground beneath me when my body slams against it. My mind is stuck on jade eyes. The same eyes that held unshed tears, and so much fucking hurt, that it made it hard to breathe.

Walking away from her was the stupidest thing I had ever done. Up until that moment, it had been sleeping with Zoe. Now it's letting Tatum quit her job in order to protect me.

Me. She wanted to protect me.

I should've been the one protecting her, not the other way around.

Phil had no right to thrust an ultimatum on me in that moment. Not when I was falling apart at the seams, desperately trying to hold on to my resolve without letting Tatum slip through my fingers. I was at a loss for words, which allowed Tatum to swoop in and make a decision for me.

I froze in that moment. The thought of losing Tatum hurt, but so did the prospect of ruining everything I had built at the club. I have put my heart and soul into achieving this dream, so when Phil dangled the possibility of losing it all in front of my face, I froze like a fucking coward.

It felt like an impossible decision at the time—one I couldn't make on the spot.

I hate myself for making Tatum feel like she had to do this for me. That she isn't as important to me as rugby. It couldn't be further from the fucking truth. Tatum has been a light in my life, brightening the darkest parts of me and revealing aspects of myself I hadn't seen in a long time. She taught me how to put myself first—something I had never done in the past. I was too busy doing what my father wanted of me, when I should've been making decisions for myself based on what *I* wanted.

And now she's gone.

I let her walk away.

Fuck.

I storm into the sheds, fists clenched at my sides and heart jackhammering in my chest. Adrenaline pumps through my veins, followed by the kind of anger that no one wants to be in the firing line of. It festers beneath my skin—hot and ready to fucking explode. The 10-22 loss to the Sharks isn't helping either. If anything, it's adding fuel to the rapidly growing fire.

"*Fuck*!" I shove my hands through my hair, ignoring the sweat and blades of grass clinging to my skin. "This is such bullshit."

Khai appears behind me, his presence doing little to ease the storm brewing inside of my chest. He doesn't touch me; he knows better than to do so when I'm in this state. It's not the first time—having dealt with many of my meltdowns all through high school and university—and I'm sure it won't be the last.

"Sin, it's okay." His voice is calm, not wanting to poke the bear. "You played a good game, but it just wasn't our night."

"I played like fucking shit." I whirl around to face him. Dirt and grass stains seep into the material of his jersey, mirroring mine. He's as much of a mess as I am, just without the internal war. "I couldn't hold onto the ball, I wasn't paying attention to the plays being set up and I missed a try conversion all because I was distracted by *her*."

Khai rolls his lips and looks around at the deflated room. Our teammates are silent as they sit in front of their locker spaces, heads hanging between their shoulders or eyes locked on the ceiling, likely replaying the game in their heads to see where we went wrong.

I know where we went wrong. It was all *me*.

"Come on." Khai clasps my shoulder, guiding me out of the room and into the adjoining training space. With everyone waiting for Coach Phil, ready for him to hand our fucking asses to us, the training room is as private of as space as we're going to get.

Khai watches, standing in front of me as I pace, eyes locked on the floor as I repeatedly shove my hand through my hair.

"What the hell is going on?" Khai demands. "This is more than just losing the game."

"I fucking lost her, man." My heart hasn't stopped racing since I walked out of the supply room before the game. I'm worried it's going to give out any second now.

"Who? Tatum?"

I nod, my pace increasing as I fight to keep her sad jade eyes out of my head.

"What happened?" my friend asks, voice even. "You told me everything was going great."

"It was," I hiss, shoulders tense. "Until someone took a photo of us at the beach last night and fucking sent it to Phil."

I stop in front of Khai, chest heaving. I'm not surprised by the shock that passes through his features. Believe me, I was the same when I saw the photo on Phil's phone. It wasn't until I had returned to the sheds that it really cemented in my mind that someone took that photo and purposefully sent it to Phil knowing it would have this desired reaction.

And as I ran out onto the field, thoughts elsewhere, I knew only one person could be behind this. The same person who told me I would regret my decision to break things off with them.

"Who would do that?" Khai murmurs, the wheels turning in his head, fighting to come up with an answer. "I mean, that's just fucking cruel."

"Who else would it be?" I roar, losing the grip I had been trying to keep on my temper. "It had to be Zoe."

Khai's eyes widen as realisation dawns on him. "That bitch! Of course she would do something like this. If she can't have you, then no one else can."

The anger simmering in my veins reaches boiling point. My surroundings blur into a hue of red, and my consciousness slips away, replaced with an entity that is filled with nothing but pure rage. Pain explodes through my fists and it takes me far too long to realise I'm beating the shit out of the curved tackle shield lying in the corner of the room.

I'm no longer in control of my actions or emotions, searching for an outlet for the pent-up rage burning in my chest. Each punch does nothing to cool me off or bring a sense of peace to the situation. I barely register the pain shooting through my arms or the ache forming in my knuckles. All I'm focused on is landing punch after punch, fighting the urge to release the scream building at the base of my throat.

It isn't until Khai wraps his arms around my torso, dragging me away from the foam shield, do I inhale a deep breath. My lungs burn and my body aches when I lock eyes with Khai. Fear flashes through his, and I feel like an asshole for losing my shit.

"Shit, Sin…"

Frowning, I follow his eyes as they drop to the ground. I see blood seeping from the open wounds split across my knuckles, sliding between my fingers and falling to the ground in droplets.

"Fuck," I wince, swallowing hard. "I didn't mean—"

"You need to hit the showers and cool off." It's not a suggestion but a demand. "If the guys see you like this, it's only going to make things worse after an already shit night."

"You're right," I rasp, chest aching. "Shit, man, you're right. I lost my shit."

Khai plants his hands on my shoulders, eyes searching my face. "I understand what happened with Tatum is shit. It's obvious how much you like her, so I understand your pain, Sin. But you can't let it get the best of you, okay? You need to keep your head in the game for the team's sake."

I know he's right, but I don't have the energy to tell him that. All I manage is a nod in response.

Khai exhales a sharp breath and guides me toward the showers in the next room over. "We have a long bus ride home, so take as long as you need in the shower. I'll cover for you with Coach Phil."

Thank God.

If I had to sit in the same room as the man who tore my girl away from me all while he rips into us about the game, I would surely lose my fucking mind.

THE BUS RIDE HOME WAS FROSTY, TO SAY THE LEAST. I avoided Phil like the plague, choosing to sit in the furthest seat at the back of the bus with my headphones in and my *'don't fucking look at me'* attitude firmly in place. My teammates are under the impression I'm in a bad mood because we lost the game, but it couldn't be further from the truth.

Khai did his best to keep everyone out of my way so I could stew in peace, but the more I listened to one of the playlists Tatum made for me, the hotter my skin got and the deeper my rage burned.

I'm angry at myself for letting her walk away. I'm angry that her father put in place a dumb fucking rule that shouldn't have existed in the first place. I'm angry that he thinks I'm not good enough for his daughter. And I'm angry that there is nothing I can do to fix this.

I stew in this anger until I step off the bus and walk to my car at the training facility without so much as saying a word to my teammates. I don't have the energy to deal with anyone right now. All I want to do is go home and be by myself. Khai told me he's going to grab a drink with Nico. I have no doubt it's because he wants to give me space, which is fair enough. I wouldn't want to be around a brewing storm either.

By the time I get back to the apartment, the twenty-one-year-old scotch in the cupboard is calling my name. It gets pulled out for special occasions, but not tonight. I need something to distract me from the turmoil in my mind. Something to ease the pain. And I need it now.

The brief moment of relief is short-lived when I step through the front door to find my father sitting on the lounge, eyes locked on me.

Fuck my life.

Could this night get any worse?

"What are you doing here?" I don't have the energy for small talk.

Not waiting for his response, I toss my gym bag on the ground beside the black leather lounge and walk through the open plan living space to the kitchen. I flick the dark grey cabinet open and reach for the scotch bottle. Dad's presence on the other side of the granite kitchen island looms, but I barely register it as I reach into another cupboard and pull out a crystal glass. Only the best for a fine scotch.

"Sin, are you serious?" Dad demands, gesturing to the scotch flowing from the bottle, half filling the glass. "Is that wise?"

I shrug and take a long sip. The liquid burns as it slips down my throat, but I welcome the pain. It's exactly what I need to relax my tense muscles and soothe the ache burning in my chest. I don't give a shit if my father disapproves of me drinking. I'll add it to the long list of things he is already disappointed in me about.

I lean against the counter behind me, swirling the amber liquid around the glass. "What do you want, Dad?"

He's dressed in another one of his many expensive suits, likely having just got done with commentating for a game and following it up with punter recaps and interviews afterwards. His hair is well-kept, along with the black leather shoes without a single mark on them. But despite his professional exterior, the anger swirling in his eyes doesn't go unnoticed by me.

Ding! Ding! Ding!

Here comes round two for the night.

"Tell me why I got a call from Phil tonight telling me you have been sleeping with his daughter behind his back for a month when he gave you and the rest of the team strict instructions to stay away from her."

There it is. The same disapproving look I have seen far too many times to count. It hasn't changed from when I was ten and didn't get my pen license in primary school with the rest of my class, when I was sixteen and got the lowest mark in my maths class, or when I was twenty-two and got my first sin bin for a high tackle. Nothing has changed.

No matter what I do, my father will find a way to be disappointed in me.

"It's none of your business," I bite out, jaw clenching.

"But it is," Dad retorts hotly, the vein at the base of his throat throbbing. "You were seconds away from losing everything you worked so hard for all because of a girl. Phil could've ripped the new contract you're gunning for at the end of the season from under your feet. What were you thinking?"

"It doesn't matter what I was thinking," I snap, heat sizzling in my veins, "because she's gone now."

God, it fucking hurts to say it out loud.

Dad runs a hand over his gelled hair, pacing in front of the island. It's not often I see him lose his cool like this, which means we could be heading for an all-out war. It's been brewing for months now, so there's no time like the present to lay it all on the line.

I have nothing else left to lose.

"I can't believe you would do something so reckless, Sin," Dad bites out, tone disapproving. "You need to focus on your career and not someone you can get a quick fuck from. Rugby is the most important thing in your life, and if you're not careful, you're going to piss it all away."

Heat burns my skin along with white-hot rage. My fingers

tighten around the glass as I bring it to my lips, sculling every last drop. My throat burns, but I welcome the pain. Every inch of my body vibrates as the last of my self-control dissipates at my fingertips.

My fingers curl around the edge of the counter, eyes locking with my father's.

"Just like how you pissed away your career with an injury?" I mock, arching a brow at him. "And now you're projecting your failed career onto me by trying to live out your glory days."

His body stills, eyelids fluttering as my words sink in. It's like watching a deer in headlights try to figure out what the fuck just happened, all before they freak out and go fucking crazy.

"What did you just say to me?" Dad's voice is low, menacing even. But it does little to faze me.

"I told you what I've been too afraid to admit for years." I push off the counter and stalk toward the island. I'm walking into the lion's den, ready to fight with my bare fists, and I could care less how much carnage is caused. "I've never been good enough for you because you're jealous you're not *me*."

"Sinnett!" he roars, chest heaving and eyes wild. "How dare you speak to me like that!"

"What? The truth?" I chuckle but it holds no humour. "You will never admit that you pushed rugby onto me because you wanted to have a career through me, not because you wanted me to love the sport. Your injury ended your life early, so to compensate for all of the goals you wanted to achieve but never could, you figured you would do it through me. But nothing I did to get to where I am was ever good enough for you because I didn't do it the way *you* wanted." I shake my head, jaw ticking. "It took me far too long to realise it."

"That's enough, Sin," Dad snaps, slamming his hands

down on the island. The contact doesn't make me flinch. "You don't know everything I've been through since that injury, and the pain I still deal with to this day."

"I understand you have your own shit to deal with, but so do I," I retort hotly. "I spent years trying to make you proud of me and all I got in return was mildly displeased looks and minimal support when I needed you the most. Now I know it's because you're jealous you never got to finish out your career while I'm at the height of mine. It pains you to see me succeed because you wish it were you instead."

"Sin..."

"No!" I shove my hands through my hair, ignoring the bite of pain from my busted knuckles. "I'm tired of being the family disappointment in your eyes when all I've ever done is my best. It's just one thing after the other and I'm fucking sick of it. I can't do it. I can't do this career for the both of us anymore."

Dad's face falls at my words, shoulders slumping forward. "Sin, I'm sorry if I made you feel that way, but..."

"I don't want to hear it," I interject, deflating with exhaustion. "Just get out."

His jaw ticks as she shoves his hands into the pockets of his dress pants. "Sin, come on. Let's talk about this."

"I'm done talking."

I turn my back to him and reach for the bottle of scotch, mostly as a distraction for my hands and because my body is fucking craving a hit of *something* to take the edge off.

"Sinnett..."

When I don't respond, focusing instead on the amber liquid filling the glass, Dad takes my silence as a hint and leaves the apartment quietly, the front door locking in place behind him. The breath I had been holding releases in a rush, and my hands flatten on the counter, head dropping between my shoulders.

How has my life become such a fucking mess in one day?

Twenty-four hours ago, I was sitting on the beach with Tatum by my side, watching the sunset. The happiness I felt in that moment, coupled with my growing feelings for her, had me contemplating risking everything just so I could make her mine.

And now I have nothing. Tatum walked out of my life, my head coach can't stand to look at me, and now I've gone and fucked my already strained relationship with my father.

Hitting rock bottom is fucking painful.

Chapter Thirty

TATUM

Avoiding my father for two days should be classed as an Olympic sport. It's not as easy as it sounds, especially when he's done everything he can to corner me into discussing what happened at the game on Saturday. The best option for me was to stay locked in my bedroom and only come out when necessary. It made it easier when Dad went to work for the day, but he would be persistent again as soon as he walked through the front door.

He's eager to clear the air, but the last thing I want to do is talk to him.

I know he means well and is trying to look out for me, but I'm not his little girl anymore who needs her father to protect her.

I flop back onto my mattress and stare at the ceiling, phone pressed to my ear. "Being unemployed sucks."

"I know the feeling," Raya murmurs on the other end of the line. "But on the bright side, now you've got some time on your hands to figure out what you want to do now. Are you going to stay in Sydney or move back to Barrenridge?"

The throbbing pain behind my eyes doesn't ease up no matter how many times I rub at my temples. I'm convinced it's caused by stress, but Raya pointed out I haven't been drinking much water these past two days, and I hate to admit that she's right. But also, it's likely from stress, too.

"I have no idea," I grumble, blinking slowly. "I moved to Sydney because Barrenridge doesn't have anything else to offer me. But now I'm back to square one of not knowing what the hell I'm doing or where to even begin looking for a job."

"You've got time," Raya reminds me. "Until you find something suitable, just live off your savings and hope for the best. I know the club paid you well."

I groan and roll on my stomach, feet moving through the air above me. "I'm so lost, Raya. I don't know what to do."

"It's what I'm here for, Tate. I'm going to help you through this and you'll come out on the other side, I promise."

My chapped lips roll together as I nod, despite my friend unable to see me. I miss working with the club. I had spent weeks getting to know the players, learning their histories and helping them in whatever way I could. The stability I had was ripped out from under me all because of that fucking photo.

What was a unforgettable memory with Sinnett, getting lost in each other's quiet company and meaningful lyrics, is now the reason why I'm jobless and we had to end things between us.

Who would do something like this?

My gut feeling tells me it was Zoe's doing—knowing her history with Sinnett—but without evidence to back me up, I'm shit out of luck.

"How are you doing?" Raya asks when I don't say anything, lost in my thoughts. "You know... with the whole Sinnett thing."

"I miss him," I admit quietly. My chest aches each time I

picture his inky, messy hair, his smile that has my insides melting or his calming presence. "A lot."

"I know you do," she murmurs. "But don't be too hard on yourself, okay? It might not seem like it now, but you did the right thing. In that moment, you were looking out for Sinnett and his career, no matter how painful the fallout of that decision was."

Tears spring to my eyes and I blink them back, tired of crying. It's all I've done the past two days. "I know. I just wish there was a better outcome, you know? One where we didn't have to break things off and we could be happy together."

It's wishful thinking, I know. In a perfect world where we met under different circumstances, maybe things would be different. No rules would be holding us back and the fear of getting caught together wouldn't be an issue.

"Has he tried to contact you?" Raya asks, breaking through my thoughts.

"Too many times to count," I whisper. "I want to reply. God, do I want to check in with him to see how he's doing, but I know I can't. If I do, we'll fall back into how it was before Saturday night and we'll be right back where we started. Dad would lose his fucking mind, especially after he forbade me from ever seeing him again."

"Why would he do that?"

I exhale a sharp breath and pinch the bridge of my nose, remembering Dad's words from two nights ago. "He thinks Sinnett isn't good for me. That he's a player and I'll end up hurt. But that couldn't be further from the truth."

"Have you tried telling him that?" Raya says, tone curious.

"I tried, but it fell on deaf ears." My eyes flutter closed. "No matter what I say or do, I won't be able to change his mind."

Raya exhales a low breath. "Gosh, this is all so messed up. I wish I knew what was going on in that head of his."

"Your guess is as good as mine. But since I'm refusing to talk to him, I don't know what he's thinking."

"You need to talk to him, Tate," Raya urges. "Clearing the air is better than letting the clouds brew until a full-blown storm is raging in the distance."

"I know, I know," I rasp out, chest tight. "I'm just not ready yet."

"If that's the case, then take your time. But don't hide from it forever, okay?"

I swallow hard. "Okay."

"Have you spoken to Noah and Nathan about this? I know they're your close friends, so I figured this would be something you'd confide in them about."

I drag my bottom lip between my teeth, thinking back on the phone call I had with my friends yesterday. Turns out, the three of us have our own shit going on and we were none the wiser. With how busy I've been, I hadn't been checking in as regularly as I would've liked, so when I learned Nathan's father is sick and Noah is having issues with Mia, guilt chewed away at my already turning stomach. I should've been there for them, but instead, I was too caught up in Sinnett that I neglected my friendship with my best friends.

Not knowing what else to do for Noah, I gave him Sinnett's phone number in the hopes he could reach Mia that way. Knowing how close Sinnett is with his sister, I have no doubt he would know where Mia is, and in turn, it would help Noah track her down.

Was it wrong of me to give out Sinnett's number without asking him first? Absolutely. It's an invasion of his privacy, but I was at a crossroads of wanting to help my friend and feeling helpless in the same breath.

I hope when Sinnett finds out, he won't be pissed with me. But if he is, I'll understand.

"They know," I tell Raya, swallowing hard. "I wish I could be with them right now."

"You can," she points out, voice even. "Barrenridge is only a three-hour drive."

The thought had crossed my mind yesterday; that I could leave to be with my friends. It would be a distraction from the pain seeping into my veins, and I wouldn't have to face Dad. But the thought of leaving the new life I had created for myself didn't sit right in my stomach. It felt wrong.

"It would mean I was running away from my problems," I murmur. "And I don't want to do that. I'm all for hiding until I'm ready to face Dad, but if I go back to Barrenridge, I'll never be ready."

Raya exhales a soft breath. "I hear you, Tate. If you can't be with your friends, just know you've got me to lean on, okay? I've got your back."

I blink back the tears stinging the corners of my eyes. "Thanks, Ray. I needed to hear that."

A few minutes later, we ended the call. Silence envelopes me, pulling me further into the depths of my mind I'm trying desperately to steer clear of. After Mum passed away, I was trapped in there for weeks, refusing to feel anything or face the world. Noah and Nathan did everything they could to drag me out of it. If it wasn't for them, I would've lost myself. Without them here now, I need to stay strong and fight the urge to sink into old habits where it's easier to be numb rather than be overcome with emotions I don't want to face.

Releasing a shaky breath, I reach for my headphones and slip them into my phone. Music has always been an escape for me—a way to switch my mind off and get lost in the lyrics of another story. My thumb hovers over the playlist Sinnett created for me.

After I left the stadium, I couldn't bear to listen to another song after "Iris", opting to drive home in silence instead. Sinnett told me the playlist is a reflection of his feelings, and he started off strong in that department. I wish I could call him, even just to hear his voice. It would soothe the ache in my chest and clear the fog in my head. All would be right.

The logical part of me knows I can't do that because it would make everything worse, but the irrational side of me is desperate to feel closer him when words aren't on the cards.

Deciding to meet in the middle, I click into the playlist and skip to the next song. "We'll Be Okay" by With Confidence blasts through my headphones as I flop onto my back, staring at the ceiling once more. It's not a song I've heard before, but when the lyrics mention we'll be okay despite facing numbered days, tears sting the corners of my eyes.

It's clear that Sinnett knew what we were facing—the end in sight that we were helpless to avoid—but he didn't care. He was willing to stand by my side in the face of time and fight tooth and nail in the hopes we didn't need to say goodbye. What he didn't account for was my inability to let him throw his life away for me. He knew we would be okay, but I didn't hold the same confidence. Instead of choosing to fight with him, I walked away. For him. I did all of this for him because it felt like the right thing to do.

As the song comes to an end, I'm starting to question whether I made the right decision or if I messed everything up.

Chapter Thirty-One

SINNETT

Sweat pours down the side of my face, tracing the curve of my jawline before landing on my training jersey. Winter has well and truly set in now, but the feverish edge to my skin has me wishing I could rip the thin material from my body. Everything feels overwhelming, and I'm struggling to keep my head afloat.

I continue to run laps around the field attached to the training facility, needing to move my body as an outlet for the pent-up frustration building in my chest. Between the tension with my dad, Phil giving me the cold shoulder, Tatum not answering my texts and Mia being back in Sydney, I haven't known a moment of peace. Not since the day I walked away from my girl.

It's just one thing after the other and I'm fucking drowning here. I can't find my bearings or push myself through to the surface no matter how hard I try. At this rate, I'm going to lose myself completely.

As I round the last bend, approaching the tunnel to the

change room, I spot Khai standing with his arms folded over his chest, his pale eyes watching me. The sun has long since returned to its hiding spot, replaced by a full moon and a cold breeze. The stadium lights guide me toward my best friend, who is rugged up in a puffer jacket and dark blue jeans. His hair is wet and not a speck of dirt or sweat clings to his skin—a stark contrast to my current appearance.

"Are you fucking insane?" Khai bites out, voice carrying across the breeze as I slow to a stop in front of him. "How long have you been running laps for?"

"Not long enough," I rasp, chest tight as I struggle to pull air into my lungs.

Khai shakes his head, concern marring his features. "I know this past week has been a lot for you, Sin, but you can't push yourself to your limits as a distraction. The last thing you want to do is irritate your quad."

I glance down at my heavily wrapped quad, hating that he's right. Ever since the game last Saturday, it has felt achy in places with the skin swelling slightly. Not wanting to worry Todd or Coach Phil, I kept it to myself, choosing to wrap it up, hoping the pain will go away with time. But with how hard I've been pushing myself this week, the pain has gotten worse.

"I'm fine." The lie tastes bitter on my tongue, but I refuse to admit that my best friend is right. "You don't need to worry about me."

Sensing he's fighting a losing battle—something he has been trying to fight me on all week—he sighs and shoves his hands into the pockets of the puffer jacket. "You don't want to talk about your feelings, that's fine. But at least tell me everything is okay with Mia. You haven't told me much about why she's been in Sydney since Monday."

"It's a long story," I murmur, bending at the waist to

snatch my water bottle and towel off the ground where I left them an hour ago. "She's got her own shit to deal with. All I can do is be there for her when she needs me."

To say I was shocked to see Mia standing in the hallway outside my apartment is an understatement. I knew she had plans to interview for a job in Sydney, but I had lost track of my days and all of a sudden, she was here. She's staying with our parents, which is something I'm glad she's doing. Mending her relationship with Mum is something that needed to happen sooner or later, so I'm glad Mia feels comfortable enough to take that next step.

When she told me about the drama with her neighbour Noah, all I could think was: *we're both fucking messes*.

I've missed my sister since she moved to Barrenridge, so it's been nice to have her back in Sydney. She has helped distract me from my churning thoughts when I'm not training, but when I'm alone in my bedroom... that's when the chaos really begins.

"Do we need to drive to Barrenridge and knock some sense into the guy who hurt her?"

I shake my head and take a long drink from the water bottle. Once satisfied, I drop the bottle to my side and exhale a sharp breath. "I've got it under control, but if I need to hide a body, I know where to find you."

"Good man." Khai claps me on the back and guides me down the tunnel. "Let's get you showered and dressed. Don't you have a family dinner to go to?"

"I told Mum I couldn't go because of training." It's a half-truth that I'm not willing to budge on. "Besides, things are still... rocky with me and my dad."

We step into the empty change room, the rest of the team having left while I was out running laps on the field. I walk to where my gym bag sits on the bench in front of my locker, rummaging around for my phone. Disappointment deflates my chest when I don't see a text from Tatum. The same as every other day this past week.

"You'll have to talk to him eventually," Khai points out, sitting on the bench beside my bag. "You can't ignore him forever."

"I can try," I mutter, running a hand through my hair. Tossing my phone into my bag, I reach for the towel hanging on the hook in the alcove space. "I've said my peace with him, which is something I never thought I'd do. But with everything going on with Tatum... I don't have the energy to continue carrying the weight of his expectations."

Khai nods. "I hear you. And look, if it's easier to push it to the back of your mind for now, then do it. But don't forget about it and hope it'll go away with time, okay?"

My jaw ticks as I nod. I hate that he's right—once again. As much as I would love to sweep this under the rug, never to be seen again, I know I can't. Not when my dad is a huge part of my life—both personally and professionally. As a commentator and punter, Dad is deep in the sport, just as I am. It would be impossible to ignore him for the rest of eternity.

If Mia can make amends with Mum, I can do the same with Dad.

Facing the music is just not something I'm ready to do yet.

Khai stands and claps me on the shoulder, a smile touching his lips. "Go shower and I'll see you at home. I'm ordering pizza, and there are beers in the fridge ready to go. You could use the pick me up."

I would normally tell him that we need to watch what we consume so we don't mess with our diets, but I could fucking care less about that right now.

"Pizza and beer sounds perfect," I tell him, returning his smile.

"That's the spirit!" He steps toward the door to the room, grinning. "See you at home."

When he leaves, I head to the showers and stay under the hot water for far too long. By the time I step out, my fingers are wrinkly and I'm starving. All of that running has worked up an appetite, something I'm eager to sate with pizza and beer.

My eyes land on a head of brown and blonde ombre hair, hazel eyes following my movement as I saunter into the changing room. She's dressed in a hoodie and black jeans, matching her reserved personality. Kind of like a black cat.

"What are you doing in here?" I ask, voice tight. My hand reaches for the towel wrapped around my waist. Water slides down my bare chest; I couldn't be bothered properly drying off when I got out.

Raya stands from the empty bench space beside my bag and waves me off with her hand. "Don't worry, I'm not here to hit on you or anything. You're not my type."

I raise a brow at her. "Not your type?"

"Not even close," she says without hesitation, eyes staying locked on my face.

"Okay, fine," I relent, walking past her to my gym bag. Retrieving my clothes, I raise a brow at her, silently asking her to turn around. Raya rolls her eyes and spins, facing away from me. "Why are you here then?"

I drop my towel and begin dressing, sliding my legs into the holes of my black jeans.

Raya rocks on the heel of her shoes, hands clasped behind her back. "I overheard something today at practice that I need to tell you about."

Pulling a black graphic T-shirt over my head, I murmur, "Yeah? What's that?"

"Zoe was telling her friends that she is the one who took the photo of you and Tate at the beach. She said she had a feeling you were seeing someone else, which would explain why you were blowing her off. And once she saw you on the beach... Anyway, she took the photo and sent it to Phil knowing it would end things between you both because she had heard from one of the guys on the team about his *no dating the players* rule."

With my hoodie half pulled over my chest, my arms still as my breath hitches in my throat. Anger bubbles in my veins, seeping into my skin.

I fucking knew it.

Raya glances over her shoulder at my silence, and upon seeing me fully dressed, she spins to face me. "I have a feeling you knew she was behind the photo."

I tug the rest of the material down and run a hand through my wet hair. "I had a feeling she did, yeah, but I had no evidence to prove it." Exhaling a sharp breath, I gesture a hand in the space between us. "How did... how did she find us? At the beach, I mean."

"From my understanding, she followed your car when you left the training centre." Raya shrugs, shoulders tense. "I have no doubt she spoke to one of the guys on the team about you. And once she saw you guys, and put two and two together about the rule Phil laid down, she found herself in a perfect position to force you away from Tatum."

"I can't fucking believe this," I bite out, shaking my head. "Why can't she take the damn hint that I'm not interested?"

"Because in her deluded mind, you belong to her." Raya states it is so plain and simple, like it's a fact. "If she can't have you, no one can."

I'm already tethering on the edge of losing my shit, having steered clear from tipping over this past week by using every ounce of restraint I possess, but the bomb Raya just dropped is the last straw. Zoe is the reason why Tatum quit her job and walked away. She knew sending the photo to Phil would put an end to us, and I'm sure she did it with great pleasure and a smile on her fucking face.

If she thinks I'm going to magically fall back into her bed like nothing has happened, then she's more deluded than I thought.

"I have to go," I rasp out, reaching for my gym bag. I don't bother zipping it up before slinging it over my shoulder. "Thank you for telling me about this."

Raya's eyes widen as she follows me out of the room, rushing to fall into step with me. My long stride makes it difficult for her to do so.

"Where are you going?" she demands breathlessly. "You better not do anything stupid, Sin."

We step into the almost empty car park, save for a few cars belonging to the staff. My Audi clicks to life as we approach it. I don't bother looking at Raya as I toss my bag into the back seat and reach for the driver's door handle.

"Just something I should've done a long time ago."

Raya watches helplessly as I get into my car, the engine roaring as I tear out of the parking lot. Hands tightening around the steering wheel, I lean back into the seat and exhale a sharp breath.

I hope I don't regret what I'm about to do. But I know if I don't do this, I'll never forgive myself for staying silent.

THE SHARP RAP ON THE DOOR IS ENOUGH TO ALERT the whole street to my presence. Having people look out their windows at the ruckus isn't enough to stop my insistent banging though. The muscles in my back tense as I straighten my spine, eyes locked on the polished wood.

Behind the door, hurried footsteps rush forward. Within seconds, I'm face to face with Zoe—honey eyes wide and confused. She's in nothing but a thin white robe, leaving nothing to the imagination. But my eyes aren't on her body, they're locked on her face, a thunderous expression mirrored in her pupils.

"Sin," Zoe chuckles nervously, eyes searching my face. Manicured fingers comb through the end of her shoulder-length hair while the other wraps firmly around her waist. "What are you doing here?"

"You took it a step too far." I'm not beating around the bush or limiting my emotions to protect hers. "What you did last week..." I shove my hand through my hair, tugging at the roots. "It was beyond fucked, Zoe. You had no right to follow me and take photos without my consent. And then to go and send it to Phil knowing what would happen..."

"You left me with no choice," she defends, voice rising an octave. "I told you that you would regret treating me the way you did, and now you're seeing the fallout from those choices." A smug grin slips onto her face. "I can't believe it was the coach's daughter you were shacking up with this whole time. I should've fucking known. It was so obvious with how you would look at her when you thought no one was watching. But I was *always* watching, Sin."

"You're psychotic," I seethe.

"And you're a fucking liar," she spits in response.

Hands fisting at my sides, jaw ticking, I hold her gaze. "This is your final warning, Zoe. If you don't stay the fuck away from me, I will make sure your ass is booted from the cheer squad."

For the first time, the colour drains from her face. *Checkmate.*

Zoe jabs her finger into my chest, features twisting in anger as she spits, "You wouldn't dare, Sin."

A smirk tilts up my mouth, one that holds so much venom it could kill a grown man. "Fucking try me. If you so much as look in my direction or speak my name, I will do what I can to get you off the team. It's not a threat, Zoe, it's a promise."

Her lips form an O as her finger falls away from my chest. She swallows hard, contemplating her next move. Threatening to have her kicked from the team wasn't something I had considered before the drive over here. But I needed something significant—something that holds a lot of meaning to her—to hold over her head. Cheerleading is all she ever talks about, next to fame and money. So what better way to get off her back than threaten to take away the one thing that brings her the most joy?

Do I have the power to get her kicked off the team? I'm not sure, but she doesn't need to know that.

"You're an asshole, Sin," Zoe seethes, a fire burning in her honey eyes.

"Yeah, an asshole who is done with your shit," I retort hotly. "Leave me alone, Zoe. I mean it, or I'm going to make life extremely difficult for you."

Zoe opens her mouth, but closes it upon seeing my arched brows, daring her to try me so I can make good on my promise.

She stays silent.

For the first time in a week, relief floods my body as one battle I've been fighting has come to an end. I take a step back and shove my hands into the front pocket of my hoodie. Zoe tracks my movement with her eyes, still at a loss for words.

I don't say a word as I turn on my heels and stalk to my car parked haphazardly on the street. Having said all I needed to, my steps feel lighter and my head a little clearer.

Winning this battle is the first of many raging around me. My biggest challenge is figuring out how I'm going to get Tatum back. She may have been willing to walk away, but I'm not. And I will fight to the end to show her just what she means to me.

Chapter Thirty-Two

SINNETT

My head is a fucking mess.

It's as if I have butter fingers tonight because I can't hold onto the ball to save my life, and every play I try to set up fails miserably.

Well, that might be a little dramatic given the Wolves are leading the Falcons 26-22, but *still*. Everything I do just doesn't feel right, and it's driving me fucking insane. And I have no doubt it has everything to do with a certain strawberry-blonde I can't get out of my head. Every time I close my eyes, her jade ones are looking back at me. When I look in the mirror, her sweet smile is right there, reminding me of everything I lost. Of *who* I fucking lost.

The ref blows his whistle, calling for a penalty on one of the Falcons' players during their third tackle. Zane gets to his feet, but not before patting the other guy on the shoulder—a silent apology for the rough tackle. He jogs over to get in formation, shaking it off.

I shove my hand through damp hair, tugging at the roots. *Fuck*. I desperately wish I could shake whatever the fuck is going on with me, but nothing I do seems to work. Is it possible to get out of this funk when my thoughts are consumed by the woman who slipped between my fingers?

It's ironic that Phil put the no-dating rule in place so the team didn't get distracted, but now my head is all messed up because I no longer have his daughter in my life.

Funny how that works.

The Falcons put a tap on the ball and rush forward. Needing to let go of the built-up tension in my shoulders, I rush into the tackle. Grabbing the guy around the waist, I drag him down to the ground, pinning him in an awkward angle that has him groaning. Pain shoots down my leg when his knee makes contact with my right quad.

Fuuuuuck. Why did I do that?

The ref calls, "Held!" and I jump to my feet, backing away from number ten. But before I can take two steps back, the burly man has his hands fisted in the front of my jersey. His deep brown eyes are filled with a rage that I've only ever seen out on the field. It's what I like to call frustration mixed with pure adrenaline pumping through your veins.

"What the fuck, man!" he shouts, spittle landing on my chin.

I clench my jaw, both from the pain throbbing in my quad and anger at the audacity of this fucking guy. It's on the tip of my tongue to tell him to get fucked, or take my aggression out in another way that could see me sin binned for ten minutes. Instead, I grit my teeth and shove at his chest, needing him away from me before I do something I might regret.

He stumbles back, heated eyes holding mine as he joins his teammates.

Huffing, I turn to join the formation on the forty-metre line. Khai shoots me a *what the fuck* look, but I shrug in return.

I don't know what he wants me to say how other than I can't think straight and I feel like I'm drowning.

Just as the whistle blows, I sweep my gaze toward the grandstand where Mia sits. I insisted on her coming to the game tonight, if only to distract her from what's happening in her life. But now she's seeing me in a state she's never seen before. I see it in her eyes. As my twin, she can read me like a book with no ink on the pages. She knows I'm distracted and playing like a pile of sloppy shit. Fuck, every Wolves fan in the crowd can see it.

And until I see Tatum, I don't know how I can snap out of this state.

"I KNOW WE WON AGAINST THE FALCONS TONIGHT, but where the fuck was your head out there?" Khai hisses from beside me, rubbing a towel over his wet hair. "Shit has hit the fan with Tatum, but don't forget what we're fighting for here."

I grimace, running a hand down the side of my face. Freshly showered, my skin is still clammy, and the cologne I sprayed moments ago clings to my skin. "I know, I know. You don't need to remind me how shit I played tonight. Trust me, I'm going to be kicking myself for the rest of the night."

Khai drops his eyes to where my hand rubs my right thigh, something that has become second nature to me these past few months. Realising my mistake, I halt my hand, but it wasn't quick enough. He saw.

Shit.

His eyes widen as he points a finger at my chest. "Did you hurt yourself again?"

Maybe. "...No."

"Sin!" Khai slaps my shoulder and shoves his hand through his hair. "When did this happen? And why didn't you say anything?"

Exhaling a sharp breath, I drop my head in my hands, left leg bouncing wildly. "It happened during one of the last tackles of the game. I copped a knee to my quad, and since then, it's been sore as fuck. Not as bad when I proper fucked it in round five, but enough that I'm worried it's going to be a problem."

"Yeah, a major fucking problem, you idiot." Khai closes his eyes, shaking his head slightly. "Sorry. That was harsh. We've been under a lot of pressure these past couple of weeks while fighting for the top spot on the leaderboard. So the last thing we need is for our star halfback to be out on injury *again*."

Sighing, I lift my head, staring at the empty row of lockers ahead. Most of the team has left the sheds, ready to celebrate the 32-22 win over the Falcons. But I haven't moved after getting back from the showers. I'm sure Mia is wondering where the hell I am, but I can't bring myself to walk out of the room. I don't want to worry her about my possible injury, nor do I want to let on to Phil or Todd about it.

If Tatum were here, she would know what to do.

My fists clench on my thighs.

But she's not here, and there's nothing I can do about it.

"Shit, man, I know. But don't worry, I'll get it sorted out."

The club is yet to replace Tatum, unable to decide on a candidate as good as her, especially after speaking with the team. Everyone sang her praises, which makes sense given how driven and passionate she is about the job. It showed in the smiles on the face of the guys when they left her office, or even how I was able to stay on track to recover from my injury in the projected timeframe. As far as the team is concerned, no one can replace her. And now we're left with a Tatum-sized hole that can't be filled.

"You need to get it checked out sooner rather than later, or else you might injure yourself further." Khai claps a hand on my shoulder, pale eyes simmering with a hint of sadness that stabs at my gut. "No word from Tatum?"

I shake my head, hands fisting the material of my athletic shorts. "Radio silence and it's fucking killing me."

My friend sighs and leans forward, resting his elbows on jean-clad thighs. "I know it's hard, Sin. You two were great together. I could see it in the way you smiled at her when you thought no one was watching, or hung on every word that came out of her mouth. It's clear you have feelings for her."

Blowing out a breath, I shove my hand through my hair, trying to ignore the ache forming in the depths of my heart. "It doesn't matter what I want. How can I get her back if she won't talk to me?"

Khai hums, tapping at his chin. "I guess you need to get creative then."

I frown. "Creative?"

Instead of explaining his words of wisdom, he reaches for him gym bag and stands, clapping my shoulder. The goofy grin on his face has me clenching my jaw. "Yes, Sin. Get creative. If you want to see her, you'll find a way to do it."

He leaves before I have the chance to call him an idiot for leaving me hanging like that.

Huffing, I push off the bench and reach for my bag. If I don't leave the sheds soon, Mia will storm in looking for me. And the last thing I need is for her to see the half-naked guys still lingering in the room, talking with some of the staff members.

When I step into the hallway, I hear Khai ask my sister, "Hey, younger Baxter. How's the hair?"

Stepping towards them, my brows furrow. "What?" My fingers graze over the ends of Mia's dark brown hair. A strange residue coats my skin. "Why is your hair all sticky?"

The three of us make our way towards the exit, where our cars are parked in the back lot of the stadium. Cool air whips at my exposed skin, and I have to fight to keep my teeth from chattering in response. The heated seats in my Audi are calling my name.

Mia chuckles. "A girl poured her drink on me, then Khai let me sit on the team bench to avoid them."

Was I that distracted during the game that I didn't notice my sister sitting on the bench?

"What? Why would they do that?" I ask, frowning

"She thought I was going to steal your attention away from her." Mia lifts her eyes to mine, and I can tell she's biting back a smile.

I huff a laugh. "The fans can be wild sometimes." Wild is an understatement. Most of the time, they're respectful and know when to not push my boundaries, and then some of them do something like they did to Mia without so much as hesitating. It's like trying to balance on a seesaw.

"More than wild. Who pours their drink on someone's head?" Mia muses, folding her arms over her chest.

"Girls who want to get laid," Khai chimes in with a cheeky smile, wiggling his brows

Mia nods in agreement, but I stay silent, not wanting to comment. Khai might like the attention he gets from the female fans, but right now, it's the last thing on my mind.

When we reach Khai's car parked a few spaces down from mine, I tell him I'll see him at home once I've dropped Mia at my parents' place. Khai nods and slides into the front seat.

Silence settles over me and Mia until we reach my car, and

words tumble from her mouth. "What happened that made you play like a distracted monkey tonight?

Opening the back door, I drop my gym bag on the seat and climb into the front seat. "I'm not a monkey." Groaning, I press my palms into my eyes, rubbing at them until I'm seeing stars. Anything to distract me from the conversation Mia seems keen on having.

When I drop my hands to my lap, I meet Mia's eyes. Her brows are raised, as if telling me she isn't dropping the topic until I answer her

Fuck me.

I sigh heavily. "Just someone I thought I was close with seems to have turned her back on me."

It's an exaggeration at best. Yes, Tatum did walk away from me without so much as letting me discuss what happened with her, but that's not what I'm frustrated about. It has nothing to do with her giving me the silent treatment, and everything to do with Phil's stupid fucking rule and Zoe putting her foot in it

Mia's gaze narrows. "A girl?"

My jaw ticks as the engine roars to life. I turn the seat warmer up high, hoping it'll ease the chill seeping into my veins and help soothe my sore quad muscles. Two birds with one stone. Pulling the car out of the space and onto the road, my hands tighten around the leather wheel. "Yes.

"Not the girl with the short brown hair I remember you mentioning once or twice."

My lips quirk. I should've never told her about Zoe, but somehow, she managed to squeeze it out of me a few months ago. "Not her, no."

A sparkle shines in her eyes. "It's Tatum, isn't it?"

"Shut it," I murmur, not wanting to entertain this conversation.

"Interesting."

"How so?"

Mia tilts my head back on the head rest, eyes searching the side of my face. "You like her."

My jaw tightens as I stare ahead. It's on the tip of my tongue to tell her she's wrong, that she doesn't know what I'm feeling. But the truth is: she's right.

Mia gasps and reaches across the console to slap my left thigh—thank God it wasn't my right—and I glare in response. "I knew it."

I scratch at my jaw, chest tightening. "Mia..."

She laughs, no doubt at the shade of pink coating my cheeks that I'm helpless to stop. I'm not opposed to talking about my love life with my sister—it's something I tend to keep private until she pulls it out of me—but when it comes to Tatum, I can't help but let my emotions show more than usual.

Flustered, I shove my fingers through my hair, avoiding Mia's eyes.

"Wow. You do love her," Mia murmurs, voice light.

Fucking hell, is it really that obvious to everyone around me?

A small smile forms on Mia's lips at my silence, and she reaches over to touch my arm. "I'm sure it'll work out, Sin."

Needing to take the spotlight off me—and so my heart rate will calm down—I nod in her direction. "Oh yeah? And how is it between you and Noah?"

Mia's face falters as she pulls her hand away, turning her attention back to the road. "I haven't spoken with him yet."

She should be taking her own advice.

"What are you waiting for, Mia?"

She sighs loudly, rubbing a hand over her forearm. "Tomorrow I'm telling Mum everything. About Ryan, my therapy, my job with Noah. Everything."

"Okay," I breathe, nodding.

"I want to know Mum's opinion before—"

"No," I interject, hands tightening around the wheel.

Mia's eyes snap to mine. "What?"

"Stop waiting for their approval. I hate to break it to you, but Mum and Dad won't ever be entirely happy with what you decide. It's how they are. Look at me. I'm the star halfback for the Wolves, a top NRL team, and Dad is still pushing me. I made it, and he's still breathing down my neck over every little thing. Don't wait for them to tell you they're satisfied, because they won't be. Not truly, anyway."

Mia drags her bottom lip between her teeth, nodding slowly as my words hover in the air between us.

Silence seeps into my skin, putting me further on edge. I want to see my sister happy after everything she's been through. Living in Barrenridge and having Noah in her life seems to have been the thing that she needed to get her life back on track, so it pains me to see her hiding from what makes her happy. *Who* makes her happy.

What are the odds that we're both having trouble in our love lives? I suppose twins do everything together, right?

"I'm proud of you, Sin."

My face flicks to the left, gaze lingering on my sister's side profile. I'm reminded of all the times Tatum said she was proud of me. It was the confidence boost I needed after constantly feeling like I wasn't good enough for my father, the club, the media, and the fans. But seeing the smile on her face and the warmth in her eyes made it easier to breathe and push away the weight settling on my shoulders.

My mouth quirks in a half smile. "I know, and I'll be proud too with whatever you decide is best *for you*, not anyone else."

Mia blows out a breath and rests her head against the window. She might not think so now, but everything will work out for her. I can feel it in my gut. Call it twin-tuition, but I have no doubt Noah will do the right thing and take care of my sister. I just know it.

My grip tightens around the wheel as Khai's earlier words sound in the back of my mind.

If you want to see her, you'll find a way to do it.

An idea slams into my head like a freight train and I can't help but smile as I turn onto my parents' street. If Khai wants me to get creative, then I know just the thing to do. I hope it doesn't blow up in my face.

Chapter Thirty-Three

TATUM

With my father out of the house for the game tonight, and Raya unable to keep me distracted because she's cheerleading, I'm left to wander around the house, moving from room to room in the hopes I'll find something to fill my time with.

Reading a book did nothing but make my mind wander, unable to focus on the words. When I couldn't find anything decent to watch on the streaming sites, every TV show or movie either not interesting enough or something I've watched far too many times that I can recite the dialogue backwards, I tried cleaning my bedroom. Clothes were strewn across the floor in desperate need of hanging, and the top of my dresser was a mess, littered with perfume bottles and random hair accessories, reflecting the chaos in my head.

My body and mind are not happy with whatever I try to do, intent instead with forcing me to ignore everything and focus on the ocean eyes that have plagued me this past week. I hate that I can't forget about Sinnett. Not that I want to. But if I'm going to move on from this and allow him to continue his career without my getting in the way of his ambitions, then I need to continue to remind myself that this is for the best. Putting him above my own needs and desires was the right call.

I've been trying to tell myself that every chance I could get this past week, and each time the reminder was like a knife to the heart. I know deep down it was what needed to happen, but my heart refuses to accept it.

Sinnett has tried to reach out multiple times, and each time I see his name on the screen, it physically pains me to not respond. We haven't spoken since the game last week, when I walked away without giving us a chance to discuss the situation. I know what he would say. He would tell me that he can have both—his career and me. But I know that it can't happen. As long as my father is hellbent on me not dating anyone on the team, whether I'm working for the club or not, Sinnett will always be out of reach.

Sighing, I flop down on my bed, staring at the ceiling. Despite the chill in the room, sweat lingers on my skin. I should go have a shower, even if it's to give myself something to do, but my body refuses to move, intent on just lying in one spot and staring at nothing.

Thinking. Feeling. Remembering.

The late-night drives with Sinnett is something I miss more than I thought I would. His comforting presence when we were in his car, laughing, talking and singing along to whatever song played from the playlist I created for him—for us—was a welcome distraction from how exhausted I was from work. It was an outlet for both of us, one that allowed us time to decompress and just be together. We didn't need to do anything sexual; we just needed each other.

My phone vibrates on the bedside table, pulling me from my thoughts. It could be Noah or Nathan. We're all riding the 'hot mess express' together, so we've been doing our best to be there for each other. They're my best friends and I would do anything for them, and vice versa. I'm always a phone call away if they need me.

I blindly reach for the device and bring it my face, expecting to see either one of my friend's names on the screen. My heart thunders in my chest when it's not either of them. I slowly push myself into a seated position, reading and re-reading the three simple words on the screen.

SIN: I need you.

I shouldn't respond to him, I know that. It'll be easier for the both of us if I continue to keep him at arm's length. But the longer the words sink into my skin, embedding themselves into my blood stream and racing toward the beating muscle in my chest, I can't help but feel as though something is wrong.

The previous texts from Sinnett have mostly been him wanting to see me so we can talk, but this one is different. It could mean anything. The uncertainty of not knowing the context and the need to know he's okay is the driving force behind my actions. My fingers move in a blur as I type out a response.

Even as I press send, I can't help but feel that this isn't just a ploy to get me talking to him again.

TATE: What's wrong?

His response comes quick, prompting me to check the time on the screen. It's far later than I thought, approaching 10 PM. If Sinnett is texting me, it means the game has ended already.

SIN: I might have hurt my quad during the game tonight. Can you please look at it?

TATE: Why me?

SIN: You're the only person I trust, Tate. Please.

Blowing out a long breath, I tap the side of my phone, weighing up my options.

Should I do this? I've spent the past week ignoring him in the hopes it'll make moving on less painful down the line. But now that I've given him that in, will I be able to pull away again?

TATE: Sin, we really shouldn't...

SIN: I just need you to check out my quad, that's it. No funny business, I promise.

I hum, rubbing at my chin. This better not be a ruse to get me talking to him. Walking away from him was hard enough last time, so to do it a second time might very well be torture. Despite this, I relent, hoping I'm not making a huge mistake.

TATE: I'll be at your place soon.

STANDING IN FRONT OF SINNETT'S APARTMENT DOOR, I'm struggling to find the strength to knock, because I know once I do, there is no turning back. Once I see his face again,

I'm going to have a hard time not falling back into hold habits. I just hope my heart is strong enough for this.

Knock, knock, knock.

Holding my breath, I stare at the wood, waiting for the sound of his footsteps to appear. When the door swings open, I'm met with pale green eyes, not the ocean ones I have grown to adore.

Khai blinks at me, leaning his shoulder against the doorframe. "Tatum," he says quietly, attention locked on my face. "He's out on the balcony."

I don't know how much he knows about us, or if anything at all, but judging by the faraway look in his eyes and tense shoulders, I have no doubt he knows all about our situation. In his eyes, I hurt his friend. With how close they are, it doesn't surprise me that Sinnett confided in him. I can't even be mad about it when I did the same with my friends.

"Thanks," I murmur as I waddle past him, rubbing my arm.

I feel his eyes on the back of my head as I walk into the open living space. The balcony door is open, almost like a gateway to the stars lingering in the sky, the moon shining bright enough that the overhead light has no need to be used.

Sinnett sits on one of the patio chairs, a black hoodie hugging his chest and the same athletic shorts that are on constant rotation in his wardrobe. The hood is pulled over his messy hair, and his hands are shoved deep into the front pocket. His right leg is propped up on a foot stool, an ice pack balancing on the taut muscles. I shiver at the sight. How is he not shivering?

He doesn't notice me at first when I step onto the balcony, the cool air whipping at my face. From up here, the lights of Sydney stretch for kilometres, creating a dazzling display that has captured Sinnett's attention. But not me.

I wrap my arms around my waist, the hoodie I threw on doing nothing to ward off the freezing air. My gaze lingers on the curve of his jaw. God, it feels almost impossible to look at him—both from guilt over pushing him away and his striking features that have me questioning if he's real.

"You know, I've been meaning to ask how you can wear shorts in weather like this." My voice carries on the wind to him, causing a delayed reaction.

Sinnett twists his head, eyes roaming my face. They linger on my lips for a brief second before lifting. Pain swirls in the depths of the sea water, and it hurts to know I'm the cause of it.

"You came." He says the words as if he genuinely thought I wouldn't show.

I take a tentative step forward, the air between us thick with unsaid words. "I promised you I would, so here I am." My eyes drop to his right thigh. "Can I take a look?"

Sinnett nods, sitting straighter in the chair. He removes the ice pack, placing it on the table beside him as I take slow and deliberate steps towards him, almost as if I'm approaching a newborn puppy that is timid and unpredictable.

Lowering to my knees in front of him, hissing at the cold bite that seeps through my pants, I focus on his thigh and not the fact that I hear his breath hitch in his throat or the subtle flex of his hand resting on his left leg. Using the light from the moon and stars, my eyes skim over the area, examining it for any sign that he has done damage to it. Visually, the skin looks a little bit inflamed, but without doing an exam, I won't know for sure if it's something in the muscle causing him pain.

"What happened?" I ask, voice barely above a whisper. My head lifts, eyes meeting his. "In the game."

Sinnett swallows hard and leans back in the chair. "I found

myself in a rough tackle. A guy from the other team jarred me right in the thigh with his knee. Hurt like a fucking bitch."

"Did you come off the field after it happened?"

Sinnett holds my gaze, jaw ticking.

His silence speaks a thousand words.

"Sin..." I press, raising a brow at him.

He shoves a hand through his hair and huffs out a sharp breath. "No, I didn't come off the field. I got it strapped during halftime and continued on like nothing happened." Lips rolling, he shakes his head. "My sister was in the crowd and I didn't want her to worry."

My eyes widen. "Oh, your sister is in Sydney?"

He nods. "She drove down last week. She's been... dealing with some personal shit. But I'm sure you know that already if you've spoken to your buddy recently."

I grimace, guilt gnawing at my sides. "I'm so sorry for giving Noah your number without asking first. I didn't know what else to do. He was desperate to get in contact with her."

Sinnett's jaw ticks. "It's fine, Tate. I don't care about that."

"Is she okay?" The question doesn't feel right the moment I ask it, but I can't stop it. "I mean, if you don't mind me asking."

"No and yes." He shrugs. "But she will be. If your friend is as good of a good guy as I've heard, Mia will be in safe hands with him, and that's all that matters to me."

"Noah is the best guy I know," I tell Sinnett, voice even. "Whatever Mia is going through, whatever that is, Noah is the guy who can give it to her. I'm sure of it."

Sinnett nods, the movement slow as if he's trying to convince himself that my words ring true. "I hope so."

A thought strikes me, one I'm surprised I hadn't thought about asking until now.

"Is that why you were in Barrenridge the night we met? To see your sister?"

"And Gran," he answers, voice tight. "I helped Mia move up there. She needed to get away, and with Gran needing help, it felt like the best decision for her."

It's on the tip of my tongue to ask what she is running from, but I refrain from doing so. His sister's business is none of mine. If Sinnett wants to tell me the details, I'll listen. He knows I'll always listen and be there to support him. But until then, I swallow the question and nod, allowing silence to consume us like a suffocating cloud.

Not wanting to focus on how intense his presence is or the fact that I feel like I'm drowning, I touch his quad, hoping to distract myself by properly examining him. His gaze watches my movements, searing holes through my skin and straight into my soul. It sets my nerves further on edge.

Wrapping my hand around his ankle, I lift his leg off the stool and go through the movements I did with him during our first session together, checking for mobility and if there are any flashes of pain.

I flick my eyes to his, but his features remain deadpan as he watches me. A shiver races down my spine—both from his stare and the fact I'm here with him, touching him, breathing in his woodsy scent.

I clear my throat and lower his leg to the ground, placing it at a 180-degree angle. "I think you might have just irritated the muscles. With the flexibility you still possess, and the fact that you've been icing it, I would suggest continuing with the exercises I've already given you to help strengthen the muscles and take it easy for the next couple of days during training. But remember to be careful in the future, okay?"

Sinnett holds my gaze, hands flexing on his thighs.

God, I wish he would say something. *Anything.* Not

knowing what's going through his mind is killing me, setting me further on edge.

Swallowing hard, I jab my thumb over my shoulder. "I... I should go."

"Why did you do it, Tate?"

His words are charged and holds too many questions. But I know exactly what he's asking.

Why did you quit your job?

Why did you end things between us?

Why did you ignore my messages the past week?

Why did you walk away?

Each one snaps off a piece of my heart, shattering me into tiny shards that feel impossible to rebuild. If only he knew how hard it was to make the decision I did at that moment. How gut wrenching it was to know there was nothing else I could've done differently.

"I had to," I murmur, unable to meet his gaze. "There was no—"

"No," Sinnett interrupts, forcing my eyes to lift to his. They're bright even in the depths of the moonlit sky. A shiver races down my spine, both from the chill in the air and the frustration simmering within the ocean pools of his irises. "Don't give me that bullshit, Tate."

I blink, too stunned to form a response.

Sinnett leans forward and scoops my hands into his. They're warm in comparison to the chill slithering across my skin, and I find myself wishing they could heat the rest of my body. But his eyes holding me captive takes on the job.

"We had options." His voice is low and firm, much like the grip he has on my hands. "You didn't need to walk away like you did."

I swallow around the lump forming in my throat. "Dad... h-he doesn't want us together. You and me." My heart thumps in my chest, rattling my ribcage. "He wanted you to choose between me and rugby. I don't want to be the reason you burn bridges with the club and your career is upended. All because of a casual hook up."

Sinnett's breath hitches as he blinks. "Is that what you think this is?"

I hold his gaze, bottom lip quivering as I search my mind for a response, but come up short. "I-I don't—"

"You mean more to me than just a quick fuck, Tate." He leans forward, minty breath fanning against my lips. Now I'm the one struggling to breathe. "It's never just been about sex for me. You..." His tongue darts out to swipe his bottom lip, searching for the right words that seem to escape him at every turn. "I wanted all of you. Your mind, your kindness, your body, your fucking smile and every inch of your soul. And once I got you, I was... lost for words."

Yeah, like how I'm at a loss for words right now.

"You have this strange ability to make me feel like I'm on top of the world but fucking drowning in the same breath," he continues, voice low. His words are for me to hear and no one else. "Having you in my life has been a breath of fresh air. I hadn't realised the air in my lungs was stale and I was longing for more. More from life. More from my career. More from my family. And there you were, telling me all I had to do was *breathe*. Now all I want is to breathe in your light."

His admission wraps around me like a python, constricting my airways. A shaky breath falls from my parted lips, the only sound heard between us. The rustle of the wind, the engine of the cars below and Khai talking loudly in his bedroom fade into the background, allowing me the space to focus on Sinnett. His eyes, his mouth, his cheekbones and the curve of his jaw. I commit every inch of him to memory, followed by his admission.

My heart stutters in my chest as I whisper, "Sin…"

"I can't do it, Tate," he rasps out, throat bobbing as he swallows. "If you reject me and walk out that door… I don't think I could handle it. I walked away from you once and it was the biggest mistake I could've made. Fighting for you should've been my top priority, but I let you slip through my fingers, and I've hated myself for it ever since."

Moisture forms in the corners of my eyes, and I fight to keep the tears from falling. Every inch of my body aches with a pain I haven't felt before. It's as if I'm being pulled apart at the centre from an entity far too large for this earth. I'm torn between wanting to do right by Sinnett and giving in to what my heart is desperately begging for.

But deep down, I know what I truly want—what feels right. And despite every rule we've broken and the boundaries we've crossed, there has always been one clear image at the end of the road, and he's staring right at me, begging me to see the light and to not run from it. To not run away from him.

Fear spikes through my heart, but not because I'm afraid to give myself to Sinnett. If we do this—say fuck it and shatter the rules keeping us apart—our lives are going to be changed forever. We'll have to face my father and the club. Everyone will know about us, including Zoe and every fan who looks up to Sinnett. Our secret meet-ups will no longer be our oasis from the craziness that is our lives. And every moment we have in public will be viewed by people across the country.

It's a fear I never thought I'd have to face, but with Sinnett by my side, it doesn't seem as daunting.

"It's always been you, Sin," I murmur, throat thick with an emotion I can't hide. "I quit my job and walked away because I thought it was the best decision for you. I spent countless hours writing up your recovery program because I wanted the best possible schedule for you. I longed to spend time with you and drive around aimlessly for hours because I knew it would bring you comfort and peace you couldn't find elsewhere. Everything I've done is for your benefit and because I care about you." My chest aches as the last word leaves my mouth.

Sinnett drops my hands to caress my cheeks, his palms warm. I melt into his touch, just like every other time he's held me like this. But this feels different. He's holding me as if he thinks I'm going to slip between his fingers like grains of sand; like if he holds me a little tighter, maybe I'll stay this time.

He doesn't need to worry. I'm not going anywhere.

"I'm going to spend every waking second of the rest of my life making it up to you," he tells me, breath fanning against my lips. "While I can't repay you for how you've helped me these past couple of months, I can remind you just how grateful I am you're here. That you chose me."

"I'll always choose you," I whisper, blinking back the tears in the corners of my eyes. "In every lifetime, it'll always be you, Sin."

The moment he crashes his lips against mine, my world returns to its axis; the storm in my mind dissipates and the tension in my muscles melt away. Being with Sinnett is like finding a ring that fits perfectly without having to try on different sizes. It's easy, effortless and a perfect match. When I'm with him, I feel whole, like he's the missing piece to my puzzle I've never been able to find. Until now.

Our lips move together feverishly, hands a flurry of movement over each other's neck, chest and shoulders. I can't get close enough to him even if I tried. Our chests brush together as my knees begin to ache from the position I've been sitting in for far too long. But I'm too scared to move for fear of shattering the moment.

My hands glide through Sinnett's hair, pushing the hood to his shoulders. Our tongues glide together as his hands find purchase on my lower back, fingers digging into the fabric of my hoodie.

Every sheltered feeling and emotion we have been holding onto over the past couple of months burst forward like a dam, soaking us in the process. But I embrace it. The words I had been too afraid to admit, and the feelings I didn't think were reciprocated. And now that it's all in the open, I can just focus on *him*.

Sinnett pulls away, resting his forehead against mine as he breathes deeply. "You have no idea what you mean to me, Tate." His eyes flick open to meet mine, a deep desire swirling in them. "Don't underestimate the lengths I'll go to in order to keep both you and my career within the club."

"But my dad..."

"I can handle him," Sinnett utters. "I'll talk to him—"

"No," I interject, shaking my head. Exhaling a sharp breath, I pull away, dropping my hands to Sinnett's thighs. "I need to speak to him on my own."

"Have you spoken to him... since, well, you know?"

I shake my head, guilt clawing its way up my throat. "Not yet. But tomorrow, okay?"

Sinnett drags his bottom lip between his teeth and nods. "Tomorrow." His hand lifts to swipe away the stray hairs flying around my face, courtesy of Sinnett's frantic movements. "But until then, will you stay with me tonight?"

My eyes widen, pulse racing. "You want me to... I mean, I can't do that, can I?"

"You can do whatever you're comfortable with, Tate," he murmurs, fingers gliding over the curve of my jaw.

"But Khai... I don't think he likes me anymore. He was a little frosty when he answered the door."

Sinnett waves his hand through the air, brushing off my concern. "Don't worry about him. He's just worried about me is all. But I also think he's in a shit mood because he has his own family drama he's working through."

Worry spikes in my chest. "Is he okay?"

"He will be. It's nothing he can't handle."

Heart thundering in my chest, the only answer smacks me in the face and presents itself in the form of a breathless, "Okay. I'll spend the night with you."

Texting my dad that I'm staying at Raya's house is my top priority, next to getting as close to this man as humanly possible. Tomorrow, the lies stop and the truth is put forth. I have zero idea of how the conversation is going to go, and if Dad will lose his shit or not, but with Sinnett smiling down at me like I'm the light of his life, the fear disappears into the darkness behind the balcony.

Sinnett grins. "I've missed you, strawberry." He presses a chaste kiss to my forehead. "Like, a lot. Listening to music on my own isn't as fun."

The mention of music has my ears perking up. "Speaking of music, I forgot to thank you for the playlist you made me."

"Did you listen to every song?" Sinnett runs the back of his knuckles over the curve of my jaw, his eyes tracing his movements. The other holds my waist firmly, his warmth melting into my skin.

I nod, leaning into his touch. "Is it embarrassing to admit that I've listened to the playlist all the way through at least twenty times in the past week?"

Sinnett grins, his hand finding purchase on my waist. "I raise you twenty-five."

My jaw drops, followed by an airy laugh. "Seriously?"

His forehead meets mine, shoulders shaking as he chuckles. "Is it less pathetic of me to say I was simply admiring my playlist making skills?"

I drag my bottom lip between my teeth, hands gliding up

and down Sinnett's thighs in a slow movement. "Well, you did learn from the best, so it only makes sense."

"See, I knew you would understand." Sinnett stands and helps me to my feet, arms circling my waist. I inhale, relishing in his woodsy scent—it's both calming and familiar. And God, have I missed it. "Tonight, you're all mine, Tate. You're not walking away from me this time."

Warmth blooms across my body as I push onto my toes and wrap my arms around his neck, smiling. "I'm not going anywhere, Sin. Never again."

Chapter Thirty-Four

TATUM

My body vibrates with a nervous energy I shouldn't possess. This is my dad for crying out loud. I shouldn't be this on edge with the prospect of finally having the conversation I have been skirting around for over a week. Maybe it's because I know what he's going to say when I bring up Sinnett. He won't change his mind, and I'm worried there is nothing I can do or say that will sway him.

But no matter what happens when I knock on his office door, I'm not walking away from Sinnett again.

"Are you sure you don't want me to come in with you?" Sinnett asked when he dropped me at the house five minutes ago. "If you need me, I can stay right here and wait for you."

"I don't think that'll be necessary," I told him, ignoring the pounding of my heart at the thought of the conversation with my dad going south. "If anything does happen, I'll call you. I know Dad. He'll be pissed and try to stand his ground, but he won't do anything to hurt me."

I exhale a sharp breath, craning my neck from side to side to relieve the tension building in the muscles, and knock sharply on the closed door. A moment later, Dad's gruff voice calls out for me to enter.

Holding my breath, I turn the handle and step into the room. Dad's eyes lock with mine from over the desktop. They're hard as they watch my movements. The conversation hasn't started yet and he already looks pissed. I suppose that's my fault for avoiding him like the plague for over a week.

"Tatum," he drawls, leaning back on the leather chair. Dad is dressed casually in a white button-down shirt with the sleeves rolled up to his elbows. The olive tint to his skin stands in stark contrast to the white, making his eyes pop. "Are you finally done with pretending like I don't exist?"

I lower myself onto one of the plush chairs in front of the desk, wringing my hands together. "Dad, I'm sorry about that. I just... wasn't ready to talk."

"But you are now?"

I nod. "I am."

Dad exhales a sharp breath and folds his hands over his stomach. "Then let's talk, Tate."

Rolling my lips together, I nod.

It's now or never.

"I'll go first," Dad says, tone even. "Let me just say—"

"Actually, let me go first," I interject. "I, um... I have a lot I need to get off my chest and if I don't do it now..."

Dad nods, allowing me to take the lead and get the ball rolling. He's not going to like the direction I'm about to take this, but I know that if I don't say what I need to, the chances of me chickening out are much higher.

"I apologise for how I've been treating you this past week, but just know it's because I was hurt," I tell him, voice wavering. Exhaling a long breath, I run a hand down the side of my face, skin inflamed. "You refused to listen to my side of the story, Dad. I thought we had a better relationship than that."

Dad sighs, the sound filled with an emotion I can only assume is frustration. "Tate... You know I trust you. I just don't trust *him*."

Heat floods my veins. "*He* has a name, Dad. And *he* is just as much part of this as I am."

"I know, and that's the problem." Dad runs a hand down the side of his face, scratching at his jaw. "Sinnett knew the rule I had put in place to protect you, and he went behind my back to break it. I trusted him, Tate. I thought out of everyone on that team, he would be the one guy who respected me enough to not go there with my daughter."

Hurt and betrayal wrap around each word, hitting me in the chest harder than I thought. I didn't know the extent of Dad's relationship with Sinnett. They've known each other for years, at least since Sinnett joined the main roster, but I was unaware of just how deep their bond ran. Turns out, it's far deeper than I thought.

"Dad, he didn't do it because he doesn't respect you," I try to reason, not knowing if it'll work or not. "Our history... It's complicated."

Dad's brows crease into a frown. "What do you mean by complicated?"

God. How am I supposed to explain this to him without giving all of the details that will want to make him stuff his fingers in his ears and scream at the top of his lungs?

"Well..." I drawl, lifting my shoulder in a half-hearted shrug. "We, uh... met in Barrenridge the night before I moved down here. He was there to help his sister move in with their grandmother. And, well..." *Why is it so hard to admit this to my father?* "We hooked up." The words tumble from my mouth before I can stop them, and judging by the way Dad's eyes widen, I should've been more delicate with my answer.

"You *what*?" he roars, making me cringe at the volume of his reaction.

"I didn't know who he was, I swear," I rush to tell him. "I promise, Dad. When I saw him... he looked vaguely familiar but I didn't know who he was until I saw him at the game a week later."

"Tate," Dad groans, rubbing a hand down the side of his face. "You really shouldn't be putting yourself in danger like that."

I can't help but roll my eyes. "Dad, I'm not a little girl anymore. I know how to look after myself. Besides, I didn't feel unsafe with Sinnett. If anything, he made me feel comfortable."

Dad groans and pinches the bridge of his nose. "Not helping, Tate."

Needing to steer the conversation from the topic of my sex life back to the problem at hand, I shift on the seat and gesture between us. "This is kind of my point exactly. The silly rule you made up to keep me from dating anyone on the team was purely for your benefit. You don't view me as a grown woman who can make decisions for myself and has my best interest at heart. In your mind, I'm still a little girl who would run to you whenever I scraped my knee and needed it to be cleaned up or whenever I was lost with my maths homework and you would help me solve the equation without so much as raising your voice when I still didn't understand."

"You'll always be my little girl," Dad says, voice even. His eyes flick across my face, as if picturing me as the same girl he remembers when I was growing up. "It doesn't matter if you're five, twenty, forty or sixty-two. No matter what, I'll do everything I can to protect you, even if you don't think you need it."

I understand where he's coming from, I do. Every father

should feel this way about their kids because it shows how far they're willing to go for them. Having that unconditional support and quiet protection can make or break a relationship. But there is also that fine line of being overbearing or too protective to the point where you can't breathe or feel as though your decisions are not yours anymore.

"Dad, I understand what you're saying and I appreciate how willing you are to help keep me safe, but listen to me when I say I don't need it in this scenario."

Dad's frown is so deep I could very well swim between the creases. "Yes, you do. I'm doing this because it's in your best interest. Your mother and I—"

"What?" I question, tone more forceful than I intended. "What would Mum say about this if she were here?"

Dad swallows, lips mashing together. "Well, she would know what to say better than I ever could, that's for sure."

"She would listen to me," I tell him, squaring my shoulders. "Mum was the best at defusing any heated situation because she knew listening to each side of the story was the only way to navigate the narrow road together."

My chest squeezes painfully at the mention of Mum. If she were here, not only would she have talked Dad out of the stupid rule, but she would support me to the end, no matter what. It was the kind of person she was. If I wanted something, she would do whatever she could to help me achieve it. She would never have stood in my way, not like how Dad is, and that's a major difference between them.

Dad exhales a sharp breath, turning his attention to the desk instead of me. "I was doing this because of her, Tate."

Now I'm the one frowning. "I'm not following."

Uncertainty seeps into his features as he rolls his lips together, contemplating his next words. The longer the silence consumes the room, the harder it is to breathe.

"I didn't want you to repeat what we did," he says, each word deliberate and soft. "Your mum and I."

And there it is. The real reason Dad hated the idea of me dating a rugby player. I had thought it was because he didn't want his players to be distracted or for me to cause friction. And then there is his issue with Sinnett's past, thinking he's not good enough for me. But it's because he didn't want me to follow in their footsteps—the one where I date a rugby player and lose myself in the process, just like Mum did.

"My situation is nothing like yours," I tell him, voice tight.

"It couldn't be more the same," Dad argues, leaning forward to rest his elbows on the table. "You gave up your job for him, Tate. Your mother did the same. She wanted me to follow my dreams and in the process she gave up on pursuing hers. I hated that she did so because I wanted her to chase her goals. All I ever wanted to see was her success."

Tears spring to my eyes, but I blink them away, refusing to cry. "She chose to do that for you, Dad. You didn't give her an ultimatum. Seeing you happy is what made her happy." I swallow around the lump in my throat, chest aching. "I didn't get a choice. At least not one that mattered. Leaving was the best choice for Sinnett because I didn't want to stand in the way of his success. But where I differ from Mum is that I plan to continue pursuing my goals with or without Sinnett in my life."

Dad rolls his lips, my words melting over him like an ice cream in the summer. The silence in the room is deafening, extenuating the erratic rhythm of my heart and the blood rushing through my veins.

Knowing Mum didn't get the chance to live out her dreams because she put my dad first, and then me when I came along, is heartbreaking. She was far too young when she left with the rest of her life still in front of her. I knew she held regrets about not pursuing her dreams, but at the end of the day, being a mother was her greatest achievement, and if that's what made her truly happy in the end, then she lived her life without regret.

"Listen, I know you don't want to see me fail or put a man first, but my relationship with Sinnett isn't a reflection of yours with Mum." I roll my lips together, searching for the right words. "I have every intention of continuing to further my career and achieve every dream I have ever wanted, but I can do that with a man by my side, using all the support I can get."

Dad exhales a sharp breath, running a hand over his gelled back hair. "I hear you, Tate. I do. But as your father, I can't help but worry. You've never given me a reason to not trust you or think that you don't need me, but ever since your mother passed..." He clears his throat and shifts on the chair. "I don't want to let her down. You're all I have left and I don't want to see you get hurt."

A tear slides down my cheek as my hands fist over my thighs. Moisture blurs my vision, creating an outline of Dad as we hold each other's gaze. He isn't the type of man to get emotional or put his heart on his sleeve, so hearing him say he doesn't want to let Mum down... It's hard.

"I'm okay, I promise," I squeeze out, teary-eyed. "When I'm with Sinnett... God, it's as if the clouds on a rainy day open up and the sun shines through, sizzling my skin, making me feel alive. We just click, you know?"

"You sound happy." It's not a question but an observation.

"I am happy," I answer, a smile slipping onto my face. "Sinnett makes me happy, Dad. Like really happy. And... I like him. A lot."

He raises a brow at me. "You do?"

Just the thought Sinnett has my heart racing with excitement and the need to be with him. Being with him is like breathing air—natural and necessary. Without him, I feel hollow, like he's taken a piece of himself with him and only returns it when we're together again.

"I do," I respond with a nod, smile growing wider. "If there is anyone you can trust me with, it's him. He has my best interest at heart and wants to see me succeed as much as you do."

Dad exhales a long drawn-out breath and nods. "I want you to be happy, Tate. I always have. And if being with Sin is what you need... I won't stand in your way." Noticing the joy splitting across my face, he points a finger at me, a serious expression melting into his weathered features. "But make no mistake, if he hurts you in anyway, I will kill him. Well, not really, but you know what I mean. I will have no regrets handing his ass to him."

With my heart in my throat and my hands clasped together in front of my chest, I widen my eyes. "So that means you're okay with this? With us?"

"Well, not entirely, but this is what you want, so I'm going to be supportive." His lifts his shoulders in a shrug. "I don't agree with how he used to spend his time, but if you're adamant that he's not the man the rumours make him out to be, then I'm willing to trust you on that."

That's all I needed to hear.

Jumping up from the chair, I race around the desk and throw my arms around his neck, hugging him close. His Lynx body wash coats my senses, a familiar scent that reminds me of when he would flip me upside down when I was six years old and walk me across the ceiling to my bedroom every night before bed. It was our night time ritual. If he was home, we would do it. I hated when he was in Sydney and I couldn't do it, Mum not being strong enough to carry me, but when Dad did come home, we'd fall into our habits like no time had passed.

"You won't regret this," I tell him, squeezing tighter. "I promise."

"I hope not," he huffs out gruffly, likely from me restricting his airway. "I'll be having a stern talking to Sinnett at training tomorrow about treating my little girl right. And if he doesn't, I'll kick his ass."

Releasing my hold on him, I step back, staring at him with a deadpan expression. "Dad, you shouldn't threaten to hurt one of your players."

"I wouldn't actually hurt him..."

Liar.

I roll my eyes. "Just trust me, okay? I've got this."

"I know," he murmurs, eyes searching my face. "Your Mum raised you to know what you want, so I have no doubt you know what you're doing. I might not agree with it one hundred percent, but I'm willing to try and understand, if that's what you want."

"It is," I say, smiling from ear to ear. "Thank you."

Dad stands from the chair and busies himself with shuffling the papers in front of the keyboard. "And for the love of God, can you come back to the club? The guys are falling apart without you."

I snort a laugh. "Now that I believe."

Dad laughs along with me, straightening his spine. "They'll be happy to have you back."

The overwhelming urge to cry has a lump forming in my throat. This conversation has been a rollercoaster ride, and now that I'm off, my emotions are creeping up on me.

I manage a smile. "I can't wait."

"And your mum would be proud of you."

Tears brim in the corner of my eyes. "I hope so."

Chapter Thirty-Five

SINNETT

"This feels weird."

Tatum turns her head, jade eyes roaming over the side of my face. "How so?"

I squeeze her small hand resting in mine, eyes locked on the sunlight streaming through the thick foliage of the oak tree. "For the first time in weeks we don't have to sneak around or hide out in the confides of my car. We're able to just... be us. It's strange."

She laughs, the sound sweet and airy. My fucking favourite.

"I agree. I almost texted Dad to say I was hanging out with Raya until I remembered that he knows about us."

Us.

It still feels like a foreign concept despite knowing it's not.

Not having to hide our relationship from Phil or the media is something I'm still getting used to.

When Tatum called me on Monday to tell me how the conversation with her dad went, I was expecting tears and a podcast length rant about how angry and upset she was. So imagine my surprise when I answered her call and she was as happy as a clam, retelling the details of the conversation with an ease and calmness that was unnerving.

Three days later and I'm still wondering how the fuck Phil is okay with me dating his daughter.

But I'm not complaining one bit.

My cheek meets the picnic blanket, eyes locked on Tatum's. I get lost in them, wondering how the fuck I got as lucky as I did. Meeting her that night at the pub was the start of my life. Before her, my world revolved around rugby. I knew what I wanted and I was willing to do anything to get it, no matter what. It didn't seem possible to allow anyone else into my space, not sure if there was room for them in my carefully laid out plans. But I was wrong. So fucking wrong.

Tatum is the best rule I could've broken. If I hadn't, I never would've learned what it means to truly live. To appreciate the value in the finer things and feel every second of the big moments.

"He's been giving me a lot of shit at training the past couple of days. It's like he wants to punish me for betraying him but is also trying to respect what you want. I can see it's slowly killing him on the inside."

I can handle the tough training drills and him pushing me harder in the gym than necessary. He has gone from giving me the cold shoulder to a slightly frosty presence, which is better than nothing. At this point, I'll take whatever he's willing to give me. It's going to take some time to gain back his trust, but I'm willing to do it if it makes Tatum happy and my life a little easier. Because fuck me, my body is aching today.

"That's his version of trying," Tatum says, biting back a smile. "He'll soften towards you, it'll just take some time."

I squeeze her hand. "I'm willing to wait."

Tatum rolls onto her stomach, kicking her feet in the air as her eyes search my face. Tendrils of strawberry-blonde hair frame her face, having fallen from the messy ponytail she threw up in the car before we got to the park.

"What about your dad?" she asks, her voice gentle. "I know things have been... tense the past two weeks."

I roll my lips together, turning my attention to the brown tinge on the tips of the leaves. With winter in full swing, the vibrant green will soon be swallowed whole by shades of brown.

"I still haven't spoken to him."

"Why?"

I exhale a sharp breath and run my free hand down the side of my face, scratching at my chin. "Because no matter what I say, he's not going to change. He's always going to put himself in my shoes and try to steer my career toward what he wants. It's never been about me, only what he wants *me* to achieve for *him*. And I'm done with trying to survive in his shadow."

Tatum's hand slips from my mine to run through my hair, her eyes watching her movements. "I'm not going to tell you how to handle this because you know your dad better than anyone else, but just know that you'll feel better once you talk it out. Take it from me."

"Maybe," I murmur, eyes fluttering close as her nails glide over my scalp, sending a shudder across my body. "But until then, I'm not going to say a word to him. He can come to me when he's ready to have a proper conversation about our relationship."

"That's your choice, Sin, and I support you."

I support you.

God, it feels fucking nice to have someone support me and be proud of what I do. Before Tatum, I had no concept of the notion, besides my sister and Gran. But now, she goes out of her way to remind me every chance she gets that she sees me and is willing to be by my side whenever I need her.

I don't deserve this woman.

Silence befalls us, and we stay in this position, listening to the rustle of leaves and the high-pitched laughter of the children running around nearby, throwing a frisbee with their golden retriever. Their mother watches from afar, eyes locked on the small children, afraid they might escape from her sight.

With how hard I've been pushing myself in training for the game in Newcastle this weekend, I needed this time with Tatum to decompress and fucking relax. Tatum returned to her position as the club's physiotherapist yesterday, which boded well for me because I got to steal a moment of her time while she did a full examination of my quad. Between kisses and knowing smiles, she concluded that I had nothing to worry about. All I need to do is strap up my quad and be mindful of how I enter tackles during the game.

The status quo has been returned, which means I can breathe a little easier.

My threat to Zoe about getting her kicked off the squad worked a treat because now she refuses to bat an eye in my direction. She has her sights set on Caleb, one of the guys on interchange. I pray the poor fucker doesn't make the same mistake I did by going there, but only time will tell. His business has nothing to do with me, so I'm determined to keep my mouth shut.

For the first time in two weeks, I feel whole again.

Needing to move or do something to redirect the adrenaline pumping through my veins, I jump to my feet and reach for the rugby ball resting at the edge of the red and black checkered blanket. Tatum's eyes track my movement as I toss the ball in the air, catching it with ease.

Wiggling my brows, a smirk spreads across my face. "You up for some fun?"

Tatum pushes off her stomach and onto her feet, her nose

barely reaching my chest. She tilts her head to the side, eyeing the ball. "What kind of fun?"

"I can run some passing drills with you."

Heat floods her lightly freckled cheeks. "I don't think I'll be very good at it."

I press a chaste kiss to her forehead and slide my fingers through hers. "You don't have to be, Tate. It's all about having fun, yeah? Letting loose."

She drags her bottom lip between her teeth, and I contemplate stealing it from her and claiming it as mine, but stop short when I realise we're not the only people in the park.

"Okay," she finally says. "But if I'm shit, don't tell my dad or anyone for that matter."

I chuckle, guiding her from under the oak tree and into the warm winter sun. "My lips are sealed, strawberry." I drop her hand and step back, flicking my wrist as a gesture to move backward. When she's a few metres away, I toss the ball in the air again. "Okay, the first drill is simple. I'll pass the ball to you, and all you have to do is catch it, okay?"

Tatum rolls her eyes. "That's it? Easy peasy."

I grin. "Just you wait, Tate."

She holds her hands up, ready to catch the ball. When it leaves my hands, spinning through the air like a spiral desperate to hit a target, fear flashes through jade eyes at the speed behind it. Tatum catches it with an *oomph*, eyes wide.

"What the hell was that?" she huffs, looking between me and the ball. "For a second there, I thought it was going to go through my stomach and out the other side."

I burst out laughing, slapping my knee as tears spring to my eyes. Tatum doesn't appreciate my reaction, scowling at me as she pops her hip, the ball tucked under her arm.

"I told you it's not as easy as it seems," I offer with a shrug.

"Remember that I'm your girlfriend and not beefy like Khai." She tosses the ball back to me, and I catch it with ease.

Girlfriend.

I've never had a proper girlfriend before. Sleeping with women on occasion is the closest I've gotten to letting a woman into my life, knowing I couldn't give them all of me, not when I was focused on furthering my career. I didn't think I was capable of caring for another person to the point I was willing to give them every ounce of my soul—until I met Tatum.

"Don't call my best friend beefy," I playfully warn, tossing the ball in the air. "And you did great. Ready for another one?"

Tatum hesitates, eyes flicking between me and the ball. My leather jacket hangs from her shoulders, covering a dark green long-sleeved shirt that pairs well with the colour of her hair. Light blue jeans hug her toned legs, reminding me of what is hidden beneath. Heat pumps through my veins at the thought of getting her into my bed tonight, naked and all mine.

"Okay, hit me," she says, her voice lacking confidence as she holds her hands up. "But be gentle."

Chuckling, I pass the ball to her, lighter than before and she catches it with more grace than the last one.

"Now pass it back." I clap my hands together, a smile claiming my lips. "You've got this."

The pass she does is terrible, but I would never tell her that. Not when she's laughing the way she is, my heart ready to explode. It's a feeling only Tatum pulls out of me.

When the ball lands in my hand after the fifth pass from Tatum, I drop it at my feet and charge towards her. Jade eyes round at the edges, and in a split second, Tatum takes off running, her laughter like a fucking drug as I chase her down. She doesn't get far before I scoop her into my arms, spinning us around until my vision blurs at the edges and my head grows dizzy.

The only clear image I see is her. With a smile only for me.

Her hands find my shoulders as I lower her to her feet, chest brushing against mine. We're breathless as we stare at each other, our silence speaking louder than any words in the dictionary.

My lips claim hers—gentle and warm. Hands sliding around my neck, we melt against each other. The kiss is slow and deliberate. For all of the times my body is fucking desperate for her, needing to feel her against me, I enjoy holding her in moments like this—close and all mine. It's a testament to how far we've come. Being able to slow down and feel these moments is not something I thought we'd get. We had a ticking clock over our heads, counting down the minutes until we'd inevitably have to part ways. But to both of our surprise, the clock is gone and we own our minutes, now able to choose what we do with them.

My hands slide over the curve of her waist and pull her body flush against me. She smiles against my mouth and I'm seconds away from combusting because *fuck me*. But also, I need to relax because if I don't, I might bust somewhere else.

"This," Tatum murmurs against my lips. "You and me... I couldn't be happier."

I grin, fingers digging into the material of her jeans. "Aren't you glad I broke your dad's rule?"

Tatum chuckles, tilting her head to the side. Her jade eyes sparkle and I find myself wanting to get lost in them for the rest of time. "Every day."

She giggles when I use her waist as leverage to hoist her off the ground, spinning us around again.

I've never been one to break the rules for fear of what the consequences might be if I did. I prided myself on my ability to follow the rules and keep a clear head. But Tatum was the one rule I was willing to break, not knowing if that decision would blow up in my face or not. If I hadn't given in to my desire to kiss her the night I walked her home, we wouldn't be here right now. I would still be on the straight and narrow, suffocating under the weight of my dad's expectations. Tatum came into my life and pulled me from the tide without realising I was slowly drowning. And she continues to hold me up without asking for anything in return.

I don't deserve this woman, but I'm going to make sure that every day she knows she won't regret the decision she made that night in Barrenridge that led us right here. Led her to me.

With the season half over, I don't know if we'll win every game or make it to the grand final, but I do know I've already won the most important thing to me. More important than a trophy or the minor premiership title. And that's the woman smiling up at me like I'm able to give her the world—my world.

Little does she know, she already holds the key to my heart. She has since the first night we met. And I have no plans to take it from her.

Epilogue

TATUM

FOUR MONTHS LATER

I'm blinded by the overhead stadium lights. Adrenaline pumps through my veins, my heartbeat skipping in time with the clock ticking down. Each second passes by too quickly, the score far too close for comfort.

Five minutes. That's all the Wolves have left to turn this game around. If they can score a try, not only will they be four points above the Melbourne Raiders, but it'll be enough to see them win the grand final.

The air in the stadium is thick, with every fan on the edge of their seat, eager to see who the winning team will be. Either way, half of the attendees will go home upset over the loss. The other half will file into the streets of Sydney, celebrating with cheers and drinks.

Sinnett's jersey from last season hangs from my frame, helping me to blend in with the Wolves fans surrounding me. He gave it to me a couple of months ago, reminding me that I can only wear his number. Not that I'm complaining. Number seven has my heart.

I swallow hard, eyes flicking from the field to the big screen with the time left in the game displayed. The Raiders are on their fourth tackle now, pushing toward their try line. But the Wolves aren't giving up that easily. Khai charges into a tackle, and somehow the big hit causes the Raiders player to fumble the ball.

With the Wolves starting their set of five tackles, the pressure is on. I hold my breath, eyes locked on the players. Sinnett is focused, head darting side to side as he searches for a gap in the Raiders' defence.

I didn't have a chance to talk to him much before the game. Dad warned me that the team would be stoic with their game faces on, ready to win. Sinnett was exactly that. Besides the good luck kiss we shared before he started warming up and a quick, "I'm so proud of you," we haven't interacted. Knowing he needed space, I took my seat in the section of the grandstand beside the tunnel the teams run out from. The Wolves staff and benched players are right in front of me, with the cheerleaders not too far away.

Raya was busy prepping for the pre-game performance when I saw her a couple of hours ago. I'm always amazed by her dancing abilities and how stunning she looks out on the field. It's clear she was born to do this, so seeing her out there shining like the star she is, in front of eighty-thousand people, was a proud friend moment for me.

We've grown closer over the past couple of months. She had my back when I needed her the most, and I still don't know how to repay her kindness. Having a friend like her has replaced the hole left in my heart after leaving Noah and Nathan. I know they're only a phone call away, but with Noah loved up with Mia and Jade, and Nathan being Nathan, hounding them with life updates doesn't feel right. They have their own stuff going on, and even though we're all busy, we still make time to catch up with each other. But with Raya, I can call or text her whenever I need and she'll be there for me.

My attention snaps back to the third tackle of the set, Nico—a front rower—going down in a pile-on tackle. I slip to the edge of my seat, hand over my heart. With less than four minutes left on the clock, I watch as Sinnett receives the ball and passes it off to Khai, who makes a run for the try line. I'm on my feet, heart slamming against my ribcage.

Three minutes.

A cheer erupts from my throat when Khai slips past two defenders and dives for the line, body sliding across the grass. The sound around me is deafening—a mixture of screams and gasps of disbelief. My hands ache from clapping, excitement electric at the tips of my fingers.

They did it.

The Wolves scored a try.

Sinnett jumps on Khai's shoulders as the rest of the team rushes to celebrate with him. A smile splits across Sinnett's face as he ruffles his friend's sweaty hair. His exterior might appear happy, but I can only imagine the pressure he's feeling right now, hidden beneath the surface.

With Sinnett's father commentating the game and the fans eagerly waiting for him to kick the try conversion, I know he'll be feeling the pressure. Anyone in his position would be.

Sinnett's relationship with his father is still strained. They've tried talking through their differences, but as Sinnett predicted, his father doesn't seem willing or able to change his mindset about how he interacts with his son. Even though they don't talk as much, the weekly family dinners long gone, much to the displeasure of his mother, Sinnett still carries the weight of his father's approval. It's not as bad as it was when I first met him and learned of what he was dealing with, but it still lingers like a shadow.

My father slowly but surely came around to the idea of me dating Sinnett. After many weeks of side glances and hesitancy to accept seeing us together—and, of course, far too many awkward conversations about me being 'safe'—he has finally stopped worrying about me dating a rugby player. Sinnett has proven to him that he is willing to do anything to protect me, taking on the job Dad had burdened himself with since Mum's passing. They're slowly mending their relationship, which is translating to their time together training. But despite this newfound acceptance, Sinnett carries the weight of my father's expectations also—something he doesn't take lightly. Despite the turmoil between them, he doesn't want to let Dad down. And in his mind, losing the grand final would do just that.

My heart is ready to burst from my chest, and my lungs ache as I hold my breath, watching as Sinnett lines up the ball a few metres from the edge of the field. This is one of the hardest positions to kick from, and with the eyes of every fan in the stadium on him, he'd be feeling the pressure.

You've got this, Sin.

Sinnett huffs out a breath and flicks his eyes to the goal post one last time before charging forward, his powerful leg sending the ball flying through the air. A collective hitch in breathe is heard around the stadium, watching as the ball soars through the goal posts.

He's done it.

The Wolves are six points ahead, bringing the score to 6-12.

I jump where I stand, watching as Sinnett rushes to his starting position. With two minutes left on the clock, the Raiders are going to need a miracle to even the score.

With my heart in my throat, and the seconds ticking by at an agonising pace, the Raiders throw everything they have at the Wolves, but in the end, they can't get past the defensive line. When the timer hits eighty minutes, a roar sounds around the stadium, and my heart nearly explodes from my chest.

They did it.

The Wolves won the grand final!

Everything happens in slow motion. The Wolves players on the bench rush onto the field, embracing the players in a flurry of hugs and claps on the back. The club's theme song sounds from the speakers, enhancing the excitement radiating from the fans. Tears spring to my eyes as I watch the players who I've spent countless months with earning their hard-fought win. It's been a long and tough season, but this win proves how strong their side is and how united they are when playing together.

I spot his ocean eyes the second they find me from across the field. Sinnett grins as he jogs towards me, his attention focused solely on me. My heart skips a beat, and the air in my lungs evaporates. Sweat coats his skin and blades of grass stick to his jersey. His hair is a mess and his face is beyond dirty, but it doesn't take away from how stunning he is. In fact, he's glowing.

Winning the grand final will do that to you.

"You did it!" I squeal when he's in hearing range. I feel the glances from the crowd around us on the back of my head, but I block them out, only seeing him. "I'm so proud of you, Sin!"

"Come here, strawberry," he rasps, arms outstretched.

Heat explodes from my chest when his arms find my waist, hoisting me off the ground and into his arms. I don't care that he's sweaty or eight-thousand people are watching us. All I care about is him and celebrating a win he has been working towards all season. In spite of his quad injury back in April, he is standing here with a grand final win under his belt.

Proud doesn't even begin to explain what I feel right now.

I don't think I could do it justice with words.

Burying my face into his neck, I allow him to pull me away over the fence line and onto the field. With my legs hooked around his waist, I focus on the rhythm of his heart and the familiar scent that feels like home.

"I couldn't have done it without you, Tate," Sinnett murmurs into my hair, his hand cupping the back of my neck as he holds me close. "This win is for you."

I hug him tighter, fighting the tears threatening to fall.

Leaning back, I grin. "You did this, Sin. Injury and all, this was all your doing."

Sinnett's grip on my thighs tighten, ocean eyes glowing under the stadium lights. They search my face as his chest heaves.

What's on his mind?

I'm sure it's a chaotic storm with everything going on. Despite the audience around us, and the celebration from the team on the field, we're in our own little bubble.

"I love you, Tate."

My breath hitches in my throat. I blink at him, the words settling into my skin.

It's the first time he's ever said those three words. They've entered my mind many times, but haven't been spoken. I was afraid that it would be too soon or the moment not right.

Truth is, Sinnett has had my heart from the moment I met him, but I was too blind to see or acknowledge it. Even if we never said the words, I still felt them deep in my core, festering into an emotion designed for him. But now that he's said them, I can't wipe the smile off my face or stop the heat exploding in my core.

There is no perfect time to tell someone you love them, but this moment right here, with adrenaline pumping through our veins, running on a high created by the most intense game of footy I've ever watched, couldn't have been more perfect.

My lips find his, electricity pumping through my veins. Hands caressing his face, Sinnett's mouth moves effortlessly with mine, responding in a way words never could. His grip tightens, somehow pulling me closer to him than physically possible.

I pull away breathlessly, my forehead dropping against his, and legs wrapped tightly around his waist. A smile tilts up my mouth. "I love you, Sin. In this life and the next."

Sinnett grins. "Winning your heart far outweighs any grand final win from tonight or ten years in the future."

I press a chaste kiss to his lips, my heart threatening to explode from my chest. "All you had to do was break some rules."

"You were worth it, Tate," he murmurs, ocean eyes roaming my face. "Loving you is the easiest thing I've ever done."

Tears spring to my eyes as every moment we've ever shared rushes to my mind.

"I hope so."

Thank you for reading Unwritten Rules! If you enjoyed this book, please check out the other novels in The Sunburnt Hearts series.

Off-Limits by Lena Moore
No Strings by Carisse Lee
Beautiful Ruins by Amanda Kade
Twisted Truths by JL Skye
Prove Me Wrong by Rebekah Bertram

Content Warning

This book contains mentions or depictions of:

Explicit sexual scenes and language
Death of a parent (off-page)
Attempted drugging

Recommended for mature audiences. Reader discretion is advised.

Also by Chloe Higgins

Blood Lover Duet

Blood Sport (Book 1)

Backstage Sinners Series

Her Dark Angel (Book 1)

Shadowed by Demons (Book 1.5)

Acknowledgments

Firstly, I want to mention just how excited I was to finally write a rugby romance novel. I grew up watching the NRL, thanks to my dad. He took me to games from the moment I could walk. I have memories of not being able to sit still during a game, annoying the hell out of my dad, to being in the crowd, on the edge of my seat, watching the Dragons vs West Tigers in the Preliminary Finals in 2010. The atmosphere was tense, and I lost my voice the moment the Dragons scored a field goal, punching their ticket to the Grand Final, which they would go on to win that year. As a St. George Illawarra fan, it was a dream come true. I've loved this sport for many years, so having the chance to write a story inspired by the league was amazing. So much so, I wrote the book in five weeks! Tatum and Sinnett have my heart.

I want to thank Carisse Lee for being the mastermind behind The Sunburnt Hearts Series. When I saw her call out for Aussie authors to join in on the project, I had no idea that the final product would be the six incredible books showcased in the series. It was an absolute pleasure getting to create a collaborative world with six amazing authors, and in turn, form a close friendship that I'll cherish. Thank you, Carisse, Rebekah, Jennah, Amanda and Lena, for making this process so much fun! You ladies are amazing.

Next, thank you to Rebekah for your help and support through every step of this process. You listened to every one of my voice memos talking about the book and how we could connect our stories and characters even more than they already were. As a fan of the sport, your insights and knowledge were invaluable. Getting to work alongside you throughout this process was so much fun, and I can't wait to continue working together in the future. This book wouldn't be what it is without your help, bestie.

Thank you to my lovely beta readers, Roxy and Abbie! I don't normally have beta readers, but the love and support you ladies showed the series was too much for me to pass on. Thank you for loving the book and characters as much as I do. Your feedback and encouragement were exactly what I needed. You ladies rock!

As always, this book wouldn't be as polished as it is without the critical eye of my editor and bestie, Anisa. Getting to work with you on my projects has been an amazing part of my whole author journey. I couldn't have written the books I have without your knowledge and guidance. Thank you for being my biggest cheerleader and loving these characters and story as if it were your own. I can't wait to continue working with you until I develop carpal tunnel and we're turning grey. Love you!

And thank you to my partner for allowing me to talk his ear off about parts of my story he understood nothing about. You've always been one of my biggest supporters, and I'm so grateful for you.

Lastly, thank you to every one of my readers who have supported me through this journey. Having you in my corner is what keeps me going. I hope you enjoy Unwritten Rules and fall in love with Tatum and Sinnett's story.

Until next time! xo

About the Author

Chloe lives by the beach in New South Wales, Australia, with her two fluffy cats, partner, and twin sister. Ever since she was young, she has always loved to read and create stories in her mind whenever an idea presented itself. She got into the romance genre in high school by reading After by Anna Todd on Wattpad. In recent years, her love for storytelling grew and she decided it was finally time to put pen to paper and share her ideas. She is always coming up with new ideas, so stay tuned for future projects.

Let's connect!

If you would like to keep up to date with me and learn about any future projects, please follow me on social media:

Instagram: @chloehigginsauthor
TikTok: @chloehigginsauthor
Goodreads: Chloe Higgins (Author)
Website: chloehigginsauthor.com.au